Praise for *The Eighth Day*:

"Frighteningly realistic. Most of Washington really works this way. Homeland Security had better read this one and take corrective action."
– U.S. Ambassador Michael Skol

"Awesome. I could not go to sleep last night because I couldn't put it down!"
– Donna Hanover, WOR Radio 710

"The author weaves a tale that will occasionally take your breath away and then cause you to sigh with re-lief.... He is a master wordsmith who knows the value of just the right phrase at just the right moment. His timing will keep you on the edge of your chair."
– Bill Twomey, CNG Newspaper Group

"A thriller with some insights into human behavior"
– Mel Robbins, CNBC

"I was fascinated. In fact, I had trouble putting it down one night and went to bed late so I could finish the book to see how it came out!"
– Otis Young, "All About Books," N.E.T. Radio

"A gripping and compelling read."
– *The Sun Daily*

THE
EIGHTH DAY

THE
EIGHTH DAY

A NOVEL BY

TOM
AVITABILE

**fiction
studio
books**

The Fiction Studio
PO Box 4613
Stamford, CT 06907

Print ISBN-13: 978-1-936558-48-3
E-book ISBN-13: 978-1-936558-49-0

Visit our website at www.fictionstudiobooks.com

Original publication: State Street Press, 2008
First Fiction Studio Paperback Printing (Author's Preferred Edition): April 2012

Printed in the United States of America

This book is dedicated to the selfless among us whose belief in something greater than themselves elevates them to the truly heroic. Be they America's teachers, first-responders, or military men and women, they are the best of us and an inspiration to the rest of us.

CHAPTER ONE
FIRST BLOOD

JUST IMAGINE THEM all sitting there in their underwear, William Jennings Hiccock thought, invoking a little trick a politician once revealed on overcoming the fear of public speaking. He scanned the three hundred expectant faces crowded into the Iroquois Banquet Room of the Westchester Hills Country Club. *On second thought, that's even more frightening.*

Braving 50,000 football fans almost every week back at Stanford did little to prepare him for this night and he harbored an unsettling feeling all day. This was a tougher crowd than the one that packed the university's stadium. Even though they were not as physical as the opposing eleven-man squad hell-bent on making him pay a painful price for every pass completion, this group was just as ominous and even more cutthroat. They were, after all, scientists.

∞§∞

Augmentation. That was the medical term.

"New Rochelle, station stop is New Rochelle," the train's public-address system cackled.

"Boob job" was what her best friend called it. "An abomination before God" was her mother's phrase. And regardless of what anyone else said, Cindy considered it a new lease on life. Ever since she was old enough to care about such things, she wanted to have a better figure. Once she entered the workforce, she noticed that all the shapely women were moving on the fast track and her career was ... flat!

∞§∞

From a distance, Hiccock did not appear tall. He possessed the proportions of a smaller person in that they were balanced, his height not all in his legs or in his trunk. It wasn't until he stood close to someone, or, as in this case, behind a podium, that his towering physical stature became apparent. This head-and-shoulders-above-the-rest quality enabled him to peg a rifle shot of a pass over the line of scrimmage. It was height and athletic ability that made him a valuable weapon to any coach on the gridiron, but those were second on his "things I like about myself" list. First place was solely occupied by his mental prowess. Perhaps his being so good at football was due to the fact that he understood every scientific aspect of the game, from the biokinetic structure of the human-propulsion mechanism to the ballistic trajectory of the leather-covered missile he launched from his rocket arm with deadly accuracy. He once concluded to himself that he didn't as much play ball as "affect" ball.

That gift of logical analysis, which was the spark and magic to his game in the arena, proved a hindrance to his life off the field, especially when it came to women. Hiccock seldom did anything without serious thought. But he often found women to be emotional beings with contradictory actions and mind-boggling logic. In the Bronx, there used to be a saying, "can't understand normal thinking." He never accepted the crude and rude tone of that obscene acronym. Lately, however, he realized there was a kernel of truth there.

What does this have to do in any way with what I'm doing now? The reason he dwelled on the great male/female divide was the blonde-haired woman in the front row. *Blondes.* They inspired two basic "looks" in the average man: the "long shot" and the "close up." For the most part, a full head of well-brushed blonde hair, dangling down and shimmering above a black dress, was indeed a head turner. Closer inspection, though, could reveal a supermodel—or your matronly Aunt Mary. As he zoomed in for the front-row woman's "close up," he noticed that Aunt Mary definitely *did not* make the trip here tonight. Glancing away from her and down at his speech notes, he folded them, slid them into his vest pocket, and winged it with a different opening. He planted his feet, took a deep breath, smiled, and went for it.

"When I drove up tonight and I saw the laser beam writing 'The Third Annual Artificial Intelligence Convention' on the low-hanging cumulus, I felt a surge of pride. Did I say felt? Wow, that's weird. I mean, scientists aren't supposed to *feel*. You know, after years of qualifying, quantifying, and qualitating facts, anomalies, and iterations, I think we wind up more like ... like efficient machines than humans. We adapt to our black-and-white environment, we join the family of exactitude and flawless logic, and we make warm friends of cold, hard facts. I mean it is drummed into our heads that in pure science there is no place for feelings, emotions, or opinions. It is 'the truth' we seek, unclouded by faulty human intervention. It's almost as though the role of scientists is to sacrifice their humanity for the *betterment of* humanity."

Where is this going, where am I going? Look at them. They don't know whether to be insulted or uncomfortably polite. This is why I should stick to the script.

An uneasy pause hung in the room. A few pairs of eyes started to wander off him and onto the curtains and up to the chandelier in the center of the room. One man was checking his BlackBerry. Bill realized, for the first time, how frightening silence was. Back in the college stadiums of his youth, there was never quiet. Even booing was a sign that somebody was following the program, being a part of it. Silence was a suffocating condition. He felt as though he had a corkscrew inside his stomach and it was twisting his insides into a tightly wound knot. He looked down at the front-row blonde. At least her eyes were still on him. Taking notes, no less! *Oh God.* Somebody was actually writing this down! He started speaking again before he knew what he was going to say.

"That's a shame." Heads and eyes turned back to him. "I know you all think that the advancements in AI are just the logical conclusion of earlier steps done methodically." He started nodding and they followed suit. "But I *did* feel something tonight. I know you felt it, too!" He delivered that line directly to a rotund man in a tuxedo who had the appearance and complexion of a vine-ripened tomato stuffed in a tight-necked, starched collar. The tomato started nodding as well. "A feeling not decipherable, not discernible or dissectible, just the unbridled pride over how far you have all come down this avenue of research."

They were smiling now. *She* was smiling. *They're with me.*

He came back more fervently. "The laser-lit heavens out front literally demonstrated just how far our field has risen from the first amassed loop matrix that I was lucky enough to be a part of, to the ..." As he went on, he thought in the back of his mind that at least this crowd, sitting there in their boxer shorts, was giving him, the ex-quarterback, a polite chance to score points.

∞§∞

From the window of the chemical lab, looking out across the nearby Metro-North station, the laser-lit cloud over the country club was little more than a glow in the night sky three miles off. However, Professor Eric Holm would never see it, being focused as he was on the end of the one-inch diamond-tipped drill bit that was simultaneously drilling in and pounding through the concrete at his feet. It was his first time ever using a rotary hammer. It would also be his last. He was amazed that he knew how to operate the drill. Although he could not recall who directed him to do this, he felt a strong compulsion to complete the task.

The buffeting noise the tool created did not concern him. Few places were as deserted as the Intellichip Building in the Central Westchester Industrial Park on Sunday night. With a jolt, the three-foot-long drill bit chewed and punched its way through the eighteen-inch slab of concrete and the drop ceiling that separated the fourth-floor chemical lab from the third-floor substrate bath. With great effort he pulled the heavy tool out of the hole and laid it on the floor. Unaccustomed to any physical labor whatsoever, he grabbed at his side as a muscle extended beyond its normal range. In pain, he didn't notice the pocket protector fall from his sweat-stained, white short-sleeved shirt.

He opened the petcock on the fifty-five-gallon drum of Freon that was propped up on a wooden cradle at an angle, like a keg of beer. He watched silently as the Freon splashed in pools on the floor.

∞§∞

"Larchmont next stop," a conductor announced from somewhere on the train. "The rear four cars only will platform at Larchmont."

After years of denial and not believing that her unlucky lot in life was due to something as trivial as the size of her chest, Cindy turned 180 degrees in her thinking. So, on this crisp, early fall night, Cindy took the 7:35 Metro-North train from Grand Central Station up through Westchester County to Port Chester, where she intended to spend the night at her sister Paula's house. The next day, with Paula accompanying her for moral support, she would check into Port

Chester Hospital. Then, five hours and one-and-one-half cup sizes later, her new life would begin.

∞§∞

"So that's the way it went all day, hit the ball, drag Bernie, hit the ball, drag Bernie."

Hiccock had the room laughing after telling a little golf joke about how terrible it is when one of your foursome has a heart attack and dies in the middle of a game. He was getting the hang of public speaking. Totally off his notes, he forged fearlessly ahead into the perils of the ad-lib.

"Before you go back to the pure logic of the labs and I go back to the pure lunacy of Washington, I'm going to borrow a page from my old college coach. Try to imagine a smelly locker room at halftime." The room laughed exactly on cue and he knew he had them. "Don't give up. Do not be distracted. Do not be lured away to defense or commercial endeavors. Do not for one second listen to the naysayers, the ill-informed, the doubting Thomases who equate your quest for artificial intelligence with that of a fool's journey. Every major advance in science has been the result of someone not following the rules, some individual thinking outside the box, someone standing up for an idea that was, at best, scientific heresy."

The room erupted as the scientific elite, engineers and programmers all at the top of their professions, reacted to their new champion and the national recognition that he would bring to their long-suffering cause. Their optimism was founded on the notion that among the many Nobel Prize winners and nominees in this Westchester country club dining room, he, Hiccock, was the only one of them who had ever won a Heisman Trophy.

∞§∞

The widening pool of Freon found the hole Eric Holm cut in the floor and started to pour through and out the ragged opening in the third-floor acoustic ceiling. Looking into the draining liquid, he was catapulted back to a time in his youth when he was running through his mother's kitchen and he hit the mop handle, knocking over the wash bucket. The soapy water found a knothole in the wood-planked floor and seeped down into the basement. He caught two beatings that day—one from his frustrated mother and another from his German immigrant father who came home and found his tools in the basement all wet.

Tonight, Holm's eyes darted around. He had the distinct impression that he was doing something wrong today as well. But he could not stop himself. As the liquid reached the open vat holding the substrate bath, it proceeded to boil. The small twinge in Holm's back caused him to twist his torso in an effort to alleviate the tightening of the complaining muscle. He was confused by the pain, having no memory of pulling it a minute earlier.

∞§∞

"For my part, as head of the Office of Science and Technology Policy, I will urge my new coach, the president, to support the legislation championed by Senator Dent of California calling for increased funding of the pure science necessary to achieve artificial intelligence in our lifetimes!"

The room combusted into a spontaneous standing ovation. They had found their hero. He was one of them, a pioneer in their field who, as the Science Advisor to the President, now held sway over the national science agenda.

∞§∞

There was a sharp thud as a southbound train sped by on an adjacent track. The doors of the car Cindy was riding in were slammed outward and yanked back by the vacuum created by the two trains passing each other. The noise took her out of her thoughts. Sitting between two men in her oversized cranberry-red sweater, she looked around at the other people on the train. There was the man standing in the doorway listening to his iPod. Tall and on the verge of forty, slightly graying at the temples, just enough to make him look distinguished. That was a pet peeve of hers. Distinguished. What a shitty deal that was. A man could out his gray for all the world to see and he's deemed *distinguished*. Let a woman try and go au naturel and she is "just giving up."

She slowly realized that "Mr. I'm-here-I'm-gray-get-used-to-it" reminded her of a guy she went on a blind date with once. What a disaster! She was an hour late, as she recalled. Always having the worst luck, that icy winter night was no different. Her car locks froze up and she spent an hour in the bitter cold trying to rectify the situation with a Bic lighter. Turned out that the guy was a putz anyway. It was one date and over, as most were.

She unconsciously looked down at her featureless contours and then raised her head to play another round of "Who's on the Train?" Her eyes landed on an older lady who gave up worrying about her hair and makeup long ago. *She's either really happy or really nuts.* The man next to her must have had some kind of Chinese food for dinner because ...

∞§∞

Eric Holm's eyes darted around rapidly in their sockets. His instincts to flee prickled at his common sense, but a strong compulsion to stay put overpowered it. He noticed that the tip of his shoe had concrete dust on it from the drilling. He reached into his pants pocket for his handkerchief. The Freon had now created a roiling surface in the substrate bath. Eric Holm leaned down to dab the tip of his shoe. As he did so, the hydrogen chloride of the substrate bath and the Freon achieved critical mass. Seven hundred gallons of docile hydrogen chloride were violently stripped of their chemical inhibitor and now became a 700-gallon fuel explosive bomb with a boiling surface. In the first hundred milliseconds of the expanding hydrogen-fueled fireball, both concrete slabs that made up the floor and ceiling were instantly pulverized, along with the professor. At 200 milliseconds, the remaining hydrogen—now an aerosol—was ignited by the 3,000-degree central fireball, turning the entire 620,000 cubic feet of the third-to-fifth floors of the building into a superbomb. In total, it took one-third of a second for the building to explode.

∞§∞

Four hundred milliseconds later, a shock wave traveling at 720 miles per hour slammed into the Metro-North station. It violently blew Cindy's departing local train off its track as if it were a toy smacked by a giant hand, leaving the railcars jutting into the adjacent express track. Cindy felt something snap in her neck as she was catapulted sideways. She found herself crushed under the weight of the man who was sitting on her right a split second before. Their bodies were thrown brutally to one side of the car, pinning the man sitting to her left between them and the window. She didn't hear well after that. Her ears had popped like on an airplane. Sounds were tightly squeezed and tinny, but she heard screams, moans, and calls for help. She knew something happened, but she had no idea what. The train car in which Cindy was sitting was now at an

uphill incline and tilting to one side, giving her the il-
lusion she was laying on her back. She was aware that
the man who only a second before was between her and
the window behind her was screaming, but his cries
were muffled by the back of her sweater. She felt pain
in her leg. When the man on top of her started grasping
at the seat back in front of him to right himself, it put
pressure on her leg and a searing pain shot through
her body. She screamed a scream that, to her now shattered eardrums, sounded like a hollow roar emanating
from somewhere else. The intense pain knifed into her
brain and she saw stars. He mumbled something but
kept clawing at the seat. Sputtering blue-white flashes
and the spotty, low-powered emergency lights were the
only illumination in the train car. The odor of ozone
from the electrical arcing outside started to pinch at
her nose. Someone had lost control of their bowels. The
metal skin of the train, having been stressed and hammered by the force of the shock wave, shed molecules
like a beaten rug shed dust, making the air taste and
smell metallic.

Cindy tried to move her head, but couldn't. A wave
of panic welled up from deep within her. Instinctively,
she lashed out, trying to push the man off her, but with
each movement, sharp slicing pains radiated through
her body.

∞§∞

Suddenly, there was a momentary dimming of the
lights. Hiccock stopped speaking, the chandelier in the
center of the room rattled, liquids in cups rippled, then
the whole room jolted. A percussive wallop attacked
the eardrums of everyone in the room, followed by a
sound like rolling thunder. The excitement felt just
seconds ago morphed into stunned silence.

∞§∞

Cindy realized that her head was turned toward the window while her body faced the other way. There was a momentary stillness within her, a split second of painless neutrality, a warm silence and quelling calm. In her mind, she wondered if this was death, numbing her in preparation for the transition from this life to ... something caught her attention. She was pinned between the two men, just barely able to see over the shoulder of the one on top of her. In awe, she marveled as she saw a white light coming through the window of the tilted car. *The White Light*, she thought as a reassuring blanket of peace covered her while she attempted to focus her tearing eyes on the bright glow approaching outside the cracked window.

∞§∞

Distracted by the huge flash off to his right, the engineer of the northbound New Haven express did not see the derailed cars of the local train at the station. Not that it would have made any difference. At 90 miles per hour, there was only time enough to brace himself.

∞§∞

Cindy watched as the bright light's halo gave way to a black hulk in the shape of the oncoming express train that rapidly filled her view through the window. The last things she sensed were a bludgeoning jolt and a cracking sound as she and her two row mates were crushed together for all of eternity.

∞§∞

As it slammed into the deadweight of the derailed train, the front of the onrushing express crumpled like a beer can under the 133-feet-per-second momentum of a million pounds of railcars behind it. The ten gleaming silver commuter cars piled up and crunched with horrendous metal groans and muffled screams. Explosive, electrical arcing from the ruptured 22,000-volt overhead catenary wires eerily illuminated the scene.

The spreading pileup sent the commuter cars, weighing 100,000 pounds each, sweeping over the platform, flattening and crushing departing passengers and collapsing the station structure. The force of the blast continued outward in an ever-widening concussive wave, eventually leaving Cindy, and 600 other commuters, dead in its wake.

∞§∞

A mile away, a small suburban neighborhood was rocked as all the windows of the two-story houses lining the street first deflected out and then imploded simultaneously as the shock wave hit. Car and house alarms were triggered instantly.

At the offices of Delta Home Security Services, a dispatcher sat in his usually catatonic state before a huge display of Westchester County. Suddenly, in a fast widening circle emanating from the exploding building's location on the map, he saw the red lights, denoting tripped alarms.

"Holy shit!" he muttered as he watched the crimson circle grow.

∞§∞

"Holy shit!" Mike Casigno said. "In all the years I've been hacking for this car service, I never saw so many flashing lights." His cab crept toward the sea of red, yellow, and blue emergency vehicle strobes that were scattered over every conceivable inch of space surrounding the train station and the industrial park beyond. From the backseat, Hiccock noticed the rising column of dark smoke, just visible against the inky black suburban sky. "This is as far as I can go. I got a cop waving me off already," Mike said.

"Thanks, I'll hoof it from here," Hiccock said as he handed him a twenty-dollar bill and slid across the backseat, not waiting for change. As he walked toward the scene of mass destruction, he noticed two areas of concentration. One was at the site a few hundred yards away that looked like it was once a building. The other was at the train station to his right. Train cars were strewn across the tracks and some had jumped the platform and collapsed the station structure. Firemen, police, and EMTs scurried all over. Guys in hard hats and cops in helmets were already cutting into the steel cars with big gas-powered saws, spewing golden sparks in firework-type arcs as they bit and chewed into the twisted metal. There was the constant chatter of police radios coming from every direction. Adding to the cacophony was the staccato interruption of "squelch," the rasping static noise from scores of transmit buttons being triggered and released.

Hiccock was impressed by the response. It had been less than thirty-five minutes since the blast and already hundreds of emergency workers were on the scene. He noticed that the ambulances and fire trucks around him were from places further out like Stamford, Connecticut, and Rescue 1 from FDNY Manhattan. This, no doubt, was an infamous benefit from the heightened alert status and coordinated efforts of all first responders in this New Age of Terrorism. He approached a cop trying hard to direct a snarled knot of ambulances, fire trucks, and other emergency vehicles. Hiccock saw the familiar metal numbers 47 on the cop's collar and realized he was NYPD, the 47th precinct, where Hiccock grew up, being the nearest Bronx cop house to Westchester County. Hiccock reached into his tuxedo back pocket and flashed his ID.

"What kind of ..." was all the distracted cop could muster.

"It's my White House ID. I work for the president."

"I dunno what I'm supposed to do with that. Wait here." He then turned and yelled, "Come around him, come on ... let's go!" at an ambulance squeezing by a rescue truck whose crew was probably atop the pile of railcars. He then keyed his radio mic, which was attached to a belt slung over his shoulders. "4-7-Charlie-portable to Central K." There was some more squelch and he added, "I need a supervisor at the north end of the station. I got a VIP here from the White House."

A noise pricked at Hiccock's right ear, turning his attention from the cop to part of the collapsed station and he wandered off in that direction. It was like a hideous light show. The arcing and sparking from the torches, saws, and short circuits made the shadows jump and images shake. He couldn't be sure, but he thought he made out a shape. He started toward it double time. At the sloping end of the fallen station roof, down in the crook created by the flattened end, was a woman screaming for help. She was in agony. He saw that her right leg was pinned under the rubble. He removed his tux jacket and covered her. "I'll be back with help. You're gonna be okay." He ran back toward the traffic jam and grabbed an FDNY Rescue 1 officer, "I got a woman pinned under the station. Come on."

"Hey pal, look around," the big bruiser of a fireman said without stopping or looking. "Everyone here is dying. I got twelve people trapped over there. I can't help you right now."

Hiccock searched for another emergency worker but he could see they were all busy. All involved in one hundred individual battles with death. He ran to the abandoned Rescue 1 truck. All the tool lockers were open and empty. No medicine, no radios. Then he got an idea. He went around the back and looked for the spare tire. *They hafta have a spare on this rig.* Off the back and below the chrome-coated diamond plate he found the tire well and the heavy-duty hydraulic jack. It felt like it weighed a ton but he cradled it in his arms, along with the pipe that fit in the jack, and headed back to the woman. Halfway there he heard the Bronx cop call out to him.

"Hey, stop. Where are you taking that thing?"

"I got a woman trapped here, get someone to help me!"

He reached the woman and assessed the situation, not sure what he was going to do next. The woman was losing consciousness. "Hey! What's your name? Lady, what's your name?"

"Shelly," she said distantly.

Hiccock saw a place where he might wedge the jack. "Shelly, huh? Is that short for Michelle?"

"Who are you?" she asked.

"Bill. At your service!" He inserted the pipe into the jack and started pumping it.

"What are you doing?"

"I'm getting you free. How are you doing?"

"I think I'm going to ... throw up. The ... pain is so ... horrible."

The jack tightened up under the twisted beam. Hiccock continued pumping. The concrete below the jack started to crack. He guessed the woman was about fifty and she was fading again. "Shelly! Shelly! Stay with me, Shelly!" He saw her snap out of it. "Shelly are you married?"

"Yes. Oh God! My leg ... it hurts."

"Just a little longer; this is starting to work." He was lying. The beam hadn't moved, but the concrete below the jack was turning to powder. He stopped. He scrambled over to the edge of the platform on his hands and knees and looked at its underside. There were steel cross-members at even intervals supporting the slabs of concrete. The jack was just a few inches to the right of one of them. He flipped the pipe and fitted the notched end to the valve on the base of the jack that released the hydraulics. The piston relaxed but didn't lower enough to free the jack. He reached in and pulled down on the piston with all his strength.

"What's your husband's name, Shelly?" His voice was strained with exertion.

"Mario."

The piston budged only about half an inch but it was enough. He repositioned the jack over the seam in the concrete right above the steel crossbeam and started pumping again.

"What's he do? Shelly! Your husband, Mario, what does he do?"

"He, he imports ... I can't feel my ... "

"Imports what, Shelly? Keep talking to me, what does he import?" The beam started to groan as the jack applied enough lift to raise a truck.

"Dried fruit and nuts."

"That's a new one on me, Shelly!" The beam was lifting ever so slowly. As it rose, other pieces of the fallen structure started to snap and buckle, each threatening to re-collapse as the pressure from the jack fought upward against the weight bearing down.

Hiccock caught sight of a cop from the corner of his eye. "Good, you're here! I almost have her free. When I say, pull her out."

The jack was now bending the beam as it lifted it. Hiccock saw that the whole thing was starting to tilt toward him. He kept pumping but tried to keep his action purely up and down.

"Officer, this is Shelly. I told her we were going to get her out of here."

"Yes we are," the cop said, as he wearily looked up at the collapsed structure.

The jack and the beam were starting to tip over. Hiccock placed his foot on the jack and pushed with all his might to keep it upright.

"I think I can pull her out now," the cop said.

"Now or never," Hiccock said, his leg fully extended. The cop grabbed Shelly under the shoulders and started to pull. She screamed. Her leg was coming out shattered, bloody, and flattened, but moving out. Hiccock felt the jack tipping, the weight of the station starting to overcome the height he had created.

"Come on. Hurry, I can't hold it much longer."

"Just another few inches," the cop said over Shelly's screams.

Hiccock looked up and saw the whole roof and structure start to fall over to crush him. From the corner of his eye, he saw the cop drag Shelly clear to the edge of the platform. Hiccock was now in a helpless situation; if he stayed where he was, he would be crushed by the tons of stuff on top of him. If he moved, the jack would give way and cause it to happen anyway. The sweat poured from his forehead. He decided he couldn't just wait for the thing to fall over. Mentally he counted to three, then pushed off from the jack in an attempt to scramble out from under the falling debris. But the jack went the other way when he pushed off from it and the whole structure started to come down.

Suddenly ten poles hit the concrete like javelins. They formed an instant wedge of protection as the weight of the roof was counter-levered by them. Hiccock got out from under the overhanging mangled roof to see ten firemen, straining with their pike poles, staving off the collapse.

As soon as he was out, the big bruiser, who didn't have time for him before, commanded, "Let her go." The firemen jumped back with their tools and the remaining part of the structure fell with a huge crash.

"Thanks," Hiccock said, watching the wreckage he could have been buried under.

"No problem," was all the fireman said before he and the rest of his Rescue 1 men went off to save someone else.

Catching his breath, Hiccock looked over at Shelly. "How's she doing?" he asked the cop.

"She's out cold but she's still breathing."

Two EMTs with Fort Lee New Jersey Volunteer Ambulance Corp patches on their sleeves appeared with a stretcher. "We'll take it from here."

Hiccock turned to survey the nightmare around him. There weren't going to be a lot of happy endings like Shelly's tonight.

CHAPTER TWO
TWO YEARS & SIX MONTHS EARLIER

"SIXTY SECONDS TO DETONATION," squawked the box.

Even in the air-conditioned, electronically filtered environment of the SSC, a slick sweat covered Professor Richard Parnes's face as the concluding stages of FINAL SWORD played out on the large-format displays in front of him. He was fully aware of the massive amount of death and destruction this operation could create. Nevertheless, for the safety of America, he had to continue with this mission in order to guarantee that the United States would remain the dominant power on earth.

"Disable safeties, arm firing circuits," Parnes said into his headset. From his raised console, he looked down at members of his team throwing switches twenty feet in front of him. Mentally he retraced his wiring design and the triggering sequence, the precise timing of which would release the initial impulse of focused energy into the dirillium base. From there on it would be nature's sequence of neutrons smashing into atoms releasing more neutrons to smash more atoms' nuclei until the whole thing exploded into a rough approximation of hell.

"10, 9, 8, 7 ..." the firing sequence officer said.

"Fluctuation in gamma 10 ... 2.34 over nominal level."

Parnes's finger instinctively flipped up the safety cover of the abort switch, as his brain calculated the effect of increased gamma on the energy budget he so painstakingly fought to preserve. Then he remembered his duty. Only a few more seconds left, and it would all be over.

"4, 3, 2 ..."

The hell with it. He withdrew his finger from the red-guarded abort switch as the count passed one. No turning back now. It must be done.

Suddenly, all the monitors in the room flashed brilliantly. A large screen in the center of the room displayed a graphic representation of what was happening. Based on estimates and experimental research the yield was expected to be 200 megajoules of energy per nanosecond, or about the output of a small star. Instead, and post analysis would tell him why, the actual yield was closer to 500. The team cheered. It was a brilliant success.

On the big screen, the image of the kill zone and collateral area reached out to a circumference of forty miles. Parnes knew it was the new hyper-shaping in the first stage that multiplied the yield so significantly. This was his team's sole focus for a year. Operation FINAL SWORD ended in victory.

"Well done, Parnes," the four-star general next to him said as he closed his mission briefing book. "Congratulations to you and your team, a truly major achievement."

"Thanks, Bob. Too bad it's all for nothing."

"That detonation didn't just wipe out Moscow, it took out the premier's dacha, thirty-seven miles away," the Bomb Damage Assessment Officer said.

Parnes nodded. "A great way to end this program."

"Well, maybe if the Cold War comes back, we'll actually build the data you just generated into an online weapons system," the general said optimistically.

"Til then it will remain a simulation exercise report in some digital archive of the DARPA library." Parnes realized he probably just wrote the epitaph of his program.

"What's next for you and your team, Parnes?" the general asked in a manner that usually accompanied opening his belt a notch after another fine meal.

"There isn't any 'next.' We spent ten billion on this simulation alone. No way that kind of money will ever be available again without a national emergency."

To the general that was a gray area, best left to the politicians. Absentmindedly he went to shake Parnes's right hand, only to realize his error mid-gesture. He turned the attitude of his hand from a shake to a pat on Parnes's shoulder, just above his severed limb.

Parnes had become the most highly paid civilian advisor to the military, despite his physical handicap. At his level, they paid the big bucks for his brain. Legend falsely accredited the loss of his right wing to a cataclysmic discharge of electrostatic plates during a cyclotron experiment gone awry. The story went that the discharge of millions of volts exploded the cells of his arm, leaving amputation the only option. In truth, he lost the limb in a Jeep accident as a young radioman drafted into the Army. However, legends die hard and professors do not get many romantic notions hung on their identities. And although he toyed with the most feared weapons of all mankind, being five-foot eight and on the thin side of fat, he hardly cut an imposing figure. So eventually he stopped denying the legend. Having long ago mastered typing and mouse clicking with just one hand, his absent limb did not impede his work on his chosen specialty, computer technology—specifically, virtual engagement protocol and anti-computational warfare. A complicated name for what simply was anything that processed strategic or tactical military data and computer simulations.

Professor Richard Parnes achieved the ultimate position in the game of military leapfrog where success and power were awarded with positions toward the outer ring of the Pentagon. He had an office, with a window, in the E-ring. Almost as impressive was his parking spot on the River Entrance side.

At first blush, nuclear weapons research seemed a relic of America's paranoid, mutually assured destructive past. Parnes's work was, however, still a matter of national security. Furthermore, his elite stature was justified, because even though the Cold War ended nearly two decades before, one tiny troublesome fact remained. It seemed someone forgot to tell the Russian Strategic Rocket Force, its commanders, and their nineteen missile divisions to go home, it was all over. Instead, the Soviet's mega death-tipped SS-20s and the like were still targeted at Main Street, U.S.A., just like in the bad old days.

Our politicians had moved this undiminished nuclear threat to the back burners of America's collective consciousness, primarily by negotiating away atmospheric and below-ground testing. It was good public relations but it did nothing to reduce the stockpile of overkill both nations stored away like dangerous nuts for a nuclear winter.

This politically expedient non-solution to humanity's nightmare made computer simulations the only way for our nuclear warriors to ply their trade and be ready to protect America with massive retaliatory force. Parnes's team was born out of this need when he approached the Pentagon with the notion of "E-plosion," detailed high-definition computer simulations of nuclear explosions. All it took was one secret, illegal underground test, officially logged as an earthquake, to prove unequivocally the accuracy of the data Parnes generated. With that baseline sample as a model, Parnes and his people were free to explore and try "what ifs" to their hearts' content, blowing up nothing more than the occasional computer chip. The data Parnes's E-plosions yielded gave America years of advancement in a nuclear arms race that was frozen in the eighties.

Accordingly, Parnes's slice of the 300-billion-dollar defense pie was the second biggest, after you removed operations. He was technically part of the old Defense Advanced Research Projects Agency. The members of his team were handpicked technicians, the cream of the crop, enlisted from schools and America's largest corporations. They were young and old, white, Asian, Indian, and black, male and female. Their personas ran the gamut from out-and-out nerds to fly fishermen. Only two things were considered when recruiting them: that they were the absolute best in their fields and that they pass the security clearance. Keeping America number one in any race was expensive. In nuclear weapons research, the cost was obscene. Team members made, on average, ten times more money than their commercial counterparts did. But true to the field, they rarely, if ever, got home early enough or took ample time off to enjoy most of it. The team had become Parnes's de facto family.

Being doggedly focused on every challenge while simultaneously planning for the next made Parnes the most boring man any woman ever had the pleasure of saying good-bye to. Even brain groupies, those women who hang around geniuses as if they were rock stars, tired quickly upon finding out they were not the center of his world. A world of microns and electrons, math and physics, and a cat named Archimedes.

He and his entire team were classified, working from black op budgets, so named because the Pentagon blacked out the name and the amounts on the line budget they submitted to Congress. Congress, for its part, exercised its power of the purse by keeping those black ops on a short leash, cutting or appropriating the monies blindly as a percentage. At the end of the day, however, the route the money took was unimportant. Regardless of how it was appropriated, through black ops or out in the open, all of the money spent on defense found its way eventually into the congressmen's districts. After a short stay in some captain of industry's bank account, a portion of the appropriation found its way into a PAC. These political action committees "laundered" the money one more time, and then contributed it into the congressmen's election campaigns. The whole thing worked without grinding to a halt because it was self-lubricating. In short, a percentage of the money Congress appropriated for war, appropriately enough, found its way into a congressman's war chest. This was proven by even those antiwar congresses who, despite being elected and given the majority to end a war, just couldn't seem to muster the votes to cut off even one penny of what the Department of Defense wanted, because in the end they would be cutting off their own funding as well.

This mission today was the last shot. It would be his last time in the Strategic Simulations Center. Détente and a weakened Russia wounded the brand of weapons research Parnes and his team worked on so diligently. The ratification of the SALT II Treaty delivered the coup de grâce. The Strategic Arms Limitations Treaty had limited his career and those of his team. Tomorrow he would awake and be without a job, without an office in the E-ring, without a parking spot, budget, and research team. He would have nothing but the severance from his contract. Not that this in itself mattered. He did not have to work another day in his life, or Archimedes' nine.

Later that day, exactly two-and-a-half years before the building exploded in Westchester County, at a small, melancholy celebration in the Parnes's home, the twenty-two members of the Nuclear Research Team gathered for the last time.

The TV was on in the den where the last few hangers-on and Parnes settled in for a cognac-and-cigar nightcap. It was the opening of the Democratic National Convention. The televised coverage eventually turned the chatter in the room briefly to the election.

34

The general reaction was ambiv
shared around the room was that
choice for president being offered to
Macordal, the team's lead mathematic
that the two most exciting candidates,
pilot James Mitchell and the wiry fresh
from Wyoming, were the ones who were ge
larity. But they had their brief moment in
light summarily snuffed out by their respec   parties' political machines.

"Do you think we will ever work on a project again, Professor?" the youngest of the team inquired. Parnes, already lost in thought, fixed his eyes on the flickering images of the convention. Maybe there was a way to leverage a little something he always thought about experimenting with. The interstitial rates would certainly be fast enough, and the architecture would be very simple.

The television report switched to James Mitchell's campaign manager. The type at the bottom of the screen identified him as former governor Ray Reynolds, but Parnes knew him on sight. Reynolds was the driving force behind Mitchell's third-party attempt. *Yes*, Parnes thought, *very doable.*

And the professor now knew exactly who would be interested in funding this new research.

CHAPTER THREE
SPIN

IT HAD BEEN TWO YEARS since the election and nine hours since the horrific blast in Westchester as dawn broke over the nation's capital. The buffeting rotor noise of the WJLA News Chopper 7 shattered the calm of the new day as it patrolled the beltway, its reporter scanning the roadway for early signs of the inevitable traffic tie-ups. To his right, the sun rose behind the Washington Monument. A quick look over his left shoulder revealed the first rays of early light washing over the front portico of the White House. This was as close as any aircraft had ever dared come since the attack on the Pentagon, the obvious exception being Marine One, the president's private helicopter. The pilot pushed his steering collective control left, veering away from the White House and its Patriot surface-to-air battery missiles that kill you first and ask questions later.

What the reporter/pilot could not see was the heavy traffic going on inside the mansion. Aides hurriedly passed the bronze busts of former presidents and antique Early American furniture that resided there since America was "early."

One of the aides, Cheryl Burston, waited at the door of a small office, fingering the edge of a manila folder, not wanting to disturb the conversation between the two men within. One of the individuals was her sixty-year-old boss, Chief of Staff Ray Reynolds. She learned from Ray that a president was able to smile in public because all the burdens of office were carried on the shoulders of his COS. To her, Reynolds's face seemed cast in stone, the turned-down ends of his mouth arching in the same direction as his bushy eyebrows. She imagined his whole countenance would crack if he were ever to hazard a smile.

Cheryl panned across from him to see—in marked contrast— William Hiccock. At forty-five years of age, he retained the confidence and dynamic persona of the starting quarterback he was in college. *He still looks good enough to be on the cereal box.* Out of so many bright, young, and even more powerful men around here, why was he the only one able to affect—often only with a nod or a boyish smile—the breathing patterns of most of the female White House staff? Most would say this was because of Hiccock's easy manner and bedroom eyes. But she recognized something else in him. Even here, outside his habitat, standing on the rocky, uneven terrain of politics, where seasoned professionals often lose their balance, she saw him take and deliver full body blows when fighting for a concept or ideal. Her intuition told her that his position in these battles was purely based on passion and not in any way manipulated to advance his own career or line his pockets. And this was hugely attractive.

Cheryl found any passion to be rare in a place where most men are just doing what it takes to move up. Those overachievers were the ones who presented you with their ego first, second, and always. One might attribute it to her lack of experience, but she could not believe Hiccock ever broadcast a false or manipulative message. He was an enigma: a political appointee, the president's national science advisor, but without a political bone in his broad-shouldered body.

"So what's your assessment of the damage to the industry?" she heard Reynolds ask Hiccock, pulling Cheryl out of her daydream.

"It was a design-and-research facility. Manufacturing is split between their Johnson City plant and a few German fabricators."

"What is the impact?"

"For the immediate future, none, because the chips and integration they were designing was tomorrow. Their current output will not be affected, so it's only down the road ..."

"Shorter sentences, Hiccock!" Reynolds interrupted and then summed up. "No immediate impact. Good. The boss cut the ribbon at that building. It was part of his high-tech initiative."

Hiccock took a sip of some Starbucks "President's Blend" coffee and Cheryl saw a chance to break in, coughing for attention.

"Yes?" Reynolds said sharply, softening it with an insincere smile when he realized it was a woman at the door. His face didn't *crack* after all.

"The proposed draft of the president's statement," she said as she handed the single page to Reynolds.

"It is with great sadness ... hmmm ..." The chief of staff had a way of mumble reading while he scanned any document, bypassing the fluff but billboarding the factual or meritorious parts. "The incredible loss of more than 600 lives both in the buildings and on the commuter trains which were caught ... uh hum ... Our prayers and thoughts go out to the families ... Yes, this is fine." He picked up a pen and scratched his initials on it. "Take it up to the residence for him to review."

Cheryl left and Reynolds resumed his conversation with Hiccock. "So you felt the blast three miles away?"

"It was massive. I went to the scene afterwards but it was too hot to get close."

"You were there?"

"I was speaking a few miles away. It didn't look like anything bigger than your fist was left, so I jumped on the late shuttle back to D.C."

"What were they working on there that could have blown up like that?"

"Not a thing. Mostly high order ..." He paused as Reynolds snapped his fingers and yelled down the hallway.

"Cheryl!" The aide returned in an instant. As if inspired by the gods of spin, Reynolds said, "Change 'passengers on the commuter train' to 'hardworking people going home on Metro-North.' The dead were more than commuters. Hell, they were voters!" He winked to Hiccock. "New York is an important vote. Don't want them to think we can't feel their pain!"

Cheryl looked to Hiccock and, although he tried to remain expressionless, she noticed his left eyebrow ripple almost imperceptibly as the sides of his mouth tightened ever so slightly, revealing a trace of disgust. She turned to deliver the speech to the president.

Hiccock asked, "Anything else?" in a way that said, "I have nothing else."

"Yes. Let's cut the crap. I know you don't like me because I didn't go along with your appointment."

"Go along? You've tried to have me fired three times, Ray."

"Chemistry, that's science. Physics, that's science. But artificial intelligence? What the hell is that? What kind of background is that for a president's science advisor?"

"I have three degrees ..."

"Please spare me. I've read your résumé. Scientific methodology, another winner."

Reynolds's dismissive tone triggered Hiccock's retaliatory instincts, but he tempered it. "Don't hold back, Ray. Real scientists don't have any feelings."

"But now you get to earn your title, Mr. Presidential Science Advisor. It is your job to see that the boss is not blindsided by any high-tech guano at the 'speak-and-smile.'"

"How about if I just write my reports and hand them in?" Hiccock said in a tone usually associated with the words "You don't pay me enough for that."

With a small explosion for emphasis, Reynolds said, "Look, I am the goddamn chief of staff around here and you are staff!"

Hiccock maintained his composure as well as his resolve. Twenty years earlier he would have told this "scuzzbucket" where to stuff it and then stuffed it up there for him.

The chief, possibly sensing some latent Bronx rage in Bill, continued in a more reasonable tone. "The boss isn't going to study all this crap in fifteen minutes and then go out there and be tested by the press corps. The need is immediate. That is why you are here, brain-boy. So forget the goddamn reports and be ready to win this press conference on your feet!"

"Why do we have to *win* anything? How about just telling the truth?" "Why is your type always so smart in gee-whiz science and so pathetically out of touch with political science?"

∞§∞

This won't be that hard, Naomi Spence thought as she prepared her final briefing papers for the earlier-than-normal daily briefing. Before her job as White House Press Secretary, there were many mornings she got the girls and her husband up before the crack of dawn and rallied them into shape to face the day. This was all before her car picked her up at 6:30 for the 25-minute drive from Georgetown to the NBC news studios in the heart of D.C. With that kind of battle-hardened experience behind her, a room full of cranky reporters presented little challenge. The decision to take the job as press secretary was made easier by the fact that she and the family could stay in their home and the kids in school with all their friends. She took one last sip of English Breakfast tea and walked the few steps from her office to the podium.

In the White House pressroom, the members of the press corps were wiping the sleep from their eyes. This session was called earlier so the White House could "weigh in" on the explosion in suburban New York in time for the network morning shows. The reporters started pelting Naomi with questions as soon as she appeared at the doorway. She essentially gave the same non-answer six times. Then, when she felt they had settled down enough, she introduced Ray. Reynolds took the podium. "As Ms. Spence said, an investigation is currently under way into a massive explosion that happened a little less than ten hours ago. Obviously we don't have all the facts yet, so please lighten up on the detail questions."

A reporter for an Internet news service said, "We have a report that Intellichip was designing a chip for the Israeli air defense system. Could this be in any way a preemptive strike by certain Middle East elements who want to keep the balance of power where it is now?"

Reynolds was caught off guard. He hated this obnoxious Internet twerp whose only journalistic experience was getting lucky on a scandal from the last administration. Reynolds looked to Hiccock, who sent back an emphatically mouthed "No!" Reynolds grabbed the edges of the podium.

"That is unsubstantiated and, as far as I am concerned, wild speculation. Intellichip would have registered that type of work with State and we received no advisory from the State Department on that. So, no, your information may need to be checked more thoroughly."

Trying to dodge that bullet, he picked on a member of the "legitimate media," a reporter from ABC.

"So what were they working on at that Westchester plant?" the ABC veteran asked.

"I am going to turn the podium over to William Hiccock, the president's science advisor, who will address that issue." He gestured to Bill with his hand. Bill was shocked, as were some members of the press corps.

"They're putting Wild Bill in the game?" a surprised UPI reporter mumbled.

"Here comes the end run!" the correspondent from Reuters said back to him under his breath.

Bill approached the podium and leaned into the mic, causing feedback. A technician backed him off. Locating the ABC reporter in the room he asked, "Could you … could you repeat the question, please?"

"What were they working on at Intellichip's Westchester plant that could have exploded like that?"

"Not a thing."

The room burst into a flurry of shouted questions. Reynolds, the blood drained from his face, rushed back to the podium.

"Too short a sentence, Ray?" Hiccock asked as he was pushed aside. Reynolds glared at him and then turned to the press. "Now hold on. As I said before, neither Mr. Hiccock nor anyone else knows for sure what that plant was engaged in."

"That's not entirely correct," Hiccock said. A trained observer would have recognized the frozen eyeballs in Reynolds's head as his life passed before his eyes. Hiccock continued, "Our records indicate Intellichip was involved in parallel processing firewall technology. That's creating chips that will protect the next generation of computers, which will be so complex that they will be even more susceptible to hacking and other nastiness."

"For Israel?" the ABC vet asked.

"We have no information of any activity in the military procurement area, which, as you know, without permission from DARPA or the State Department, would be tantamount to treason." The room broke into a frenzy upon the use of the word *treason*. Reynolds buried his head.

"Someone's going to swing for this. You can't tell the truth here," said the Reuters correspondent, summing up the moment.

∞§∞

"Good God, Ray, what the hell were you thinking, putting Hiccock up there?" Spence asked, brandishing a fanfold of wire copy with a death grip. Watching her, Hiccock figured that whatever finishing school network anchors go to didn't cover getting so worked up that your neck veins showed.

"It was a gut call. I expected him to snow 'em."

"I don't snow people, Ray."

"Grow up."

"'White House leaves terrorism question open in Intellichip blast,'" the press secretary read from a headline. She continued, "'Science geek number one scares nation ... Arabs protest accusation they planted bomb.' Sweet Jesus, what a mess." She threw the copy down.

"I asked you what they were working on," Reynolds said angrily to Hiccock.

"And I told you."

"Gentlemen, please," the press secretary said. She turned to Hiccock. "Mr. Hiccock, please don't ever talk to the press directly again, and any releases are to be cleared through my office first." Without looking, she held a finger out in the chief of staff's direction, "Do I have your support on this, Ray?"

"Of course."

"Does this mean you don't want me to accept the request to go on *Geraldo?*" The vicious looks he received in response to that quip dissolved Hiccock's little smile.

∞§∞

Carly Simone made it to the press briefing room just after the briefing ended. It took her 30 minutes to get through White House security and obtain her press pass. Her original papers were back at the hotel by now, the airline having lost them with the rest of her check-in baggage. So there she stood outside the empty pressroom in the same clothes she wore last night. She also didn't have a clue where you went after a briefing was finished. But she didn't panic; after all it was only her first day as White House correspondent for Scientific American. Suddenly she saw him, William Hiccock, the reason she got this new assignment. If things had gone as planned last night, she would have introduced herself at the A.I. Convention, and this morning would not be the first time, but the explosion ruined everyone's night.

She pitched her story angle to the editors, on the basis that never before had anyone in the American public even known there was a science advisor to the president. This guy was a an ex-football hero, and that meant that the science-minded Americans who read their magazine might be interested in who he was, what he would and what he could do to advance the cause of science in America today. Last night her premise was proven when the technocratic elite warmly embraced Hiccock.

She had already written 300 words on last night alone. She promised her editor 2500. With 700 more going to background, she only had 1500 or so more to write. *Might as well get this over with,* she thought as she steeled up for her introduction, attempting to smooth a night's worth of wrinkles from the dress she wore at the dinner. She walked towards Hiccock. He looked like he had something on his mind. She turned on the smile.

As for Hiccock, he was running through a whole bunch of scenarios in his mind about any future encounters with the press. All at once he was looking into a vaguely familiar face, a really pretty face framed with blonde hair.

"William Hiccock, I'd like to introduce myself;, Carly Simone, from *Scientific American.*" She extended her hand.

"Pleasure to meet you." *A real pleasure.* What brings you to the White House?"

"Actually, you."

"Me?"

"Well, your story."

"I wasn't aware that I had a story."

"Wait until you read it in *Sci-Am*."

"Oh I get it; you are going to do a story on me for *Scientific American*."

"Hopefully with your cooperation."

I don't think you'll have any trouble getting anything out of me. "Sure, whatever I can do to help." *Wow, that was easy.* "Thank you. Can we sit somewhere for a while and talk?"

"That sounds nice... er fine."

"I think three times would do it."

"Excuse me?"

"Three interviews. I think that's all it would take. The third would probably just be a follow up to clarify."

"What are you writing, a novel?" I hope it ends with me getting the girl. Stop that, William, she's serious.

She doesn't know how to read the little smile that just rippled across his face. *Is he taking me seriously? Has it just hit him that I am in the same dress?* "I assure you, I only offer that as a measure of ensuring accuracy. Our readers demand it, as do my bosses."

"I completely understand." What a great dress... Oh crap! I can't do this.

"Of course you'll just have to clear everything through the Press Secretary." *Sorry babe.*

"Well, of course; how do you think I got this pass?" She said, holding up the pass dangling on a strap between her décolleté covered breasts.

"Well, that's very impressive," *My God you are healthy,* "but I think you should really review that with her one more time, especially after today."

"What happened today?" Oh shit, I should have been here.

"You really are new around here. Cover that with her; she's nice in a mean sort of way. Good to have met you. I've really gotta run." *If I talk to you any longer we are going to be picking out china patterns and registering at Macys,* he thought as he walked off in a deliberately more self-important rush than was necessary.

Leaving Carly to say to his back, "And nice meeting you, too. I look forward to working together." *Nice butt,* she thought as he turned and walked down the corridor. She was pleased having just had her first encounter with her subject.

On the way back to his office something about her was nagging at him. She looked familiar, although he couldn't place from where. As soon as he reached his office, the pile of memos, press releases, and position papers nudged any further thoughts of... Was it Carly Simon? Wasn't that the name of a singer? *Like I should talk,* thought Wild Bill Hiccock. He dove right into a position paper on "The Health Issues of Power Line Proximity in Niagara County." Somewhere between "effective radiated power coefficients" and "the field effect of electromagnetism on cellular membranes", it hit him. Aunt Mary! She was the blonde from last night. The one sitting up front! *Damn, why didn't I remember her? I hope she wasn't offended.* "...the fluxivity of the domain within the nucleus alternates between two..." *So she followed me here?* He read the next four dry, technically precise pages with a smile.

CHAPTER FOUR
GIFT FROM HEAVEN

THERE WAS A SOFT, early fall breeze blowing into his face. That was good; he wanted to be downwind of his target. Dennis Mallory's eyebrows knitted as he strained to listen for any crack of a twig or brush-by of a bush that would reveal the position of his prey. Not wishing to betray his location by the slightest move, he didn't dare check his watch. Instead he judged by the position of the sun that he'd been waiting for at least two hours. The only movement he did risk was the rippling of his fingers over the main part of the weapon that hung comfortably in his lowered hands. An eagle circled above, catching a thermal with outstretched wings. The hot sun baked the valley and created huge heated updrafts upon which a bird of prey could hitchhike. *Two hunters*, he thought. *Only the bird doesn't need contacts.*

The quiet rustle of the forest was soothing. A few years back, at just about this time of day, he would be traipsing through some god-awful neighborhood. Suddenly, a movement caught his attention. As he had been trained to do with so many other weapons, his mind was immediately flushed of any and all thought save one: lining up his shot. The antlers and head of a magnificent eight-point buck peeked over the bramble about thirty yards ahead. Having long ago gotten over buck fever, he exhaled, eliminating even the remotest possibility that the holding of a breath could affect his body mechanics when he released the arrow. He silently coaxed the "venison on hoof" a little more out into the open, where he would be able to get a good shot. He slowly brought his arms up and lined up the "peep site" with green fiber-optic pin of his Titan site. The eagle above suddenly started flapping his wings in an almost silent flurry of whooshes. It didn't faze the buck, which lazily strode out another two feet into the clearing. Dennis pulled back the remaining tension of the 70-pound draw, Bowtech Guardian Compound bow, making them one single, deadly weapon system and was waiting for the next foot of revealed buck to cross his sights when a cry came from above them.

"Shit!"

Dennis and the buck looked up. There was the sound of breaking branches as the eight-point buck's flag went up and the white underside of his tail disappeared into cover. Dennis watched, both amazed and perturbed, as a swatch of colors, lines, and ropes came crashing down into the opening. At the center of the ball of color and cloth was a helmeted man rolling in agony.

"Aw, fer christsake!" was all Dennis said as he replaced the arrow in his quiver. He then unstrapped his safety belt from the trunk of the tree and climbed down from the stand that required an hour of positioning. He approached the man on the ground and saw that he was rapidly losing blood from his upper leg. Dennis quickly opened his own belt, yanked it through the loops of his camouflage pants, and dropped to his knees. He used the shaft of an arrow as the turnbuckle of a makeshift belt-tourniquet. The man on the ground was going into shock and shuddering. The twisting of the tourniquet stemmed the flow of blood. Dennis determined that this daredevil had lost quite a bit of blood, but not as much as he had seen other men, including himself, lose and still survive.

"You're going to be okay. You're bleeding a lot and you might have a concussion. Don't worry, I'll get you out of here." He removed his Gerber Skinner knife from its sheath and slit the man's parachute. *Was it a parasail or para-glide?* He couldn't remember what the hot dogs who jumped off of cliffs called these things. Making a blanket of the multicolored fabric, he covered the crumpled body, deciding to leave the man's helmet on but loosening the neck strap a bit. Dennis figured if he could at least keep him warm, the guy might not go into total shock. Dennis reached into his pocket to retrieve his cell phone. There was no signal. That's when the man's eyes met his.

"I'm going to a campsite about a mile back to get help." As he walked away, the man grunted and tried to talk. Dennis came back and leaned down to listen.

"My ... poc ... ket."

Dennis felt all the man's pockets and found a cell phone in his right front. "I already tried but there is no sig ..." Dennis was surprised to see a full signal until he read the name of the phone. It was a Comsat 310. "No shit, a satellite phone. Well, buddy, this is the best three grand you ever spent."

Dennis was lucky to have drawn a tag from the Montana lottery and called the park rangers with the number printed on his out-of-state hunting license. He then reached in his pocket and retrieved his own personal Radio Shack GPS system. A gift from his wife, Cynthia, with a note that said "So you can always find your way back to me." In the past, the only thing that got in the way of his coming home to her every night was the ritual at the watering hole, three blocks from the precinct that was his office for twenty-five years.

"My name is Dennis Mallory. I have a wounded man here, at 45 degrees, 37 minutes, 4.36 seconds, north, 110 degrees, 33 minutes,

35.82 seconds. Need air-evac, he's lost a lot of blood."

"Hold on." The ranger didn't put his phone down and Dennis could hear him calling to the chopper whose scratchy response was followed by a repeat of Dennis's coordinates. The ranger got back on the line. "Is the victim conscious?"

"He's going in and out."

"Are you by a clearing or place for the helicopter to land?"

"We're about 300 yards west of a nice clear patch. I'll mark it with a part of this guy's parachute."

"Parachute?"

"Yeah, a little present from heaven dropped down here with a thud ... cut up his leg on a broken branch as he was coming in, probably busted a couple of bones to boot."

"That's a first!"

"For me, too, buddy. For me, too!"

∞§∞

The chopper was four minutes out, and Dennis was packing up his gear when he heard a sound that freezes all hunters dead in their tracks. He turned and saw a giant chestnut-brown grizzly three yards from the downed man. Instinctively, Dennis started shouting, trying to distract the mammoth beast from the smell of blood. He knew that, at sixty yards, the .38 strapped to his ankle would do little more than piss off the thing.

The bear turned around as it got wind of yet another predator in his domain.

"Now what do I do?" Dennis said to the trees as he quickly unzipped the bag into which he had just stowed his bow. He cut himself on the razor-tipped edge of a Carbon Express, three-veined arrow as he snagged it out from the quiver. The bear started toward him. Then, as if the animal had calculated the distance between them, it turned to go back to the raw meat writhing on the ground only a few feet away. Like an Indian brave, with his bow out in front of him, Dennis began running toward the bear as he nocked the arrow to the string. To get the bear's attention he started screaming again ... to no avail. It hovered over the bleeding fellow for a second, sniffing at the brightly colored blanket.

While running, Dennis observed the bear's hesitation, the nylon chute momentarily confusing the bear. The scent of fresh blood, however, overcame the grizzly's visual disorientation and it began to prod and poke the bright fabric covering the newly butchered prey it was so fortunate to stumble upon. Then the grizzly got a handle on something that looked edible. With a snap of his head, the bear chomped down on the man's arm.

Dennis stopped momentarily, just long enough to take a shot, then continued running. As soon as the arrow left his bow, he feared that he might hit the man he was trying to save. The bear swung the man out of harm's way just as the arrow punctured the animal right above its left shoulder. The pain pulling the beast sideways created the image of the man being dragged like a rag doll.

This time, Dennis got down on one knee as he nocked the next arrow. Taking a deep breath, he retracted the bow and aimed. On exhale, he loosed the arrow. The animal cried out, dropping the man's arm. Having been hit right in the chest it rolled backwards, snapping off both arrows that lodged deep in its body. The 1,200-pound grizzly roared as he beat the ground with massive paws and tried to shake away the pain that stung him like giant bees. Dennis approached the man and saw he was still breathing. Although his arm was gnawed, it was still intact.

Dennis fit the string into the notch of one more arrow. Cautiously, he advanced toward the wounded animal. It lay helpless, its breathing rapid and short, its thick fur rippling with spasms. Its eyes wide, the bear was choking on its own blood, the arrow having punctured the right lung. Dennis, a hunter all his life, of men, as well as animals, felt a genuine sadness for this great creature's agonizing confusion.

"Sorry, pal, but this is for your own good," he said as he let go of an arrow that went right into the beast's heart. The giant bear stopped moving as if a switch was thrown off. Dennis gazed upon the grizzly for a moment. How sad that such a glorious animal had to be wasted like that. He had to put his daughter's dog, Patches, to sleep when it contracted a tumor in its old age. She grew up with the dog and even though she was sixteen, he still had to explain to her that it was for Patches' own good that he be put to sleep. His daughter didn't buy it. It took a year before their relationship normalized again. Normal only for a brief second because then she was seventeen and discovered a completely new set of ways to test him.

Dennis heard the rotors of the approaching chopper and ran to the clearing to flag down the paramedics.

CHAPTER FIVE
CAKE AND SOUFFLÉ

THERE WAS A TIME when people actually took tours of the Mason Chemical Plant Number Five. But that was long ago, before the National Football League decided that Canton, Ohio, was the perfect place for the Football Hall of Fame. Now *they* give all the tours. As with most industrial plants that are not working on anything of vital national or corporate security interest, the chemical plant had minimal security, mostly to keep out mischief-makers and give the employees the sense that they were being protected. This unseasonably warm fall evening, that protection was the responsibility of Eugene Harns, one of Canton's finest, retired some fifteen years now from active duty, filling out his pension check on the night shift three days a week in the guard shack. It was an easy job. He wound up being more like the old guys at Kmart, a smiling, welcoming face waving folks through as long as the picture on their ID was a close-enough match.

It was only natural, then, that the appearance at his guard booth of a petite woman carrying a cake provided a good excuse for him to act official.

"Hold on, Ma'am," he said as he stepped out of his shack. "No unauthorized access past this point."

"Oh, hi. Listen, my husband Jim, he works the night shift. Anyway, it's his birthday tonight, and I made him this little cake so he and Andy and the other boys could celebrate." She finished with a smile that would have gotten the Army to open the door at Fort Knox.

"What's your name?"

"Eugenia Nichols. What's yours?" She extended the hand that wasn't holding the cake on the plastic tray.

"Well, I'll be ... I'm *Eugene*. Eugene Harns." He allowed a smile at the seeming coincidence, not realizing that she read his name badge a split second earlier. "I'll just call the night desk and see if they'll come down to escort you."

As Eugene picked up the telephone to call the night manager, she politely protested. "Gosh, don't spoil it. It's supposed to be a surprise!" Eugene looked the suburban mom up and down, her shyness causing her eyes to avert then reconnect during his scrutiny. If it hadn't been dark, he might have noticed that her eyes kept moving rapidly when she wasn't focused on him. Nevertheless, even in bright sunlight, Eugene would not have seen beyond her incandescent smile, her happy blue skirt, and her sensible shoes. His thirty-two years as a cop told him that she was as sweet as the cake. Her promising him a piece of the chocolate seven-layer on her way out also persuaded him to let her have her little surprise. He nodded his head as he allowed her through. She gave him a kiss on the cheek, which made him feel old, as if she thought of him as a grandfather or something.

Maybe I'm getting soft, he thought as she sauntered toward the main building.

∞§∞

Upon entering the main room, the woman looked up to find dozens of brightly painted pipes of all sizes crisscrossing at different levels above her head. The tops of huge, three-story-high chemical vats jetted thin streams of vapor. She climbed up the aluminum stairs, her sensible shoes clanking all the way, onto a grated metal walkway. Walking directly to a valve-control panel box, she noticed a 6,000-gallon vat behind her, standing tall from the floor below. A red label read "Caution: Super Corrosive Content." She placed the cake on top of the metal box and opened the panel. Inside was a large red valve held in check by a safety rod with a red flag on it, reading, "DO NOT REMOVE." She pulled the rod out and turned the wheel. Immediately, the giant spigot at the bottom of the tank opened and a torrent of acid poured out—instantly vaporizing everything in its path.

A technician ran down the catwalk toward the woman. "Turn it back! Close the valve!" he screamed.

Without flinching, she pushed her hand into the cake and lifted it up, pieces of cake and icing falling off, revealing the .38 caliber snub-nose revolver she so painstakingly placed between the layers this afternoon. As she pulled the trigger, the loud report of the gun startled her, causing her to ask herself, *where did this gun come from?* Yet she was compelled to continue as the remaining cake in the front of the pistol blew off while she pumped three holes in the technician's chest. He tumbled into the acid, dissolving like a pat of butter on a hot skillet. As the structure on which she was standing weakened and started to buckle from the same acid, she sat down in her very confused state, her jittery eyes bouncing in her head. *Wasn't there a meeting at Jenny's school tonight? Where's the cake I baked for it?* Seconds later Doris Polk, aka Eugenia Nichols, slid off into the same corrosive mix.

∞§∞

That was a different sound, Eugene thought as he poured a fresh cup of coffee in anticipation of the slice of cake. He looked over to the little single-cup Mr. Coffee in the guard shack, as if that were the source of the rumbling thunder. Then he heard a noise he had never encountered in his life, something like a gigantic squeaky door accompanied by the low guttural rumble a Trident nuclear submarine would make if you dragged it across Interstate 80. He didn't even notice the hot liquid burning his leg from the coffee cup that slipped through his hand. Mesmerized, he watched as the entire Plant Number Five collapsed in and on itself like a startled soufflé dissolving into oozing goo right before his eyes.

CHAPTER SIX
SPIN

200 YEARS AGO it must have made sense, but the hard marble steps and floors of the former military academy were killing the Captain's legs. He calculated that he must walk 30 kilometers a day over these things that were half the rise of normal stairs. The "standard issue" boots he wore as part of his daily uniform were designed for tramping through terrain, not over polished marble. The steps and floors were designed this way so that generals and commanders of the legions of Italy, who once occupied this country, could ride their mounts right up the stairs to their offices. That perk of command was now causing his legs to ache two centuries later. The closest anyone in this compound ever came to a horse lately was a 4x4 Toyota Land Cruiser. The steed-inspired length of each step caused him to hobble up the stairs in a manner not unlike a small boy, with both feet landing on every center-worn tread. This small annoyance piled up to once again have him doubt his lot in life. He had risen to the rank of Captain early, and with pride, only to have his career stalled at that level. Younger men than he were now his superiors. He considered himself a glorified office boy running antiquated Teletype messages, deemed secret, to various parts of the massive military structure. It was that level of sensitivity, which demanded that no underling, beneath the rank of Captain could ferry these signals to the Command staff. He hurried past statues of great former generals and busts of other old men whose bones were now dust, those marble effigies keeping them in eternal service to a country that had been occupied more times than a hotel room in Paris.

He stopped at the desk of the assistant to General Nandeserra. The Captain hated the General's clerk, who had adopted an air of royalty, simply because he was the lackey of a commanding officer (an elevation in life to which his goat herder of a father could never have imagined).

"Is he in?" the Captain asked flatly.

"He's busy," the little snit replied.

"It's a communiqué."

With an almost disgusted sigh, the aide laboriously lifted the phone and buzzed into the inner office. "Captain Falad, with a telex."

As he entered the room, Falad was surprised to see 10 high commanders in conference around a map of the United States. There were pins inserted at various places, one in a place called Ohio. He stood waiting to be recognized as the men discussed something about the effect on their plan.

"So, are you saying that the Americans won't look this way?" General Nandeserra asked in an accusatory tone meant to belittle any opinion that didn't originate within his brain.

"I am saying, General, that they have established no links or any connection to us or Samovar." A slight-of-build, mustached Colonel, in an ill-fitting uniform, explained.

Falad surmised that he must be in the intelligence service, since intelligence officers were not warriors, just brains. The army could make a uniform fit the body of a man of action, but could not make a dress shirt for a brain. *Brains*, Falad thought, *required a private tailor.* He noticed the copy of an intelligence report; it was in Arabic but the words "Canton Ohio," which had no Arabic translation, remained in English. He then heard Nandeserra mutter, "Yes."

Falad stepped forward, put his feet together, as is appropriate when addressing an officer of flag rank, and handed the papers to him. The General put on his half-height reading glasses and gave the paper a quick scan, "That will be all, Captain." He dismissed Falad without looking up from the Teletype impacted paper.

As the Captain headed for the door he heard the General announce, "It appears the Americans do not have any idea that they are under attack, at least from the disposition of their military assets in the world. There has been..." the door shut behind him, cutting off the General's words.

Falad walked across more than 1,000 meters of unforgiving Turkish marble back to his desk in the basement. Falad was stationed in the "Eyes and Ears," the nickname he and his unit called the modern listening post that was finally approved for installation. It was really nothing more than a few satellite dishes with K-band receivers hooked up to a distribution system that allowed for many television sets along with many video tape recorders to monitor worldwide satellite broadcasts. It was crammed into a small space amidst the clanking metal Teletype machines that still carried encrypted communications to various levels of the government and military.

Ever since the Gulf War of the last century, nation states of the world realized that much intelligence was flying around the globe in the form of satellite news networks like CNN. Critical information regarding operations, troop movements, and the future deployment of forces were the common fodder of American journalism. Falad estimated that America's lust for news had saved nations around the world billions in intelligence gathering costs. Having lived for a short time in the U.S., Falad was well aware of the open nature indicative of that society as well as its puppet governments throughout Europe. That's how he got this assignment. To his chagrin, he was pulled from an active field artillery unit on the western border only to shuttle papers and culturally interpret the programming they were receiving.

America had made a sport of political and governmental news coverage. They just couldn't help themselves from broadcasting these matches to the rest of
the world. Falad had been brought in to separate the
dung from the fertile soil. There was much dung on
these programs. People, who had no idea of what was
truly going on in government or military affairs, were
given airtime and the privilege of discussing pressing matters of the day with anchors and hosts of talk
shows. For the most part, those moderators' only apparent reason to exist was to fill up the spaces between
Weight Watchers advertisements and recorded music
offers. This massive amount of uninformed guessing
and supposition was confusing to standard, direct
translators. It became clear that "who was talking?"
and "what true knowledge did they have?" were more
cultural questions than ones of fact. Many horse's ass-
es were allowed to pontificate on matters of the day,
essentially polluting the well of information which was
originally so pure when Peter Arnett broadcast direct
from Baghdad. One could plainly see, in night vision
green and white, the air war happening over his shoulder. Today 90 percent was garbage and people speaking merely to hear themselves talk. Falad's job was to
monitor, decipher, and rate the relative importance
and political power of the various heads that spoke so
that the "intelligence" they spewed could be either dismissed or considered.

Getting the hang of the White House could certainly
be a daunting task; her level of security pass clearance
had its limitations unless a senior person accompanied
her. The first thing she learned was that Hiccock had
"All Access." He seemed to have a direct line right to
the president, a truly rare circumstance between a science advisor and POTUS, which is what she learned

the insiders called the President Of The United States. It was a carry over from the abbreviation used on the old White House interoffice phone system.

She thought she was heading down to the White House mess when she found herself in the little room, off the pressroom, filled with reporters filing their stories. The United Press International correspondent immediately zeroed in on the blonde as she entered the room, appearing somewhat bewildered.

"Can I help you?" Dave Higgins asked.

"I can't believe I wound up back here," Carly admitted out loud.

"New here, aren't you?" he asked seeing the special badge hanging from her neck. It was a "short term" issue, usually for reporters whose newspapers didn't have a permanent reporter assigned to the press corp.

"Yes, my second day." She extended her hand. "Carly Simmone from *Scientific American*."

"Dave Higgins, UPI. Want a cup of coffee?"

"Actually, I was heading to the mess for an interview."

"Ah... that's the next door over, then make a left."

"Thanks." she turned to leave.

"Who are you interviewing?"

"William Hiccock."

"Right, *Scientific American!*" he made a gesture with his finger like a gun and shot her a wink. She reciprocated, shot him back a pressed grin, and left.

∞§∞

It took all of five minutes. Wally Smith, the producer of MSNBC, found his way into Naomi Spence's office.

"What can I do for you, Wally?"

"Naomi, we all play by the rules here. You say hands off Hiccock and we back off."

"Thank you for reminding me of my own rules"

"...Well today this girl shows up with a special, and Dave Higgins tells me she's having lunch with Hiccock, doing an exclusive egghead piece for *American Science* magazine. What gives?"

"First off, it's *Scientific American*. Secondly, she is not a girl, she is a woman, a reporter, and, for your information, the story was set way before anything blew up."

"Listen, Naomi, I represent over four million viewers. Throw in NBC and CNBC and we got 30 million adults 25 - 54 watching. I don't think I like the idea of being scooped by some monthly journal of a science rag, when we are covering hard news here."

"Yesterday you did a seven-minute package on the president's daughter Marie's poodle and how she got better doggy health care being the daughter of the president. Real hard there, Wally"

"So that's what this is about, revenge for a little human interest?"

"The only thing human about that piece was the cute shot of the dog, Wally! Otherwise you were going for PoodleGATE."

"You know, Naomi, when we were back at 30 Rock, you understood how tight this business is..."

"Stop right there, Wally. We worked together back in New York 15 years ago. You have cashed that chip more than a few times, and now it's done."

"You can be so infuriating."

"My husband tells me that all the time."

"How's Larry doing?"

"The doctors say as long as he walks the straight and narrow, his kidneys will be with him 'til we own a place in Miami."

"Say hi for me, and think about what you are going to do to make this up to me."

"Up yours, Wally. I'll tell him you said hello."

"See ya round, Spence."

"See ya round, Wal."

As soon as he left, Naomi called her assistant. "Sue, pull the *Scientific American* file. I want to see last month's request for access letter one more time."

"Do you ever regret not playing in the NFL?" Carly asked a half-hour into her interview with Hiccock.

"I never connected with football the way I have connected with science. Football was a game, a diversion. I have always been a scientist."

"Are you just saying that because we are doing a *SciAm* article right now?"

"No, I told the same thing to *Sports Illustrated.*"

"When?" she asked. "I didn't see any article from *S.I.* in my research."

"Exactly. I told them the same thing I just told you. Took all the fun out of it for them, I guess."

Carly was smiling. "So then you learned from *that*, what to say to me?"

They both laughed.

∞§∞

Wally Smith was getting a cup of coffee when the laughter turned him around. As he looked at this *girl*, this blonde, very attractive blonde, with a great smile... he felt inspired.

CHAPTER SEVEN
FALL INTO THE GAP

THERE THEY ARE, right where Walter said they would be. *Rusty and filthy, enough to beat the band, but they will do,* Martha thought as she put the jumper cables into the backseat of the car. She returned to the garage and opened an old, dusty Army footlocker. She was inundated with the intense smell of mothballs. Again, there where her dear departed Walter left it, tucked under the heavy brown cloth of his sergeant's uniform, lay his illegal war prize. It was still oily, situated next to a magazine. The magazine held nine bullets. When inserted into the German Luger, it would be transformed from a dead war relic to a deadly weapon.

She shut off the light in the garage and went out to her car as the setting sun drew long shadows on everything in her quiet little neighborhood. Walter needed her. Soon she would see him again and help him with the dead battery in his car.

∞§∞

Mr. Quimby was watering his lawn when he noticed Martha backing out of her driveway cautiously. "Eh, Martha," he called out across the picket fence that separated these neighbors for thirty-five years. "Going to the grandkids?" He chalked up her lack of response to the widow Krummel being hard of hearing of late. As her taillights disappeared around the corner, he turned back to his meticulously manicured lawn. The last few days of Indian summer had been brutally hot and that meant lawn-browning weather if one wasn't careful. Maybe he would water Martha's as well.

∞§∞

She drove as dusk turned into darkness. When Martha got sight of the highway sign for the Waukesha Gap, new thoughts filled her brain. Her eyes fluttered momentarily, causing her to refocus on the dirt road and a farm stand just ahead. Making a left-hand turn onto the service road, she thought, *big juicy strawberries will make an excellent jam.* She followed the bumpy and dusty road for eight miles.

This was an access road for the railroad's right-of-way maintenance crews. Ahead of her, lit by her headlights, she could barely make out the two big metal cabinets that sat on concrete footings alongside the track. As soon as these cabinets came clearly into view, new thoughts filled her head. *There is a little baby in the big cabinet crying for its mother.* She shut the engine off but left the lights on as she retrieved the jumper cables, crowbar, and a big old flashlight and made her way toward the control boxes. Her nose twitched from the pungent odor of creosote, a petroleum derivative with which the wooden rail ties were saturated. Not remembering how she knew this, she recalled that this tarlike goo was meant to dissuade termites and mushrooms from making homes in the vital wooden cross members.

Using all her effort, she managed to pry open the small hasp lock on the bigger panel. She then placed the crowbar on top of the smaller cabinet along with the Luger. After positioning the flashlight on the ground, the tiltable head pointing up at the box, she opened the cabinet. For a brief moment, she was befuddled by a wave of fear washing over her. Then, as quickly as it came upon her, it was gone. With the confidence of a veteran track-and-signals railroad man, she traced the circuitry, her hand hovering just above the copper-clad contacts and relays. She identified her first contact point and clamped one end of the jumper cable to it. She attached the other end of the cable a foot to the right and about four feet lower, which sent sparks flying. A solenoid began to clank as relays flipped.

Three hundred feet down the track, a switch machine cycled through its positions, first sliding the rails left with a metallic clunk, then slamming right back to the original position. Lights on a signal bridge above the switch followed suit, going from green to red and back to green. The lights on the dwarf signal beside the track alternated in an "L" configuration, first one over the other, indicating straight through, then side by side: turnout to the left. At this point the switch machine threw the rails left again, but this time the signal did not turn red. It stayed green. As the rumble of an approaching train echoed through the valley, Martha walked precariously down the track along the sloping loose-gravel roadbed to a point in front of the signal bridge. The dwarf signal displayed two lights, one on top of the other, indicating that the switch was set for straight ahead. She made sure the light was set on green and turned her back to the white fog created by the glow of the oncoming train's headlight. As she walked back to the control boxes, two tracer-like bands of light raced toward her, the reflection of the train's powerful headlight, first seen off the stropped-steel 155-pound main line rails, as the locomotive came around the bend and into view.

Having completed her task, a slight shaking overcame her body. She felt conflicted over the thing she knew she must do next. With a sense of dread welling up from somewhere deep within her, she turned and approached the cabinets again. She watched in stunned silence as her hand extended out into the night, on its own, reaching for something. The flashlight on the ground in front of her shone in her eyes, which darted to and fro. This degraded her night vision so much that, as she reached for the Luger, she smashed her head right into the crowbar she didn't see. The old woman staggered, falling to the ground in the gap between the control cabinets.

Unconscious, with a deep gash in her forehead, her last thought was of her husband Walter, who died twenty years ago.

∞§∞

Train 7210, its consist made of only tank cars, was high-balling through the flat valley at sixty miles per hour. The lead engine, running short hood forward, being a General Electric C40-8W, was known on the road as a Dash 8 Diesel. It was coupled with four other Dash 8s, which gave her a combined pull of 20,000 horsepower, enough to pull the eighty cars across the country. Two additional locomotives, older Dash 7s, were hitched to the rear of the train and served as helpers in a push-pull arrangement that generated an additional 2,250 horsepower each, enough power to climb up and over the Waukesha Gap. Jim Crowley, a third-generation railroad man, was at the controls. One of his last living actions would be to ease his grip on the brake handle when coming around a banked-curve section of track at full speed. He did this secure in the fact that the signal at the Waukesha interlock was "clean and green." The vertical lights of the dwarf signal indicated the switch was set for the straight. At seventy miles per hour, the two miles of arrow straight track ahead gave him just under two minutes to bend over and get his thermos to cut the chill of the night with some hot coffee. But before he was able to grab the thermos, his cab jerked suddenly, veering hard left as his engine raced over the thrown switch meant to be taken at five miles per hour.

He was already dead from his head slamming into the throttle pedestal before his body crumpled to the floor. The half-ton wheels of the engine ripped through the frogs and railroad ties that made up the track-and-switch roadbed. Pandrol clips, which long ago replaced spikes, popped and sprung from the cleats below the rail. The massive force of the millions-plus tons of tank cars coupled behind it pushed the engine like a plow into the dirt as the other engines began to jackknife. With the pneumatic brake lines leading from the engines to the rest of the train severed, the cars had no way of slowing down and proceeded to derail and collapse, spilling their liquid contents out onto the countryside. The ruptured tanks were ignited by the sparks flying from the grinding metal, setting off a hundred fires in the vegetation and bramble along the right of way. The faster conduction of sound through the steel rails made each cry of bending steel and groan of folding iron sound as if it were a spring twanging underwater—the kind of pre-echo that one usually only hears in monster movies. It took a full minute for all the cars to come to a moaning, squeaky halt or to randomly explode. When they finally stopped, a quarter mile of devastation and destruction lay strewn about the woods of Waukesha Gap.

Amazingly, Martha had fallen between the two concrete footings, and the engines and cars piled up away from where she lay. Rescue workers were astonished and confused when they found her there three hours later.

CHAPTER EIGHT
OPTIONS

BILL ENTERED HIS OFFICE and there on his desk was a huge, enormous gift basket. He pulled the card.

"Mr. Hiccock?"

Bill turned as he finished reading the card, "Yes."

"Joan Duma, from the Office of Protocol."

"Hello, Ms. Duma. What can I do for you? Would you like a dried fruit or nut, I seem to have a ton of them?"

"Actually that's why I am here."

He smiled as he read the signatures, Shelly and Mario Singorelli. "I'm sorry, I am not following you."

"White House protocol forbids any member of the administration from receiving gifts without full disclosure and receipt of value authorized."

"Wow." Then Bill got deadly serious. "You're talking forms to fill out, right?"

"Actually it's more like a small booklet with addendums to the GAO, IRS, and eventually the Mitchell presidential museum."

"Okay. So what's the alternative?"

"Alternative?"

"Come on, Ms. Duma, all a terrorist would have to do is send spiced hams or fruitcakes to every member of government, every day. The whole thing would grind to a halt in forms and rigmarole."

"I don't think I like your tone, Mr. Hiccock."

"Sorry. What's my option? How do I get out of this nightmare?"

"Well, you could donate the basket to a food bank or to the homeless."

"Done. They'll be eating dried apricots and almonds by this afternoon."

"Good. And, I assure you, we in protocol would never be party to any terrorist action."

"You don't laugh a lot, do you, Ms. Duma?"

∞§∞

"Seventeen events in two weeks," Wallace Tate, the Director of the FBI said. "No credible group claiming responsibility. No rhyme or reason to the targets, no escalation. Seemingly isolated incidents." A fifty-five-year-old, well-tanned, and taut-skinned former Boston police chief, he was a political survivor of two administration changeovers. Where former directors administrated their way through their tenures, Tate ruled over his bureau with a dictatorial style not seen since the iron-fist days of J. Edgar Hoover. The combination of his police training and his executive acumen made him a field agent's worst nightmare: a boss who might be in your face or looking over your shoulder at any time.

Ray Reynolds, Press Secretary Spence, and Hiccock listened intently to the report.

"What about the terrorists?" Reynolds asked.

"Wrong handle, Ray," the director said. "Terrorists have a cause, a common belief that binds them. All these acts were carried out by people posing as homegrown U.S. citizens." He inserted a CD into his laptop and punched the pad. He preferred to use a laptop when he made these White House briefings. It was HASP and password protected and if someone tried to monkey with it, a program shredded everything on the hard drive, insuring FBI secrets wouldn't be compromised. A screen came up containing Professor Holm's uncomplimentary driver's license photo, next to which appeared a black-and-white security video made virtually unwatchable by a blizzard of static.

"Prior to this mangled security tape, which provided enough evidence to prove him guilty in the destruction of the Intellichip building, this man's most violent behavior was slamming the side of his computer when it locked up on him."

He hit the touch pad, bringing up Martha Krummel's photo. A picture of a smoldering freight train pileup was displayed in an adjacent box on the screen.

"Martha Krummel, a grandmother, derailed an eighty-car train. As far as we have learned, the only thing that seemed to make her angry was the weeds in her garden."

Displayed next on the screen was Doris Polk. "This woman was a secretary and taught Sunday school. After she opened two valves as if she were a trained technician, the entire Mason Chemical Plant dissolved into liquid muck."

Her photograph was replaced by that of a young boy. "This Boy Scout merit badge holder started a fire that destroyed the corporate office of the number two accounting firm in the country. On his FaceBook page he said he wanted to be president someday."

Tate clicked repeatedly now, his point made. "And thirteen others, every single one of them exhibiting no known ties or sympathies to any group, real or imagined; just average citizens."

"You said imagined?" Hiccock questioned.

"Mr. Hitchcock, I don't have the time …"

"It's Hiccock," Ray Reynolds said. "I asked Bill to attend because he was there when Intellichip blew. Ever since, he has been weeding through any science issues and advising us on policy."

"Very well," Tate nodded to Ray stiffly. "Field agent reports have indicated …"

"Excuse me," Bill interrupted again, "a moment ago you said 'imagined.' I would still like to know what that means in this context."

Suffering fools was not the director's strong suit, and he sized up this science whiz as being nothing short of a nuisance. "We have teams at Quantico that stay up all night thinking up the wildest scenarios, and this one's got them stymied."

"Okay, but this level of devastation isn't something you learn on the Discovery Channel or in a YouTube video. In every case these people knew something intimate about the means of destruction."

"We know that," the director said. "We utilize cutting-edge modern police procedure and we show nothing, nothing in common."

"Except one thing." All heads turned to Hiccock. "They're all dead."

There was a perceptible smirk on the director's face as he punched the pad once more and Martha Krummel's photograph reappeared. "Except her."

"Are we talking suicide terrorists now?" Reynolds asked. "How do they get these people to do this?"

"Because these perpetrators all have squeaky clean backgrounds, we believe they are deep-cover moles. Agent provocateurs lying quietly until they are called on to act."

"How could you possibly reach that conclusion?" Hiccock said agitatedly.

The director closed his eyes for a second and swallowed deeply. "Deep cover. We have recognized and prepared for the possibility for years. The Russians were constantly getting caught trying to plant moles in the United States. In fact, they even had an American town built in Russia where they would train their agents to live in our society without raising suspicions."

"Does the Office of Homeland Security concur with your scenario?" Ray asked, prompting a confident nod from the director. "Then that's good enough for me. Let's go see the president immediately and inform him of your investigation's focus. Hiccock, you can go back to your office."

Hiccock was about to say something but held his tongue.

"Ray, I'll get started on background so when, and if, the boss decides to share this we'll be ready," Spence said. She left, followed by the two men.

Hiccock just sat there stewing, an argument raging in his head.

∞§∞

The President's Council on Physical Fitness would have to rewrite its bylaws if it saw what the president of the United States was doing in the White House gym. James Mitchell, a younger-looking man than his fifty-eight years, was working out on the rowing machine. A cigarette dangled from his mouth as he strained on the oars while receiving the report from Tate and Reynolds. The man's own doctors had of course warned him about his smoking, but he had been a fighter pilot and an ace in both Vietnam and the first Gulf War. He was shot down deep in Indian Country in the former and managed to evade the enemy, in their own backyard, for a month, ultimately returning to America a true hero. A little thing like a cigarette wasn't going to land him in Arlington National Cemetery.

James Mitchell was probably the most surprised man in America on election night. Although he had been the popular favorite early in the campaign, he was nearly ground up in the political machinery. The party bigwigs thrust their will on America and limited the field of who *could* become president to two—and Mitchell wasn't one of them. The millions of dollars in each party's war chest were bequeathed to the two prep school boys who were groomed for presidential service since they were still shitting in their diapers.

Failing to get his party's nomination meant he was boxed out of the big money and the essential television time those dollars bought. He and Reynolds revised their goal to achieving a decent enough double-digit independent turnout in this election to possibly pave the way for another run in four years. Mitchell's little fledgling campaign turned to grassroots town meetings and tried to make the most of the Internet, including a personal blog he hammered out every day between campaign stops. But gaining a ten to eleven percent foothold into the next election wasn't the way it played out. Because a *fourth* candidate, a Democrat from way out left, siphoned off enough votes that when the counting was over, the scrappy little fighter pilot with no money became President elect of the United States.

The big three networks spent all of election night reporting that the vote was too close to call between the Democrat and Republican, with Mitchell not even breaking into his vaunted double digits. Their prognostications came back to bite them in their collective rear ends, when the actual vote tally came up in Mitchell's favor.

A karmic retribution of sorts ensued as the whole affair sent tremors throughout the media elite who earlier cast their "big vote" pronouncing Mitchell's campaign as "dead on arrival" in Iowa. The first shock was felt in cable where many a verbose and traditionally aligned pundit found himself now out of favor and out of work. A new political reality swept its way onto the deeply rooted, bipartisan American scene on President Mitchell's independent coattails.

The cable news channels reengineered themselves, practically overnight, as the suits in those cable network's executive offices unceremoniously jettisoned the established, venerated pillars of the conservative and liberal status quo. They immediately embraced anyone who ever hesitated long enough to utter, "um" when asked, "Are you a liberal or conservative?" Big salaries and signing bonuses soon followed. This newly hatched brood of "indies," realizing that their newfound wealth and fame were directly connected to James Mitchell's success, cut him slack, running interference on his behalf whenever some righty or lefty tried to convince the American people that being politically ambidextrous was some kind of deep character flaw.

In this volatile environment, the entrenched broadcast networks and newspapers, which had long since plastered their political leanings across their front pages in 90-point type and evening lead stories, had but one recourse—attack. They argued that, since Mitchell's name never registered on any of their beloved exit polls, the election had to be fixed. This accusation was easy to prosecute, because in any national election millions of ballots were cast and some voter irregularity was to be expected. The networks jumped all over these even though, statistically speaking, the numbers were miniscule making the allegations insignificant enough to be practically a myth. But good myths sell papers and commercial airtime.

For the first six months of his administration, reporters investigated every ward and precinct. The news corporations dispatched them with an implied warning: "Do not come back empty-handed." Every allegation or actual fact of irregularity was scrutinized and reported with an intensity that in and of itself screamed "scandal." Even inconsequential screw-up's that normally would never pass muster with a small town paper's editor were now suddenly being served up nationally as potential "smoking guns."

Eventually, two factors defeated the media's onslaught. For one, the many false alarms and cries of wolf started to dilute the public's interest. But more importantly, Mitchell's middle-of-the-road brand of politics and quiet ability to get things done with both parties were getting noticed. Slowly, over the next eighteen months, his approval numbers crept up.

That was in the good old days of two weeks ago.

Now acts of domestic terrorism, the magnitude and frequency of which this country had never known, were challenging Mitchell's administration midterm. The frequency and randomness of the events of the last few weeks were more heinous, more terrorizing, and more devastating to the national psyche than even the unbelievable destruction of 9/11. Mitchell was the man the entire nation now looked to as the only person who could stop the nightmare. In fact, for the majority of Americans, it was the first time many bothered to look in his direction at all.

Deep in his bones, James Mitchell knew that this kind of crisis could either make or break a presidency. The connection with the American public that any White House resident needed to govern and improve the nation was based on the way he performed in a crisis. In a warped manner of thinking, the smartest thing Ronald Reagan ever did was get shot. His political capital went through the roof when he uttered to his wife, "Honey, I guess I forgot to duck." Legislatively he became unstoppable with that one-liner.

The decision he made today would be seen by history as Mitchell's defining moment. As he listened to the head of the FBI and his Chief of Staff, he realized that the solution they came up with was really going to be his solution. If the FBI was right, then so was he. He would become a powerful force that his congressional enemies would disagree with at their own political peril. It was called "bounce," the political lift an officeholder gets when he comes up on the right side of a critical national issue. As was the case with George W. Bush who limped into office after a messy election only to enjoy peak, albeit short-lived, record approval ratings in the wake of his handling of the terrorist attack on the World Trade Center, leading the country out of this crisis would be all Mitchell needed to hold sway on important issues like welfare, education, deficit control, and arms. If the FBI was wrong, however, the whole kettle of rotten fish heads would follow just as assuredly. He planted his feet firmly on the floor and set his backbone absolutely straight, a trick the fighter jockey learned in the preflight briefing rooms that helped him focus on every minute detail of the mission.

His was either a yes or no vote. It would probably be yes because, although he was the most powerful man in the world, he really hadn't been given any choice. To vote no would be to vote for inaction until another plan was submitted. He continued to focus acutely on every word the FBI director said.

"Under my direction, the FBI will be turning up the heat on suspected cells and known affiliations of any ..."

The director stopped speaking, distracted by a commotion outside the front door of the gym. The Secret Service agent on post grabbed his holster and stood in front of the president. Reynolds turned toward the muffled sound of the ruckus. The argument outside the gym got louder.

"What's going on?" the Commander in Chief yelled.

The door opened and a Secret Service agent stuck his head in. "Sir, Mr. Hiccock is demanding to see you. Mrs. Lamson says he doesn't have an appointment."

"Let him in, Jim."

"Mr. President, there's no need for him to be in attendance," the director protested.

The president didn't acknowledge the director. Hiccock marched in, adjusting his suit, obviously having been physically restrained.

"Geez, Bill, you got my man here ready to take a bullet. Why all the fuss?"

"Mr. President, sir. I serve at your pleasure. If I have lost your confidence then there are plenty of swell teaching positions just waiting for me out there in the real world."

The confused president looked to his chief of staff for clarity.

"Sir, your national science advisor doesn't agree with the director's analysis of the threat we face."

"I wasn't aware you had any experience in law enforcement, Bill."

"No, Sir, I don't. My degrees are in science and engineering, but you don't have to know Dick, er ... Tracy to see that we are using outmoded paradigms and Cold War fighting tactics to define an enemy that may literally have been born yesterday."

"Wow, that's a mouthful. Did you rehearse that all the way down here?"

Hiccock smiled. "Maybe just the gist of it."

"Do you have any proof, Bill?"

"No, Sir. But neither does the FBI. They're just rounding up the usual suspects."

This comment pushed Tate into nuclear mode. "How dare you! This is FBI jurisdiction. We have more experience in this kind of crime than any agency in the world!"

"Listen, when it comes to this type of anarchy there is no track record. The first World Trade Center attack, the Olympic bombings, and September 11th taught us that."

"What's your point then, Mr. Hiccock?" the director said sharply.

"I see his point," the president said. "Your agency and the traditional intelligence channels blew all those cases." He turned to Hiccock. "Go on, Bill, this is almost refreshing."

"Actually, Sir, I don't know what to say next. I didn't think I'd get this far. But I suppose I would not like to have alternate theories dismissed so quickly. It's a new world, getting newer every day, Sir."

"Nonsense," the director said. "You're just an intellectual chauvinist who thinks that science is the answer to everything."

Hiccock bristled. "Then you explain to me how long ago an eleven-year-old Boy Scout, or 'agent provocateur' as you called him, would have to have been indoctrinated, trained, and stationed in proximity to the accounting firm that he eventually incinerated."

"Perhaps his was an isolated incident, nothing more than a boy with matches."

Hiccock's Bronx attitude started to kick at its cage. "Come on, will ya? You'd have to be out of your friggin' mind to think that a boy who bypassed security and disabled multiple floors of sprinkler and fire reporting systems didn't have the smarts to hightail it out of there before becoming toast!"

After a moment's silence, the president let out a long breath. "Okay, Bill, be careful what you wish for. As of now, you are in charge of your own investigation."

"Excuse me? I didn't ask, nor do I want ..."

"Ray, come up with a way to fund him. Call it a ... Scientific Ramifications Inquiry or whatever."

"You could issue an executive order establishing the Office of Scientific Investigator," the chief of staff said.

"Give him direct-line access to me, Ray."

"What does that mean?" The slight indignation in the director's voice was all too apparent.

"It means he reports directly to me and I expect you to offer him your bureau's fullest cooperation."

"Wow," Hiccock said. "You can do that? I mean, of course you can. You are the president."

"Ray, I can do that, right?"

"I'll run it by counsel, but it sounds just like the Biotech thing you did last month."

A light went on in the president's brain as he remembered the Biotech initiative as being "cinchy," a term a young female aid used to describe the constitutional and political realities of such a move. "Yeah, I can do that."

∞§∞

A Marine guard was standing mute outside the gym, eyes front as Reynolds and the director of the FBI had it out.

"Thank you for your support in there, Ray."

"First of all, I don't work for you, I work for the president. And if he likes the idea of this geek running around the country under his authority, then I am duty-bound to love it."

"You've managed to undermine my authority and the bureau's reputation."

"Get off that horse, right now. You had every opportunity to present your case and counter any of his arguments. You failed to convince the boss. Hiccock beat you, even when we stacked the deck against him."

"Ray, I have been here through two administrations and I will not ..."

"... Well then, you know how the game is played. I know James Mitchell and I know what he was thinking in there. He was thinking how his whole presidency is in your hands. And then Hiccock comes in and points out a flaw in your logic. And you had no good answer. You were blindsided. The boss is a man who likes to have options, Tate. Hiccock at least gives him an option."

"But Ray, that little display by that uncouth character in there was mere grandstanding. I'm amazed he fell for it. Maybe you can point that out to him later?"

"I am not going down to the mat with the man just so your feelings won't be hurt. Now go find the bad guys ... before Hiccock does."

CHAPTER NINE
POST DEPRESSION

ACCEPT, ACCEPT, ACCEPT, reject, reject, accept, accept, accept, 1-0-0-1-2 enter, accept, reject. Seven hours a day, forty-nine weeks a year. That was the rhythm of his work as well as the lot in life of U.S. Postal Service mail sorter Bernard Keyes. With sixteen years in, he was relegated the post of senior sort operator. His $38,000-a-year salary limited his life, like a small bowl stunts the growth of the fish in it. He was better than this and he knew it. As he heard his supervisor coming up behind him, he laid out his plan. He would grab the prodding tool used to un-jam the sorter and turn and smack him with it right across his fat, redneck face, and he would continue beating him until there was nothing but brains everywhere. He glanced down at the stick as the footsteps got closer.

"Bernie, what the fuck did you screw up now, you dipshit?"

He turned around with nothing more than a meek smile and a swallow. "It wasn't me, Burt. Wanda up the line's been screwing up the opcodes. Here, look." His hand reached out toward the heavy prodding tool but passed it by, grabbing a mangled envelope instead. "She over inked the pads again! The shit's smearing everywhere." He pointed to the blob of ink where sharply defined lines should have been. Knowing even his lunkhead boss could see that these smeared bar codes would not be easily recognized by the laser reader, he felt he successfully defended his turf.

"Well then, get back to work, and try to be more productive."

I'll produce a bat right up your ass, you cocksucker, he thought. But out loud he whined, "It ain't me, it's up the line." He went back to sorting. As he stood there accepting, rejecting, and revising the zip codes on a million letters, he was thinking of how his boss would cower if he knew what Bernard Keyes did when he wasn't on the sorters.

It started seven years ago in a chat room called "Going Postal," where U.S. postal workers logged on mostly to gripe about everything. An irony not lost on Keyes was the fact that in the chat room, the soldiers of paper mail used e-mail—the realm of the enemy—to communicate.

It was in the "Going Postal" room that the calling first came to him. A web surfer spouted off about actually "going postal" by getting a gun and wiping out his substation. At first, Bernie thought it was just a guy acting big, but as the rest of the room discounted him as a nut, Bernie read something that resonated between the lines of his rants. The man spoke truths about the threats everyone faced— potential losses of freedoms, property, and lives. Bernie instant messaged him. The man responded to Bernie's IM and they started chatting without anyone else knowing what they discussed.

Bernie found his battle cry that night. This was a cry so loud that the crazy interloper, who was all set to buy an Uzi and spray his workplace, became, instead, satiated by the beginnings of a plan that would, in the end, be much more satisfying.

CHAPTER TEN
OLD FLAMES HOME FIRES

YOU MAKE YOUR BED and you sleep in it, but you don't always make your bed during the week, unless you are expecting company or your mother to drop by. Therefore, it was only sensible for Hiccock to have his usual once-a-week dinner with his ex-wife, Janice, at his home on Wednesdays, which just so happened to be the same day Mrs. Phelps, his combination cleaning woman, plant waterer, and surrogate mom, worked a full day sprucing up the Hiccock residence.

Having dinner with your ex-wife every week certainly made some people question either the dinner part or the "ex" part. Hiccock married Janice Tyler because she was the best person he ever knew. She was the best lover he ever had, and remained, to this day, his best friend. He wasn't at all sure what he brought to the union.

He thought for a while it was a case of reading the wrong signals; two people, temporarily appearing to be going in the same direction at the same moment, only to realize they were on a course that would separate them.

Actually, he was the one who veered away. He allowed himself to become besieged with work. It was almost as if getting married checked off the relationship box on his "Things in Life to Do" list and made more room for work. And so they became the other half of the American Dream, the one nobody likes to acknowledge, the divorced couple. Nevertheless, Janice still possessed all those wonderful things he admired about her in the first place. Not having her to talk to was not an option. He *needed* her feedback on his ideas.

Watching her while she focused on the pasta before her and the almost mechanical precision of each fork twirl, perfectly sized to slip into her mouth without requiring her to open it too far, his mind returned to their time together at Stanford.

It had been the start of a new research project, ambitious in scope and grand in scale. 2,000 sets of twins were to be interviewed and studied. An adjunct professor of statistical analysis had recommended Bill to the head of the project, Janice Tyler. Bill had heard of Janice. She was almost famous. Apparently she was a brilliant undergrad student who distinguished herself in behavioral sciences and won an unprecedented full project grant from the National Science Foundation. She even had office space in the Human Sciences building. Bill found the room number on an open door leading into a space that even an optimist would call cramped, and knocked on the doorframe.

"Hello," he said as he entered into the tiny empty office. As he took a step inside, Janice came from around the back of the door with a pile of books and almost crashed into him.

"Here, let me get those," he offered.

"I got it," she said.

"You sure?"

"I said I have them." They stood together for a second, then she squinched her nose. "What's that I smell? Curry!"

"Uh, yeah I guess I had Indian food for lunch."

"Yuck. I hate Indian food. You walk around smelling like *you* all day." She waved away the "curry-fied" air from her nostrils as she walked off to put the books down on her desk.

"Maybe I should step outside and come in again?"

"Okay, do it." Janice encouraged.

Bill stepped back outside into the linoleum-tiled hallway and rapped on the doorframe again.

"Who is it?"

"Miss Janice Tyler?"

"Yes."

"I'm delivering your order from the Bombay Palace, with extra curry."

When she laughed, he knew it was going to be okay. She wasn't the stick in the mud she first appeared to be.

"I'm William Hiccock, referred to you by Professor Parnes. He said you could use a Scientific Methodologist on your team."

"Well, listen buckaroo, I am the quarterback, coach, and manager of this team. We are going to generate a lot of data. Do you think you can handle the workload and still play your little mindless reenactment of warfare every weekend?"

"You know who I am?" the quarterback said with just a little self-satisfaction.

"I know that you are supposed to be good. Do you think you can handle crucial data and keep your facts straight?"

"GM"

"What?"

"You said quarterback, coach and manager of this team. There is an aberration in the framework of the hierarchical order of succession you just employed to establish your archetypal position. Stemming from the fact that there are no managers in football, that titled position would be better suited to a baseball analogy."

"So what do I want to be in that analogy?"

"I dunno... how about 'bitch!'"

Janice was stunned. He could read all kinds of changes of mood and thought on her face. He wondered whether he had just blown it or blown it wide open. She took a deep breath as he waited for the explosion.

"Two rules, One. I am the high, exulted queen bitch of this team and you are nothing more than a subservient, scum sucking, drone worker bee. Two. You just used up the one and only time you can *ever* call me a bitch again... until I give birth to a litter!"

"I can live with that," William said as he turned and walked out.

"I think that went well," Janice said as she sat down and started reading through the pile of books.

∞§∞

"Janice! Janice!" The call cut across the campus as Hillary Dennison ran with her book clasped to her bosom. Janice turned and waited for her to flurry across the green.

"Are you coming to the pep rally tonight?"

"It's so retro, and I think I have some socks to de-lint tonight."

"Come on, it's the biggest game of the year Saturday, and the boys need our support." She actually stood taller when she said that making her chest stick out like an obscene version of Shirley Temple saluting in a sailor suit. It made Janice laugh.

"Who's pitching?"

"Pitching? I'm not sure. Isn't that baseball? All I know is Brad's playing and that's all I care about."

"Oh, now I understand your sudden team spirit. Hillary, he's a jock and you are on your way to being a brain surgeon. Don't you see the irony in that?"

"Don't you see his buns in those tight little pants when they're running around the field?"

"Good point! Is that 'wild' guy going to be there?"

"You mean Wild Bill Hiccock. Yeah! He's such a hunk a dory."

"Hunk a what? When did you turn into 'Gidget' goes to college?'"

"When did you turn into my mom?"

"Okay what time?"

"It's at 8, in the big gym. I'll pass by at quarter to and we'll walk over together."

"Fine!" Janice replied reluctantly. As Hillary bounced off, Janice started to call after her. She managed to get her mouth open, but couldn't utter the words, "On second thought." Relaxing her stance, she attempted to persuade herself that she wasn't going for any other reason than to show a modicum of school spirit. *Oh God, what will I wear?*

∞§∞

At 8:45 Janice sneaked into the back of the gym. The pageantry and theatrics of the band, the drill squad, and the cheerleaders having long since finished their routines, the rally turned into an unofficial social event. She took in the ambiance of the crepe-paper-and-cardboard-decorated gymnasium, enhanced by scratchy music coming from a tinny P.A. system. Soft drinks were being served. Pretzels and potato chips crushed under her feet into the hardwood floor as she searched for Hillary and finally spotted her. The young Ms. Tyler checked her sweater and shifted her skirt one last time before making the walk across the "gauntlet," diagonally across the gym where she would be seen and noticed by everyone. As she crossed the circle in the middle of the floor that they used for hockey or basketball, or whatever, she once again agonized over whether she had made the right choice in shoes. Should she have stayed with the longer dress being a sure fire match to her sling back pumps? She decided on shorter over matching but only after an hour of "in front of the mirror" indecision. She smiled as she approached Hillary standing there with dopey Brad.

"What happened to you? I waited till five of," Hillary said

"I was caught up with something and I got here as soon as I could. Hello, Brad."

"Hi ya" was the double syllabic response which she was sure was a big step for him over the grunts that must pass for communications between Hillary and he. Then she looked at him again and realized this shortstop, linebacker, or whatever he was, was quite a male specimen. *Maybe Hillary was on to something,* she thought.

In the awkward silence that followed, Janice realized that Brad had noticed her looking at him and turned to scan the crowd. Small clutches and groups had partitioned off talking about this and that. Janice didn't recognize anyone she particularly wanted to converse with. Then she saw "him," his protuberant head and shoulders appearing above the four or five obviously "star struck" girls, their mouths open wide as he pontificated on the process of throwing a perfect slider to the catcher-guy. She burnt that image into her retinas for one second longer before forcing her eyes off the spectacle, and continued scanning the room. Her eyes focused back on Hillary who was in the midst of having a heaping helping of Brad's tongue. *God, how can she get her mouth open that wide?* Once again, she pried herself away from an image she was riveted to. She found herself looking at Bill again, with his little cheerleaders hanging on every word he spoke. *Wonder which one he'll try to choke with his tongue,* she thought as she fixed her gaze at the clock at the end of the gym. *What am I doing here? I've got to get out of here!* She pivoted towards Hillary and the Tongue Monster to say goodbye. It was evident at this point; they wouldn't have stopped if she had set herself on fire.

Janice left vowing she would never, ever delude herself into going anywhere or doing anything that included Mr. William Hiccock again.

∞§∞

It wasn't easy and she didn't know what even possessed her to do it, but she sweet-talked the guy

in the ticket booth something awful. The final negotiation to get a 50-yard line seat, right behind where
the home team stood during the game, was complete
when Janice agreed to relinquish her number. Another
thing, out of character for Janice, was that she wore
her politically correct school sweatshirt over her big
sweater, cinched at the waist by her flared skirt making her appear more... ample. The stadium went crazy
when Wild Bill Hiccock was announced over the loud
speaker. As he trotted out of the tunnel and over to the
sidelines in front of her, the roar of the crowd gave her
goose bumps. The goose bumps led to a warm feeling
that enveloped her body from head to toe, even on this
very cold November day. She suddenly realized that
out of the 80,000 people in the stands who were yelling their heads off, it was _she_ who possessed a special,
direct relationship with this man they adored.

He was, after all, her subservient worker bee. She
was almost dizzy when she realized her mouth was
open.

For the first two "innings," she knew Bill had not
seen her, even though she was only some 30 feet away.
During the halftime break, as the marching band was
finishing a tortured rendition of a song she used to like,
Bill returned to the sideline. He glanced over her way
and caught her eye. She was pleased when he smiled.
She returned his smile and nodded back. Luckily, she
started waving a split second after he turned toward
the field. She pulled in her hand, reprimanding it for
being silly and thankful that he hadn't noticed. For the
rest of the game, they exchanged glances, he to her after a play and she finding him when he came back to
the side as Brad's guys were sent out to stop the other
team's quarterback.

Janice figured it must have been an exciting game
because the score was tied and the teams just stopped
to rest with only two minutes left to play. People started shouting "Wild Bill." The guy next to her, his face

painted in school colors, said to his buddy, "It's time for Wild Bill's shoot out."

"What do you mean by that?" she asked.

"Lady, if we're lucky, we are going to see a master of the two-minute drill. This guy calls the plays with no huddles. He's won four games in the last two minutes like that."

"Sounds impressive," was all she could think of to say.

At one point, Bill got the ball and the other team started coming aggressively toward him. The players were being thrown and pushed. Helmets were clacking as the skulls inside of them must surely have been cracked. *That would explain Brad's cognitive skills challenge,* she thought. Then one of the biggest, meanest guys from the other team got a hold of Bill and spun him around; Bill almost danced around him and caused the big guy to fall right on his face. Bill then scampered around to the other side of the field and threw the ball from mid-air while he was jumping over a player who had been wrestled to the ground. Bill then turned to the stands where Janice stood. He looked right at her and smiled a big, goofy grin like a little boy who just caught a big fish. Janice was touched. He was showing off to *her*.

Suddenly, he became a blur as two "tackle men" slammed him to the ground. She winced as she heard the noise that the bodies made as they pummeled him into the dirt. A whistle was blown by one of the judges as he threw out his hankie again. Bill got up really slowly.

It amazed Janice that in this mindless contest of testosterone based violence, which pitted one color shirt against another, the man in black and white stripes was chiding them all for "*unnecessary* roughness!" *As if any of this really necessary at all.*

Bill made his way to the sideline, as his team was now downfield without him, preparing to kick the ball through the goal post. Then another whistle was blown and both teams rested once again.

During the time out, Bill walked over to the edge of the stands where Janice was seated.

"Are you okay?" Janice asked, catching herself just before reaching over to brush dirt off his shoulder-padded uniform.

"Yeah, I'm okay."

"What did you say to those guys?"

Bill just looked at her and laughed. She laughed, not really knowing why.

"You disappeared last night," he said nonchalantly.

"Oh, were you there?" she said in a lame attempt to appear aloof.

"Yeah, as unreasonable as it may seem, they kind of make you go to the football rally when you're the starting quarterback. Nice shoes, I remember thinking."

"You noticed my shoes?"

"Hey, if I can see a receiver's hands 75 yards downfield, you bet I won't miss your, "catch-me-kiss-me" pumps from across a gym!"

"They weren't "catch-me-kiss-me" pumps, and that's not even the right terminology, Mr. Football."

"I know, but I didn't figure you for the other terminology type," he said as the whistle blew summoning him back to his team to watch the ball get kicked through the goal post.

She didn't know whether to be insulted or complimented. *Did he just scratch me off his list, or decide to take me home to mother?*

The crowd went crazy; fans and security people swallowed up Bill and his teammates as they hustled off to their locker rooms.

∞§∞

One of the reasons Janice had been awarded the grant for her research was her sense of commitment.

She gave her all to the subject. That was especially hard to do here in California. The entire state was almost one giant distraction for anyone under 30. If you were looking for a reason not to do anything, California delivered it. So her dogmatic approach to further her studies stood out amongst those who allowed the Golden State to modulate their biorhythms.

It was Monday night, the day after the big game. Janice hadn't seen or heard from Bill, not that she should have. He had been assigned from Tuesday night to Friday afternoons and Saturday mornings only on the weekends when he had a home game. He, otherwise, had to fit his classes and commitments around her project. It was working out well. His job was to make sure the scientific accuracy of her study remained beyond reproach. Far too many scientists, who had actually done good work, were frustrated in the end by some scientific committee or board finding a non-scientific method used in either the accumulation or handling of data. For her it was like being handed a winning lottery ticket, living like a millionaire, then finding out there was an audit at the end where every cent and every reason for spending the money was scrutinized under penalty of having to pay it back. So there she was, well past 7 p.m., in her office reviewing the questionnaires the volunteer students from five participating universities had mailed in. She was surprised when Hillary, eyes swollen and bloodshot, entered her office. "What's wrong?" she asked.

"Why are men so childish?" she said with a slightly quivering bottom lip.

"Because they think it will increase their chances of us nursing them."

"Be serious."

How come everyone comes to me with their man problems? Hello, do you see a ring on my finger?

"Want to tell me about it?"

"It's Brad."

"Why am I not surprised?"

"Last night after the game, we spent the whole night together."

"Oh, I see. And he hasn't called you yet today?"

"No, that's the problem. He *did* call and told me he was going to Santa Clara, tonight."

"What's in Santa Clara?"

"Some sluts from Santa Clara lost a bet on the game and are throwing an orgy to have sex with all the players," she said starting to hyperventilate.

"Wow, their parents must be so proud, a whole football team. Why don't you tell the dean? I'm sure that would get the whole team expelled. They'd certainly think twice about going..."

"Are you crazy? Then Brad would hate me forever!"

Janice was dumbfounded. She immediately foresaw all kinds of problems for Hillary. The poor girl was conflicted and had esteem issues in proportions usually found in Greek tragedy.

"Well, I don't know what to tell you then, except Brad is a dick head and you better get your head out from between his legs or you are going to get pissed on!"

Mascara was running down her cheeks as Hillary laughed and looked at Janice in a sisterly way. "I know I am being silly and unreasonable; it's just that I love him so."

Janice grabbed Hillary by the shoulders. "Hillary, listen to me. While you were making love last night, he was getting laid. Got that? You: love; him: sex. Why do you think they call it getting fucked! You had sex with the guy. That's all! Love comes from somewhere else. Don't ask me where, ...damned if I know."

"But I *know* Brad loves me." She protested through heaving breaths.

"Listen to me! Oxytosin."

"What?"

"Oxytosin. It is an enzyme that is released in a female during sex affecting her brain. Its purpose is to produce a nesting urge. Prehistorically speaking it was 'necessary' to keep women in the dark cave while the men went out in the sunshine, to hunt and kill food. Get it. You don't love him. You are just being drugged by a million years of non-evolution."

Talking about the brain suddenly brought back the medical student inside Hillary. "You're saying a chemical imbalance in my brain is causing feelings of need and intimacy. Where?"

"The cerebral cortex. There is a gland that..." she stopped dead in her pathology as she caught sight of Bill standing in the doorway.

"What are you doing here?" she asked.

"I heard we got a lot of questionnaires in, and I finished my paper on chaos theory and its relevance to applied physics. Thought I'd come here and have some real fun with..." his words trailed off as he recognized the person Janice had been addressing, "Oh hi, Hill." *Please don't ask me where Brad is.*

"Hi, Bill; surprised to see you here," Hillary said as she dabbed at her nose with her hankie.

"Really? Oh. Anyway I didn't mean to interrupt, just let me grab a pile of these and I'll go down the hall..."

"No, Hillary was just leaving..."

Hillary turned to her, surprised, then catching up. "I'm going to de-tox my brain. Happy researching, you two. Thanks, Janice, for being a real friend. Bye, Bill."

"Have you gone through these yet?" Bill said as he reached for a ream of questionnaires.

Janice stared at him with a mixture of wonder and caution. He couldn't decide which, but it prompted him to ask, "What?"

"Nothing; it's just that you are here."

"Well, you know, you've got that whole location specific awareness thing down pretty well. I am here; you are there; we are both here. That about covers it."

"How come you aren't in Santa Clara?" she asked instantly making him the poster boy for irresponsible males everywhere.

"Do you know how I got to this school?"

"No, how?"

"Well it wasn't on a subway driver's income. I won a football scholarship. I could have gone to Notre Dame, but the science program here is the best of all the schools who wanted me."

"Can we get back to the Santa Clara tar pits?"

"Those guys played a great game; they want to let off a little steam. Let 'em. I've got work to do."

"Oh, is that it? The work. But aren't you their General? Shouldn't you be *with* your men as they go into battle?"

"It's Captain, and that's only on the football field. Santa Clara is an extracurricular activity. Look, are you perturbed that I am here? Am I interrupting your plans for the evening?"

Just then, Janice noticed that when Bill grabbed the pile of papers, he had uncovered the book she bought that day. Suddenly feeling stupid, she wanted to hide that book from Bill's eyes.

Bill took her temporary distraction to mean that she didn't want to see him at that moment. "Well, I'll go. I'll take these back to my room and bring them back tomorrow."

And he was off!

Janice sat stunned, as she had no idea what had just happened. She was so happy to see him. What had she done to make him angry? Why did he leave? She plopped herself in her chair and mindlessly thumbed the page edges of a new copy of *The Football Widow's Guide to Football.*

∞§∞

Tonight was Hiccock's attempt at Fettuccine Alfredo. With candles on his table and *Geraldo* on TV in the background, the former college sweethearts now sat in his "bachelor" apartment as a snapshot of what they used to be.

"This is really good," Janice said after two mouthfuls.

"Yeah, it came out pretty good. Must be the cream cheese."

His words stopped her cold, right in the middle of her fork twirl. She almost spit out her pasta. "Cream cheese?"

"Yeah, I went all-out and got the Philly instead of the no-frills stuff."

"I watch a lot of those cooking shows on cable, but this sounds like a recipe from the Cartoon Channel."

"You just said it was really good."

"And you just told me you made it with cream cheese. Alfredo must be spinning in his grave!"

"Want more?"

"Definitely."

Bill gave her another serving. "You know what I was just thinking about?"

"No, what?" she asked after swallowing a fork full of the Ronzoni Number 14 and cream cheese based culinary masterwork.

"When we first met."

Janice smiled and her eyes met his the same way they had that night when he showed up in her office, "You mean our first fight?"

"No, I was wondering what ever happened to Brad?"

Janice's mind recoiled. "Brad? What made you think of him out of the blue?"

"It wasn't a fight. I thought you were meeting some other guy there and I was in the way."

"You know, you didn't know anything about women then and you don't know anything about them now?"

"Where did that come from?"

"You were the smartest dumb jerk in the world. It took you a year to realize how crazy I was for you."

"Oh yeah? Well, I came to you that night because I decided I had enough of the wildcatting and partying. I realized all I wanted was to see you."

"Do you know I never went to a football game in all my years of high school and college because I was afraid I'd want more, want it bad! And I thought I could never get it. Maybe I wasn't cool enough to have a guy like Brad, or you! But, I overcame that to see you play. No, that's a lie; I came *solely* to see you. You know, I had to go out to dinner with the jerk who sold the tickets just to get close to mid-field so I could see you!"

"You never told me that!"

"It wasn't important. We went Dutch actually; I didn't want to owe that sleaze anything."

"So, I guess we both sacrificed for each other," Hiccock summed up the last few minutes and was ready to move on. Janice however, was still processing.

"Wait," she retorted, "Are you taking the position that not going to a slut infested, mass groupie suck and fuck-fest with sexually transmitting diseased tramps was somehow a sacrifice? On second thought, don't answer that! So, how was your day at the office, dear?"

The evening's conversation continued, focused on his day at the office, that being the office of the president's science advisor.

"So you think the FBI's theory is wrong?"

"First off, they'd kill me if they knew I was discussing this with you. And, yes, when any part of an assumption doesn't test true to the operational model of the proposition, it must be deemed false."

"Well, that may be true in a purely scientific sense, but I know of cases where eleven-year-old boys have the intellect and adaptive skills to do great tasks."

"Are you suggesting that I am not considering the human factor?"

"You pretty much live your whole life ignoring the human factor." She smiled to take the point off the little dagger she just inserted, but Hiccock felt it all the same.

"Is this going to turn into the 'soulless' argument again?"

"Am I getting too predictable for you? Listen, artificial intelligence is half the package. Without a conscience or other mediated value structure, it has no more potential to be useful than a, a ... serial killer." She dug a little more pasta out of the serving bowl.

"AI can be the tool that helps man crack the biggest mysteries of life and the universe, unfettered by human bias. It can help us reach beyond the limits of three-dimensional thinking."

"That's what I am afraid of. Without all those messy, sloppy biases or without some moral or spiritual guidance package, it will never be intelligent, just belligerent."

Hiccock was lost. Tyler seemed distracted by something on TV.

"Well, at least they can't blame this one on hip-hop," she said, still looking at the TV.

He looked over his shoulder to see what she was watching. Geraldo displayed a mug shot of Martha Krummel, the gardening grandmother who derailed the freight train.

"Grandma Martha didn't hang with the homies around the beat box."

"You know, having an ex with a Ph.D. in behavioral sciences might be an advantage after all. At least we'll ..." He stopped when he saw a video clip, taken with a telephoto lens, of himself as he had left the White House today.

"Once again, ladies and gentlemen," Geraldo said, "I have a confirmed report from an inside White House source close to the president that this man—can we slow that tape down?" The video image on the screen strobed and flickered as it slowed down to catch Hiccock walking from the side door of the East Wing to a waiting car. Geraldo continued to speak over what in the business is called a "package," a pre-produced piece featuring old footage and stills of Hiccock in his college days. "William Hiccock, the former Heisman Trophy–winning quarterback who abandoned what everyone agreed would have been a brilliant career in the pros to follow his love of science"—the picture switched to footage of Bill among a group of administration appointees—"has now been named as independent investigator of these same terrorist attacks. This despite the objections of the FBI and the Office of Homeland Security. It seems, ladies and gentlemen, as we sit here tonight, that a classic old-fashioned turf war is heating up within the administration.

"Forgive me for saying this, but have we not learned anything from the other attacks? As you recall, there had been ample warnings, but each held tight by various government agencies leaving us vulnerable, while bureaucrats protected their precious areas of autonomy. In this latest round of more random, more sporadic but unrelenting attacks, we still have no idea who or for what purpose Americans are losing their lives. Let's hope the squabbling ends soon so we can catch the people who are doing these horrific deeds. I am being told right now from the control room that my producers are trying to get Dr. William Hiccock on the phone. We'll try to get him on the air and see if he can provide further insight into this segment, which we're calling 'The Quarterback Gets in the Game.' We'll be back after this break. Stay tuned, lots of news to come."

The telephone started to ring.

"*Over* the objection of the FBI?" Janice said.

"It pays to have enemies in high places." The telephone kept ringing. "And I am not going to answer that. I am actually under orders not to."

"Then you'll have time to do the dishes."

CHAPTER ELEVEN
MEETINGS

NOBODY STEALS CLOTHES anymore, right? Carly asked herself as she looked out the diner window at the harsh green tinted fluorescent spill from the laundromat across the street. As her *private* unmentionables tumbled in the *public* dryer, she sat sipping hot tea with lemon from her "sick tray" before her. No cross-dressing transvestite or out of work Victoria's Secret model was going to steal her intimate garments and get away with it. *This is ridiculous!* She thought, yet she still couldn't get herself to deposit them in the hotel laundry service bag. *Why can't I ever remember if it's cold or hot water that gets blood out?*

As if she were instantly cast into one of her worst nightmares, she recognized the face of a man she knew, entering the diner. In her particular version of the common nightmare, she would find herself naked in front of a laughing and snickering 6th grade assembly. In the dream she would nearly die of embarrassment, although she always awoke, in a cold sweat, before meeting the grim reaper, naked. Tonight, she was bloated, retaining water. Her hair unceremoniously lobbed on top of her head, she was in the old ripped sweatshirt with, *Oh God*, old spaghetti sauce stains on her chest. The warm-up pants she wore were a wonderland of lint balls and, on her face, the last remnants of a day's make-up had, at this point, been reduced to an echo of eyeliner. Her lipstick had long since dissolved away from her normally accented lips.

Although he wasn't laughing at her yet, her heart stopped when she realized he was someone from the

White House, the press corps, somebody from cable. *Please don't let him see me.* She buried her face in the cup and mentally tried to be smaller than her 5'10 frame. Although at that moment, she was in the middle of a little real life nightmare, later, upon reflection, she would come to appreciate the evening as the night that changed her life in ways she could never have dreamt possible.

"Hello there; Carly isn't it?" the voice said.

Shit. "Yes, Carly Simone," she said. Then waited for him to fill in the blank look she wasn't trying very hard to conceal. He was on the far side of fifty, and could have been Regis Philbin's brother. There was a warmth in his eyes, but a perpetual sneer to his mouth. She wondered which one was dominant.

"Wallace Smith, MSNBC. May I join you?" He flashed a winning smile.

Carly was surprised. "Well, actually, I was just leaving."

"*Actually* this will only take a few minutes."

"What will?"

He smiled as he invited himself into the booth sitting across the table from her. "I have an idea. Do you watch MSNBC?"

"Sometimes, not lately. I haven't had time to watch anything lately."

"Are you permanent here now?"

"No, I am on assignment." *Why didn't I comb my goddamn hair?*

"Do you like it here in Washington?"

"It's got a personality all its own... more than any other place in America. The buildings and what they represent are old and stationary, but the people in them are always new and constantly changing. Even New York has natives. Here in D.C. if you find a native, there's a good chance they are not involved in the only business *in* this town."

"Well, I can see you are not opinionated."

"I do objectivity for a living, I live subjectively."

Wallace, who 25 years ago started out as a copy boy at the *New York Post* instead of going to college, recognized the journalism school jargon. "What school did you come out of?"

"Andover, then NYU Journalism for post grad."

"Well, Carly, I'll get right to the point. How would you like to work at MSNBC?"

"I wouldn't know how to write for television."

"No, Carly, I mean, go on camera, become a reporter."

"Me? I have always done print. I am used to hundreds of words; you guys deal in hundredths of seconds."

"Look, we have producers like me who handle all that. TV requires someone who can speak extemporaneously about an issue only when the earpiece falls out of their ears. You know Brian Williams, or Scott Pelley?"

"Yeah."

"Sometimes I am reading the script right into their ear, two words ahead of what they are speaking. It's called audio prompting. We of course only do it when things are happening so fast that there isn't enough time to even teleprompt it to them."

"So, are you saying you will put the words into my mouth?"

"Only if we are live and you couldn't possibly know everything that's going on."

"But if I don't know, why would I be talking about it?"

He held up his hands in a "no-contest" gesture, "Okay, so that's a deal breaker right there, Carly. If you are going to spew forth journalistic ethics to me, then maybe you should stay in the virginal, unadulterated, pristine world of magazine writing. So you can be as God intended, one girl, talking to a few readers with nothing between you and them but a pencil and notebook."

Carly let the "girl" remark go. But she grabbed onto the magazine slam. "So if I remember correctly, the top shows any network actually produces themselves with consistent top ratings are the ones they laughingly call 'Magazine Shows.' Tell me, is that just a way of buying credibility, 'print' credibility, the credibility won by those reporters who apply pencil to notebook?"

Wallace was amazed at the moxie this girl had. Maybe she didn't know who he was. "You know as the head of the Washington news operations I would love to debate this all night, but you look like you got other things to do tonight and so do I. I'll just leave it at this. I would like you to come work for us and cover the science beat. Since we deal in hundredths of a second in my business, I'll give you a few hundred thousand to decide. Here's my card. Or you can always find me around the press room."

"Okay, I'll think about it."

As he stood looking down at her, he began negotiations. "You haven't asked me how much we pay."

"You haven't asked me how much I want."

Wally used his poker face and smiled, then turned away, thinking *She is some piece of work. She'll probably be great on camera.*

Carly tried not to watch him leave. She sat still for a minute or two reviewing the conversation. Hundredths, hundreds. Girl. Print. Ask me what I want. Credibility. Then it hit her, *this wasn't a chance meeting.* He must have had her followed. He didn't even order a coffee to go. Besides, he wouldn't be in this neighborhood at night. So he came after me... That was a good point from which to start her negotiation for salary and benefits. As she sat there the echoes of another nocturnal fantasy started resounding within her. She always thought about being on TV. Reaching millions. Gaining the trust of millions. Making millions. She plopped down a ten, more than enough to cover the tab for tea and dry toast plus tip. She walked out of the diner and headed for the hotel. As she walked her head slowly rose from looking down at the cherry blossoms, which were falling like a gentle spring snow onto the sidewalks of Washington, D.C. Their unmistakable scent that filled the soft warm breeze, and the realization that what just happened was a good thing, lifted her head and spirit. The Washington Monument, brilliantly lit against the inky black sky, became an exclamation point to the evening that had started out with a period.

She was a block from the hotel when she stopped to retrace her steps, realizing she left her panties in the laundromat.

∞§∞

"Bill, are you sure you want to keep this small?" Reynolds said.

"Ray, if it gets too big, I'll wind up filling out forms and running a bureaucracy instead of trying to figure out what the hell's going on. Thank you, but no thank you. I don't want to move into the Department of the Interior. I'll work out of my office. I don't want a staff of 300. I don't want to do anything but get started."

"It's your show, Bill. Do you at least want a car and driver?"

"I'll manage on my own, thanks."

"Hey, that makes my job easier. Anything else?"

"No, I just need the one gov-ops person to handle the forms. Which reminds me, what's the story with Cheryl?"

"She's bright and she's a self-starter, why?"

"How about her?"

"You want one of my assistants to be your gov-ops?"

"Especially one of your assistants, one who knows how things work around here. Besides, she can spy on you for me."

Spying being a two-way street, Reynolds shook his head. "Okay, Cheryl will be assigned to your group."

The intercom beeped and Reynolds picked up the receiver. "Ah, yes. Send him right in." He hung up the phone. "When I called Tate to do the vetting on Janice, he hit the ceiling and said he'd be right over."

On cue, FBI Director Tate entered. "This is preposterous."

Hiccock concealed his slight delight at Tate's rage and remained focused on the chief of staff.

"Just run the usual background check on her, please," Reynolds said calmly.

"Sure, why not? I am sure the president whole-heartedly supports Hiccock's efforts to rekindle his marriage."

"Forget the fact that she's my ex-wife," Hiccock said brusquely. "She's the best on anyone's list."

Tate rolled his eyes. Reynolds looked Hiccock deeply in his. "Bill, I think the question is whether both of *you* can forget the fact that you are exes?"

"Are you kidding? We're like the best of friends. We still have dinner once a week. There isn't anything we wouldn't do for each other ..."

∞§∞

"Fuck you! No way!" Janice said resolutely. "I've got a practice, a funded study, and a neurotic, type-A personality male with a great talent for finding superior wines with whom I am trying to wash you out of my hair. No!"

"The lawyer?" Hiccock asked incredulously.

"He's an arbitrator."

"He's arbitrary, all right. I thought that was over."

"It was under review."

"See, it's not even a relationship, it's a - a - a thing! Under review."

"If you remember, we agreed not to talk about our other relationships."

"What do you mean, *we*?"

"Listen, Bill, we would still be a we if you didn't throw yourself so totally into that artificial intelligence thing and now this White House job. Christ, even the president gets time off!"

"Would you have liked it better if I sold out and took that Defense Department job with Robert Parnes right out of college, in a think tank, trying to figure out how to get more fucking mega-death from atomic weapons?"

"Or signed with the Giants! First off, what's so goddamn wrong with money? And yes, a little more bringing home the bacon and a little less worrying about the pig would have been nice!"

"Wait, I'm lost again," he said in exasperation, fingers splayed out on his forehead.

He could see she was trying to conceal a little smile. "Forget it, that analogy didn't test well to the operational model so it must be deemed false. Here's a better postulate, buckaroo! You got a degree in engineering, your first Master's was in physics, your second Master's in scientific methods. You are not a Bachelor of Science, you are a goddamn husband of science and you cannot have two wives."

"Give me a fucking break. You're jealous of my work?"

"Angry! I'm angry at it because it took you away from me. So I am out there," her arm shot out pointing toward the window, "and if you haven't gotten the message yet and you haven't been dating anyone, don't shit on my good luck!"

"Good luck! He's old enough to be your father's ... younger brother." He squeezed his eyes as soon as he said it, knowing he crossed a line—a receding hairline—with that remark.

"End it here and now." Her face was daring him. "Not one step further," she said, wagging her finger.

Hiccock felt he landed some good shots and received the TKO, so his mind reverted to his original reason for all this. "You're right. I am not handling this well. I'll try to do better. But Janice, this investigation is the most important thing in America. I need you. The president needs you. Your country needs you."

"Two strikes out of three, Bill. I didn't vote for him and I divorced you."

"I know that face. You *are* going to help me, aren't you?"

"You got me on the country thing."

CHAPTER TWELVE
TERROR FIRMA

CARLY ADJUSTED HERSELF in the chair as Wally finished a phone call in the little office afforded MS-NBC in the cramped quarters of the surprisingly small White House. Its initial design never considered the exponential growth of journalism outlets that would clamor for representation in the longest running story in American history, the office of the chief executive. Carly had played out the way she imagined this meeting was going to go at least 20 times in her head.

Wally was probably going to play the card that print journalists make crap for salary, whereas broadcast is the money train. Dangling the carrot of future big paydays once she established herself, he would then try to get her for the cheapest possible price. She was ready for his argument and felt she was prepared to walk if she didn't get what she wanted.

Wally hung up the phone and mentally switched gears; a smile suddenly appeared on his face indicating he was ready to iron out the details with her. She let the silence grow, not wanting to start the negotiation.

Then Wally broke the ice, "So I assume we aren't doing this over the phone because you have decided to join us."

"Let's just say I am interested," Carly replied as neutrally as she could.

"Okay, let's cut to the chase; your salary will be $120, 000 a year. You will have total editorial control over any piece you initiate. If you are assigned to a story, however, then the producer and the editor of that story have final say."

The $38,000 a year print reporter was stunned. All her objections evaporated right before her eyes. Having to say something, all she could muster was, "Can I stay with *SciAm?*"

"I'd insist. It gives you more credibility for your beat."

That's $158,000 a year. "What's my beat?"

"Science. I got a feeling this Hiccock guy is on a fast track with all this terrorist stuff and I can't make the guy out. You seem to have a way with him."

Carly was mildly amazed at this comment. *Do I have a way with him?* "So let me get this straight. I get paid and have control if I deliver Hiccock to MSNBC."

"For now, yes. That's the deal. You scoop every other cable network in town and you get to renegotiate for millions in a year or two. This is a good deal, Carly."

Was he willing to go higher? It was worth a shot. "Is that all you are prepared to offer me?"

Wally smiled, paused for effect, and then said in a low voice. "Carly, let's make believe I offered you the standard 60,000 starting salary and you countered with 180 and we spent weeks to get to 120,000. Now let's make believe you feel good about beating me for 60 Gs and can get to work."

"Fair enough. When can I see the contract?" Carly inquired.

"Give me your lawyer's name and we'll stay out the nitty-gritty; from this point forward we have to work together. Let our business affairs department and your lawyer hash it out."

Carly smiled. *I don't have a fucking lawyer.*

Wally smiled as they shook hands.

∞§∞

The long abandoned Bufford farm was off the interstate and down a road that only deer and, before he died, Bufford would normally ever travel on. But tonight was an exception. Seven trucks and three cars went down this deserted road, noticed only by a doe and her fawn. Inside the barn, the dank smell of straw, sawdust, and animal droppings attacked the olfactory senses. The rotting timbers, with their deeply etched, distorted grain gave the wood plank walls and cross members the gnarled look of the twisted souls from Dante's *Inferno*. Bernard and the others listened to a report by RedBarron348. Everyone in the group used their chat room handles, never any real names. Bernard set this up as a security precaution; if captured, no one could divulge the identity of the others. His nom-de-web was Sabot. He thought it was a little obvious, but it would be looked upon as a bold and brash snub to the authorities when the time came to write his memoirs or, better yet, have them written by an adoring, thankful public.

World movements usually happened in synchronicity, as if the collective consciousness of mankind arrived at a single notion at the same time. America had already sustained and repelled attacks by fundamentalist zealots who made their statements on religious or political grounds. But now, for the first time, the high-tech mongers and "industrial rapists of humanity" were being attacked. Bernard acknowledged it as a signal that the great struggle was nearing. If they didn't stop the advancement of technology taking over human life now, it would soon be too late.

In its seven-year history, the Supreme Council of the Sabot Society normally met twice a year. Tonight's meeting, however, was special. Called last week, the cell leaders from across America converged on the farm to ascertain their position in the new movement that had exploded across America. Bernard opened the meeting to a room full of grinning faces. He reviewed the agenda he held in his hand. First, he would ask if anyone was responsible for any of the seemingly anti-technology "statements" that literally blasted their way onto the front pages. Then he would poll the group to see where they stood on showing further support and solidarity with the cause. He would follow with a suggested list of targets to "supplement" the already-initiated campaign, after which he would conclude with a report from the treasurer.

Looking up from his pad, he thought he knew the reason for the smiles around the room. The attacks escalated their struggle to national prominence. In a way, that legitimized this group's existence. It also assured the communication of its message to the other warriors out there—those who realized the true depth of this impending crisis and could take demonstrable action and rally the fight. As soon as he had everyone's eye, he began.

"I'd like to call to order this meeting of the Sabot Society. It is an exciting time ..."

"Sabot, excuse me," DuneMist interrupted.

"Yes," Bernard responded, caught off guard.

"We have all decided to commend you on your recent initiative." The room erupted into applause. Sabot was stunned, but his confusion was not apparent to the attendees. DuneMist continued, "Last meeting, when you singled out Intellichip and Mason Chemical as the advanced guard of the forces of enslavement, we thought you were asking us for recommendations on how to address them. Now we see that you have struck mightily and struck deep into their very hearts. We know our bylaws forbid each cell from knowing the activities or identity of the others, but all of us who were not involved in the operations applaud those of us who were. And Sabot, to you, a special note of appreciation for advancing the cause." Once more, the room convulsed with applause.

Bernard just stood there, his mind racing. They were thanking *him*. They figured out that he masterminded the acts of insurgency being perpetrated on American high-tech companies. They were cheering him on. That never happened to Bernard in his whole life. Nobody ever gave him credit for anything. They were giving him their vote of confidence, and there was only one thing to do.

Bernard raised his hands and the ovation stuttered to a halt. He took his time, looked at them with a serious stare, and made a show of having just made a decision. "I will allow this one breach of security, and simply say thank you to those of you—you know who you are—for your contribution, and ask for a moment of silence for those who gave the supreme sacrifice in the Ultimate Battle." Everyone in the room was moved by his words. Bernard's head swam as he decided he liked the adulation.

"I have prepared a list of other targets. I will discuss these with each and every one of you independently. Some of your tasks may not be as grand or as risky as those that have been achieved thus far, but I want each of you to know that no matter the size or status, every mission will be just as vital to our goal."

∞§∞

Through the extremely small, highly placed window, one could see the guards patrol the catwalks around the compound. Hiccock figured the window's diminutive size and location—about six feet from the floor—were to deter the prisoners from using it to escape from Leavenworth Penitentiary. A heavy metal sound clanked, a buzzer sounded, and a female federal corrections officer escorted the bound and shackled seventy-seven-year-old Martha Krummel, aka "The Gardening Grandma Terrorist," to a desk in the visiting room. Hiccock and Janice took their seats across from her.

"Are those necessary?" Hiccock asked the guard, pointing to the chains.

"She's on suicide watch," the guard said plainly.

"Hello, Martha," Hiccock said to the gentle-looking woman. "I'm William Hiccock and this is Janice Tyler."

"Are you lawyers?"

"No, Martha, we are investigators for the president."

"Don't like him. Didn't vote for him."

"Well, there's one thing we agree upon already, Martha," Janice said. "Do you fully comprehend the seriousness of your situation?"

"Like I told that lawyer fellow, I know I did it. I don't know *why* I did it, but I know I did. It was like I was dreaming or sleepwalking it. I did things and knew things I didn't even know I knew."

"Like what?" Hiccock asked.

"How to cross-connect wires in a signal block vault, thus reversing the polarity and the direction of a main line interlock cutout relay switch." She stopped, frozen, and shook her head. "You see! I don't even know what I just said but I knew how to do it."

"Do you listen to rap music?"

That remark earned Hiccock a swift kick under the table from Janice as she asked, "What were you going to do after you derailed the train? Did you have an escape plan?"

Martha started to tremble and cry. "I knew I had to kill myself. I don't want to die. But I know I have to kill myself. I got knocked out by a piece of something or other from the wreck or I would have."

The short hairs on Hiccock's neck prickled up while Janice turned white and shivered as if it were twenty degrees cooler in the eight-by-eight cubicle.

"She tried to off herself the moment she woke up in the hospital. Twice more since she's been here," the guard said, nodding to the shackles around her thin wrists.

"I don't want to die," Martha said, looking down at eternity through the tabletop.

Hiccock's eyes sank, too, and then rolled over to Janice. He expected her to be as moved by this as he was, but she sat intensely focused, observing Martha.

∞§∞

The flowers were well-tended and thriving, Hiccock thought, as he and Janice strolled the colorful little garden area off the prison exercise yard. It was a peaceful respite after the chilling interrogation of Martha. Hiccock realized the "free" labor here at Leavenworth must be the reason for the meticulously maintained patch. For a second he imagined that Martha's gardening talents could be put to good use here. Then he remembered that she would kill herself as soon as someone put a shovel or rake in her hand. *Maybe when this was all over, Janice could help her.* They stopped at a bench looking over some kind of flowers. Maybe they're irises, he thought.

"So, doc?" he asked.

"She is a case study in and of herself."

"Glad I got you mixed up in it now, aren't you?"

"Don't push it. I think Martha might be exhibiting bi-stable concurrent schizophrenia. It's rare."

"Because if I remember correctly schizos don't remember the other personality," he said, dragging up Psych 101 from some obscure part of his brain.

"Yet she is fully cognizant of both her realities. Amend that. She is aware of her violent side. I want to call in Professor Wallace Jenkins from Harvard."

"Can't. He's not on the list of cleared consultants."

"What is this, a friggin' HMO? Bill, he's the guy!"

"No, you're the guy! They want this contained."

"What if …?"

"Listen, you can do this. I know you can."

CHAPTER THIRTEEN
BA DA BING'S

JOEY PALUMBO HAD BEEN the coolest guy on Gunhill Road. He was part bad boy, part Franciscan monk. He managed the perfect balance between good and mischievous. If you were a young male, you could do worse than trying to be like Joey. To the surprise of no one, Joey became an FBI agent. He was really the perfect cut for one. He had smarts, kept his wits, and made everyone feel as if he had everything under control. He must have had a canary, Hiccock thought, when the director of the FBI called him to Washington, D.C., from his field office in San Francisco just to discuss his old friend, Bill from the Bronx, whom he hadn't seen in eight years.

Hiccock sat at the bar in "The Prime Rib" on K Street. It was a Georgetown approximation of a place on Webster Avenue where they used to throw back a few and add two-inch, medium-rare increments to their LDL cholesterol count, way before anybody was counting. The waitress brought him his Dewar's and soda, snapping Hiccock out of his thoughts.

"What, no egg cream? Who friggin' ordered that?"

Hiccock made a 90-degree turn on the rotating bar stool to see Special Agent in Charge Joseph Palumbo standing behind him. Hiccock got up and, unexpectedly for both of them, gave his old schoolyard buddy a hug. Joey still wore cologne.

They ordered Joey a drink and took a table in the corner. As they sat, Hiccock almost forgot that Joey was here in an official capacity. Hiccock noticed a whole size difference in Joey's face; not fat, but more filled out from the skinny Italian kid who could take

a broomstick and smack a "Spaldeen" over three sew-
ers with ease. Hiccock wondered what game they were
going to play tonight. He chided himself for not having brought a Spalding rubber ball with him just for
laughs.

"So how ya been, Billy Boy?" Joey said with a warm
smile.

"I can't complain."

"Understatement of the century. You've come a
long way from Bing's."

That was a name Bill hadn't heard in a while.
Bing's Carousel was a candy store on Burke Avenue.
It became the official headquarters of the Red Wings,
a two-hand-touch football team that played its home
games on the cracked cement of the big schoolyard
on Bronxwood Avenue. Because of the concrete, the
player who had the ball wasn't tackled. Of course, the
young stallions of the Bronx were not delicate in their
application of the two-hand touch and turned it into
various forms of two-hand crunch, two-hand crack,
and two-hand smash. The results usually ended up
like a tackle. For years the only equipment the players employed was a football shirt bought from Gunhill
Sporting Supply. They asked Joe Mastruzzi's mother
to sew on the letters to save the 25-cents-a-letter sew-
on charge. Eventually shoulder pads were used, but
not by the real tough, real stupid guys. Bill's basic athletic ability was hard crafted on the cold, sometimes
snow-covered concrete "field" with spray-painted hash
marks. When he got to Spellman High School and tried
out for varsity, he was already the most experienced
quarterback, including seniors, in the New York High
School Football League.

"Football was your game and I hit a pretty mean
stickball, but let me show you the future MVP, Gold
Glove, batting 'champeen' of all time." Joey reached
into his wallet and pulled out a picture of Joseph Palumbo Jr. in a Bay Area Little League outfit, a small

aluminum Louisville Slugger propped over his right shoulder. The kid had the same look his father had in the old days, confident and cocky.

"Geez, Joey, he's got your ugly mug and probably your gift for swinging at the high ones." Hiccock smiled to show Joey he was kidding. "He's a great-looking kid. You must be out of your mind with all that Italian macho pride shit."

"Better that than the WASP, ice-water shit you got flowing through your veins."

"Irish and English ya Dago bastard!" Hiccock accentuated the familiar ethnic slur by flicking his right thumb under his top teeth, then adding Joey's mom's favorite exclamation "Fa!"

"You fucking hard-on, it's good to see ya," Joey said, his right cheek tightening as he half-smiled in that cool, I am straight but *I still missed ya, way.*

"You, too, Joey, you too."

"So I figured your big mouth got you into this?"

"Geez, if I only kept it shut, I probably wouldn't be seeing you for another few years," Bill said, offering an opening for Joey to get down to business. But Joey decided not to take it. Instead he laughed. Bill looked over at him, "What?"

Joey sat up straight in his chair. Affecting a proper British accent emulating Sister Eugenia, he said, "I was just thinking. What are the odds of two ruffians from the Bronx winding up working for Uncle Sam?" Bill smiled as he recognized the voice of the primary authority figure in black and white from their Catholic past.

"So how'd you wind up at the White House?" Joey asked as he tore off a piece of bread.

"The House Committee on Science, Space, and Technology had asked me to take part in a project. They were trying to get funding for the Super Collider-Accelerator Ring. The one in Texas."

"Oh, not the one on the Grand Concourse?" Joey jibbed.

"Anyway, I got to brief some people from the administration and I guess they liked my no-nonsense straightforward way of taking complicated, technological subjects and making them wholly unfathomable and totally boring."

"You were always good at curing insomnia when you got into one of your smart guy rants."

"So since I wasn't a Democrat or a Republican, Mitchell's people nominated me for SciAd. I think there was one other guy who actually wanted the job, but he had a tendency to wear fruit on his head. Ergo, they reluctantly settled on me."

"I dunno, I always figured you for NASA or some nuclear shit."

"Not on your fucking life. I had the chance to work with a guy I met back in college. Think-tank stuff on nuclear weapons and research. But I didn't warm up to the idea of doing clean little calculations on messy mega-death yields."

"Parnes?"

"Yeah, how'd you know that?" Then it hit him. "You dickhead! You read my file. I've got an FBI file?"

"One of our primary functions is the vetting of anyone working for the higher end of government. I actually recertified this Parnes guy two years ago."

"Recertified?"

"Yeah, he changed jobs and we just made sure he was still a good security risk."

"Yeah? What's he doing now?"

"Classified, buddy. Couldn't tell ya even if I knew."

"Anyway, so now I get to affect the national science agenda, make sure important work isn't ignored and that science in the schools doesn't go the way of religion, music, and art."

"God forbid. So how'd ya get on the FBI's shit list?"

"Don't you have that in your stinking file?"

"I'm trained as a field agent. I only trust reports when and if I can't investigate myself."

"Aw geez, Joey, I not only stuck my foot in my mouth, I managed to get it in up to my knee."

A passing waiter gave Joey pause, then he asked, "Bill, I read what you said to the president, but I want to know *why* you said it?"

"I said it because I saw it happening all over again."

"What?" Joey asked.

"Us, putting on the blinders. There were no less than three warnings leading up to the September 11th attacks. The first one was in the court papers of the Blind Sheik case back in '95. You guys came a cat's whisker away from nailing him for, and I quote the Justice Department indictment, 'planning to hijack and crash a *civilian airliner* into CIA headquarters.' Then there was the Al-Qaeda hijacking of the Air France A320 Airbus in Algiers that was foiled when the pilot realized they were going to fly the plane, loaded with fuel, into the Eiffel Tower. So he faked an emergency and landed in Marseilles."

"Our hostage and rescue teams study the French paratrooper's retaking of that airbus on the tarmac. It was a textbook example of overcoming terrorists who hold a plane."

"That's what gave that bastard Bin Laden the idea that his boys needed to learn to fly. The day after the dead hijackers were dragged from that plane onto the tarmac in Marseilles, Mohamed Atta, the asshole who led the attack, enrolled in flight school."

"Hindsight is 20-20."

"Awww bullshit! Bureaucratic insulation and turf wars blinded us."

"Whoa! I thought you were a science guy, where'd all this political venom come from?"

"That's the point, Joey boy. It ain't political. It's our lives we are talking here, our security. As far as science goes, the whole key is the exchange of ideas and experimental results good or bad. All the advances came from standing on the shoulders of scientists and philosophers who came before. If science were run like the FBI, the Secret Service, and the NSA, we'd still be treating disease with leeches and taking six months to cross the ocean."

Bill paused and saw Joey appraising him. He wondered what he thought. "The final unbelievably stupid lapse of governmental oversight came in July 2001, two months prior to the attack. No less an event than Italy closing their airspace went unreported to anyone! Egyptian intelligence caught wind of a plot to hijack a civilian airliner and crash it into the G-8 summit in Genoa, killing President Bush and the other world leaders attending that little shindig."

"Hey, that was under Secret Service's authority."

"That's my fucking point! Did the Secret Service, the FBI, or the NSA ever tell the fucking FAA? You think those pilots in the airliners that hit the towers and the Pentagon would have gone along with a hijacking, thinking it was only a political exercise, if one asshole from the government had told the FAA, 'Hey, the next hijacking might be with the intent to use your plane as a missile.' Those pilots would have flipped the plane the moment anyone got up to rush the cockpit, whose doors, by the way, would have already been fortified. On top of this, if the public had been informed, those passengers on either of those flights would have stopped things from getting that far—like those brave souls on Flight 93 in Pennsylvania. Do you realize that the window of opportunity to hijack a plane and use it as a flying bomb lasted less than an hour? That was the time it took for the Flight 93 passengers to find out about what happened to the World Trade Center and say, 'Let's roll.'"

"Are you laying September 11th at the FBI's feet?"

"The FBI and the rest of the agencies laid the welcome mat at the terrorists' feet by keeping their tight-assed, 'agency first,' bullheaded, bullshit attitudes."

"Come on, Bill, don't hold back. Tell me what you really think!"

"Sorry, but that whole thing gets me started."

"So now I see why Tate hates your guts."

Hiccock nodded. "What about you, do you hate me?"

"Me? Nah. Look, even though I'm an agent for the FBI, I get your point. I'm not supposed to, but I do. Personally, I think you're chasing fairy tales, but hey, it's a free country."

"So what's the message you're supposed to deliver to your old pal here, Joey?" Hiccock figured he might as well save his friend some anguish. He expected Joey to ask him to go away, to drop the whole thing.

"Fairy tales can come true, it can happen to you. And if it happens I want you to promise me you'll notify the bureau."

"Gee, Joey, I appreciate your position and all, and I really would like to help out the old bureau there, but I got two problems with this." *Let's see who can fake sincere better.*

"Well, let's see if we can work those out."

"One, your boss is, like you used to say, a *strunz-a-menz*. And two, I work directly for, and report directly to, the president. Period. You got a problem with that, take it up with the Commander in Chief." Having put the last nail in that coffin, Hiccock sat back and hoped it was over. It wasn't.

"Then can I ask you something as an old friend from the neighborhood?"

Hiccock picked up his right index finger and started wagging it at him. "Don't start with that ..."

"C'mon, from one Boulevard Blade to another." He then gave the secret club gesture, making a fist but with the thumb between the index and middle fingers. Hiccock could not believe Joey was actually invoking schoolyard ethics but his face softened. "Here's my card, Bill. I'm the head of the San Francisco office now, so call me personally, please. Despite my asshole political boss, us worker bees actually do know what we're doing, you know."

Hiccock was about to decline, but then flashed on the fact that with his three science degrees, he didn't know diddly-squat when it came to investigations. A lifeline to an experienced agent could be a good thing. "Deal."

Joey smiled. "So I heard you got married ... to a doctor, no less." Hiccock took a deep swallow from his drink and proceeded to relate the ballad of Billy and the head doctor.

Three drinks later, there was a lull in the conversation. Joey fingered the edge of his glass as Bill swirled the last bit of liquor around the ice cubes.

"You're right, you know," Joey said. "We really blew it."

"Forget the fact that on September 10, 2001, the whole country cared more about some congressman's zipper than Bin Laden's attack on the U.S.S. *Cole*. We stopped appreciating how good we had it and that there was someone out there who wanted to take it all away from us."

"But we were supposed to be the guardians, the ones on watch while others slept. Hell, we got seduced too."

"Bullshit, you got declawed, de-balled, and de-fanged by politically correct, political bullshit that took the war out of warrior, the police out of policeman, and the secret out of secret agent."

"So you really think you'll get these fuckers, Bill?"

"*Think* is the operative word. I'll leave the guns and the bombs to you guys. I just want to make sure they don't get away with this because I *didn't* think, didn't consider every possibility."

"So is that how a brain guy fights crime?"

"Nope, that's how a dumb guy tries to get out of something he has no right being in the middle of in the first place."

∞§∞

Joey's FBI sedan, probably borrowed right out of the Washington D.C. motor pool, was pulled around first. Bill was waiting for the valet to fetch his car when his cell phone rang.

"Mr. Hiccock, Carly Simone."

Hiccock was glad to hear from her, but his radar was bristling a bit. "Nice to hear from you, Carly. What's up?"

"Can I get 10 minutes tomorrow? Something's come up and I would like to run it by you."

"I can do that, around three maybe?"

"Fine, I'll be there.

"I will be too!"

His Ford Expedition pulled up. He threw the car jockey a five spot. He rolled down the driver's side window and opened the moon roof; it had turned into a warm and clear evening. He hoped the fresh air would diminish the slight buzz he had going. He was starting to have sssssdsecond thoughts about refusing a personal car and driver. As head of a presidential commission he was entitled to one, but his blue-collar upbringing made him think it was a little too much. Then, a sobering thought crossed his mind. If the cops stopped him right now, it would mean a DWI for sure. There was little doubt Tate would make a federal case out of it. His brief career as a special investigator for the president and, to a lesser extent, a mole for Joey from Gunhill Road would be even briefer. He instinctively slowed down and put his hands at the prescribed ten and two o'clock positions on the wheel and made doubly sure he obeyed all traffic laws.

Pulling into his spot, he shut off the engine and took a deep breath. He was home safe and sound, promising himself he would never do that again. As Hiccock stepped away from the car, his head turned to the sound of a branch snapping. He was startled by a man coming toward him from the bushes. Instinctively, Bill ducked low and, extending his right leg, swept the man's legs out from under him.

As he fell to the ground, the man protested, "Hey, what the ... ahh. Owww." Hiccock was about to stomp on his face when the "Ow" caused him to hesitate.

"Ow? What kind of mugger are you?" Bill's fists were still poised to punch his lights out.

"I'm not a mugger. I need to speak with you."

"Why did you jump out at me like that?" He grabbed the man's shirt pulling him halfway up, with his arm cocked, ready to clock him, for emphasis.

"I'm not too good at all this cloak-and-dagger stuff," the man explained nervously, his hands up protecting his face.

Bill sized him up as no real threat and extended his hand. "Here, let me help you get up there, Mr. Bond."

"Wendell, Wendell Simmons."

"What's so cloak-and-dagger that you need to ambush me from my own bushes?"

Rubbing his knee, Wendell looked around. "Inside?"

Twenty minutes later, Wendell was holding a bag of frozen peas on his knee as Hiccock attempted to restore his own equilibrium with strong black coffee. Wendell was a short man who seemed better suited to be an air-conditioning and refrigeration repairman than the research scientist he claimed to be. Seated across from him, Hiccock couldn't help but imagine this late-forty-something balding man in a blue uniform shirt with "Chuck" or some such name embroidered on it, his shirt pocket holding a dial thermometer and an AC current tester. That image faded as Wendell got deeper into his story. Was this man offering Hiccock the smoking gun evidence he needed? If so, the Intellichip explosion was indeed a case of sabotage.

"My job was to ensure the formula's integrity as we ramped up to higher volume production runs."

"Did you work in quality control?" Bill inquired, remembering his brief series of courses in chemical-industrial techniques.

"That was the first flag that something was amiss. I was a technician before I became a project manager. I didn't have any latitude on the rules. I followed them because I knew they meant scientific repeatability and safety. Then, suddenly I'm meeting with the CEO, who is not a chemist I might add, asking me to fudge results."

"And did you?"

"Most of the stuff was budgetary. But then he hit me with a doozy. He wanted me to increase the amount of suspension in the formulation originally intended for a plant in Arkansas."

"And why was that strange?"

"That amount of suspension wasn't necessary, because the load was being delivered in a matter of days. We suspend to decrease the possibility of unintended combustion or impurities affecting the batch during shipping."

"So this level of suspension was better suited for something that would take how long?"

"Months—like the shipment was going real far. We had already registered the shipment with the ICC for interstate travel, but to me it seemed as though this batch was going outside the country."

"And the amount of suspension you added to the batch in the Intellichip building should have inhibited it from exploding that night?

"Absolutely. That formulation was stable and would have remained so until the suspension was intentionally stripped at the point of delivery."

"How would that have been done?"

"Lots of ways. Any low-boiling-point liquid would destabilize the suspension."

"Like Freon?"

"That would do nicely."

"That's an incredible story," Hiccock said as he sat back from the edge of his chair. "And you were an engineer on this project?"

Wendell nodded. "The *head* of the project. Thank you for not calling the cops."

"Mr. Simmons, why are you risking so much to help?"

"Heather Simmons ... you wouldn't know her or recognize her name ..." He stared down at the floor. "She was twelve, asleep, safe in her bed, when the windows ... the windows imploded, that's the term. Her carotid artery was severed. By the time I came to, she was so white ... and the sheets soaked red ..." He looked up at Hiccock, tears in his eyes.

∞§∞

General Nandesera felt a pain in his back. It was his first consciously aware moment since he sat down three hours earlier to review the final operational plans for Samovar. The lactic acid in his muscles made him stiff. His body was used to the military regimen. Sitting still had been an acquired talent –one that he struggled to conquer every day that he sat and thought rather than stood and fought. It had been a while. The last time he actually fought was Afghanistan in '89. Overall, he was pleased with the report he had read. His assets were in position. The retribution for the American cruise missile strikes deep within his country would soon be rained down on the imperialist giant that felt it could kill without consequences. The General was about to sign an order making America pay dearly for those punitive attacks carried out towards the end of the last century. All that was needed was an exact position and time in which to execute. That, he was hoping, would be provided by the new "eyes and ears" center supplying the much-needed intelligence. As an old soldier, he would have much preferred hard human intelligence over electronic eavesdropping, especially when the eaves one was dropping in on were public media outlets.

Alone in his office, he signed the order without fanfare or ceremony. As he removed his reading glasses, he sat silent for a moment. Very quietly, his nation had just gone to war with the United States of America, which was already under attack by somebody else; he didn't know who, maybe the North Koreans, but he knew those events were the perfect diversion and cover for Samovar, his Master Plan.

CHAPTER FOURTEEN
CONNECTIONS

"YOU'RE TELLING ME that the CEO of Intellichip was illegally exporting chemicals from Mason Chemical to Iran?" said Reynolds. "I don't believe it!"

"I don't know if I do either but there are two separate issues here. The illegality aside, if the mixture in the building that night was going overseas, and it was heavily suspended, then it couldn't have spontaneously combusted or been accidentally ignited by the employee. It had to have been sabotaged. On the other hand, Wendell could just be a disgruntled employee of Intellichip. I think the FBI should check out his story, whether he actually did lose a daughter on the night of the explosion and so on."

Reynolds raised an eyebrow, announcing that Hiccock just impressed him in some way. "FBI? Handing the ball over to the other team?"

"Let's just say I don't want that factory to blow up again, this time in *our* faces. Besides, Tate strong-armed an old friend of mine to grovel for the FBI. They don't want to be left out of my loop."

"It's your call. You know, Bill, your FBI pal probably wrote a report that found its way to Tate's desk already."

"Then they better have a good infirmary in the old FBI building there, because if Joey wrote a blow by blow of everything I said, Tate's going to have a coronary."

"Now why doesn't that surprise me? Listen, you aren't in the pristine realm of science now. You are into an area populated by power-hungry men. Being right isn't always as important as surviving the political shit storms around here."

Bill was confused. Reynolds was the last guy he expected to give fatherly political birds-and-bees speeches. "Thank you, Ray, for that insight. I'll try to remember to always have my umbrella out."

"Look, whether I like it or not you are now part of my team. I have a vested interest in your survival and Tate knows it. Be careful!"

Bill knew that Reynolds was covering his bets, straddling both sides of the loyalty issue. After all, he, the dumb political guy, could be right. Reynolds was making sure there wasn't anything more than a few feathers left in his potential serving of crow. Or was he keeping a murky access road open for his boss, President Mitchell, to take as an escape route? Hiccock was stunned to catch himself in the middle of such political calculations and reverie. *Maybe this place is rubbing off on me.*

"How's it going with the wife ... ex-wife?"

"Fine. She's onto something."

"Has she found the common tie yet?"

"No, but this is either two-dozen, separate one-in-a-billion coincidences of individual schizophrenia or ..." He paused as the scientist in him demanded more empirical data before even speculating on a conclusion. His last words hung awkwardly for a moment. "That's all I am prepared to say at this time."

"Very politically astute answer, Bill. You're learning. I got to hit the head." Reynolds made his exit, totally misreading Bill's intention. It would not be the last time.

∞§∞

As William Hiccock left Ray Reynolds' office he looked at his watch and realized it was five past three.

He decided to skip a pit stop to the men's room and get back to his office to meet Carly.

When he reached his office, she was sitting there, filling his office with a French perfume he should probably learn the name of. He made a small apology and sat behind his desk. She was looking very attractive today. Her hair color had changed. It was now a constant shimmering hue. It almost didn't look real. "Well, what's on your mind, Ms. Simone?"

"Carly, please." Hiccock nodded and she continued. "Well, things are happening so fast here at the White House. Yesterday I was offered a job at MSNBC."

"Congratulations!"

"Thank you. Actually it was in no small part because of you."

"Me?"

"Yes. You are drawing a lot of attention and they want me to cover you."

Hiccock was intrigued by her directness. "I'm flattered, but I'm doing classified work here."

"That's why I wanted to talk with you first. Do you see any way of me covering what you do while you maintain your need for secrecy?"

Hiccock liked that she was clearing it with him… But wait! He caught himself. "Carly, that's really a question for Naomi's press office."

"Mr. Hiccock, I know what she'll say. That's why I am coming to you. You can grant me access, I believe, if you feel that you are being treated fairly."

"Pardon, but the news media has been anything but fair with me. And don't quote me on that, please."

"Trust starts here, Mr. Hiccock. I won't breathe a word of it. After all, I am a print journalist at heart. I like to believe we hold ourselves to a higher standard."

Hiccock took in the new television reporter for a moment. *Now* the hair color made sense. He imagined that someone spent two or three hundred dollars on a "colorist" to bring luminosity, highlight, and tone to her soon-to-be nationally broadcast, locks. He found himself smiling at her and her 300-dollar dye job. *It was worth it.*

He forced himself to look beyond her good looks and tried to look into her heart to see if she harbored good or evil. He gave that up in short order realizing probably only God could do that. *Were her eyes always that blue?* was the thought that capped his mortal failing at being God-like.

"I'll talk to Naomi and see what we can do. But, if I say I can't divulge or talk about something you'll have to respect that."

"I wouldn't have it any other way. I'll let you get back to work."

She stood and extended her hand. Hiccock was amazed at how soft it was. Something was said through the brief eye contact that followed but Hiccock had no idea what that was. She then turned toward the door; he consciously avoided watching her as she left.

CHAPTER FIFTEEN
RECRUITMENT

CYNTHIA MALLORY RETRIEVED the mail from the box in front of their two-family house in Hollis, Queens. She could hear Dennis out back, trying to get the lawn mower started. She smiled as each pull of the starting cord was followed by chugging, then silence, then some swearing. She entered the house through the front door and proceeded to leaf through the envelopes. One, addressed to her, from Queens Metropolitan Hospital Neurologic Institute, caused her breath to catch slightly. She stuffed it into the pocket of her housecoat. An unfamiliar envelope, addressed to Dennis, caught her eye. She headed out the back door to see her husband adjusting a screw on the top of the uncooperative mower.

"Come on ya piece of ... junk," he barked as he whipped the cord so hard this time it snapped. "Ahhh ... crud!"

"Denny, why don't you just go down to Sears and get a new one?"

"Do you know what they're asking for one that's not *half* as good as this?"

"No, I don't. But how much do they want for one that works?"

That stopped him. She could always stop him. He threw in the towel and the broken cord, smiled, and asked, "What's up?"

"There's a letter addressed to you from GlobalSync."

"Junk mail?" he asked, wiping his hands and heading toward her.

"No, I don't think so. It looks serious."

He grabbed it and tore it open. "Holy Christmas!"

Cynthia was glad that he'd been heeding her admonishments to cut down on the swearing. "What dear?"

"Look at this!"

It was a check. There, next to a big greasy thumbprint was the computer-printed amount of $100,000.

"Holy shit!" Cynthia said, violating her own edict. "What's this for?"

"I dunno. Probably some computer screw-up. I never heard of this company."

"My God, that's an awfully big mistake."

"Let me go call them and see what this is all about."

"How about we cash it first and wait 'til they call us?"

He smiled and kissed her on the forehead. "Sometimes you exhibit the heart of a jewel thief, you know that?"

"Just think of the shiny new lawn mower we can get you with that. You deserve it."

"Don't cozy up to me just because I'm suddenly rich." He put his arm around her as they headed toward the house. His hand dropped to her behind where he stole a few soft pats then held on, adding, "A small fortune in my hands."

Six frustrating minutes later, Dennis hung up the phone having made no progress. He decided he needed to go to the GlobalSync offices himself. Cynthia went with him, the letter from the hospital forgotten for the moment.

∞§∞

Janice and Hiccock were escorted by two-uniformed Madison, Wisconsin, cops past the crime scene tape into Martha Krummel's home. Although the local police already broomed the house, Hiccock and Janice flew here to see it firsthand. There was a chance that Janice could pick up some psychological clues as well. Once inside, the smell reminded Hiccock of his grandmother's house: it evinced the same Cashmere Bouquet–scented memory. He fingered through a candy dish, found and unwrapped a cherry red sourball, and took one more nostalgic deep breath. They studied each room. The kitchen was locked in a time warp, every appliance the cutting edge of 1960's Westinghouse technology. Hiccock imagined a woman dressed in a Pat Perkins day dress or in Capri pants like Mary Tyler Moore in the old *Dick Van Dyke Show*, with a casserole and pink oven mitts, singing a song from the 1964 World's Fair. *"The future will be dandy. The kitchen will be handy. At the Westinghouse hall of ..."*

The living room possessed the quiet comfort of a cozy place where someone smoked a pipe while Martha read or did needlepoint. As he appraised the room, his eyes were drawn to the huge RCA furniture console color television and hi-fi stereo unit. Then, it struck him. In the whole house there wasn't a stick of furniture, or anything else for that matter, that was acquired after the 1970s. Bill examined her collection of books, all garden-related, while Tyler searched through the drawers.

"There's nothing here," he said, his head tilted sideways, reading spines.

"So how did a seventy-something grandma master railroad signaling and control?" Janice asked as she rummaged through a drawer full of hatpins and hair combs.

Out of frustration, Hiccock collapsed in the chair behind Martha's desk situated in front of the picture window overlooking her garden. To Janice, who was standing behind him, it appeared that he was looking through the window at the now abandoned flowers and shrubs. He wasn't.

"What's wrong with this picture?" he said.

"Nothing. She had a great life. I'd like to have it set up like this when I'm her age. Without the federal charges, of course."

"C'mon, we're looking right at it!"

∞§∞

"Carly Simone, the White House. Back to you Brian. How was that?"

"You blew it at the end by asking me 'how was that?' Never break your attitude until the cameraman says 'cut!' You just showed 10 million Americans that you are worried. Now let's try it again and here's a trick. Practice a completion face, the face that you will put on when you are finished. It should say, 'there I've told you, but I stand ready to answer any questions you might have on follow up.' Okay. And camera's rolling, speed!"

Carly counted down to two then silently to zero and began, "...in 3, 2, ... Good evening, Brian. In a move that caught Washington by surprise today, the White House was sold at auction to a bidder from Boulder, Colorado on Ebay!" As she read another gibberish story into the camera that was only feeding a tape machine for her review, Carly's rehearsal for her new job as White House science beat reporter for MSNBC was taking shape. She was learning "on camera" etiquette, in a crash course, from one of the best field producers at NBC. He had been flown *in* specially from his ranch in Montana and *out* of semi-retirement. The network was hot on Carly and wanted her "on-air" in record time. They worked for two days on when to smile and when not to smile. She mastered the skill of listening to the earpiece and talking at the same time. Eventually they moved on to audio prompting, where she practiced becoming a ventriloquist's dummy for a producer who would put words in her ear only to be regurgitated a split second later.

∞§∞

Hiccock and Tyler came blasting through the doors that identified the FBI's Washington, D.C., Electronic Crimes Lab as an "authorized personnel only" area, pushing Martha's computer on a rolling cart. Kyle Hansen, thirty-two and already the top computer expert for the FBI, followed.

"Is that all of it?"

Hiccock nodded yes. "What's a seventy-year-old gardening grandmother need with a computer?"

"Careful, Bill. You'll have the AARP all over you for that insensitive remark," Janice said.

The technicians hooked up the machine and rebooted it in record time. Hansen got to work.

"You're looking for any activity that would bring her close to railroad info and practices," Hiccock said.

"One of our Cyber Action Teams obtained a warrant and secured the ISP's records from her account. We know when she logged on and for how long, but we only know the material that she downloaded, which was supplied by her internet service provider," Hansen explained as he typed away.

"We're going to need more than that and maybe her hard drive will tell us."

∞§∞

DuneMist: There was a man and a woman poking around the Krummel house today.

SABOT: Were they police, FBI, or real estate agents?

DuneMist: Definitely investigators of some kind. They had a police escort.

SABOT: Interesting.

DuneMist: I watched from across the street. They left with a computer from the house.

SABOT: That's a good point. I shall instruct our members to erase all communications.

DuneMist: That would be a good thing.

SABOT: Thank you for this information.

DuneMist: :)

SABOT: Signing off.

DuneMist: TTFN

As Bernard shut down his computer, a flood of thoughts invaded his mind. First, DuneMist must live in Wisconsin because that's where the Gardening Grandmother lived. Second, if one of his own members had figured that Martha was carrying out his orders, then maybe he should become more proactive.

He rebooted his computer and went to the web site of an Illinois ISP. He decided to open an account and to use the name, address, and credit card number of Terrance Johansen of Decatur, Illinois. Terrance's letter to the May Company, demanding credit to his card

#2314-012312-9090 expiration date 09/30/13, had been mangled and was inadvertently ripped open and resealed with a cellophane tape bearing the words "Received in damaged condition, re-wrapped at Parkerville Station." It was then sent on its way after Bernard photocopied the letter and the envelope containing Terrance's return address. The online system required either a phone number for billing confirmation, a debit card, or a credit card. Of those three choices, the easiest identity for Bernard to steal was the credit card. The online registration form accepted the "borrowed" information, and Bernard picked the ISP because they offered a seven-day free trial. Bernard knew that as long as he cancelled the account before the free trial was up, Terrance would never see a bill or even know he had an account opened in his name. Bernard already knew this trial period would last only a few minutes, just long enough to e-mail the chief of police in Madison, Wisconsin, whose address was conveniently located at the bottom of the Madison Police Department web site.

∞§∞

With any international corporation, twenty-four-hour buildings were a necessity. The White House was no exception. Late-night staffers and hangers-on from day shifts, attempting to whittle down the millions of tasks the administration was duty-bound to fulfill, populated the halls and basement apart from the president's residence. Even chiefs of staff sometimes had to burn midnight oil; it was not unusual for Reynolds to turn off his desk lamp at 12:00 AM. He grabbed his coat and walked down the hall to find Hiccock bent over reams of printouts.

"It's midnight, Bill."

Hiccock rubbed his eyes. "There's something trying to knock on my brain here, but so far ..."

"Bill, go home and catch a few winks. Then maybe you'll hear the doorbell."

"Do you think this is odd?"

"What?"

"We checked. Martha had a computer. The kid had a computer. Every one of these 'homegrowns' had a computer."

"You think they were all wired up to an organization on the web?"

"No, that goes back to the mole theory. What if they were all recruited, trained, and coordinated on the web?"

"How's that different from what I said?"

"What if none of them knew it?"

Reynolds sat with his coat over his lap as his mind began to race. "Have you been able to confirm this?"

"That's going to be tough. Every one of them but Martha is dead."

"Then where's this coming from?"

"It's the only plausible common denominator."

"Let me see if I follow your thinking. You are alleging that somebody—we don't know who—is recruiting random people on the web—but we don't know how. These random recruits are attacking this country— without knowing why. Is that it?"

"Yeah, I know it's off the charts. But it's the only scenario that ties together all the loose ends. Could be a whole new method of recruitment, training, and deployment. One that is airtight."

"So what's the wife—" Hiccock held up his pointer finger— "ex-wife think about this?"

"She feels there is an external behavioral moderator at work here."

"Inglese, por favor."

Just then Janice entered the office rubbing the bridge of her nose and yawning. "I just finished reading all the profiles. These people exhibit a hybrid schism"—she noticed Reynolds and "dumbed down" for his sake—"they all have no connection to their targets and no apparent aptitude in the means of destruction. In my opinion, it's safe to assume that all these people were aware of their actions but probably would have had no recollection of how or why they did it— or how they knew how to do what they did, for that matter."

"If that's true that makes them the perfect operatives," Reynolds said. "Even if you catch them, they don't know anything. That only leaves how they are being recruited and trained."

"That's why I've got that meeting tomorrow with someone who might be able to shed some light on the subject," Hiccock said.

"Speaking of which, the boss has approved your wild idea of bringing him into this, but for Christ's sake, Bill, he's not even in the government. Couldn't you find a smart guy who's already on the payroll?"

"Wow, that's a floater just waiting to be creamed, Ray."

Reynolds simply smirked. It was too late at night for this.

CHAPTER SIXTEEN
PEN AND SWORD

THE EXCLAMATION "PULL!" was followed shortly by an ear-piercing shotgun blast that shattered a clay pigeon. The pieces fell serenely into the Chesapeake Bay. The skeeter, in shooting goggles, ear protectors, duck hunter's hat, and red flannel jacket, was best-selling author Frank Harris. When he was forty-five, he started fooling around with some military-styled video games and a year later wrote his first thriller, which became a huge hit. At the age of fifty-five, the former bank manager was a multimillion-dollar word machine churning out high-tech spy and political novels. Although Harris never served in the military, when his publisher dressed him up in pseudo military casual attire for the picture on his dust jackets, he looked every bit the part of a retired flag officer. He had handsome features, and the peaked cap covering his balding head made him appear years younger.

He was firing from the jetty that extended into the bay from his twenty-five-acre waterfront estate. Hiccock, standing next to him, recoiled from the kickback as the next blast emptied out of the double-barrel shotgun.

"This is about the terrorists, isn't it?" Harris asked as he removed his ear protectors and walked over to the gun table.

Hiccock smiled. How could he have expected this guy not to figure it out? "Let's make believe you didn't ask that and I didn't nod, okay?"

"Just like in one of my books. What's the Washington brain trust think?"

"They're looking for the ghost of cold wars past. They are so inside that box, a light goes on when you open the door. That's why I'm here."

"Generals always lose the start of the next war because they fight it like the last war. After a few licks, they'll catch on." Harris wiped down the shotgun and placed it on the table.

"Something tells me the clock may run out before we get off the last shot."

"Well, I think I know what you're looking for, but it's going to cost you."

Hiccock surveyed the vast accumulated wealth of Harris's surroundings. A quarter of a mile behind him, knights in armor, forever mounted on stuffed horses, stood on motionless display behind the twenty-foot glass windows of Harris's armaments room. A Sherman tank was propped up like a statue with a landscaped circular garden surrounding it amidst original Remington sculptures with a few Robert

E. Lee pieces thrown in for good measure. It was Harris's private homage to man's largest and longest-running endeavor: war.

"Forgive me, but what else could you possibly need or want?"

"The U.S.S. *Iowa*."

"The what now?"

"I want one magazine battery, three cycles, nine rounds," Harris said matter-of-factly as he reset his earmuffs and heaved a shotgun into the ready position. "Pull!" he called to his houseboy, butler, or whoever was launching the clay pigeons, fifty yards downrange from them. The clay pigeon disappeared in a smear of powder. "I get to squeeze 'em off."

"Let me get this straight, Mr. Harris. You want the United States battleship Iowa for target practice?"

"Each shell weighs 2,700 pounds, is 16 inches around, and can hit a target 20 miles away. Ever hear one of those babies go off as it belches out flame and smoke? What a sight! What a sound!" He gently wiped down his prize shotgun. He picked up a smaller weapon.

"How about a million dollars, a plane, and enough fuel to make it to a sympathetic country?"

"Okay, one cruise missile?"

"I can't believe I flew down here to negotiate weapons of mass destruction with you!"

"That's what you need to afford the best-selling author who has everything."

"Deal. I hope."

"Trance-inducing visual graphics," Harris said plainly.

Hiccock smiled. "That's certainly outside the box. You mean brainwashing by computer?"

"If it was my novel and I was writing it, I would have the bad guys lulling regular people in with hypnotic graphics, the kind only a computer can make. Clicking the mouse would make the graphics swirl and perform. When their mouse click responses start to lag or match a predetermined rhythm, then I'd know they were going under and ready to accept input. All that would be left to do is implant the commands. Maybe by telephone."

"That is *brilliant*. I'll order a check of the phone company logs."

"Yeah, maybe I shouldn't have told you. It would have made a great book. Well, it's yours now. Time to feed more fish."

"Feed more fish?"

Harris picked up one of the target pigeons. "I have them specially made from freeze-dried compressed fish food. Mixed with a little egg, they harden like clay. The minute they hit the water they rehydrate into fish food." He brandished an Uzi submachine gun. "Watch this." He smiled at Hiccock. "Pull!" he barked. With the sound of a zipper, the gun spit out thirty rounds per second. The plate was not exactly shattered as much as separated in midair, continuing in the rough shape of a plate until gravity pulled the falling pieces apart. "Neat huh?" he asked with the excitement of a schoolboy.

∞§∞

"Last night they burned the midnight oil as they have for so many nights since the terrible rash of terrorist attacks besieged the country. Still in the apparent center of the government's efforts to find out who the perpetrators of these horrific events are, stands the president's science advisor, William Hiccock. Normally the science advisor to the president is a backroom political appointee who the public hardly, if ever, sees. In my exclusive report tonight, we'll explore how the government is using newer, more scientific, techniques to catch a bad guy and how a former college quarterback sensation turned science advisor is calling the plays..."

Watching in his "eyes and ears" center, a bleary eyed Falad made note of this new face, this Carly Simone reporting. She was sharing intelligence on the "Hiccock" he had heard of when he accused certain Moslem countries of pre-emptive strikes against American corporations trading with the Israelis. He wrote up the content of her report, and noted she was new to the network. He made a note to do a Nexus-Lexus search on her to see where she came from and if she knew of what she spoke.

∞§∞

"We have traced back through the worms we found on Grandma's hard drive," Hansen explained as he set up more tests in the FBI's ECL. "We'll sign on to the same sites she did."

"What's a worm?" Tyler asked.

"Originally it was a mole that hackers planted in your computer to track and retrieve what you're doing on the web."

"Like my E-bay, bank accounts, and dirty e-mails."

Hiccock raised his right eyebrow, "You?"

"Didn't know I banked online, did you?" she said, winking.

"Now legitimate web sites use a form of them to implant redundant information, images, and personal preferences to make their pages load faster."

"Oh, like a cookie?" Hiccock asked.

"Only not as passive."

"So we got a record of everywhere she went on the web?" Hiccock said, trying to follow along.

"Parents love it because they know what sites Junior's been visiting," the Electronics Crime Lab tech replied as he pulled up site after site.

Tyler leaned into Hiccock. "Remind me to clean my hard drive when I get home."

The tech navigated through MyGarden.com. The site recognized Martha and displayed the greeting, "Hello, Martha, haven't seen you for two weeks. How are the petunias?" It waited for a response.

"So the web site doesn't really know about her flowers or how long she's been away?" Tyler said.

"Correct! The web site is reading the worm, the cookie as you say, in her machine. Otherwise the site would require enough memory to remember all of this for every person who logged on."

"So it's like a distributed form of intelligence?" Hiccock had some notion of this structure.

"Yes, data are spread throughout the Internet in every user's machine."

"Are you finding anything unusual?"

"We've run routines all day. It all looks normal. No hypnotic or trance-inducing graphics of any kind have come up. Of course we'll go through all the content again with a fine-tooth comb." Hansen didn't sound in the least bit optimistic.

Hiccock felt a wave of defeat wash over him. "You know, a cruise missile just doesn't buy what it used to."

∞§∞

Habibe Al Rassam Assad hated shaving. It was one of so many new skills he had to learn. He and his team members had to pray in private, plan in private, and speak Arabic only when they were in the deep room. That was the name of the room in the house consisting of all interior walls, void of windows and any kind of electronic equipment. He had been training for this for three years. When he was recruited he was told that his mission was to carry out the great will of Allah, that he would be a hero, a man whose name would be taught in Madrassas from Teheran to Indonesia. He and the team were ready and released for action. All they needed now was one critical piece of intelligence.

In the corner of the kitchen there was one cell phone. Constantly plugged in, it had a number known only to General Nandessera. It was intended to be used only once. Now that they were released, one of the team members had to remain in the house next to the phone at all times, periodically checking it to make sure the signal strength bars were showing strong. The long awaited message would be in code. The key to the code was based on the Arabic translation of the American book, *Chesapeake*. The code would be in numbers and written down by hand. Every other number was a page number. The one in between was the ordinal number of a word on that page. A zero anywhere in the code indicated that the previous word's first letter only was to be used. Any American reference or non-Arabic translatable words could be spelled out by using only the first letters of words ear marked with a zero. It was an old key code style. But only two people knew

the book chosen, he and the General. The General himself would code the message and hand place a call to a
trusted aide half a world away. That aide would then
dial up the cell phone number of the safe house and
repeat the series of numbers twice. By using this form
of layers or cutouts, there was no chance of any electronic trace or pattern, which could be established by
the American NSA; the National Security Agency having the task of listening in on the millions of electronic
signals generated every minute throughout the world.

∞§∞

Asaad checked the "package." It was not really
necessary, but he was trained to be a professional and
leave nothing to chance. He performed the checkout
for the hundredth time and found all the elements in
their proper and ready state. He proceeded into the
deep room to join his clean-shaven team for afternoon
prayers.

∞§∞

Joey Palumbo was reviewing the stuff in his overnight in-box between sips of herbal tea instead of the
usual morning coffee that was killing his stomach lately. He hoped to delay the ulcer he was working hard to
have just one day farther into the future. Having been
added to the very tightly controlled distribution list on
all "Homegrown" traffic, he was more than interested
in the report he held in his hand. It seemed the Madison PD received an anonymous e-mail from someone
who knew Martha Krummel's computer was now in
the hands of the authorities. That in and of itself was
unsettling. The e-mail reffered to a Sabot Society but
fell short of taking credit for the recent wave of events.
The most interesting part of the message, which prickled his cop's nerve endings, indicated that this would

not be the last: "Furthermore, for purposes of verification, this and all future Sabot Society communications would carry the code word "ultimate." Palumbo picked up the phone to dial Billy Hiccock, but thought better of it. He called the Washington headquarters of the FBI instead.

∞§∞

Tyler seemed to love her Tandoori Chicken and Hiccock was working his Lamb Biryani. One of their evolved passions was Indian food—that still cracked up Bill, considering that Janice almost kicked him out of her office the first time they met just because he had it for lunch—and now they were dining in the best Indian restaurant in D.C. He popped his finger into a properly puffed poori, the steam inside escaping from the hollow bread made the same way it had been for dozens of centuries.

Hiccock was a little depressed and Tyler obviously noticed. "Wanna talk about it?"

"No," he muttered as he ripped off another piece of steaming bread. "It's just that, well, I really don't have a clue about what the hell I'm doing. What makes me think I'm right and Tate and the entire national security system is wrong?"

"I didn't think it was about that."

"What did you think it was about?"

"I thought you were just investigating the possibility that you could be right."

"So you're saying that they are not mutually exclusive conclusions?"

"Yes, I know what you, what we, are doing is applying scientific methodology to a case that has more than one connection with science."

"So you're saying it's not necessarily me against them. I just happen to represent a different set of assumptions than theirs."

"Exactly."

She watched him as he pondered this way of thought for a second and then shook his head. "No, no, nothing scientific about it. I wanted to cream that bastard at the FBI. This is personal!" Hiccock noticed the hint of a smile on Tyler's face. "How do you do that?"

"Do what?"

"Manipulate me like that?"

"Was I manipulating you?" Her eyes couldn't have appeared more innocent.

He nodded then tried a little reverse psychology of his own. "There's something I've been meaning to tell you."

"Yes?"

"I think that you have been doing a great job."

"That's very nice of you to say."

"Well, I know what it's like to work under someone who never acknowledges your contribution." Hiccock let it hang.

"How do you do *that*?"

"Do what?"

"Compliment me and insult me in the same breath," Janice, Bill's former boss at school, said.

"Was I doing that?" Bill said, certain his eyes couldn't have appeared more innocent.

"Okay, truce!"

They both focused on their plates. After a minute, Janice looked up. "Do you trust your FBI friend?"

"Joey? Sure. Why do you ask?"

"Well, today when I left the Electronic Crime Lab, I walked to the Psychological Profile Division. I attended a seminar last year with the assistant there, Helen Davis, and I went to look her up. When I entered the office, she immediately closed a file marked 'Homegrown.' She seemed to know I was working with you. She was pretty closemouthed."

"Like she was ordered not to divulge squat to you?"

"Yeah, squat, that was the word I was looking for."

Hiccock glanced away for a second, then rejoined Janice's gaze. "You think this 'Homegrown' file is about what we are investigating?" He slammed his hand down on the table and spilled the tamarind sauce in a shallow plate. People near them turned toward the table. "Of course it is! Damn. We were supposed to share information."

"What are you going to do about it?"

"I'm going to kick Joey's ass."

CHAPTER SEVENTEEN
THE PIANO LESSON

FROZEN FOR ALL ETERNITY with his right arm fully extended, forever warding off would-be tacklers, as the ball is clutched tightly in the left, torso twisted mid-sidestep, was the figure atop one of the many football trophies that lived on a glass shelf in William Hiccock's apartment. Their only human contact now was when Mrs. Phelps dusted them every so often. Wild Bill barely paid them any notice any more. His Heisman Trophy was not the first won by a player from Stanford. That path had been cut by Jim Plunkett. Nevertheless, this trophy along with other prizes stood guard to his illustrious past, a history of his glory days in gold, brass, wood, and chrome.

The kid with the golden arm was asleep in his armchair, the TV flickering in front of him. His sleepless nights and stress over the lack of progress in the investigation were taking their toll. The remote fell from his hand, awaking him startled. In a groggy haze, with one eye open and the other closed, he checked his watch. As he rubbed the sleep from his face with one hand, he searched the floor for the remote with the other. Finding it, he pointed it at the set, about to shut it off when he was caught up in an old black-and-white film on TV. A clichéd old Viennese music professor, replete with little white goatee, was giving a young girl a piano lesson.

"You see, the spaces between the notes are as important as the notes themselves. Now once more, only let the notes 'breathe' this time. Feel the rhythm left by the spaces." The actor recited his line with an accent, probably his own from Germany, but being pawned off as Austrian to the movie-going public of 1940 or so. The professor's lesson for the day was not lost on Hiccock. As the young girl tickled the ivories on her way to Mozartville, Hiccock picked up the phone and punched in a number he knew well, thinking, *the spaces between.*

"Like this, professor?" the young actress, destined for anonymity in later years, asked as she precisely paced each note.

Ten minutes later he was in the shower when the cordless phone he left on the bathroom sink started to ring. His wet hand reached out from behind the glass shower door to pick it up.

"Thanks for getting back to me so early," he said as he directed the showerhead away from him.

Tyler was at home sitting at her vanity in a robe, a towel turbaned around her wet hair. She held her beloved pink princess phone in one hand as she put on makeup with the other. "So what are you all excited about?"

Hiccock looked down, about to say something, but thought better of it. "In your travels, ever bump into anyone monkeying around with or involved in high-speed interstitial image retention research?"

"It's a little early, but are you referring to subliminal advertising?"

"Essentially yes."

Extending the long, pink-coiled cord, she rose from the tufted, crimson velvet covered bench, walked over to the closet, untying the silk belt of the red Norma Kamali wrap. Exposing one shoulder then two until the robe tumbled to the floor, she caught a glimpse of herself in the mirror. *Not too bad,* she thought. "Back in the sixties, advertisers were starting to experiment with slipping in quick cuts of beautiful women during cigarette commercials."

Hiccock ran a towel over his hair with the phone tucked under his chin. "And dry, desert scenes into beer commercials," he added. "It worked, too. Until

Congress got wind of it, made it illegal, and financed research for building monitoring machines."

"But, Bill, the head guy on that was out of your old graduate school, what was his name ... Walters ... Watkins. Wallenford!" She resumed her task of eyelining.

"Yeah, that rings a bell. They had one of those machines right there I bet."

"Sure. That stuff is probably collecting dust in the basement of the Media Lab. So why this sudden interest?" she asked, pulling the towel off her hair.

"Something came to me as I was waking up."

"Really?" she inquired with a naughtiness that surprised her.

"Down girl, this is work. You sure his name was Wallenford?" He was imagining her finishing her morning routine in her bra and panties. He loved the way she looked when he caught her doing something perfectly plain and ordinary. How sexy she was, even when she wasn't trying. That brought a smile to his face that waned with a twinge of sadness. He was, after all, just imagining.

"It's always work with you ... Jack! No! John. John Wallenford."

"Thanks, Janice. See ya tonight for dinner?"

"Um ... not tonight, Bill."

"What's up?"

"Nothing, I just can't make dinner tonight."

"Oh ... Okay." He clicked off, taking a deep breath. Tyler hung up, also taking a deep breath.

∞§∞

Sperling High Voltage made large capacitors for use mainly in research projects. One of those was the particle accelerator being assembled on Long Island at the Brookhaven National Lab. Opponents of the project claimed that the research being done right there on Long Island could create a black hole that would suck

Long Island, the entire Earth, the sun, and this whole corner of the galaxy into it. Most of the protests took the form of sign-toting students and others who managed to acquire the delivery schedules of the supply trucks. They blocked the main gates for a short time and a few spoke over the various media outlets on the dangers of screwing with the basic glue that held everything in the universe together.

The idea came to Bernard after reading about the protests in *Time* magazine. He logged onto a bulletin board the society now ran under the guise of a hardware-trading web site for people who had old Olivetti word processors. The subject matter ensured that no one but the lost or stupidly curious would ever bother with the site. He typed in the message: "The weather on Long Island is getting better." Voyeurger noticed immediately and responded to Sabot via Instant Messenger.

> Voyeurger: What can I do for the cause?
>
> SABOT: Hold on. I am reading your file now.
>
> Voyeurger: What are you looking for?
>
> SABOT: Do you have any experience with explosives?
>
> Voyeurger: Yes, I remove tree stumps with them.
>
> SABOT: Very good. Here's my plan.

Although Bernard couldn't see him, Voyeurger was smiling as he outlined his idea. It was Bernard's turn to smile when Voyeurger typed back that he could do this within a week.

∞§∞

Hiccock was on his way to a military aircraft. He would shoot up to Boston, then an Air Force helicopter, already having arrived at Logan airport, would shuttle him to Cambridge. As he was leaving his office, Carly appeared at the door. "Can we chat?"

"Gee, I am out of here. I'll be back tonight."

"Can I buy you dinner?"

"No, I have plans for dinner... No I don't." Hiccock caught himself remembering that Janice had a date. "Sure! I'll call you on my way back to D.C. this afternoon."

He walked out to the car waiting for him in the portico wondering if this was a good idea, but not in any mood to cancel his spur-of-the moment acceptance of dinner. *Did I just say yes to a date?*

∞§∞

The offices of GlobalSync were the epitome of downtown chic. After following the prescribed protocol, a series of security guards and receptionists, Dennis and Cynthia finally stood in front of the company's comptroller in her office.

"Can you tell us what this check is for?" Dennis asked the lady who probably worked her way up from assistant bookkeeper.

"Let's see, the code here—23765—should tell us." She entered the numbers into her computer. Her expression changed when the screen came up. "Oh, dear!" She picked up the phone, "Mr. Freidland, can you come into my office? You're going to want to handle this yourself." She hung up the phone, then hung "smile number three" on her face, and politely asked, "Would you kindly just wait here a minute?" Dennis caught Cynthia's eye and shrugged.

Ten seconds later, Mr. Freidland, in a suit that cost half of Dennis's Detective's Benevolent Association pension, entered the carpeted, midlevel executive office.

"Ah, Mr. and Mrs. Mallory, nice to meet you. Would you follow me, please?" With the air of a maître d' he turned and led them into a small private elevator. There were only two floor buttons. The mirror-polished, stainless steel doors opened onto a vast space. Floor-to-ceiling windows revealed the cityscape of lower Manhattan Island. The vista was reflected in the highly polished black-marble flooring that, to Dennis, had the unintended effect of making the entire floor look like it was covered in an oil slick. Way down, at the other end of the space, was a desk that was a replica of the "con" on *Star Trek*. A skinny man in a red turtleneck, green pants, and white shoes swung his feet around and off the side return where they had been planted while he talked on a wireless headset. Upon seeing the Mallorys, he removed the headset, stood up from his desk, and approached them. Dennis gave a glance to Cynthia that said, "*Now* I get it!"

"How's the leg?" Dennis said to the man.

"Hurts when it rains, but I stopped limping about a month ago.

It took me a while to track you down, Mr. Mallory, and *I* can find anybody." He smiled at Cynthia. "And you must be Cynthia. It's a pleasure to meet you."

Cynthia returned the warm smile.

"I appreciate the two of you wanting to come here to thank me but believe me, it is I who should thank you, more than any amount of money could ever express."

Cynthia caught on. "Oh, you must be the young man Dennis helped in the woods."

"A lot more than helped, Mrs. Mallory. Your husband saved my life twice in one afternoon."

"Well, thank you Mr...?" Dennis fished for the name.

"Oh, God, how rude of me! Miles, Miles Taggert."

"Well, Mr. Taggert, I appreciate your generosity, but I came here to tell you that I can't accept this money."

The maître d' gasped as if Dennis had just used a salad fork to cut into a chateaubriand.

Taggert shook the smile off his face. "Why not? Is it not enough?"

"Oh, no, no. That's not it. It's very generous. It's just that I can't accept money for helping you. It wouldn't be right."

"Wow, you really are a hero," Taggert said.

"Yes, he is," Cynthia said. "And thank you, but really, there is no need."

Taggert walked back around and sat behind his desk. He gestured for the Mallorys to take the seats facing him. He pondered for a second. Then he reached his hand across the titanium desktop. "May I have the check, please?"

Dennis patted the pockets of his off-the-rack Macy's sport coat, having absentmindedly stuffed the check in his breast pocket. He handed it over.

Taggert ripped it up. Then he turned to his keyboard. Typing quickly, he finished with a double tap on the return key. He then swiveled his high-tech, ergonomic chair and faced the Mallorys once again. "Okay, so let's talk about you for a minute, Mr. Mallory. You were a decorated New York City detective, shot three times in the line of duty and retired with thirty-five years under your belt. I don't know for sure, but my dad was a cop and I know your last three years couldn't have been padded up too much, so I figure you're making do with a comfortable but not great pension."

Dennis bristled.

"Please don't take offense," Taggert added. "I just like to know things about people. All from the public record, by the way, and what I have learned from my father."

"Who is your father?" Mallory asked.

"He was a sergeant, the seven-eight in Queens. He retired when I went past 500 million in personal wealth. It was my idea. I didn't want my mom to lose him to some junkie or hoodlum after she worked so hard and sacrificed so much for all of us."

"Wow, aren't you the son of the century," Cynthia said. "Dennis, I like this boy."

"Anyway, so here's my next idea. Do you know what we do here, Mr. Mallory?"

"Haven't a clue," Dennis said, turning his palms up.

"We protect secrets, our own and those of clients. We protect secrets that have to be out in the open to have any value. We make it safe for trillions of dollars to find its way from point A to point B."

"Okay, so that explains all of this."

"Then hopefully it also explains why I'd like to hire you as a consultant."

"Me? I don't know anything about your business."

"You don't have to. I need what you already know. Security, police procedure, and how to keep my secrets *secret*."

"What about your dad?"

"We're not talking."

"Now you are down to son of the *month*," Cynthia said.

"He objects to my hang gliding."

"With good reason," Dennis said.

"He just doesn't want your mother to lose you, after all they did to grow you up," Cynthia said.

Taggert ceded their point. "You should meet them sometime. You'll get along swimmingly!"

Just then, Dennis noticed the lady comptroller had silently glided across the "oil slick" and appeared in his periphery. If he was in an undercover operation, he could have been dead. It had been twenty years since he worked undercover, and upon reflection—the wavy one of the comptroller reflected in the slick black floor—that was a good thing. She handed Taggert an envelope. He peeked inside, nodded, and slid the envelope across the desk to Dennis.

"Here, I hope you'll agree to work with us."

Dennis opened the envelope to find a check for $100,000. He dropped his hands, wrinkling the check. "It's another check for 100 grand!"

"Yes, but this one is different. It is an advance on your salary."

"Are you some kind of a wiseguy?"

"Actually, yes! Three degrees and four patents. But if you are asking me if I am being a smart aleck, no. Look at this, please." He gestured to the maître d', who surrendered a note to Dennis. Scanning it, he quickly surmised it to be a nasty letter from some nutcase threatening Taggert.

"Have you heard about Intellichip?" Taggert asked.

"That place that blew up in Westchester?"

"Yes, well I did business with them and a company called Mason Chemical."

"Never heard of *them*."

"They were destroyed last month."

"Have you notified the police about this note? It is a threat."

"I'd rather not. They probe around, and I keep secrets, remember?"

"So does the mob."

"I assure you everything we do is legal and within not only the letter, but the spirit of any law."

"So, why me?"

"Why not? You saved my life twice already."

"You think your life is in danger?"

"You tell me."

"Look, I'm retired." Dennis grabbed his wife's hand. "*We* are retired."

"Will you at least consider helping me?"

Dennis tapped the new check on his knee. "We'll think about it." He placed the check back on the desk in front of Taggert. "Meanwhile, you can hold on to this for a while, 'til we decide."

"Fair enough. And whatever you decide, thank you for everything you have done for me. I hope you'll at least be my guests from time to time for a weekend in the country."

"Why, thank you very much, Mr. Taggert," Cynthia said.

As the Mallorys turned to make their exit, Dennis hesitated. Glancing back at Taggert, he said, "When did you receive that note?"

"A minute before you entered my office." Dennis noted the tinge of anxiety in Taggert's voice.

Dennis now saw this man, a billionaire who was half his age, as a vulnerable, scared young boy. His immediate thought was of Taggert's father. Or more correctly, himself in Taggert's father's shoes. After being a cop all those years, how would he feel if his daughter sought protection from some other cop? He knew that would never happen because ... he couldn't think of why it would never happen, which had the effect of softening Dennis's demeanor. "We'll let you know soon."

CHAPTER EIGHTTEEN
ONE MAN'S JUNK ...

THE COLLEGIATE CALM AND SERENITY of the MIT campus were suddenly disrupted by the thumping sound of heavy composite resin rotors chopping through air. Hiccock looked down at the bike path he used to pedal between classes during his graduate study here at the nation's premiere brain trust of genius. Leaves and dirt swirled, causing tiny whirlwinds that eventually developed into mini-tornadoes. A Marine Huey helicopter made an unscheduled landing on the highway in front of the vaunted institution, the commonwealth's state police having closed both the Massachusetts Avenue Bridge and Memorial Drive to give wide berth to the hurriedly arranged arrival of the president's science advisor. Hiccock emerged and was greeted by a school administrator and the head of school security. He was hurried into the gym.

At the front doors was a sign that read, "AUCTION TODAY 3–5 PM INSPECTION 9 AM–2 PM." He was met at the door by John Wallenford, a man with long gray hair that was not in a ponytail, green-gray eyes, and a body alignment that made you think he was listening for baseball scores through the static of a table radio with one ear.

"I don't know if this means you have good or bad timing," Wallenford said, "but thanks to your government at work, 20 million dollars worth of 1960's era state-of-the-art equipment is right this second up for surplus auction at pennies on a dollar."

"What? Right now? We've got to stop the auction!"

In the gym, the auctioneer waved his gavel. On the small stage sat lot 112, a mass of two-inch videotape recorders, spectrographs, cameras, and racks of time-base correctors—the former subliminal research equipment now on forklift skids. "3,800 going once … going twice … sold! To the esteemed gentleman in the plaid jacket from Boris Reclamation Services."

Nearly as soon as the word *sold* reverberated off the gym's tiled walls and hardwood floor, Hiccock and Wallenford walked up to the recycling czar in plaid who just won the lot. Hiccock immediately sized this guy up as the A/V monitor from high school, now all grown up. "Excuse me, Sir?"

"Yes?"

"We arrived here late. We need this equipment."

"Who's we?"

"My name is Hiccock. I work for the president of the United States, and all I can tell you is that this equipment is needed for a matter of national security."

"I just bought this *from* the government as scrap. Why didn't you just hold onto it while you had it?"

"I'm willing to reimburse you for it."

As they walked away, Hiccock placed his checkbook back into his vest pocket with prejudice. "I can't believe I just paid 20,000 dollars for that pile of junk."

"One man's junk is another man's dubious obsession, I gather," Wallenford said wryly.

"I wonder if I can claim this as an expense," Hiccock thought aloud while fingering the receipt and dreading the inevitable reams of paperwork to follow.

∞§∞

A huge crate and six pallets of what the untrained eye would categorize as junk were conspicuously plopped in the center of the FBI's Electronic Crimes Lab. Hansen, returning from lunch, was shocked to see Hiccock standing beside the pile.

"What are we supposed to do with this junk?"

"Hook it up and test the computers," Hiccock directed.

"How?"

Hiccock grabbed a curled, yellowed manual as thick as a phone book and slapped it into Hansen's chest. "Here. Partial assembly required."

∞§∞

Tommy was not concerned that the rear quarter panels of his Camaro were rotted out as he sat in the diner parking lot. It matched the rest of his life. Seemed ever since the seventies ended, his life was just a big pile of rot. He tried a few different get-rich-quick schemes: phone cards, Nutralite products, at-home distribution of cleaning products, and ten others that turned out to be stay-poor-longer schemes. At this point, the notion of lashing out, getting even with anything, had struck a receptive chord in his twisted mass of internal wiring. Three days ago he waited outside the Sperling Plant and decided that truck number seven was his baby. For the next three mornings he followed number seven, studying the driver's habits. The teamster religiously stopped at the Dunkin' Donuts on Sunrise Highway. Lunch, however, would present the real opportunity.

The twenty-six-foot truck that Sperling used was a Freightliner M2-106, the same make and model that anyone with a driver's license and a pocket full of non-traceable cash could hire from most any truck rental company. He went to Ryder. Scanning the application, he smiled inside when he came across the section requesting information regarding "materials to be transported." Tommy dismissed the application and asked the clerk if he could see the truck, his well-rehearsed cover story being that he had to deliver custom cabinets to a client down poorly maintained roads and he needed to measure the clearance before renting. The clerk, who could not give a shit, said, "Yeah, go ahead. Knock yourself out."

Out in the lot, Tommy crawled under the truck and measured not the clearance, but the area right ahead of the rear wheels and the distance between the main chassis rails, which ran the length of the truck. Those rails had facing flanges that formed a natural shelf support.

∞§∞

Twenty-four sticks of dynamite were stashed under the oil drum out back in his yard. He had accumulated them one stick at a time from uprooting jobs. His design was quite ingenious. He filled a four-inch-wide cardboard mailing tube with the twenty-four sticks. Precisely packaged in six bundles of four, they were wired to a kitchen timer set for ten hours from now. He then went to buy a pack of cigarettes, even though he didn't smoke.

Setting the charge in broad daylight wouldn't have been his first choice. Doing it at night, however, would have necessitated breaking and entering, since the trucks were garaged and locked then. That would have brought with it a whole slew of issues and risks he was not prepared to deal with.

With the loaded tube in the trunk of his car, Tommy sat in the diner's parking lot waiting while the driver lunched. Five minutes earlier, he dropped a matchbook with a lit cigarette sticking through it into the dumpster on the side of the diner. The glowing tobacco reached the first match tip, igniting the book and in short order the grease-drenched paper products that filled the container.

Within two minutes, everyone who was outside the diner and anyone coming out of it turned away from Tom and his car to look at the burning dumpster.

He walked between the Sperling truck and his Camaro. Squatting down, he fitted the black spray-painted tube between the rails. He attached the bungee cord from the tube to two of the many holes along the rails, one to each side. The bungee spanned the other end of the tube that was resting on the far rail flange. This last piece of ingenuity would hold the tube in place as it bounced and rumbled through its last day.

Twenty seconds later, he was up from under the truck. He quickly surveyed the location and determined that no one had been watching him. He walked off without looking back, confident that, unless the truck was to go in for rear-end service, no one would ever notice the tube. He got into his car and pulled away.

∞§∞

Do I call and cancel or bring flowers? Hiccock toiled extra hard through the afternoon in an attempt to avoid making that decision, until it was too late to call and maintain any shred of decency. Having cornered himself into a no-choice situation, he showed up at 8:30 at the Watergate Apartments, sans flowers. Carly came down looking great. That made him smile and change his whole attitude about the night. They took a cab over to M street. Carly had picked the place. It was a quiet establishment where politicians and lobbyists could converse in relatively secure high backed booths significantly minimizing the risk of being overheard. To him, this practical setting played against the notion that this was somehow intended to be a romantic encounter.

Dinner was pleasant enough and off the record. Then, Carly asked if they could go "on record."

"Sure," Hiccock responded.

"Is there a rift between you and the FBI?"

Hiccock thought long then said, "My area of expertise is the scientific ramifications of these attacks. The FBI is the investigative arm of the Justice Department. They have their methods and practices which have served this country well for the last century."

"Fair enough, but is there a rift?"

"There might be occasional disagreements as to the value of certain data."

"What would be some examples of data you disagree on?"

"I think that's as much as I want to say."

"Is there any cooperation between you and the bureau?"

"Yes, in fact I have an old friend there and he and I get along like 'old friends.'"

"Are you close to finding the culprits of these attacks?"

"In that regard, this is more like chess than football. It's sometimes hard to tell how close the victory is just by looking at the board. The move/countermove nature of this investigation makes 'predicting' a fool's endeavor."

"Is there any progress?"

"Only in the elimination of certain people or groups as suspects, but the list of potentials is so long it doesn't make a dent. Besides, all you need to do is find the right one. That can happen in the next minute or years from now. There is no way of knowing."

"When is your next report to the president?"

"I report to him every day."

"Personally?"

"Yes, whenever possible."

"Tomorrow?"

"I suppose."

"May I come along?"

Hiccock was a little thrown, "That seems like a silly question. You can check with Naomi, but my instinct says, 'No way!'"

"You're probably right."

"Yeah, probably."

"Off the record?" Carly prodded. "Where will you meet with the president?"

"I'm afraid that ever since the attacks the location and schedule of the president is a national security issue. I cannot divulge anything about his plans on or off the record. But don't you know that?"

"I am sorry. You're right. It's just that this is all so new to me."

"Why would you want to know that?"

"My next question was to ask if I could interview you tomorrow, and I was hoping that might be right after your meeting with the president."

"Oh, I don't want any more publicity than I already have, thank you."

"Can I call you tomorrow and just get a quote?"

"Sure… but I'll have to call you. I'll be on the road."

"Fine. Now can we go back on the record?"

"Why not?"

The evening lasted 45 minutes more and ended with a handshake and separate cabs. Hiccock didn't know if he was relieved or perturbed. Somewhere deep down in his maleness, he wanted something to help offset the slight nudge that he felt over Janice having a date and being out there, living her life. As for Carly, at an intellectual level he knew he was playing with fire. Especially since the only time he'd gotten burned on this job was when he got too close to the press. Now he was dining with it!

As he got into the cab, he wrote the night off as a pleasant enough diversion and totally harmless.

CHAPTER NINETEEN
THE PAPER CHASE

ALTHOUGH A FIVE-MAN TEAM would normally do this kind of preliminary surveillance of a suspect, the full compliment of agents on this case was a straight result of the director of the FBI being intimately involved with this operation. Scuttlebutt had it that he had some issue with the president and wanted to make sure the bureau cracked the case in short order. All the stops were pulled. Terrance Johansen, the original suspect, turned out to be totally unaware and unconnected to the e-mails that originated from a temporary online account created with his credit card. It required a federal court judge ordering the Illinois ISP to release those billing records.

Suspicion fell on the current target, Bernard Keyes, when the bureau painstakingly deconstructed Mr. Johansen's credit card life. Every transaction, every purchase in every store, and every salesclerk still working or fired had their background combed and analyzed. It all came up a dead end, until Terrance recalled, in his sixth interrogation, about having a problem with the May Company.

It concerned a credit he was seeking on a dress his wife had purchased but never wore to their son's graduation from medical school. She had brought the dress back to the store, but the credit to his American Express card never went through. After many frustrating phone calls, mostly navigating through automated customer service, he finally reached a human being who simply told him to write a letter including all the facts and pertinent information. She would personally see to it that the credit was applied to his account.

The FBI spent two days with Doris Welch, the assistant comptroller of the May Company. They investigated her husband, Wilbur, with the thought that he might have appropriated the number. But again, nothing out of the ordinary arose. Of course, the first thing the agents asked for was the letter. It was ultimately found in the company archives at the end of the second day. It was of little physical evidentiary value because it had been exposed to scores of fingers, each leaving a set of prints or a partial. Still, everyone who could have possibly touched it was printed, as the FBI forensic lab went "by the numbers." The letter was torn and crumpled. When questioned, Doris finally remembered that the envelope had been ripped and resealed at the post office, now inferring a new potential suspect.

The chain of evidence took a new turn. Not having the original envelope was a bad break. Ever since the anthrax cases, the post office had become very serious regarding opcodes being stamped on every piece of mail that went through the system. Those codes would have told the FBI exactly what path the letter traveled. Without those imprinted telltales to go on, finding the route of the letter from Johansen's home to Doris Welch's office involved three distinct possible courses, each one implicating many postal employees. Although the scope of the investigation jumped to hundreds of individuals, the task actually became easier. As postal employees, they were known entities, with fingerprints and closer tabs kept on them than random citizens.

The trick, of course, was not to arouse suspicion among the postal workers. "Friendlies" were identified at the highest level of management. Again, military service records were the best place to go. The bureau looked for former officers who had distinguished themselves. There were no guarantees, but any police work had to make certain assumptions in order to move ahead. Three supervisors were found to have good military service records in the nine suspected places where the letter could have been opened. They were contacted surreptitiously by SACs. Those special agents in charge personally met with each one and made the call that, first, these supervisors were not suspects themselves and, second, that they could be trusted with a certain degree of information. These men having been military commanders and serving in the chain of command made the agents' tasks easier. Their cooperation was as good as any cop in the world could expect. All three concurred that the highest possibility of a piece of mail being damaged was in the handling that occurred "in the house," as they called it. Although not impossible, once the piece was routed and sorted, it was hand-delivered and the chance of damage reduced significantly with the personal touch of letter carriers. In addition, if the envelope was sealed in a clear plastic tape with lettering on it, this also boded well for the damage to have happened in the house, since carriers didn't carry reseal tape.

Manual sorting and machine sorting being the essence of the postal system, the investigation focused on these choke points of mail flow. A letter got from here to there by someone or some machine deciding that it went into this pile or that. Twelve people were identified as highly probable to have come in contact with the Johansen letter. The date of the letter and the "date received" rubber-stamped at the May Company eliminated four people from the list because it traversed the system midweek and therefore excluded those on weekend shifts. Two more fell from the list, one on vacation and one on sick leave that week. That left six people in three substations covering two shifts. The Sumpterville and Hattings offices were eliminated after nothing in the personnel files or supervisor interviews pointed to anything suspicious. However, the Parkersville station had the "Dip Shit," his supervisor's name for a man that fit the profile—a real nonachiever,

given to rants and rages against the machine, literally. His supervisor and coworkers all acknowledged
the fact that he was bitter and harbored much anger
toward everything. Thus, Bernard Keyes became the
insect under the huge microscope that was the FBI.

With thirty agents in the field, 300 more in offices
and headquarters, aerial reconnaissance, and dedicated satellite time, every move Bernard Keyes made was
now a matter of national security. His place of work,
home, car, garage, and even his favorite bar were now
more wired than most local TV stations. Millions of
dollars worth of electronic gear was sending the FBI's
central nervous system every impulse of Bernard's life.
The most productive device, however, and the one that
would prove to be the best few hundred dollars invest-
ed, was the keystroke transmitter. NCIJTF technicians attached it to Keyes' Dell computer during a sur-
reptitious, court-ordered break-in. It transmitted every
keystroke he made to a "bread truck" parked near his
house. The truck was equipped with a satellite up-link
patched directly into the FBI Electronics Crime Lab in
Washington, D.C. There, other National Cyber Investigative Joint Task Force technicians would eavesdrop
on every chat room and web site Bernard visited, including the e-mails he sent out announcing an emergency meeting of the Sabot Society.

∞§∞

Mallory's Chrysler Concord was parked in front of
his daughter Kelly's house. Inside, Cynthia and Kelly
spoke in hushed tones in the kitchen as Kelly's husband Jim and her father tinkered with Jim's Jeep out
in the garage.

"Does Daddy know?"

"No, I didn't want him to worry."

"How did you hide the dizzy spells?"

"They only happened a few times. It was the head-aches that made me go to the hospital."

With tears in her eyes, the daughter reached across the table, grabbing the hand of the mother she loved, then hated, then loved again and had now come to cherish, since she herself became a mother. "It's so in-furiating. It isn't fair, it just isn't fair." Anger replaced Kelly's tears.

"Kelly, this is God's plan. It's been there since be-fore I was born and decided to act up now."

"You know, you are going to have to tell Daddy sooner or later."

"Tell Daddy what?" Dennis asked, as he and Jim stepped into the kitchen.

∞§∞

As their grandson John worked a Tonka bulldozer into a pile of dirt in the corner of the yard, Dennis and Cynthia sat on a stone bench near a sleeping rose bush.

Dennis read the letter for the third time. "I've paid into the health plan for thirty-five years, and they won't cover the type of procedure you really need? I'll go down there and raise hell."

"Dennis, the doctors at the hospital and the admin-istrators all tried. No health insurance will cover it, it's too expensive. Those words in that letter, severe aortic stenosis, complicate every treatment option that we could ever afford."

Dennis picked at one of the thorns as the gravity of Cynthia's situation sank into his chest. He closed his eyes in one last-ditch effort to test whether or not this was just a bad dream from which he could awaken. Cynthia's sigh brought him back to the inescapable reality of the nightmare already in progress. The sun was setting, the day's final light illuminating Cyn-thia's graying blonde hair and affording her a radiant glow. Her eyes were large and sparkling. *She's never looked more beautiful,* he thought. He couldn't let her go without a fight. He spent his whole life protecting strangers, the great unwashed, the hoity-toity, the average working stiff. If he could do that for them, it was his duty to protect his gal Cynthia. Hell, there were doctors all over the world working on this. Surely, they could help. He'd find a way to save her life.

∞§∞

Truck seven returned to the loading bay of Sperling High Voltage at 4:18 PM. At 7 AM the next morning, it was scheduled to be reloaded and ready to roll by eight, but instead of going to Brookhaven Labs, it would be making a delivery to Con Ed in Shirley. The dispatcher, seeing number seven back into the loading dock, glanced at the clock and decided that there was plenty of time to load up before the 5:00 PM punch-out and directed the dock men to do so. A forklift specially set up with a curved saddle and claw to hold 55-gallon drums loaded fifty of them filled with Translyte. At 4:55 PM, the load was completed, and the workers closed the truck's rear door. The crew all punched out before 5 PM. One of the workers noticed some people still up in the office as he steered his Ford Focus toward the employee parking lot exit.

∞§∞

Dennis squinted as the late afternoon sun glared through the window behind Miles Taggert, silhouetting him in his own palatial offices. "Mr. Taggert, I'm here to propose a trade."

"Go on," Taggert prompted across a teepee of fingers, two dabbing at his chin.

"You want me to keep you alive; I want you to keep my wife alive."

"Whoa, wait a minute. What's the matter with Mrs. Mallory?"

"She has ..." Dennis reached into his coat and retrieved the hospital letter, not wanting to get this wrong, "arterio-venous malformation in her head. Traditional surgery, the kind my Detective's Endowment medical will cover is very risky because of ..." he found the other words in the letter, "Severe aortic stenosis, they'd have to lower her body temperature during an already risky operation. She probably couldn't survive that."

"What can I do?"

"You travel in high circles, with people who are always running off to Liechtenstein or Sweden to try new radical therapies that aren't available here in the United States. I'll work for free, but you pay all the travel, medical, or whatever bills to make sure Cynthia beats this thing."

"You'll draw a salary and we'll do everything we can for your wife ... as long as I am alive. Deal?" Taggert extended his hand. Dennis did the same, worried that his might be shaking from nerves. He had been in tight situations before, even helped negotiate a Detective's Endowment contract once, but this was different. He was negotiating for Cynthia's best shot at survival. It was a pressure he had never known, even when he was undercover.

"Deal."

CHAPTER TWENTY
TAPPING KEYS, TAPPING FAVORS

GLORIA SANTIAGO, SPERLING'S assistant comptroller, was getting more and more frustrated. Her computer was not cooperating today. She had entered the same numbers into a spreadsheet three times already, only to have the computer lock up when she tried to print it. The only way out was powering down. To her dismay, every time she rebooted, the spreadsheet was gone. This time, at 5:30, she saved it every step of the way.

"Gloria, why are you still here?" her boss asked on his way out the door.

"Dave, this friggin' computer is going out the goddamn window in a minute."

"Are you not thinking pleasant thoughts? You know these things read your mind and if you don't think pleasant thoughts they can be vindictive."

"Dave, please, I am in no mood."

"Sorry, what's the problem?"

"I have been working all day on this spreadsheet for the meeting tomorrow and this piece of crap keeps losing it."

"Did you save it?"

She turned and shot him a look that could burn out his eyeballs.

And when he tried the spreadsheet himself, he had no better luck. Finally, she resolved to do it by hand.

Dave patted her on the shoulder. "Your dedication will pay off someday, Gloria. Try not to work too late."

She watched him leave, muttering under her breath, "Try not to drink too much."

At 8:50, she was still standing in front of the Xerox machine, breaking company policy. One good thing about working late was there were no pansies around to object to secondhand smoke.

One floor below, under truck number seven in the loading bay, the kitchen timer counted down the ten remaining seconds.

As she took a drag from her third and final cigarette of the night, the ash fell onto the sixth copy of the handwritten spreadsheet.

As she bent over slightly to blow the ash off the sheets in the sorter, the whole machine suddenly rose up, lifting her off her feet. Her confusion lasted less than a tenth of a second as her back met the ceiling and her spine snapped. She and the machine continued their ascension through the roof, which had already ruptured from the blast wave that instantaneously took out the entire front of the building.

The first responding fire units were warned that this was an industrial site containing level-four contaminants. As the pumper truck rolled with its siren wailing, Captain Horace Kelso read the MSDS on file for the plant. This Material Safety Data Sheet indicated they were speeding toward a potentially deadly scenario: vaporized Translyte, a coolant for high-voltage transformers, one of its constituents being PCBs. *Nasty shit*, he thought as he remembered, back when he was a lieutenant, how just a few gallons of this chemical, inside one overheated transformer located under Hempstead Turnpike, turned a whole square mile into "no man's land" for twelve hours. This place manufactured the shit and could have tons of the stuff.

As his rig approached the scene, he witnessed something that scared the bejesus out of him. People were strewn all over the street. These spectators who were attracted to the fire had been overcome by something. Judging from the pale color of their faces and foam around their mouths, it was definitely airborne.

He picked up the radio mic to speak to the men in the trucks with him and those heading in. "Full contamination area. All units. This is a hot zone! Respirators only. Repeat. Full contamination!" His men had drilled for disasters such as this since 1974, when three firefighters died because a garage burnt down igniting some barrels of similar crud.

His next call was to Suffolk Fire Control. It would be their job to evacuate the area. *This is going to be a big mess*, he thought as he put on his respirator mask.

∞§∞

The e-mail received by the FBI five minutes earlier was short and to the point. "Sperling. Ultimate."

∞§∞

Captain Kelso was surprised when the man in the suit flashed an FBI ID card, informing him that they would be taking over the crime scene investigation from here. *How did they know it was a crime this fast? A federal crime no less!* This news came to him two minutes after his men, having worked in full turnout gear plus respirators, finally managed to snuff out the chemically fed blaze after an arduous nine-hour battle. Being too tired to argue, he watched as the thirty or so prissy Feds—all clean, rested, and gas mask equipped—poked, prodded, and assessed the still-smoldering scene.

∞§∞

General Nandeserra would just as soon have lined these clerics up against a wall and shot them, but since they were the main source of funding for his nation's military, he patiently suffered through all their ill-informed questions.

"Allah be praised, is this the time in which to strike at America?" The mullah from the mountains asked as if he already decided it wasn't.

"Sheik, the timing has never been more perfect. America is in a state of confusion. They have no idea who is attacking them. For years we have waited, waited for the opportunity to weaken her without unleashing her wrath upon us. Samovar is ready to strike. In the current confusion, they will never know it was our initiative."

"How can you be certain of that, General?"

"Samovar has been in training for years. There is no physical evidence or monetary connection linking Samovar to us in any way."

"Are you sure he can carry out this mission?"

That question set off an alarm inside the General's head. He was very careful to never let on to all but his most trusted men that Samovar was not the name of an operation but that of one single assassin. This mullah had methods of intelligence that reached into his core of officers. He made a mental note to find out who the traitor was later.

"How do you mean?" It made no sense attempting to deny that this was, in fact, one man. Maybe it would go unnoticed by the others.

"Men usually chosen for these missions, Allah be praised, are young and full of rage and spirit. I suspect your man is more mature, softer then. Will he be able to carry out the mission? It is plain that a young man straight from the Madrasasas is blinded to the corruption of the west; all he sees is his glory before God, but an older man might be seduced by its devil's comforts."

"I do not dispute your words, Sheik, but the man was selected by Allah himself, as he lost a great deal in the American missile attack...both his brother and mother. His spirit is beyond question, and his resolve is that of the great Jihad, Allah be praised."

"Very well, General. How soon will he strike?"

"We have one last operational detail to conclude after which it would only be a matter of hours."

They seemed to arrive at a consensus throughout the room. The General had addressed and satisfactorily eliminated all of their concerns. Reading this on their faces, he requested to be excused.

A nod from the Sheik bid him leave. As a servant opened the door, the mullah asked one last question, "General, there will be no loose threads then?"

"Absolutely none."

"Allah be praised."

∞§∞

As Taggert entered his office, he was startled to find a mini construction crew there. Dennis was in the center of the activity, instructing the foreman.

"What's all this?" the young entrepreneur said.

"Phase one of keeping my end of the deal."

Taggert surveyed the room as huge thick panes of glass were installed inside the grand windows of his office.

"Two-inch-thick laminated acrylic, sixty-four sandwiched layers, optically clear, but with the stopping power of an ought 30-30 at ten yards."

Taggert took it all in, then focused on his desk. "Hey, where's my Vaccaro chair?"

"High-back, Kevlar, and armor steel-plated. Can stop a .38 at point-blank range. Same kind the president uses in the oval office." Dennis knocked on the back of the regrettably conventional-looking leather chair.

"Mr. Mallory, I guess I am going to have to get used to you protecting me." Taggert tried the chair on for size. He found it vastly different from his Vaccaro, the one he had custom-made by the Italian designer who had also been commissioned by Ferrari. "You can sleep in this chair," he said, surprised, and then swiveled around. "The president, you say?" He thought about this for a second and smiled. "How much is all this costing me?"

"One hundred forty-seven thousand, plus four hundred and twenty thousand for your new Mercedes."

"Let me guess, bulletproof?"

"Grenade-proof!"

"What color?"

"Same as your old one, Midnight Blue."

"Good catch, Dennis!" Taggert grinned, then scrunched into his new chair, a content, safe expression washing over his face.

Five men appeared at the doorway. Dennis waved them in. "Mr. Taggert, here is your security detail. These men have all worked with me on the job and, I assure you, are still the finest of New York City's finest. They will alternate shifts and be your bodyguards twenty-four hours, seven days a week."

Miles stood and, like an inspector general, worked his way down the line of armed nursemaids. Dennis reflected on how well this had all gone so far and how hopeful Cynthia had been these last couple of days. His wife was now seeing doctors who weren't even listed, thanks to Taggert's powerful friends and connections. She was amazed to share a waiting room with Ivana Trump. Dennis knew that even rich people died, but he suspected they didn't die as often as those reliant on HMOs. Many years before, he made a promise before God and all their family and friends that he would love, honor, and protect her, and he was damned determined that death would not part them, at least not yet.

After work, Dennis made a pit stop at Harrigan's, his old stomping ground down from his precinct. Jack Flanagan was there, in his usual booth.

"Saints preserve us! If it isn't Dennis Mallory come all the way from retirement to hobnob with the working stiffs."

"Semiretired, you old leather-pounder," Dennis said as he patted Jack on the shoulder and slid into the booth.

"Semi?"

"Picked up a little job on my days off."

Jack stopped mid-swallow, "Hey, wait, you're off everyday."

"See how bad I need your help."

"What's this going to cost me?"

"Not a thing, just a little time ... and maybe a phone call or two, some lab time. Nothing much."

"What kind of job?" Jack asked suspiciously.

"Now keep this under your hat, will ya?"

"My lips are sealed."

"Yeah, around the rim of that glass."

"If I remember correctly, you threw back a few with the best of them, old friend."

"I made a deal with some big shot named Miles Taggert who runs a computer company. Seems he's been getting some threats and with what's happening lately, let's just say he wants a little added protection."

"So are you working for him?"

"Security consultant. Ain't too bad. Got Benton and Davis and those guys full-time jobs bird-dogging him twenty-four/seven. I get to play with all the new gadgets and what I say goes. Pretty good deal overall."

"So what are you pulling in from this?"

"Oh, we got a trade deal of sorts going."

Dennis reached into his sport coat pocket and produced a second threat letter that Taggert received earlier that morning. He handed the evidence, now sealed in a plastic bag, to Jack. "Could you run this through forensics?"

"Fan mail from some flounder?" Jack said, invoking an old cartoon line.

"Huh?"

"Forget it, Bullwinkle. What are we looking for?"

"Unfortunately, it's been touched by Taggert, but only him." He placed a fingerprint card in front of Jack. "Here's Taggert's set. I just tightened the mail handling so this won't happen again. I'm hoping to find the perpetrator's latent print. Also do a run on the paper, the writing, anything you can offer."

"Give me two days. I'll send it in as one of my sleeping cases."

"Thanks, Jack."

"How's the wife?"

"Not so good. They found a thing in her head that could ... that could take her away from me."

"Ah, Jesus, Dennis. Cynthia's a saint, a regular saint. She don't deserve that, not after all she's been through. How's she taking it?"

"She's got more balls than you, me, and the whole squad put together. But that's the trade deal. I got this billionaire to pull all kinds of strings to get her some of that real top-shelf medical treatment. All I got to do is make sure his secret admirer never gets any closer than this letter."

"I'll run it first thing in the morning. Tell Cynthia that Joanie's and my thoughts and prayers are with her."

∞§∞

"Your piece is cut," Wally informed Carly with cold indifference.

"What do you mean?"

"I got two packages and three talking heads on the chemical factory in Long Island. You're bumped."

"But Wally, don't you see? This is exactly the perfect segue into my piece. What did that factory make?"

"Chemicals that help eggheads make black holes. Or so the propaganda goes."

"Exactly. That's science, Wally, and my story is about how the number one science man is investigating. It's the perfect sidebar."

"Sidebar is a print term. In TV we call that ...er... well, I don't remember. Okay, cut it down to three minutes and I'll slot you in before we go to the heads. But it better be good and you better have the scoop of all time!"

"Thanks, Wally; you won't be sorry."

"Famous last words," Wally said to her departing, wiggling backside as he picked up his phone. "Jennie, tell Dave the talking heads are cut back three minutes and tell video tape to expect a roll-in from Carly. Three minutes."

Carly went to the pressroom and called her cousin, Harry.

"AT&T long lines," the unemotional voice at the other end spoke.

"Harry Edmonds, please," Carly requested as she pulled out her cell phone.

"Test, Edmonds," Harry said from his testers desk in what they called the NOC in Bedminster, New Jersey.

"Harry, Carly. How are you doing, cousin?"

"Not as good as you I see, cuz. Saw you on the news last night. Wooo hooo!"

"You did! Cool, ain't it?"

"You always were the coolest, even when you were spooning out smashed Cheez Doodles from the bottom of your Coca Cola."

"You know, if you forget that, I promise to forget you wet your pants when I jumped out of the closet in your room that night."

"You scared me to death!"

"So wanna do me a favor?"

"What do you need, kiddo?"

"If I told you a phone number, could you tell me who it belongs to?"

"Sure; it's called a reverse directory."

"What if it's a cell phone?"

"Well, I got a friend over in Wireless that can maybe give me a location down to a cell."

"Good. I'll call you at about 4 o'clock."

"Hey Carly, is this for a news story?"

"No, I had dinner with a guy last night. I just want to check to see that he is where he said he was going to be." She little white lied with a lascivious lilt in her voice.

"Oh, okay, I got it."

"Thanks, Harry; talk to you later."

CHAPTER TWENTY-ONE
RIPPLES

SECRET SERVICE AGENTS had surreptitiously visited the facility the day before and made their quiet plans. No one, except the head of security and the CEO, were aware of their true identities and mission. Local hospitals were stocked with Type AB blood. Major overpasses were identified and would be manned along the route. People along that route would momentarily be inconvenienced as their cell phones dropped calls. A new, high-tech addition to the "bubble." The reason for this security was because the president was here. He had come to this remote Virginia facility to witness the top secret testing of a revolutionary new weapon in the war on drugs. The head of the White House security detail referred to all the president's mobile security needs as the "bubble." It was an unseen sphere of security in which the Commander-in-Chief traveled.

Hiccock was driven to the secluded location by the Secret Service. He had to pass through a magnetometer and have his White House I.D. card swiped through a portable scanner. The resident ordered him in attendance to get an unbiased assessment and explanation of the science behind the satellite-based defoliant. Hiccock was briefed only four hours earlier. From what he gathered, the device worked from 100 miles up in space. It could bathe up to 200 acres with protoplasm-inhibiting beta rays. Once it was positioned into geosynchronous orbit over a target country, it could wither and brown that nation's vegetation. The farmers on the ground would never suspect anything more than blight or Hot Soil.

The test on this day was accelerated. 100 times the normal exposure was being beamed to a field of sprouts. The president watched as 10 technicians stood in the field as proof of this device's safety for humans, while it killed the lifeblood of the flora and fauna around them. The president, however, was 300 yards away from the target.

"What is the principle behind the beam?" Hiccock asked, sitting ten feet from the president.

The head of the project, Professor Di Consini, explained the process to the president's science advisor, who would have known this already if he weren't chasing bad guys. "We modulate a band within the ultraviolet spectrum by the square of its base frequency. The wavelength variations dilate the photosynthesis receptors of the organism. This causes the protoplasm to disperse as in the natural life cycle of the plant cell."

The president looked to Hiccock as a UN delegate would look to a translator for the interpretation of something a foreign dignitary had spoken.

"They put the plant through thousands of day-night cycles in a very short period of time, in effect accelerating the life cycle of the plant and bringing it to an early old age."

"Precisely. Except it all happens without the plant maturing."

"Wow, if you could lick that, you could grow forests overnight!" Hiccock blurted out, impressed.

"Yes, we got here trying to make a 'super grow light' if you will. All we managed to do was to kill the plants without them growing at all. Unfortunately. the laws of thermodynamics prohibit us from also accelerating the maturity process which would have led to growth."

"So the plants die of old age on the inside while never sprouting on the outside," Hiccock concluded.

"That's why this is such a destructive device," Di Consini said, topping off Bill's observation.

"Are there any downsides to this process, Professor?" the president inquired.

"Just one. Photosynthesis creates oxygen from carbon monoxide. Thus the accelerated oxygen production also starves the plants of monoxides, contributing to their early demise."

"But you are also creating an oxygen-rich environment as a by-product," Hiccock pointed out.

"Exactly, and that can aid a spontaneous combustion." Di Consini liked Hiccock. He was smart.

"So, will a target field suddenly combust into an inferno?" The president caught the drift of the conversation between the two scientists.

Di Consini resisted the temptation to coddle the president too much for following the science jargon. So he didn't say, "Why yes, my boy, I think you've got it!" Instead he flatly informed him, "It's possible, given a windless day, high solar heat, or electric storm. We found that if we slow the process, we also reduce the combustible risk, but lengthen the kill time."

"I see." The president pondered this as he observed the field being bombarded by silent, invisible plant killing rays.

Di Consini continued, "Sir, we are 10 minutes into this hi-powered test. Each ten-minute segment roughly equals a week under normal exposure. Six weeks in application or 60 minutes in this test will kill off approximately 98 percent of the crop."

"Hiccock, do you see any downside?"

"Three big issues sir; one practical, one legal, the other ethical."

"Go on," the president urged, impressed at the speed with which Hiccock's mind had processed this new invention and already categorized and outlined his thoughts into three distinct talking points.

"The professor has given us a powerful weapon. Legally I would think it amounts to an act of war against the country we point it at. I would imagine we must keep this totally top secret or the planters can cover their crops or farm hydroponically in caves or underground. But lastly, this can be used to throw a country into famine, sir--turning green fertile fields into dust bowls. Will we ever be tempted to turn off the food supply of a country whose politics we don't like?"

"Bill, that's why I like keeping you around. You never let the fact that I am your boss sugar coat your logic."

"I know *you* wouldn't do such a thing, sir. But will your successors be tempted?"

The president mulled this over as he watched the field of sprouts through binoculars and the 10 "guinea pigs" standing out there being, *what was it?* - Modulated.

Hiccock saw this as his chance to make his call. "Sir, I need to make a call. I'll be right back." Hiccock stepped some thirty feet away and tried to use his cell but got no signal. Then he remembered "the bubble." The Secret Service was experimenting with an electronic jamming device that would make it impossible for anyone to signal or give real time intelligence to any would-be conspirators using an ordinary cell phone, or other electronic surveillance equipment. So he went inside the building and asked permission to use the phone on a secretary's desk.

∞§∞

"Thank you for remembering," Carly spoke through the receiver.

"I only have a second," Hiccock said as he placed her number back in his wallet.

"So can you tell me what you've briefed the president on today?"

Hiccock held the phone out and looked at it like he just heard a squealing noise. "Carly, is that one of those stupid questions reporters just have to ask in case your subject has an instant brain tumor and forgets what this is all about?"

"Come on, Bill, give me something. I go on the air in three minutes."

"Nothing like cutting it close, huh?"

"I promise. I will credit whatever you tell me to an anonymous high-placed administration official."

"Okay. The president is considering asking Congress for additional funding for homeland security to raise the level of preparedness of our National Guard and Coast Guard," Hiccock informed her, knowing the president himself had told 10 members of Congress this already and they would probably beat Carly to the air in the next two minutes to blab it to their constituents. By tomorrow it would be old news. But it gave her what she wanted. Bill still didn't know why he wanted to give her anything at all. She was cute; still, she showed no interest in him. He was just being a little silly here and he knew it. But she was cute!

Carly didn't care about the questionable value of the "insight" she was getting from her "high-placed source;" she looked at her cell phone hoping the number would appear. Instead it read "private call," meaning the caller ID feature had been turned off at the other end.

"How much, Bill?"

"58 billion but you definitely didn't hear that from me."

"I understand."

"Look, I got to get back. This squares us right?" Hiccock said as he started pulling the phone from his ear.

"For what?"

"For whatever reason I feel the need to help you."

Carly laughed, "See ya around, Bill." She pressed end then called her cousin Harry.

"Harry, can you tell me where the last call on my phone came from?"

It took about one half of a minute, then she heard Harry say, "Got it," with some satisfaction. "He was on a land line, real simple. Arco Systems and Design, Alexandria, Virginia."

"Thanks, honey. Love ya, bye."

She had 30 seconds 'til airtime. Just enough to rehearse her opening line as she checked her hair in the news van window.

"Carly, 15 seconds!" The cameraman informed her.

She adjusted her blazer and planted her feet. She turned around and checked her background. The portico of the White House was right behind her.

"Stand by," her cameraman said.

Carly waited to see the tally lights on the Beta-Cam camera nestled on her cameraman's shoulder. Although he was rolling tape, the feed from the camera was simultaneously being up-linked to a microwave tower in D.C. It was then routed through the master control switcher in the D.C. control room of MSNBC. From there it went by broadcast cable to their satellite up-link facility in Fort Lee, New Jersey. Through 130 miles of space, up to Weststar 7. Known in the business as a bird, the satellite sits in geo-synchronous orbit above the equator, capable of distributing broadcast signals to thousands of dishes around the country and the world.

∞§∞

MSNBC has learned exclusively today that the president, who is at this hour in Alexandria Virginia, at Arco Systems, is considering asking Congress for 58 billion dollars in additional funding to ..."

Falad almost fell off his chair. He looked once again at the corner of the screen that held the little geometric design with the word 'LIVE' in it. He ran as fast as his regulation boots would carry him across the marble.

CHAPTER TWENTY-TWO
LOOSE ENDS

GENERAL NANDESERRA was taking a bath when he forced his way in. Falad had no qualms about this breach of the man's privacy, because the General himself ordered Falad to find him immediately as soon as the U.S. President's whereabouts were known, no matter what time of day.

Falad used an apologetic tone anyway. "General, we have a location on the American President outside the White House and in range of Samovar." The general immediately stood and stepped out of the bath, Falad looked around and handed him a towel.

He went straight to his computer and opened a Word document of the Arabic translation of Chesapeake. He typed in the word "execute" in Arabic and the computer jumped to the 32nd word on page 217. He wrote down 217,32. He then entered Alexandria. That was a lucky break, because that proper name was in the book. 495, 56. He searched for the letters V (0,4,107) and A (0,1,34). Then he found the letters A, R, C, and O. Falad picked up a regular, non-secure phone and called AT&T international information. In his best American accent he responded to the automated audio prompts, "What city and state?"

"Alexandria, Virginia."

"What listing?"

"Arco Systems."

A young woman operator cut into the line and said, "Hold for your number..."

"Excuse me, but I am also looking for the address," Falad stated in a tone and manner consistent with some businessman from Norfolk.

"I have Arco Systems and Design, 1401 Juno Boulevard in Alexandria. Hold for your number." A computerized voice then spewed out the 10-digit number to his already hung up phone.

One of the General's aides entered with the map, which Falad had instructed him to fetch as he rushed in. The aide was already studying it and called out the address' coordinates in Alexandria. The General wrote them down in a coded way that had been designed to indicate the end of the message. He picked up the phone and dialed a number he alone knew and had memorized.

∞§∞

It was mid-afternoon in Quebec, Canada when Muhammad Al Kazir's cell phone rang. Like the Samovar team, he was paid a handsome wage while all manner of his life was subjugated to one and only one purpose: watch, wait, and answer the phone when it rang. He had been waiting for five months, since he had entered Canada on a student visa.

"Yes, General," Muhammad said, knowing the General would be the only caller ever on this phone. The General started reading off the numbers as Muhammad wrote them down, then repeated them. He knew not what the numbers were, or what they meant, or even to whom he was about to call and relay them to. When they checked the numbers, he simply said, "Fargo Bank. Allah Be Praised," and hung up. He waited five seconds then dialed the number, which he too had never written down, only memorized.

∞§∞

At the "safe house" in Washington D.C., four of the five members of the Samovar team were off in their own respective areas of the large six-room apartment.

One was out getting toilet paper and other necessities. Samovar happened to be looking at the phone when it rang. He caught it on the first ring. "Yes?"

After he had double-checked the numbers, he opened the James Michener tome and started with page 217, the 32nd word. It took all of three minutes as the long-anticipated message was finally unfolded before him in Arabic. He looked up the address on a map identical to that of the General's. He knew how to get there for he had spent months driving around, studying Washington D.C. and exploring its surrounding areas, only to find technology, which he could download to his smart phone, had all but rendered that exercise a mere curiosity.

With his bedroom door closed behind him, he opened his closet. There, hanging in meticulous military order, with color-coded tags, two inches apart so as not to wrinkle, were 27 uniforms, all custom tailored to his size. A tag on each one identified the municipality it had been crafted for. That information had been a gift from a Moslem student who got a job working the night shift at the biggest dry-cleaning company in the Washington D.C. area. As they came in for cleaning, he painstakingly photographed and measured each uniform. Those pictures and measurements were sent back to the General's staff, where women, plying needles, replicated the uniforms from dyed bolts and other garment industry staples. The badges were crafted by metal workers in the desert of his country. Each uniform was shipped to him via international Fed-Ex, as innocently as any three-pound large box.

Getting the right holsters and guns was a little more problematic, but, here again, one of his team members, posing as a tourist, took telephoto pictures of actual officers on duty. He then simply went to various police supply stores and bought the leatherwear. The guns were as easy to get by attending one of the hundreds of gun shows the Americans loved to convene. Complying with the "waiting period" rules, which were purposely made impotent by the pressure of the gun lobbies in the U.S., was not an issue for a foreign national with nothing but time on his hands with which to build his arsenal.

He chose the uniform with the tag "Alexandria," and pulled the leather that was similarly marked from a series of drawers. He found the appropriately tagged gun in the footlocker that held all the guns and ammunition. He also took out a Walther PPK and screwed on a silencer. As he adjusted the tie he had learned to make like a good soldier, he gave himself one more full inspection in the mirror. Stepping out of his bedroom, he found one of his men sitting on the couch watching a satellite feed of Al-Jazeera. An anti-American protest was being covered. The sounds of the shouting and guns being fired in the air, which normally accompanied these planned "spontaneous" uprisings, provided a background noise that would help with the next step. He approached him, silently raising the Walther, and pulled the trigger. There was a small popping sound, which was lost in the cacophony emanating from the TV; the top of his head rippled as the bullet went straight through, his blood then pouring out. Before the body had time to slump over, he walked into the kitchen as team member two was just turning with a cup of tea. "I made you a cup..."

The cup shattered washing his shirt in tea, and then blood as two more bullets slammed into his body. He fell back with a crash. That brought the third member of the team out from his room. He was shocked to see his comrade slumped over on the couch, the cushions soaked red with blood. His eyes slowly rose up and he flinched upon seeing Samovar pointing the gun at him. It all became clear to him at that instant. He held up his hand in the gesture that means "wait" and got down on his knees as he started praying. The man closed his eyes as Samovar put the gun to his forehead and fired. Samovar then heard a key turning in the lock of the main entrance. As the young man entered, Samovar fired three times. The grocery bag dimpled with each shot as the door was splattered with exit wound blood. Without so much as a sigh, Samovar wiped down the gun, and strategically placed it on the floor next to the first victim, for the authorities to find. He opened a drawer and took out a kilo of cocaine. He ripped one side of it and dropped it on the table to appear as if it had haphazardly fallen.

He went back to the closet and lit the sleeves of six of the uniforms; he dropped one onto the carpet that ran throughout the apartment, the flame instantly catching the nap. He watched for a brief second as the doorway to the room was consumed with the spreading fire. Retrieving the phone, he left closing, but not locking, the door. There was nothing in the house, on the dead men, or in their aliases that would connect them to the General or his country.

Samovar went down to the garage and collected the Ford Taurus he had rented weekly from Hertz for the last six months. He placed the cell phone under the rear tire of the car, which was parked facing outward in the spot. Inside he entered Arco's street address into the GPS app on his smart phone. He put the Ford into reverse and released his foot from the brake momentarily; the car inched back slightly. Through the open window he could hear the cell phone crunch. He then slipped it into drive and punched the accelerator hard. The rear wheels spun and screeched as the cell phone was catapulted out from under the tire, smashing into the concrete wall of the garage into a million pieces.

Samovar drove in accordance with all traffic laws and resisted the urge to speed. Following the female computerized voice of the app through the series of "right turn ahead" and "exit ahead" prompts, directed him, with Global Positioning accuracy, to his appointment with history.

∞§∞

The Barclay's Bank in Quebec was Mohammed's last stop in Canada before he would return home. Having served his country, and now retrieving his $50,000 bonus for making that one phone call for the General, he entered the bank and proceeded directly to the safe deposit boxes. The key had been sent to him five months prior. He hadn't known which bank it belonged to until the General disclosed this tidbit at the end of the phone call. As he returned to his car with an attaché case full of 500 one hundred-dollar bills, he had visions of living like a wealthy man at home, with the ability to pray openly, and re-grow his beard, and maybe marry and have sons. He didn't notice the man following him in the underground parking lot. He too had received a call from the General today.

The man had been sent a photograph of Muhammad Al Kazir five months ago. He had been waiting since then for his message to execute. He didn't know who this man he followed was, or why the General wanted him silenced. He didn't know if the man who he just "drew a bead" on was a Moslem or an infidel. All he knew was that his $50,000 assassin's fee was in the man's briefcase. That would be enough for him to disappear down in the islands until this murder had "cooled off" and long since been relegated to the open case file as a robbery-homicide.

In less than 30 minutes of his phone call, the General's word to the mullahs, that there would be "no loose ends," was carried out. Five people, potential loose ends, had been eliminated and at least two more would die in the next hour or so.

∞§∞

In the Virginia countryside, the modern offices of Arco Systems and Design stood out like an off-white slab of halvah. Samovar wished he could taste the sweet dessert cake one more time before meeting Allah, but he was sure sweeter and tastier delights awaited him in the next life.

He pulled up to the guardhouse at the main gate and addressed the officer, "I'm here to help out with the security detail. I'm Johnson, how are you?" He extended his hand as he affected the perfect mid-Atlantic accent which he studied and had mastered two years earlier. Samovar's eyes fixed on the man standing 20 feet ahead in the unmistakable regalia of a Secret Service agent, long brown rain coat, sunglasses and a curly wire coming from his ear.

The guard, recognizing the uniform and badge, accepted him as what he appeared to be. The fact that the president's visit had been kept secret actually made the guard more easily accept the last-minute appearance of this cop. No one at the company had been informed of the intended arrival until the Secret Service showed up at 8 a.m. making sure no one could call out, even to tell their wives, that Mitchell was expected. It only made sense that some cops were caught off guard and had to scramble to work. "Well Johnson, the Secret Service is all over the inside; your guys are out on the walkway." He checked his clipboard. "There's Captain Yates up there."

"He's a good boss. Thanks. I'll report to him. Where can I park?"

"Right over there in the visitor's spot."

Samovar offered a short salute and drove towards to the designated spot. The agent in the raincoat held up his hand. Samovar pulled up to the man. "I'm supposed to report to Captain Yates up ahead."

The agent said nothing but scanned every detail of the man, the uniform, and the interior of the car. Avoiding his gaze, Samovar saw in the rear view mirror that the guard at the gate was waving him through. The agent glanced up at the guard, and didn't pay him any attention. The agent didn't really care if this Johnson cop was the guard's brother-in-law.

"I.D." was all the agent had to say.

Samovar's hand grazed the butt of his service weapon on the way to his shirt pocket. Readily placed there, as it was in every uniform, was the appropriate photo I.D. A driver's license was tucked into every wallet in each pair of uniform pants back at the apartment. Family photos, two hundred in assorted bills, credit and Social Security cards were also duplicated in every billfold. This precaution was taken in the event a cop, during a routine traffic stop, happened to catch a glimpse of its contents.

After checking the photo on the Alexandria Police Department I.D. against the face before him, the agent handed the card back. "How come you're late?"

"Had a court appearance, and a judge who wanted to give the jerk-off I arrested every possible chance to walk, based on me being a fuck-up! Shot the whole morning to shit!" Samovar, a.k.a. Johnson, gave him a look that said, 'You know what I mean?'

The agent waved him by without saying a word.

He prayed to Allah that the agent hadn't seen the crime movie in which Robert Duvall and that "black actor" played policemen and from which he borrowed, verbatim, the line of dialog concerning the judge. As he got out of the car, he adjusted his holster and put on his cap, briefly hesitating to inspect his reflection in the side view mirror. This act was purely for the sake of the guard and president's security man, who, still watching, would surely read it as the actions of a man about to meet his boss and ...maybe the president.

∞§∞

The test had gone well. One hour and twenty minutes, after the beam was turned on from the satellite that had been launched from a Department of Defense shuttle mission three years earlier, the sprouts were dead. The 10 test dummies, as Hiccock thought of the technicians who built and believed in this thing, were seemingly fine and no worse for the wear.

The president was impressed. "Professor Di Concini, you have made a substantial scientific development here. On behalf of America, I thank you for all your efforts." He then shook the hands of a few of the research team members before he, Hiccock and a few other military men exited the demonstration area.

As they walked through the building, the president queried Hiccock, "So you think we shouldn't put this weapon system on-line?"

"No sir; I didn't say that. I would just suggest ensuring some safeguards against its abuse."

"Bill, there's a man who's always within 20 feet of me with the 'football.' At any moment, anywhere I am in the world, I can authorize the launch of nuclear weapons aimed at any point on the globe. The safeguard against me being crazy, is the NCA; the National Command Authority."

∞§∞

Back at the White House, Naomi Spence hit the roof when one of her aides reported seeing a rerun of an MSNBC piece in which the reporter gave accurate information on the president's location. First, she called the Secret Service office down the hall. She hadn't even hung up when they immediately sprang into action. She then called Wally to chew him a new asshole!

∞§∞

"With all respect, sir," Hiccock said. The presidential contingent was now on the other side of the building heading for the presidential limousines. There was a line of local cops looking outward and Secret Service agents all along the route. "Nuclear weapons are big, noisy, and leave a giant mess. You also don't need to send a card along with them. The recipient will know who sent them. The weapon we have just seen is a stealth system; as long as it is secret it can be used with impunity. That may be too great a temptation, sir."

"Bill, you are a real piece of work," the president said as he turned to a Two Star General who had accompanied him to the test.

Samovar was 25 feet from the president, who was walking his way and chatting with a soldier and another man. There were seven agents loosely around the president and in three more seconds Samovar would be inside that ring of men. His hand stealthily unsnapped the leather holster's strap, his hand flexed not unlike the mannerism displayed by gunfighters in the old west right before a gunfight. His hand was on the butt of his gun when his simple plan dismantled before his very eyes.

A Secret Service agent suddenly put his hand to his ear and requested, "Repeat!" He then dropped his hand and yelled, "Close ranks!"

Instantly ten agents surrounded the president. The pace picked up as the now small, tight circle of agents almost swept him off his feet and rushed towards the limousine. Hiccock didn't know what had happened as he was left in the dust. Then he saw one of the police officers turn and pull his weapon out of its holster. The cop fired just as someone yelled "gun." An agent, blocking the line of fire, went down. The cop, now crouching, fired again and was immediately hit by return fire. It was like a bad movie seeming to play back in slow motion. The cop's arms and legs were shattered. The agents, and there must have been ten firing at him, didn't aim for his vital organs. It was immediately apparent to Hiccock that they wanted him alive! The local cops reacted as well, albeit not as quick on the draw, and a split second later, three fired. One of the officer's bullets slammed into the ground and skidded off the asphalt a foot in front of Hiccock. Another one of the cop's bullets caught the shooter cop in his head; just as the Secret Service was yelling "hold your fire!"

The president was immediately flung into the back of the limousine. It peeled away, as Hiccock watched the rear door slam hard on one agent's leg. The man grunted as he continued to shield the president with his body and re-shut the door after pulling in his leg. Agents brandishing blue metal and black machine guns were now yelling for everyone to get down. Hiccock hit the dirt. The Secret Service then ordered all the cops to drop their weapons. Captain Yates repeated the order, and the cops placed their weapons on the ground. Agents collected them and had the Captain identify each of his men until the Service allowed them to stand again.

∞§∞

In the limo, one Secret Service agent checked the president for wounds, while the other two had their sub-machine guns trained out the partially opened bulletproof glass windows. Soon other Secret Service cars joined the limo.

"Where's the football?" the driver shouted to the agents in the back seat, as sirens blaring from more and more police and unmarked cars cleared the way for the limo's return to the White House.

∞§∞

Eventually, Hiccock was allowed to get up. As he passed the bullet-riddled body of the cop on the ground, he was struck by the wild look in the man's eyes frozen there by death. He wondered if he had just seen the common face of the enemy; the one who was unleashing terror on his country, attempting to assassinate the national courage as well as our leaders. He never thought much about the face of the man or men he was after. He now had a reference from which to draw upon for any future nightmares he might have.

He was driven back to the White House by the same agent who drove him out. This time he shared his ride with the Two Star who had arrived with the president.

CHAPTER TWENTY-THREE
UP THE CHAIN

THE LETTER that Dennis Mallory entrusted to Jack Flanagan for analysis set off a number of alarms at the NYPD forensics lab. Federal watch lists and a dozen other law enforcement advisories were tripped when it was analyzed. This was more than Flanagan had bargained for and he had to cover his tracks. As a senior detective he had the juice downtown to have any forensic guy's curiosity over the origin and purpose of the letter squashed. The Feds, however, would be rabid dogs looking for an ass to bite. To save his own, he reached out to an agent he once helped "get on the right track" many years back. As the operator at the FBI connected him, he hoped the agent on the other end would remember his hometown roots and an NYPD detective sergeant who looked the other way when the young G-man made a small mistake.

"SAC Palumbo."

Jack felt an immediate cold wind through the receiver. *This might not be easy.* This guy sounded hardened, in that been-a-fed-too-long way. "Joe Palumbo? It's Jack Flanagan, Manhattan North squad."

"Hi ya, Jack. How ya doing?"

That glimmer of familiarity gave Jack new hope that he just might be able to pull this off. "Joe, it's been a long time. SAC, huh? Good going."

"Nah, they just couldn't get anyone else to head up the San Fran office, so they got down to me on the list. You're still gumshoeing, I see."

"Yeah, still can't get it right after thirty-six years, so I keep trying."

"So what can I do for the finest of New York's finest?"

"It's a long story, but essentially, one of the good guys here, an ex-detective, needed some help with a case he took on freelance. His wife's dying ..." Jack caught himself and, not wanting to will anything in, amended his words "... fighting a brain tumor or something. So he needed money. He took a private security job. His protectee received a threat letter. He asked me to run the letter through our lab."

"I see, go on."

"Anyway, the letter he gave me to do a scratch and sniff on wound up getting the bureau's attention."

"Hold on," Joey said as he riffled through his in-box. "Yeah, I got a report here. A threat letter to one Miles Taggert. You're damn right we are interested. It might be tied into the recent wave of terrorist attacks."

"Yeah, I got all that. Look, I'll take a lecture from the chief of detectives on misuse of police assets. Hell, I'll even pay the lab bill. But what I need is to get my ass out of this loop and for Dennis to be kept in it directly. It's his case, you know, and he ain't a cop no more. So can you help me out here, Joe?"

"That's a pickle. I got the director all over my butt on this one."

Jack could read from the tone of the agent's voice that he was going to do something. He added a little incentive. "You know, Joe, at the end of the day, we are all after the bad guys, not the good cops."

"I hear you, Jack. I still got some friends in the New York bureau. I'll see what I can do. What's this guy's name and number?"

As Jack filled in Joey, a tradition as old as law enforcement itself was once again celebrated. A cop tapping a favor for an old partner or boss, which in turn causes another favor to be called upon, and maybe three or four more until the task was done, or covered or even buried. Each step along the way, although not by the book, was definitely written into the margins. With each new pass-along, a new set of debt and obligations was created ensuring the continuance of an economy deeply rooted within every police organization in the world.

∞§∞

Janice came rushing into Bill's office half an hour after he returned to the White House. She ran up to him and gave him a hug. "I'm glad you weren't hurt."

"Yeah, it was close."

"Were you next to the president?"

"No, I was ten feet behind him. We had been chatting but I fell back because he started talking to a General, and I wanted to give them some room. But one of the bullets hit about a foot in front of me."

Janice closed her eyes as she rested her head on Bill's shoulder.

A Secret Service agent appeared at the door. "Mr. Hiccock will you come with us, please?"

Hiccock gave her one last squeeze and followed the men down the hall. They entered the Secret Service office to find the Chief of Presidential Detail waiting, along with Naomi Spence.

"Mr. Hiccock, you excused yourself from the president's side early during the demonstration today. Can you tell us what you did in that time?"

"Yes. I called Carly Simone, the reporter. She had asked me to give her a quote on the president."

"And did you?" Naomi asked.

"Yes, Ms. Spence. I told her about the president's funding bill. I thought it was an important issue and I knew he had already briefed Congress. I was only giving her a couple of hours lead."

"If anybody gives out plums to the press, Hiccock, it's me, so I can keep the books. Otherwise every reporter would work that deal with every member of this administration," Naomi said barely containing her rage.

"Well, that's a good point. I'll remember that next time."

"Did you tell her where you were calling from?" The head of the Detail asked.

You could see the neon sign flashing "Stupid" across Bill's forehead as he realized that even though he didn't tell her where he was, he did. "Oh God, don't tell me she had my call traced?"

"I am afraid so. We don't know how yet, but we'll find out soon."

"So who tried to kill the president?" Hiccock, still comatose from the revelation, asked the Agent.

"Right now we have nothing solid. The gunman wasn't an officer. His badge was a phony, and he's got no history we can find."

"A foreign operative?"

The Agent made a decision that Hiccock was one of the good guys. Even though he proceeded by not really imparting facts, only conjecture. "Too early to tell but a guy with a clock this clean doesn't just pop out of the cabbage patch. Somebody spent a lot of money on brooming his past. It might have been a plan hatched and executed solely by him, but that's not likely, unless he found a ton of cash in a brown paper bag on his doorstep one day."

"I don't follow that," Naomi said.

Hiccock jumped in thinking out loud before he caught himself, "He'd have left some kind of trail making the kind of money that disappearing from society requires. Sorry." He yielded to the head Secret Service agent.

"That's okay; you're right. It's just too early to tell."

Naomi steered the discussion to her pressing matter. "I have a press briefing in five minutes. The scanners caught all the local police radio traffic, and all the networks are already live, speculating on the attempted assassination."

"We're in lockdown here, Naomi. Where's the conference?" The head agent asked.

"At State. Everybody is shifting there now. I leave in two minutes. Anything I need to know or not know?"

"Keep it calm for now. We are investigating. We have no names or any reason to believe this wasn't just a lone nut."

"They know he was dressed as a cop. It leaked from the hospital," Naomi informed the agent.

"Damn" was all the man who trained to work in secret could say as the veil was lifting on that which he wanted to hold confidential forever.

"Last question, then I have to go to the press conference. Two agents were hit. How are they doing?" Naomi queried, knowing it was a question she would be asked.

"We have two men down; both were wearing their vests and are expected to fully recover. Try not to mention the vests. Why tell the next guy where to shoot?"

"Thanks. Wish me luck," Naomi said as she exited.

"Am I needed any longer?" Hiccock asked the head of the detail.

"We'll talk later."

As he left the office he could not get over the fact that he may have been an unwitting accomplice to the attempted assassination of the President of the United States.

CHAPTER TWENTY-FOUR
REPERCUSSIONS

AN ABSURDITY was in progress at Foggy Bottom. Since the White House went into "lockdown" the minute the Secret Service heard the gunshots in Alexandria and ordered the crash, the press conference was hastily moved to the facilities at the State Department. This was no easy task for myriad reasons, not the least of which was that for every reporter the networks had covering the White House there were an equal number assigned to the State Department. The displaced White House beat reporters were invading their counterparts' turf at State, consequently wrinkling a few egos, which had to be ironed out. Oddly enough, the woman creating the most disturbance was a blonde whose limited access White House pass was being questioned at the gates of the State Department's entrance.

"You obviously don't recognize me. I cover the White House for MSNBC," she protested.

"That ain't the problem lady. I was told green and white passes only. You got yellow there and nobody said nothing to me about no yellow pass," the Wankenhut security guard explained. "Besides, there's a crew from MSNBC inside already!"

"There is? Well, they'll vouch for me."

"They're inside already and they ain't going to come out again till they're leaving." The guard was beyond being courteous at this point.

"Do you have a supervisor?" Carly asked in a tone that really meant, *Is there someone with a brain who I can speak to?*

The guard keyed his radio, "Len, I got a reporter here wants to see you." He placed his radio mic back in its belt clip and motioned with his hand to Carly. "He's coming, ma'am. In the meantime, will you please step aside so I can help these other people?"

It took two minutes, but a guard with gold captain's bars on his epaulets arrived at the guard's station. "What's the situation here?" the Captain asked, looking Carly up and down and hoping it was something to do with her.

"I'm Carly Simone from MSNBC and I need to get into that press conference right now!"

"You're Carly Simone? Please wait right here." He keyed his radio. "Base, this is Captain. Tell the detail I got Ms. Simone here at northwest entrance.

"Just a minute ma'am," the older guard related.

Carly was relieved that she was finally getting the treatment consistent with a member of the 4th estate. A minute later, two men in suits appeared and asked to see Carly's I.D. She showed them and one of them said, "Follow us, please." As she left the area with her personal escorts, Carly shot a glance to the guard who had given her such a bad time and said, "See I told you that you were wrong!" She couldn't figure out the strange smile she saw on the guard's face. She would in just a moment.

Having never before been in the State Department, Carly had no way of knowing that her two male escorts were not delivering her to her rightful place in the press room. Instead, they entered the State Department security office. There she was introduced to a bald headed man who was too mean looking and too serious to ever mistake for anything but a cop.

"What's this all about; where's the press room?"

"Miss Simone, I am assistant agent in charge, Glenn Durban. I am placing you under arrest for violation of the National Security Act. You have the right to remain silent; anything you say can and will…"

Carly's head started to spin. She couldn't comprehend what was going on. "What are you doing? This must be a mistake!"

"You have the right to an attorney...," the bald man continued on in a drone more accustomed to a common criminal than Carly Simone, ace reporter from MSNBC.

"Do you understand these rights as I have explained them to you?"

Stunned and shocked, Carly instinctively just nodded, her eyes frozen in space.

"Agent Grimes, you are witness to the fact the prisoner nodded in the affirmative as to the understanding of her rights." The word "prisoner" ripped through Carly's brain like a jagged-edged knife. She quailed as her arms were suddenly grabbed and she felt the cold hardness of handcuffs clamping down on her wrists; the burly agent behind her sliding her bracelet up so it wouldn't interfere with the ratcheting action she heard and felt as the restraints were tightened.

She was led through the halls of the building and out onto the steps with her hands secured behind her, an agent on each arm. As additional news vans and satellite trucks were pulling up past the C Street North West entrance, the MSNBC guys caught sight of Carly being loaded into the back seat of a Secret Service black car, and watched it leave with its grill lights and rear deck array flashing. Bill, a CBS technician keyed his PL line that connected him with his network's Washington control room. *They're gonna love this*, he thought as he dialed, anxious to report on what he had just witnessed. Members of other news organizations were also making calls.

∞§∞

Naomi was handling the impromptu conference well, especially since there were already conspiracy questions abounding. For her part, she stayed on the "this is what we know at this moment" and "that's all I can speak to" disciplines which prompted repetitive, probing questions on the same topic. Although it was an effective way for the press, as a body, to hammer away at the "talking points," to the outside observer it made the press look bad, not the press secretary. Of course, if in the heat of repetition, Naomi changed any part of her answer even one iota, it could open a door to an onslaught of news.

"Naomi, are you saying this man acted alone?" a practicing member of the art of repetition asked.

"Gill, again, it's just too early to know that for sure. We do know he was the only one arrested at the scene."

She then called on a reporter from Fox news. "Harry."

"Naomi, my producer just informed me that Carly Simone from MSNBC was just led away from this building in handcuffs. Can you comment on that report?"

"What aspect of it would you like me to comment on?"

"Is it true?"

"I don't know. I have been in here with you."

"Why would she be arrested?"

Naomi glanced in the direction of the Secret Service's public information officer. He nodded, having just heard that Carly was in their custody over his earpiece. She planted her feet and spoke. "Miss Simone has been taken into custody for alleged National Security Violations." The room erupted. As bad as the events of the last 24 hours had been for the country with the explosion and deaths on Long Island and now the attempt on the president's life, no one in the room would have believed it was soon going to get worse.

CHAPTER TWENTY-FIVE
OUT OF THE FOG

IT WAS A SHIT JOB and Jerry knew it. Especially out here on the cold, damp tarmac on this foggy night. The only good news was that this was his last plane. A 767 with 300-plus-passenger capacity. Six bathrooms. Jerry watched as the four-inch flexible pipe started to constrict, telling him what the gauge on his lav-cart's pump confirmed. The waste holding tanks on the big Boeing jet were sucked dry of the 1,200 pounds of human waste deposited during its last flight. Judging from the amount he just pumped, Jerry figured the plane had just completed a seven-hour flight. *What's seven hours from SFO*, he thought as he mentally drew a compass circle from San Francisco International Airport out 4,000 or so miles. Jerry climbed to the platform at the front of the lav-cart, which put his head directly under the fuselage of the giant bird. *Maybe Hawaii or Argentina.* He disengaged the internal release valve first. That closed the petcock within the outlet housing, making it safe to disconnect the hose's main fitting without having the formaldehyde-laced blue liquid and residue pour out over him. *Does this airline even go to South America?*

Having topped off the fuel tanks of the 767, the fuel truck operator proceeded to disconnect his single-point refueling hose. The flight line, turn-around ground operation was smoothly and routinely nearing completion.

On board, the passengers were settling in and surely fighting for what little overhead compartment space was left. Jodi, a female baggage handler, pulled her motorized luggage ramp back from the closing cargo door;

otherwise, Jerry would have seen him. A man in a long coat, both hands in his pockets, had just blown by the inner door marked "Authorized Personnel Only." The man had not responded when a security guard called out, "Sir, that's a restricted area!"

Instead, he wheeled around pulling a 9mm automatic from the right pocket of his coat and fired two shots into the guard, whose bulletproof vest temporarily saved his life. The kick of getting hit, even wearing a Kevlar vest, caused the guard to fall back stunned as he fumbled for his fallen gun. The gunman continued through the glass doors that led to the flight line. Walking behind Jodi as she backed up her luggage conveyor belt, he passed most of the ground crew. The roar of the turning engines from an MD-80 pushing back from the next gate drowned out all sound on the ramp. That, however, was not the reason the man disregarded another security guard blasting through the door wielding his gun and commanding, "Freeze. Drop your weapon!"

The workers scrambled and hit the deck. The man pulled something from his left pocket while simultaneously drawing the gun again from his right and firing. The second guard's shot slammed into the man's shoulder, spinning him around and sending him down. The guard ran toward the downed man with his gun fully extended, his eyes wide and heart pounding in his chest, as this was the first man he ever shot. He was less than a yard from him when he realized what was in the wounded man's other hand.

"Oh, my God!"

It was too late. The man released his grip on a grenade and flipped it with his last ounce of strength. It rolled ten feet, under the fuel truck. Just as the guard registered what the dying man had done, his face was flashed by the blast as his entire body was lifted and blown back, along with flaming debris and an expanding ball of flame engulfing the area. The female

baggage handler's body, perforated by grenade fragments, was also thrown back like a rag doll from the
force of the explosion. Her ton-and-a-half conveyor belt
truck was cart wheeling end-over-end, eventually rip-
ping open the bottom of the plane's huge wing, which
contained a completely filled and topped off fuel tank.
The machine landed on top of Jodi, wedging her body
into the corner of the terminal building. The breached
wing tank exploded and the plane split in two, each
200,000-pound section lifting fifty feet into the air and
crashing back down. The rising orange ball of flame
was visible for fifty miles, and falling debris shattered
the twenty-six-foot-high glass windows and crashed
through the roof of the terminal building. The aluminum halves of fuselage that were once the giant plane
melted away instantly in the intense heat, dropping
the 324 already-dead passengers and crew into the
pyre of flaming Jet-A fuel.

They would find Jerry's mangled body 400 feet east
on a taxiway.

∞§∞

There was fog coming through the air-conditioning
vents. It was so hot in this part of the desert that condensation was forming in the car. Winding through the
barren landscape, Hiccock drove a rented four-door sedan. The car's radio was tuned to the news.

"... engulfing the plane and the terminal. There are
at least 320 dead on the plane and as many as 50 others in the terminal and on the tarmac. It is known that
the plane was being refueled at the time and speculation is rising that possibly a spark of some ..."

His cell phone started to ring and he lowered the
radio. "Hello, Ray."

"Where are you now?" the chief said.

"I think I'm about five minutes away."

"Call when you get there; I have a fax for you to read."

"If the Admiral has a fax machine."

"Do you even know if the Admiral still lives there?"

"No, I don't know if anyone will even be there…"

"Did you check with local utilities or police?"

"I tried that, but the Admiral's deed, mortgage, phone, and electric bill must be in another name, as far as I can tell."

"Wonderful, and this is your last great high-tech hope?" Reynolds added, not trying to hide his lack of confidence in the whole idea.

"I've got a hunch about this. What's in the fax?"

"Basically it's a get out of jail free card for you. The head of the Presidential Detail of the Secret Service has determined that you were not materially connected in the plot to assassinate the boss. Although a congressional oversight committee might censure you and Naomi wants to spank you in Macy's window for all the world to see, I think you've heard the end of this.

"What about Carly? How did she backtrack my location?"

"The FBI has found she has a family relative who works for the phone company. The FCC is applying pressure now, but she hasn't given her cousin up yet."

"Why do I feel responsible for her?"

"Were you fucking her?"

Hiccock was taken aback by that question. "No. What makes you think…?"

"Bill, I've seen the girl; she's a looker. If I were your age and single, I'd have been tempted."

"No, nothing like that happened."

"Well, Tate at the FBI was trying to make a meal out of your dinner with her the other night."

"How did they find out about that?"

"She expensed you out. It was on her T and E report."

"Wow, everybody gets receipts for things. I gotta learn that lesson soon." Hiccock shot glance towards the rental contract on the seat next to him.

"Hear the news out of S.F.?"

"It must have been a horrific way to die. I don't think I can remember when a plane exploded refueling."

"It's happened a few times in the military. Static. It builds up on the truck frame, then discharges. Unless the FBI discovers evidence of terrorist activity, I bet when the wreckage cools they'll find the fuel truck had no static strap dangling to the floor."

"Gee, I almost forgot about that, it's such a low-tech thing."

"Yeah, easy to miss. Poor bastards never knew what hit 'em."

"I can't imagine the horror ..."

"Boss is calling, don't waste too much time with your high-tech hermit, okay, Bill?"

∞§∞

Navajo Gully 1 mile. *There actually were places with names like that*, Hiccock thought as he passed the highway sign.

A million miles from civilization, with a backdrop of purple mountains off in the hazy distance, Hiccock noticed a rare patch of green and color in the dusty, dry New Mexican desert. He stopped his car and walked up the hillside toward the humble house. The plantings provided a welcome mat of sorts. He noticed someone in the thick of them and approached respectfully, as he realized this was an older woman. Trying not to startle her as she bent over tending the yuccas and some other plants, he said, "Excuse me." She continued working with a trowel. He upped his volume. "Excuse me ..." She stood, her left hand pushing against her lower back, the hand tool in her right. He smiled. "I'm looking for Admiral Parks?" he said, making a question out of the statement.

Squinting in the noonday sun, she regarded him and started to pull off her work gloves. "No one has called me 'Admiral' in thirty years." A half-smile momentarily flashed from under her Katharine Hepburnish hat. In that moment, Hiccock saw in her mature, sunburned face the traces of the younger woman he'd only seen in her black-and-white file photo.

∞§∞

It was tea for two as the pot sat on a wood-burning stove in the center of the two-room house. A cup was passed between Hiccock and Admiral Henrietta Parks, USN retired. She was a serious-looking woman with rugged skin, her blue eyes set off by the long gray ponytail hanging down one shoulder. She could have been a pioneer a hundred years earlier.

"People are blowing up things?" she asked.

"It's been all over the media ..."

"I don't get any TV, radio, or newspapers."

"How can you manage to unplug like that?"

"After I was invited to leave the Navy, I just stayed away from anything technical or mechanical."

"I'm amazed. A lot of people fantasize about disconnecting from our crazy world, but you are the first person I have ever heard of who has actually done it."

"What do you want from me, Mr. Hiccock?"

"Call me Bill, please." Her directness reminded Bill that she was an Admiral. "I'm here because you wrote about this thirty years ago. You practically predicted what's happening now."

"How did you know about that?"

"I used your paper—your premise actually—as the principal source in my thesis."

"You wrote a thesis on naval computational warfare?"

"No, it was on predicted validity and baseline sampling. I quoted from your work extensively ... with footnotes." Bill felt like he was suddenly defending himself.

"Because of that little manifesto they forced me to take my pension," she said, looking off at the setting sun.

"Like Kaczynski ..."

"Who?"

"Ted Kaczynski ... the Unabomber."

"Can't say I know the gentleman."

A slight shadow of concern darkened Hiccock's face. Something had nagged at him since he entered the house, but now he knew what it was. He pushed his chair back, got up, and, walking off the porch, proceeded to scan the outside of the house. After inspecting all four corners, he returned. "There's probably not a chance in hell that your power, telephone, and cable are shot under the ground, right?"

"No electricity, no phone, no telegrams."

"Telegrams?"

"Cables."

He tried to squeeze the unbelievability of the situation from his eyes. He walked down to the car past a load of firewood. Retrieving his satellite phone from the front seat, he hit autodial.

"Yes, Bill?" Reynolds said impatiently.

"I need a few things."

∞§∞

One Corps Slice Signal Support Package was delivered. It consisted of three army trucks and a communications van with camouflage, netting, and a satellite dish array out of Fort Hood, Texas, and was parked in front of Henrietta's cabin. A generator truck whined in the background as a few military technicians milled about. The shoulder patch on one of the shirts read

"3rd Signal Brigade." A mass of camouflage-wrapped wires and fiber-optic cable packs connected to the trucks was snaked into the cabin. They were connected to two four-foot-high shock-mounted mobile rack units containing routers and codecs. From there, two lines ran to a twin-screen Sun Microsystems minicomputer that sat in front of Admiral Parks. And sat ... and sat.

"What's the matter?" Hiccock said, concerned.

"How do you turn it on?" she asked, looking at the racks, not realizing the power switch was hidden in the design of the twin monitors nowadays.

Hiccock breathed deeply.

"Listen, Mr. Hiccock, you came after me. I didn't ask you to come here. Now I am sorry if I don't know how to get this contraption going. In fact, I don't know why the hell you think I can help you at all. So maybe you just better pack up all this equipment and make sure not to scratch my floors when you haul it out of here."

Hiccock studied her, trying to figure out if this was her way of signing off or just negotiating. "Admiral, I believe in you and your theories. I want you on my team because I believe you have a contribution to make. The nation is suffering right now. No one has a clue what's going on. Thirty years ago, you did the basic analysis of what I think might be happening today. I want you to be familiar with what's gone on since then."

"Bilgewater!"

"Excuse me?"

"That's a load of backwash. You happened to pull my report to the Joint Chiefs out of some dusty old pile and now you have elevated it to the status of 'scripture.' I think it's got more to do with your pride than my writings."

"Fair enough. Maybe I am a little biased toward your paper, but the president has given me the job of finding an alternate causality. My intuition tells me computers somehow play a role here."

"So why do you think I can help?"

"Maybe you can give this a fresh new look from an old perspective."

"Old? Try ancient! I can't even recognize this apparatus here as a computer. In my day they were enormous."

Hiccock pondered this for a moment. "I got a better idea." He removed his laptop from its case. "Let's start small." He opened the PowerBook and pointed to the "on" button. "You press this circle here; it's actually a momentary contact push button, they like the design to be sleek and smooth so they hide it."

Later that evening, as Hiccock was leaving, he said, "I'll be back from Washington in two days. Just fool around with the laptop before you tackle the big one. These men will camp outside and won't bother you unless you have questions."

"I haven't touched a computer in three decades. I wouldn't get your hopes up."

"All I can ask is that you give it a try."

∞§∞

The smell of burnt flesh, scorched asphalt, spent jet fuel, melted plastic, and halogen foam was nauseating, but after a few minutes of exposure and some retching, the average person would be able to control the gag reflex. The reason for the HAZMAT suits, however, was the unconfirmed whereabouts of three pounds of dicloromonothoromethane that, if it were in the cargo hold of the now-disintegrated 767, would have boiled into a crude form of nerve gas. *Cute what they allow to fly on planes these days*, Joey Palumbo thought, as he heard nothing but his own breathing inside the helmet of his regulation HM4 plastic disposable contamination unit. As the head of the FBI's San Francisco office, this was his jurisdiction. Normally, any event at SFO airport would first be NTSB territory, but due to the recent events, any major loss of life was now considered a potential terrorist act. That was fine with the National Transportation Safety Board. If this had been an accident, it was one of the worst ever.

The white foam sprayed from the crash trucks to smother the fire would have given the entire scene the look of a fresh December snow were it not for the twisted, jagged metal struts, charred bodies, and dismembered parts. As he scanned the devastation, there, lying in the "snow," he spotted something, but couldn't quite make it out through the HAZMAT plastic face shield. He stepped closer to it. As the shape and texture came into focus, it tugged on a memory string, untying some old recollections.

Gunhill Road provided the perfect sled ride, a quarter-mile straight downhill run. On the morning of the first snow, there was not a car or truck in sight. He was trudging up the steep hill, through the three feet of new snow, his Flexible Flyer skidding along behind him on a frayed rope. The only sounds he heard were the muffled footfalls and squeals of delight coming from kids making forts, having snowball fights, and zooming by him on their sleds and garbage-can covers. Reaching the corner of Decatur Avenue, he turned and saw the great snow-covered way stretching out beneath him. The only mar on the pristine white cover was the dirty brown girders of the Third Avenue El, making a hard left turn south onto Webster Avenue.

Holding the sled up at an angle, he started running as fast as his galoshes-covered feet would carry him. When he reached his maximum velocity, he belly flopped down onto the sled he threw out ahead. Grabbing the steering handles in each hand, he sped down the hill, increasing speed with every second, his body prone on the sled, the cold wind and stinging snow lashing his face. Being an advanced sledder at age ten, he used the more difficult rear-foot-drag method of turning the sled. To do it you had to pull hard on the steering handle while dragging the toe of your foot on that side. The combination of this one-sided braking action and bending the runners in that direction gave the sled the handling control of a Ferrari turning on a lira. As the day progressed, nothing affected him or his friends—not the bitter cold, the runny noses, or the minor cuts and scrapes that were the occupational hazards of belly flopping in the Bronx, 1972.

As the winter sun was setting early in the afternoon, Joey pulled his little sister Gina on his sled while she held her teddy bear, Bobo. Crossing 212th Street, a kid on a sled sped out of nowhere. This kid, not being a master of the toe-drag-turn technique, couldn't avoid ramming into the sled, sending Gina flying.

Joey ran to his sister as she lay there, still, not breathing. Panic arose within him, but then, almost as suddenly, a new feeling came over him, even stronger—the need for action. He knew he could not just stand there. He immediately scooped her up in his arms and started running back toward Gunhill Road. There he hailed a passing garbage truck and implored the driver to rush him to the hospital. The doctors in the ER resuscitated Gina, everyone involved praising Joey for his fast action and for keeping his head.

The next day, Joey's mom made him her special, once-a-year, Easter morning blueberry pancakes for breakfast. This was her way of honoring her little hero. Gina was resting now in the hospital, Joey's mom having spent the night, leaving only to come home to make her breakfast for Joey. She'd be going right back.

After breakfast and more hugs than a guy should get, Joey, all bundled up, left for school. As he crossed 212th Street, there, in the snow, dirty from being run over, lay Gina's teddy bear Bobo.

Now it was an Elmo doll. There in the white foam, dirty with soot, lay somebody's little girl's Elmo. *Shit!* The FBI agent cursed to himself and the Virgin Mary. He didn't cry much growing up, but now the man fought back the tightening in his throat and the fluttering in his chest and focused on the next action he needed to take. A shout from behind turned him around.

A crane lifted a mangled motorized luggage conveyor belt, which had been blown into the corner of the ramp area, up against the terminal building wall. He moved cautiously over to the other agents supervising the recovery.

"What do we have, Ned?" he said loudly to overcome his helmet's muffling effect.

"We found another body. Looks like ground crew. Could be the belt operator." Joey bent down. The piece of equipment had shielded her upper body from the fire; the lower half, which was not behind the machine, was gone. *Action*, he thought, to steady himself as he blocked out the human horror he now probed. "What's this?" He waited for the click of the crime scene camera, recording the position of each element before investigators touched it, then moved her hairless head with his gloved hand, revealing a hole in the right side.

"Look at the thorax, more punctures," Ned said.

Joey called for the forensic pathologist who was piecing together a human remains jigsaw puzzle twenty feet from him.

CHAPTER TWENTY-SIX
TWEAKS AND GEEKS

"WHAT KIND OF DRUGS were you on?" the fuming chief of staff said.

Hiccock avoided the burning stare by taking in the objects on Reynolds's credenza. There on a wooden pedestal was a baseball autographed by Carl Yastr-zemski. "Thirty years ago she predicted exactly what's happening now."

"Aw come on, Bill. The woman wrote an anti-tech-nology thesis when the cutting edge of technology was a five-tube table radio ... and the Navy canned her ass."

"The Navy was attempting to secure congressional funding for new ASROC shipboard computers. They didn't want the doves in Congress using the Admiral's writing to sink their programs." He jutted his chin out toward the prized baseball. "Did you ever meet him?"

Reynolds turned his head to see what Bill was talk-ing about. "You mean Yaz? Sure."

"My father took me to see him when he played against the Yankees."

"Don't change the subject, Hiccock." The telephone rang, and, picking up the receiver, Reynolds listened for a second, then relinquished it to Hiccock.

"Joey? No shit! Are all the forensics in? Can you fax that to me? Okay, as soon as you know. Thanks, buddy." He hung up.

"Forensics? I guess that means the fuel truck did have a static strap," Reynolds said wryly. "Is this new event something tied into your investigation?"

"There are two troublesome issues that could point it our way. One, the forensic team thinks they have ex-tracted grenade fragments from the bodies of a guard and baggage handler. Two, the plane had a handful of top computer scientists from Santa Clara onboard."

"Major brain drain for Silicon Valley." Reynolds got up and grabbed the ball, rotating it like a pitcher, feeling for the seams behind his back. "Somehow computers are playing heavy into this. I have to admit your theory seems more on the money every day."

Hiccock was impressed. The man just came as close to contrition as a hooker gets to fashion and he never even flinched. *I guess that's why he's the second most powerful man in the White House.*

"Yaz was past his prime when I saw him, but my dad said it didn't matter, 'cause the basics stay the same. That's why I need people like Admiral Parks on my team. She practically wrote the basics."

"Just be right about her." Reynolds tossed and caught the ball with a snap and replaced it on its pedestal. "Oh, Justice called. They sprung that hacker you wanted out of Elmira and have him over at the FBI ECL. Don't you know any normal people?"

∞§∞

Chivalry and honor having been relegated mostly to the legends of the Knights of the Round Table or the Japanese samurai warriors, anyone would be hard-pressed to argue those values were alive and well today. The exception was in the underground network of cop-to-cop favors. Dennis especially believed this to be so after his phone call from Brooke Burrell, an FBI agent stationed in New York. She would become his contact into the Fed's lab results and any further threats the bureau received that could affect his new job. He knew that he now owed Jack big-time. This old buddy of his had tapped a favor from the FBI, and that, to him, was a debt of honor.

The FBI lab results cross-correlated the letter to Taggert with ones received by a few high-tech companies throughout the New York area, seven on Long Island, four in New York, three in New Jersey. Although they didn't have the name of the writer yet, they had deciphered a pattern. That news gave Dennis a little comfort in their numbers. It meant his protectee, Miles Taggert, was one of fourteen. In those numbers there was a little security. He asked Brooke if he could be alerted if any moves were made on any of the other thirteen.

She repeated the wishes of her boss, "'Whatever he wants,' he said." She did not have to add *so long as it doesn't violate agency or federal guidelines.* It was enough for Dennis to know that his juice, and that of Jack and whomever else he had tapped, was still fresh and had some kick left in it.

∞§∞

Hiccock arrived at the FBI electronics lab and immediately spotted and approached a longhaired, geeky-looking guy. "You must be Vincent DeMayo."

"No, I am Special Agent Foster. I think you are looking for him." He pointed in the direction of Brooklyn, New York, or so it seemed to Hiccock, as he followed the finger to a man who could've been right out of the mob movie *Goodfellas*. Black shirt, black tie, black, black, black. He was thirty-something and, obviously, still cocky after three years in Club Fed. He was seated in front of Krummel's computer.

"Vincent DeMayo?"

"The name's Kronos, man. It's my online persona. Kronos, the keeper of time." He made a clockwise motion with his right index finger as if he were tracing the second hand of his watch.

"William Hiccock. I am your bailee, the one keeping you from doing time." Hiccock made a counterclockwise motion around his watch. For an instant, Hiccock thought he might have made a mistake pulling the strings with the president to get this mob-nerd freed from prison. But his research showed Vinny DeMayo had beat the best encryption software and blasted through firewalls guaranteed impenetrable by the world's largest banks and governments, all in the name of organized crime. Hiccock was counting on the fact that all a computer whiz like "Kronos" cared about was cracking code—the bigger the better—and using cool equipment. Hiccock's mob, the U.S. government, could probably lure him with bigger machines and harder codes to crack than that other mob.

Their eyes locked in a kind of macho stare down. After a few seconds, Hiccock nodded toward the computer. "Anything unusual?"

"There are no obvious hack or chop marks in any of this freakin' code."

"What about the not-too-obvious?"

"That is my specialty. And I don't see anything at my level of genius in this pile of crap here either."

"Modesty becomes you."

"Mr. Hiccock," Hansen said, interrupting, "I think this is something you'll want to see."

Hiccock and Kronos followed him into another room that contained the equipment Hiccock had purchased at the auction. Somehow, the equipment, older than the FBI techs themselves, was working, albeit with wires and cords everywhere. Duct tape and wire ties seemed to be holding it all together.

"Whoa!" Kronos said, "look at all this crap."

"Crap is a relative word. You can't use a computer to find out what's happening inside a computer if you don't know what you are looking for. This old collection of analog equipment works on the output, not the insides."

"So you're looking for something that is happening between the digital clicks of a computer's internal clock?"

"Exactly. And you can't see that with something that's ticking the same way, but an analog device, working like the human eye, which is ..."

"Accumualtes how much of something, not how many of something."

"Essentially yes, and also because it's running at a much slower scan rate."

"So we can see the interstitial data between the digital blanking rate," Kronos said.

"What do you have?" Hiccock asked Hansen.

"After a lot of tweaking, we pointed the camera at the screen and ran a copy of Mrs. Krummel's cookies through their paces." He pushed the button on the huge two-inch Ampex videotape recorder. The giant reels turned at a very fast speed, almost fast forward. "We essentially visited every page she had and recorded it at high speed. We didn't see anything while scanning it. But when we played it back ..." He hit "Stop," rewound, and hit "Play." Now the tape reels were spinning ever so slowly. "... under slow-speed playback, we found this."

The Conrac TV before them displayed an electronic image of Martha Krummel's computer monitor screen. It was blinking with black flashes. The web page looked normal but after a few black flashes, a message popped onto the entire screen. After the next black flash, it was gone. "Those flashes are the refresh rate of the computer and happen approximately seventy or so times a second, too fast for the human eye to catch. To see this, we have to play back at a speed one hundred times slower."

"Persistence of vision," Hiccock said. "It's how movies, TVs, and computers show images. It happens so fast that we don't see the blinking. Unless you do something like this." Hiccock waved his hand in front of the monitor causing the image to strobe.

"That's the between the clicks that another computer could never see," Kronos said.

"Let's see that one message frame."

The tech now turned to a computer. "Once your contraption caught the image, it was easy for us to capture it as standard NTSC video and freeze it on the screen." On the computer screen the now-frozen message appeared.

Hiccock read the screen aloud: "The time has come, Martha. Derail the Train at 8:30 PM."

"So far we've found 200 others. All big type, all one sentence, some diagrams."

"Diagrams of what?"

"Train track wiring, signal and switch circuits ..."

Hiccock felt a surge of adrenaline.

"And then there's this."

As the pages flipped, images of a gun in someone's hand, having been downloaded from a web site, flashed across the screen. Next, a scene from some HBO gorefest movie came into view, showing an older woman lifting a pistol to her temple and shooting herself in the head. Hiccock read aloud another message on the screen.

"After you have done your task, Martha, place the gun to your temple and fire."

"Whoa, the shit they put on the net nowadays!" Kronos declared in disgust.

∞§∞

"Absolutely. Behavior and even hypnosis can readily be achieved at interstitial rates of less than one-fortieth of a second." Tyler said this as if she had written the paper herself. Seated in the FBI cafeteria across from Hiccock, Hansen, and Kronos, she sipped her third coffee of the morning.

"So the president is now fully aware that each homegrown act of terror—including Martha Krummel's—was predetermined, suggested, and induced by their computers?" Hansen said.

"Yes, I briefed him just before I came here," Hiccock said. "But that's not the question. The question is ..."

"Who programmed the computer to 'program' Martha?" Tyler said, completing his sentence.

"Kronos?" Hiccock turned in time to see him downing half a sugar donut in one bite, a dash of white powder on his nose. It was times like this that renewed his doubts over getting Kronos sprung from prison.

"Well, once we knew what the hell we were looking for it got a little easier. Me and the head geek here ran a few virus scans and interpolated file arrays. We dug up the line of code in the worm that calls for the messages and even the switcher routine to flash them." Kronos said this while licking the powdered sugar from his fingertips.

"There's a high-tech 'but' coming," Tyler said.

Hansen provided it. "When Kronos here tried to trace it back to the source, he hit a firewall."

"Sounds serious."

"Can't breach it. Ain't never seen nothing like it and neither has number one geek here."

"Hey, c'mon with that," Hiccock said in protest.

"It's okay," Hansen said. "I *am* the number one geek because I de-tangled his algorithm and nailed his URL to the wall."

"Is *that* how they caught you, Kronos?" Janice asked as innocently as she could manage.

"Ahh, so!" Hiccock said, borrowing from a famous stereotype. "Number one geek smarter than you, Mr. Number One Genius Ego."

"Eat crap and die. I was sleepwalking when I wrote that friggin' code!" Kronos stuffed the last of the donut into his mouth.

Hiccock turned to Hansen. "You ever see a firewall like this?"

"No. I create them for the bureau and every other gov.net function, but it's beyond me."

"Is there anyone else who might know more?"

"Hey, you got the best in the country right here," Kronos said, then patted Hansen's shoulder, "and the geek that caught him. Ain't no one else."

Hiccock rolled his eyes and then held his finger up. "There might be one other person."

CHAPTER TWENTY-SEVEN
BLACK TIE, RED-HANDED

THE WALDORF-ASTORIA has legendary security and means of egress. It has been a favorite of presidents since it opened back in the thirties. FDR's private armored train car would be shunted under the hotel in the vast underground rail network that comprises New York's Grand Central Station. Roosevelt's custom-made Pierce-Arrow was off-loaded onto a specially constructed secret elevator right under the Waldorf and opened onto the street. It was the safest way to enter New York City. Of course, that level of protection was only afforded to heads of state. Tonight, the security of the main ballroom was in the hands of the normal hotel dicks and whatever odd security men came with the participants.

Dennis had reviewed the venue for two days. Three of his men were on detail this evening. He wasn't pleased with the hotel's refusal to install metal detectors. They felt the nature of the festivities, tied to the price of a ticket, made it unlikely that anyone in the crowd would pose a problem. Dennis was there as another set of eyes. Cynthia had been taking treatments well. The biggest and most dangerous was scheduled for tomorrow. Having a job to keep him occupied tonight helped him fight off the sense of helplessness a mere man is prone to feel in the face of an act of God. So there he stood, his particular brand of therapy being to scan the crowd for the author of the poison inkjet letter.

His "cop's sense" bristled—out of a sea of faces in attendance to honor Taggert for the benefit of the Work with Pride Foundation, one man stood out. His appearance was just unkempt enough to tell the ex-detective that $250-a-plate dinners were not this guy's normal social activity. He also didn't seem to be with anyone at the table.

Speaker after speaker respectfully stood and awaited their turn at the dais to praise not only the foundation's efforts to help homeless people attain and maintain good, steady jobs, but also the merits, generosity, and overall good fellowship of Miles Taggert. *Miles could run for Pope after this*, Dennis thought, as he observed his bearded suspect and a few others. Dennis walked over to Harvey Davis, one of the ex-cops he wrangled to be on Taggert's detail. Harv was a photographer of sorts, and Dennis had him get a press pass.

"Hey, Harv, snap a few of the beard at table fifteen in the back. I got a feeling."

"Yeah, I noticed him, too. Wonder who's watching the farm while he's here?"

Harvey stepped away, shooting toward the stage, disconnecting any attention to the beard with the interaction he and Dennis just displayed. A minute later, he casually turned and snapped the shot with a long telephoto lens from across the room. No one even noticed at the beard's table.

As the event came to a close, Miles Taggert was barraged by do-gooders and well wishers wanting to connect with the man of the hour and bask in his glow. Dennis and his three men formed a Secret Service–style perimeter around Taggert. People were shaking his hand or speaking to Miles over, under, or through his or his men's outstretched arms. As they proceeded toward the door, the people at table fifteen approached to congratulate Taggert. Dennis noticed the beard moving closer. He spent half his attention on him but continued to scan the rest of the crowd. After all, the cost of being wrong about the beard could be a dead Miles Taggert.

When the beard moved in a little too close for comfort, Dennis applied his considerable weight and muscle behind his request. "Do you want to step back, please?" As he placed his hand on the beard's torso to accentuate his command, he detected something hard. He immediately called out to Benton and Davis, "He's packing!" The two bodyguards immediately formed a barrier between him and Taggert. Harv proceeded to usher Miles out unceremoniously, a move the rest of the partygoers and admirers considered downright rude.

Dennis looked the beard in the eyes. He sensed a coldness and distance that gave him more impetus to further invade the man's space. "Keep your hands at your side. Step to the rear of the room please."

The beard stood frozen with a look of confusion on his face; his body stance hinted at the desire to run, but the combined girth of Mallory and Benton effectively sealed the tiny opening between tables in which he would have to pass. Their cop's sixth sense, turning on all eight cyclinders, they moved on the beard as one. The man's one second of hesitation was not tolerated well by the former cop who was used to having his wishes granted—one-way or the other. He chose the other. Benton got hold of the beard's arm. Swinging him around, he grabbed the collar of his shirt as Dennis reached behind his rumpled sport coat only to find ... a Blackberry. Steered by Benton's hand on his belt and collar, the beard was thrust up against a column as Dennis continued patting him down, and then spun him around announcing, "He's clean." Dennis handed him back his digital palm-thingy and asked to see his identification.

"Are you cops?" the beard asked.

"Don't worry about us, pal, worry about your situation," Benton said.

"You aren't cops, and you have no right to search me. I am leaving now and if you try to stop me I will have you brought up on charges." With that, the beard adjusted his wrinkled and frayed sport coat. He tucked his checkered shirt into his faded, black jeans. Those second-hand-store Levis didn't, by any stretch of the imagination, go with the old, brown dirt-caked walking shoes that had seen better days. Definitely not the ensemble one wears to a high-society shindig.

∞§∞

That night, Tom (aka the beard, aka Voyeurger) went home and got online. The scuffle with Taggert's security guards made a choice he had been agonizing over for the past week easier. The path of least resistance was the key to success. Those bonehead security jerks had proven a little too resistant to his plan to strike out for the cause.

> Voyeurger: My primary target is too well protected.
> I had to abort.
>
> SABOT: That is a shame.
>
> Voyeurger: I will move on to target two.
>
> SABOT: Keep me informed.
>
> Voyeurger: Will do.

∞§∞

A day later, Dennis received a call from the Waldorf's head of security. A .25 caliber Saturday night special was found taped under a table in the ballroom. Table fifteen.

"Son of a bitch!" was Harv's reaction as he fished out six pictures of the beard from his desk drawer and headed to the scanner.

∞§∞

The bitmapped printout of the beard was forwarded to Joe Palumbo's desk from the New York office. His decision to help out a cop who helped him one July day fifteen years ago was an idea that was starting to look better and better.

At Joe's direction, the bureau immediately input the picture into their image recognition system. There it was compared and cross-checked with millions of National Crime Information Center pictures, as well as hundreds of thousands more from other world police organizations. Unfortunately, the NCIC computers didn't make a high-confidence match. Joey knew that if every state department of motor vehicles had digitized photographs for every driver's license in their database, the search would have been almost foolproof. But, that was a political issue. Although the mood of the nation was in favor of tightening up a little on personal liberties since 9/11, state DMVs fell under the issue of state's rights, a thorny constitutional issue in the best of times.

∞§∞

At his office at GlobalSync, Dennis Mallory conducted a meeting of his team. He had already handed out six different computer projections of the beard—without his beard, with different hair colors, with and without glasses, and other options.

Benton spoke for the team. "Dennis, go home. We know how to do all this. You should be home, waiting for word, or at the hospital."

"I know, but I can't do nothing there but just sit around feeling helpless. Normally they do this while you're awake—it's amazing. But Cynthia is claustrophobic. The machine they're using is more intimidating than an MRI, and she can't last ten seconds in one of those. So they sedated her, she should be up in a few hours. So I figured ..."

"You figured you'd break our balls a little. Listen, Miles will chopper straight to the house in the Hamptons tonight. Harv gets there an hour ahead. I am in the copter with him and then he's nestled tight for the weekend. So forget about this and go be there when Cynthia comes out of it. Send her all our love, too."

"Thanks. I hate feeling useless. This whole thing is just ... well, thanks guys, if anything shakes call me."

Alone in the elevator, Dennis started reviewing the events of the last few weeks. Miles had proven to be a man of, and beyond, his word. He took up Cynthia's cause as though she was his own mother. Today, three of the world's top radiotherapists were at her side, employing a technique the Detective Endowment Association medical plan wouldn't cover. They used 201 beams of deadly radiation. Each beam's dose was a minute fraction of the strength that healthy tissue would find lethal. By using computers and other gizmos, the beams would then converge somewhere within her head. At that intersection, their strengths would combine and affect only the targeted blood vessels that made up her AVM. That made this "gamma knife" technique a kind of sharpshooter picking off the dangerously abnormal blood vessels in crowds of healthy ones. The process was very expensive and not an easy list to get on. Once again, were it not for Miles Taggert's substantial weight as a benefactor to the university and his subsequent clout with the directors, doctors, and companies responsible for the Stereotactic thingamajig, they would not be involved with this level of medicine at all.

From Dennis's side of the bargain, the guys had all been doing a good job. With the big exception of letting the beard slip through their fingers, their police work was flawless. Now, if Cynthia had a good outcome with this procedure, she will have avoided the invasive brain surgery that, with her other conditions, would almost certainly be fatal, and all this would have been worth it.

When he arrived at NYU Medical Center, he bought some blue flowers in the lobby. He headed up to the floor where his wife, his love, his partner for the last thirty-eight years was recuperating. The instant he entered the room and caught sight of her lying there, a shapeless lump under the sheets, wired to the electronic equipment all around her, his eyes welled up. She was so brave. He had been shot three times in the line of duty. He had received five department commendations for bravery, three awarded by three of the four mayors that had spanned his career. He was brave by accident. Each time was a surprise; he had not expected to get shot that day. Cynthia, on the other hand, faced her dragon, looked it right in the eye, and went forward fearlessly.

No, that's not true. She experienced fear, but she was brave enough to not let it stop her.

Dennis didn't know if he would have had the grit to look into the maw of eternity with the dignity and calm she exhibited. Unlike him, she quietly steeled herself, without anger, agitation, or any of the male testosterone-laced peer pressure that always diluted his initial instinct to run and hide under the covers. As he tiptoed over to her, she appeared as if she were about twelve years old and in the middle of a sweet dream. He caressed her hair with gentleness out of character with his big, meaty mitts. At that moment, she *was* his little girl and he was her daddy. This was as vulnerable as he'd ever seen his wife and it brought up feelings that he'd only known with his Kelly when she was much younger. He wanted her to have no pain, no fears, no worries—all the unreasonable requests a father would make to God as he sits marveling at a sleeping daughter.

She began to stir. Dennis withdrew his hand, fearing he had brought her back to *this* reality, with all its pain and scary, grown-up consequences. He placed his palm on her pale hand and focused on it, trying to direct into her any life energy and other stuff he never believed in 'til now. Her eyes opened and he was glad that he was there. He liked being the first thing she saw.

"Hi, baby. You did great!" This was the same thing he'd said to Cynthia's opening eyes back when Kelly was born and she awakened after her caesarean delivery. He kissed Cynthia on the forehead. She felt warm and smelled of some kind of ointment. She managed a smile. He placed his head next to hers and stayed bent over like that, in silence, for more than thirty minutes.

Within an hour, Cynthia was talking. Even though the test results wouldn't be known for a week, they dangerously entertained the notion of a European holiday, perhaps a house in Italy, possibly sharing it with her sister and brother-in-law. She and her sister were the only two left in their family. It would be good for them to spend time together, now that they realized how precious time was.

And so the night progressed. Eventually she fell off into a restful sleep. After a while, he stopped hearing the soft beep of her heart monitor. He slept in the chair that he had moved close to her bed, awaking whenever he shifted only to realize he wasn't in their own bed. Cynthia awoke around 4 AM. Automatically, as happens after years of sleeping together, Dennis slowly awoke looking right at her.

She had a look of contentment as she lay there and just looked at him for a long time, then smiled. "Hey, handsome, I'm hungry. What does a girl have to do to get bacon and eggs around here?"

Appetite being one of the best signs of recovery, he determined a little thank-you prayer to God was appropriate.

CHAPTER TWENTY-EIGHT
THE HARD WAY

IT HAD BEEN TWO WEEKS since Cynthia's procedure and the news was looking good. Although the doctors made the usual disclaimers about being vigilant against any recurrences, it was as clean a bill of health as anyone given her history could expect. Dennis wanted to shake the hand of every doctor and nurse involved. Instead, he wrote a check for two thousand dollars to the National Institute for Neurologic Disorders and Stroke.

In keeping with that good news, there came another break in the case. Benton had shown several photographs of the beard to the office workers of the Work with Pride Foundation. The staff didn't recognize him as anyone who purchased a ticket. Dennis experienced an inspiration only bestowed on a cop who has had his antenna fine-tuned to crime as long as he had. *Did anyone report losing a ticket?* Indeed, someone did recall a man who claimed to have lost his ticket. His name was Enrico Hernandez of the Bronx.

Dennis went to Enrico's Body Shop at 2935 Southern Boulevard. There he found Enrico screaming at a guy who was having difficulty smoothing the Bondo on a hammered-out fender of an '87 Impala with a sanding wheel. The man was making a mess of the compound filler. Eventually, Dennis got Enrico to focus on the missing ticket.

"Yeah, I lost the ticket, but the girl at the table outside remembered me and let me go in."

"Why did you go to the dinner?"

"You see this neighborhood? The homeless people here were coming out of the woodwork. This Work with

Pride thing really helped them. Two of their guys work across the street. I might hire one myself next month. So, yeah, I wanted to go and support them." He then gave an exasperated gasp as he yelled to the worker, "Hey pendejo, large slow circles, por favor!" He waved his hand in big round motions to emphasize his point to the hard-of-Spanglish. Dennis tried to get him back on track.

"Did you know Mr. Taggert?"

"Who?"

"The man that was being honored that evening."

"Oh, him. No. I was there because they give Jimmy an award."

"Who's Jimmy?"

"One of the guys from across the street. I chased him away a few times. I mean every day he was here with his hand out. After a while it got to be too much, you know?"

"Tell me about it."

"Then one day I don't see him come around anymore. I figured he's dead. Then he shows up one day working across the street for Julio. Now, he brings me coffee most mornings, says it makes him feel good to hand me a cup, instead of the other way around."

"Yeah, I remember that guy. They gave him that plaque."

"You were there?"

"Yes."

"I thought you were a cop!" Enrico said with a laugh.

"You're good. No, I retired three years ago."

"So why you asking me all these questions?"

Dennis pulled out the picture of the beard. "You ever see this man?"

"No."

"We have reason to believe he was in the office when you went to purchase your ticket."

"Let me see that again. Yeah, now that you mention it, he looks like the guy that was hanging out while I was there. I remember thinking he looked too clean to be homeless, but not by much. I thought he must have been a new program member."

"When did you lose your ticket?"

"Don't know. Could've been anytime before the dinner."

"When was the last time you saw it?"

"The day I got it. Then I forgot about it until that night."

"Did you have any robberies or break-ins during that time?"

"No."

"Mind if we check your home?"

"Yes, I do."

"Sorry to hear that."

∞§∞

Agent Brooke Burrell exited her car first. The NYPD Tactical Patrol Force emptied out of a step van as five more agents surrounded her. She knocked on the door. Enrico answered as expected, it being 6 AM, after all.

Holding up a folded piece of paper, she identified herself. "Mr. Hernandez, I'm Agent Burrell of the FBI. I have a warrant to search these premises for material evidence in a matter of national security. Would you step aside, Sir?"

Maybe because he was groggy, or maybe because he was pissed at being awakened, or maybe it was just that no woman was going to come into his castle and start giving him orders in his underwear, he responded, "Hell no, get away from my house!" He attempted to shut the door. All Brooke had to do was tilt her head toward the door to get the three big bulls in flak jackets and helmets to slam a battering ram into the door, smashing it open. Two more team members hustled a bikini-brief-clad Enrico to the floor and cuffed him. Bringing him upright and sitting on his couch, the forensic teams went to work straightaway, dusting for prints and retrieving fibers. One cop secured the unwilling Enrico's fingerprints.

∞§∞

When Brooke left two hours later, Dennis, who had watched the operation go down, took the opportunity to cross the street and introduce himself. She was smaller than he expected; more refined than the policewomen he had known in New York. She greeted him with a welcoming smile.

"Hello, Mr. Mallory, nice to meet you."

"Pleasure. How did it go?"

"Like in the book. Got a lot of latents. Maybe one of those prints will be your bearded wonder's."

"How was Hernandez?"

"He chose the hard way, but we persuaded him to see our point. He's just an angry citizen. He'll get a suspended sentence for obstruction and no jail time."

"Thanks for all your help," Dennis said. This agent was no older than his daughter.

"No problem. I hear you were an above-grade cop."

"I had my moments. You'll let me know if you turn up any interesting evidence?"

"As long as my supervisor approves, you'll know what I know."

"Thanks."

∞§∞

"One latent print lifted from Enrico's drawer matched an ex-Army Corps of Engineers grunt named Thomas Regan," Brooke Burrell told Mallory a few days later in her FBI office. "He received the Purple

Heart for being wounded during the invasion of Grenada while attempting to rescue medical students who
had been taken hostage. The Army photo of him was a
rough match to the pictures Harv took, when you allow
for the twenty-five years, twenty pounds, a beard, and
thinning hair that separated them. His last known address was in Thousand Oaks, California, in 1989. No
record since. No credit cards, no license, no police records, and no death certificate. He just vanished into
the American fabric."

"Until he went shopping in Enrico's dresser
drawer."

Burrell nodded. "So Regan risks a break-in and covers his tracks for the sole purpose of stealing a 250-dol-
lar ticket to a high-society wingding?"

"This guy is focused and dedicated. I have to assume he has thought this out. I can't believe he left a
partial. Probably missed it in his wipe down."

"You think he's that careful?"

"The .25 caliber revolver that was found in the ballroom was wiped clean. And that would have been before he intended to use it."

"It isn't a dead match but it looks like your 'beard'
is Thomas Regan. We'll have all the airports and train
and bus stations alerted with composites."

Brooke's cell phone rang. "Yes, he's here right now."
She passed the phone to Dennis. "It's Special Agent in
Charge Palumbo."

"Hello, Mallory here."

"Mr. Mallory, we've never met, but Jack Flanagan
asked me to extend the professional courtesy. How are
they treating you back there in New York?"

"Like a VIP. Can't complain. I'm guessing this is
not a customer satisfaction survey."

That got an audible laugh. "Fair enough. The fact
is that your lead is bringing us into an area of national
security. I might not be able to keep the door swinging
both ways much longer."

"I hear you. I won't expect anything further, then."

"Of course, I now also have to make a pitch to appeal to your sense of patriotism. If you find out anything that can help us, you'll be forthwith." Joey employed the grammar of New York cops to stress his point.

"Of course. And thank you for everything you've done to help me thus far."

"We are all on the same team here."

"Do you want to speak to Agent Burrell?"

"I'll call her back later. You be good ... oh, how's your wife?"

That genuinely surprised Dennis. "Why, fine thank you. I'm touched that you asked."

"From what Flanagan said, she's one tough lady."

"Amen to that, brother."

CHAPTER TWENTY-NINE
CATS & BUGS

BLOWING UP Sperling High Voltage was an extra-points project because, with one blast, Tommy Regan not only struck a blow against technology, he made an object lesson of man's cruelty to the environment. The people who died from noxious fumes resulting from the fire became poster children for America's disregard for chemical and biological safeguards. In one fell swoop, he had won the admiration of the Sabot Society and ELM, the Earth Liberation Movement. This next attack would be spectacular, in the aftermath of which no politician or government official could deny the danger or ignore the raping of this planet any longer.

Luckily, magnets were not on any federal agency's watch list. There were no public outcries to regulate magnets. They just cost a bundle. So Tommy reached out to the Sabot Society.

Voyeurger: In order to prepare the Cat, I will need $7,000 to cover veterinary costs.

SABOT: I don't think that will be a problem, especially after how well your last pet project was received.

Voyeurger: Have them priority mail their intentions to me.

SABOT: I will alert all our members.

It was amazing. Within three days, the post office box he rented from Pack, Wrap, and Mail on Sunrise Highway was stuffed with U.S. Post Office blue-and-red

Priority Mail packets. They were the perfect carriers, these solid cardboard envelopes that offered not a hint of their contents. Less than five dollars' worth of stamps got second-day delivery. They were dropped in standard, anonymous mailboxes leaving no way to trace the sender.

Outside the store in his rotting Camaro, Tommy opened envelope after envelope, calculating their contents. There were twenties, fifties, fives, and tens, some wrapped in newspaper in a further, though unnecessary, attempt to hide the contents. Within two weeks, he had $8,432 dollars in cash all collected, transported, and delivered through the courtesy of Uncle Sam's post office. What a great country!

Alinco permanent magnets were awesome devices. A one-pound magnet could lift an engine block. The two magnets he needed cost $1,200 each, for which he paid cash, no questions and not even a raised eyebrow. Edmund Scientific out of Tonawanda, New York, supplied the next crucial element of his surprise package, a four-pound gyroscope. It was a 24-volt model. He had already located eight-ounce RV model batteries that put out 24 volts from Radio Shack. Designed for model planes and boats, they were lightweight. Each one cost $189. He bought four. The expensive part was the C-4. It took him three weeks to locate the guy on the Internet who once said it would not be a challenge to acquire certain "plastics" for rapid remodeling work. Rapid being the three ten millionths of a second it would take to detonate the four pounds of deadly putty.

It was a devilishly simple device, once he figured it out. The basic principle was based on a cat's ability to land on its feet. Of course, making something that performed like a cat was no small task. He even toyed with the notion of using an actual cat, but he thought it might bring about unfavorable Karma to initiate the genocide of possibly 10 million with the death of one of

God's innocent creatures. No, he would not sacrifice a cat to help man pay for his sins.

The cat solution came to him as he was watching some kids play Frisbee in the park. The disc always flew level as long as it was launched level. It was, he reasoned, because of the angular momentum of the spinning disk.

∞§∞

"Five dead including one who was in the Sperling plant. She was a bookkeeper working late," Nichols, the assistant to the director, told his boss. "The other four were poisoned watching the flames. Nitro traces are leading our agents on the scene to suspect dynamite. They are focusing on one of the delivery trucks as the point of origin, and that truck was loaded with a chemical used as a coolant for high-voltage transformers."

"Anything from EI on this?" EI was Electronic Intelligence, a once small, now major part of the bureau's crime-fighting arsenal. The whiz kids down there had ways of determining what some online pervert trolling for twelve-year-old boys in a chat room had for lunch. EI provided the big payoff on Bernard Keyes, the FBI's number one suspect in the rash of recent homegrown events.

"Yes, Sir. Homegrown 1 sent this e-mail at 9:04 PM EST. It only contained two words, 'Sperling. Ultimate.'" The suspects on a big case like this were code-named in their order of discovery. Homegrown 1 was actually Homegrown 1 and only.

"Have you confirmed that it's a genuine claim of responsibility?"

"The timing is close, but it is incontrovertible. The factory blew at nine, four minutes before the e-mail was received. However, it wasn't on the fire call boxes or radio frequencies until 9:05, a minute after. So no way it was just someone responding to a scanner call.

The first report didn't get out to the media until twenty minutes after that. We got 'em, Sir."

"What is the operational plan then?"

Nichols smiled. "Sir, something's fallen into our laps. E-traffic out of Keyes's location indicates a meeting of their top cell leaders has been called."

"When?"

"Three days."

"Can we identify whomever he e-mailed the meeting notice to?"

"EI was able to pick up his outgoing keystrokes. They have determined he posted the call for the meeting to an old bulletin board."

"Meaning?"

"They communicate without leaving a routing trail but we're watching the billboard. It's a challenge because people don't have to enter one or reveal themselves in any way in order to read the postings. Our guys are working on it."

"The good news is we know the location of the meeting place, so we stand a good chance of apprehending the entire ring."

"Seems probable, Sir, especially since we've kept security on Homegrown airtight. The Sabot will have no reason to suspect we are on to them."

"Nichols, I want you to personally call everyone with knowledge of Homegrown and remind them one more time how critical containment is on this. And let them know you are calling for me!"

"Yes, Sir."

"You have my approval to wait for the meet to get all of them. One proviso: if we learn of any bombings or potential acts of terror in the next three days, we jump all over Homegrown 1, stop it cold, and chase down these cells some other way."

"Of course, Sir. I'll write up the operational guidelines and have them on your desk for you to sign in fifteen minutes."

"Take twenty, I don't want any mistakes."

"Yes, Sir," Nichols nodded as he took leave.

Alone in his office, Tate ran through the next few steps in his mind. He reached for the telephone to call Reynolds to ask for a sit-down so he could see the president's face when he told him he had solved the case. Better yet, Homegrown 1 was about to be joined by Homegrown 2 through 10 or 20.

On second thought, he decided to call the San Francisco office.

∞§∞

It was 6:30 PM in Oakland. The setting sun, hanging low over the Pacific, bathed the ball field in an amber wash. Joey Palumbo was sitting on a dusty bench watching his nine-year-old master the strategy and mechanics of playing Little League second base. This was the perfect time, watching his son grow up. Joe Jr. was the greatest achievement of his and his wife Phyllis's lives. Watching his son turn two and discovering that birthday cake wasn't just intended for one's mouth, Joey had an epiphany and suddenly understood what true selflessness meant. This was someone he would gladly die for.

Although he loved his wife and intellectually knew he would sacrifice himself for her as well, their love was somehow, somewhere, at some point far out in the abstract, conditional. Especially if she divorced him or, someday, God forbid, she turned against life and went on a self-destructive path. But there was no limit, no threshold that his son could cross that would erode Joey's selfless devotion to Joe Jr. Down deep in his soul, at the very center of his being, he would be willing to make a draconian deal with any devil to trade his life for that of his son's.

His secure bureau cell phone rang. He got up and distanced himself from the other parents. "Palumbo."

"How are you, Joe?"

He knew the director's voice. "Fine, Sir, and you?"

"I'm having a great day, Joe. We got a concrete match to Homegrown 1 on the explosion and fire on Long Island."

"When did this happen?"

"Within the last hour. NCIJTF has him typing the credit note four minutes after the blast."

"It is a good day, Sir." There was an awkward pause, Joey trying to decide why he got this call, probably before the president. Then he found out.

"Has your friend come up with anything?"

"Our agent Hansen tells me they have found the means of recruitment."

"The subliminal thing?"

"Yes."

"Do you believe that?"

"Hiccock's not dumb, Sir. If he is going that way, there's probably something there."

"Of course, that doesn't rule out Homegrown 1. I mean he could be behind Hiccock's subliminal theory."

"That's true, Sir. Should I call him and see?"

"Joe, I need you to find out what you can, but I don't want to tip him off that we are as close as we are."

Joey didn't like the sound of this. "Can I ask why?"

"Homegrown is about to expand. We found out the perpetrators are having a big meet in three days and we expect to be there when they do."

"Sir, Hiccock has clearance." Joey had the unsettling thought that he may have just pushed a little too far.

"Joe, I am asking you to ascertain what he knows without jeopardizing Homegrown."

Joey resented the implication that his friend was a security risk and considered telling his boss to go to hell. But looking toward the infield as his son bobbled a routine ball to second, it was all too plain to him that his little second baseman wasn't going to get a baseball scholarship to Harvard. After a deep breath, the father in the agent said, "Yes, Sir."

"Let me know as soon as you know anything, okay, Joe?"

"Certainly. Good night, Sir."

As he folded his encrypted phone, Palumbo seriously considered his next action. He had pretty much kept his old buddy out of the loop, feeding him nothing of any consequence. Now he was being asked to see if Hiccock was going to scoop the FBI before they could have their little dog-and-pony show in three days.

How do I do this?

∞§∞

Kronos was confused. He had flown all the way to bum-fuck New Mexico and then was driven two hours and 300 minutes to this place in the middle of nowhere. He knew Hiccock was summoning him here to meet some kind of Navy Admiral, but as the car drove up, he saw nothing but Army crap: soldier jerks, trucks, and satellite dishes. He thought about it and laughed to himself. *What did I expect? To see them pull a ship up to this shack in the middle of the desert.* Hiccock and Tyler stepped off the small porch into the desert's oppressive midday heat to greet him.

They entered Parks's home. Looking around the inside, the sparse furniture, curtains on the windows, and wood burning stove reminded Kronos of a family trap restaurant on Route 4 in Paramus, New Jersey. The politically correct environment of the eatery was corporately designed to look like a country home. It was a ploy to get people's minds off the portion-controlled servings as mandated by the head office in Milwaukee or someplace. Except for the Sun Microsystems minicomputer in anvil cases, this house looked like a small corner of that restaurant, complete with an old grandmother.

Taking it all in, Kronos turned to Hiccock. "So where's the Admiral?"

"She's at the computer," Hiccock said, pointing.

Kronos was enraged. "She? She's, she's ... she's an old broad!"

"Mind that tongue, boy. She is an old *Admiral* broad. And she forgot more than you'll ever know."

Kronos felt the skin on his face start to heat up. He bit the inside of his cheek, pivoted on his heels, and stormed out the door.

"Come on, Kronos," Hiccock said, following him. "This isn't some hacking competition. People are dying out there wholesale. We have to try everything."

"Look, I hacked for the mob. I made them millions. I was Electronic Enemy Number One for four years. I got pride. Why do I have to work with her? What could she possibly know?"

"Let's go find out. I left her with her first computer four days ago."

Kronos planted himself, not moving. "What? She didn't have a computer? Are you whacked out of your freaking mind?"

"Look, in the early days she was in Naval Administration, a fancy name for the secretarial pool in the Navy."

"Is this going to be a long freaking story?"

"When the computer first came along, the torpedo heads didn't know what it was and assigned it to her command."

"You are boring me here."

"Well, when they started aiming guns and figuring out missile arcs with the damn things, her department grew. She had the first machine, an ENIAC.

"Electronic numerical integrator and computer, yeah, so? I had a Commodore 64, big whoop!" Kronos crossed his arms, assuming a petulant stance.

"The story goes that one day the whole machine went down. Couldn't get it running. Techs and engineers all over it. No go. Then she got this idea. She walked over to a big rack, reached inside, and found a moth had flown into the cabinet and got stuck in a relay contact. She removed it and the thing started right up. She logged it officially as 'Computer not functioning. It had a bug in it'!"

Slowly Kronos turned. "That was this broad?"

"Wherever you are, young grasshopper, she got there first."

"Yeah, so what's with the no box till four days ago?"

"She abandoned all technology. I read her papers when I was in college. She called for a halt to further computer research and enhancements, claiming that one day they would become too fast and too smart to overcome, and then whoever controlled the boxes could control the world."

"So they kicked her ass out of the Navy for that?"

"If anybody was going to control anybody, Uncle Sam wanted to make sure it was us. C'mon 'couzeen,' let's go see if she can help us."

"That's 'cucheen.'"

Kronos looked back through the doorway. The old woman was busy doing something at the keyboard. He thought of Elmira. He had won the trust of the assistant warden when he fixed the warden's son's laptop, saving the old man a few hundred from a rip-off repair shop. Although he then became the de facto IT guy at the prison, he still had to return to his cell three times a day and report to the workout yard whenever the screws wanted him out there. Since he was a white-collar criminal, the macho guards didn't fuck with him much. With the assistant warden's blessing, his life there was better than most inmates', but the crummiest, worst day of freedom was still a million times better than the best day in jail. Hiccock had gotten him out of there and Kronos didn't want to go back. Reluctantly, he re-entered the house. Parks was at Hiccock's

laptop as the familiar audio signature for Microsoft
Windows tinkled out of the machine.

"Whoever came up with this was a pretty smart fellow," she said to the two men as they approached.

"Windows?" Hiccock said. "Yeah, I'd say so."

"It's the Killer App of all time!" Kronos added.

"The what?" Parks scrunched her nose, looking up
over her bifocals.

"Killer application?" Kronos sighed, not believing
he had to explain this. "Software so hot, people buy the
hardware just to use it."

"I think he's agreeing with you that this guy was
smart," Hiccock said.

"Yep, except he missed a few things like right ..."
she typed a few keystrokes, "... here. He's got a big hole
here ..."

Suddenly Kronos felt like he was falling. He experienced the sensation of wind whipping past his ears
as he looked at the screen beyond the Admiral's gray
hair. Right there in uncompiled language was a nested
loop error that had been missed by legions of proofers
and beta-test site weenies who must have been paid
millions by Microsoft.

"He'd pay you a king's ransom for finding that little
bug," Hiccock said.

Kronos spun his head to Hiccock on the word bug.
Whatever Parks had seen was forever lost as she hit
the power button and said, "Ah, he's a smart fella. He'll
figure it out on his own sooner or later."

Kronos was in awe. He had found a new guru. He
pulled Hiccock aside. "She didn't have a computer 'til
four days ago?"

Hiccock checked his watch. "Three days and twen-
ty-one-and-one-half-hours, actually."

Kronos sat down and powered up the Sun System,
positioning himself next to Parks. "Yo, how you doin',
Admiral? I'm Kronos. We're going to work together and
blast through that freaking firewall."

"What's a firewall?" she asked.

After a deep breath, Kronos started typing a hundred words per minute as he proceeded to teach and preach "Computers 102." "It's a form of active encryption."

"Like the Enigma code of World War Two?"

"Yes, only those codes were passive, waiting for someone to figure out the key. A firewall actively rejects any attempt to decode it by changing itself and confusing the destructuring logic of the code breaker."

"So it slithers and slides when you probe it?"

"Exactly."

"Show me how far you got when you hit this firewall," Parks commanded.

He typed like a machine gun as Parks watched the screen.

CHAPTER THIRTY
TRAFFIC PATTERNS

THE REST STOP on the Jersey Turnpike provided an excellent observation point from which Tommy could research and plan his attack. At the end of the cracked asphalt parking lot, through the scratched windshield of his Camaro, he could observe the comings and goings of the stainless steel tanker trucks at night. The trucks formed a mobile pipeline into the storage tanks. This specific tank facility had already been earmarked by groups like Greenpeace and Earth First as one of the world's most dangerous ecological time bombs. The intent of these organizations was to merely alert the citizenry to the obscene violations big corporations were imposing on Mother Earth. The most they envisioned, or could hope for as a result of their efforts, was the occasional protest or letter-writing campaign. They never in their worst nightmares counted on Tommy and his dedication to bringing instant justice and notoriety for the cause.

Tommy's mother died of breast cancer. Later it was learned that he had grown up in a "cancer cluster," a cute name to define living over a biological and chemical atrocity. American Cyanamid, the behemoth chemical conglomerate, eventually settled out of court with no admission of guilt or assumption of responsibility on their part. After all the "incidental" legal expenses were siphoned off, in addition to the incurred attorney's fees, the remaining dollars were distributed among the affected families. Tommy was awarded the paltry sum of $5,000 for his mother's life, on which he was taxed.

The righteous indignation over all of this didn't co-alesce in his mind until after he was hit with shrapnel during the Grenada incursion. His head wound terminated his military career ... and gave him a remarkable new sense of perspective. He spent months in and out of veteran hospitals during recovery and rehabilitation. The doctors were encouraged when he showed a voracious appetite for reading. Of all that he read, it was the radical literature and the rants and ravings of eco-terrorists like the ELM that found a home in his newly ventilated brain. Eventually Tommy came to understand that he was also a wounded veteran of their "Great Cause." His moment of epiphany came with the realization that his family had actually been attacked, raped, and pillaged by corporate greed and disregard for the sacred Earth.

Over the previous two weeks, he had observed no less than three trucks, sometimes as many as five, drive through the gates into the facility after 12:30 AM. Inside there was a portico strategically located a quarter-mile away from the main tank farm. At this safe distance, every truck was inspected before it entered. Bomb-sniffing dogs were used, as were mirrors on long poles to check the undercarriage. The driver was wanded for any weapons.

Tommy noticed, to his great satisfaction, that they only checked the lower half of the cab and undercarriage of the trailer. They never looked higher than the roof of the cab. He panned his Nikon high-powered binoculars left and up the turnpike. There, approximately a quarter-mile from the turnoff the trucks took to get to the tank farm, was a pedestrian overpass. Although the span was fenced and wired to stop evil kids and other miscreants from hurling bricks into speeding windshields for fun, the access stairs, parallel to the turnpike, were only blocked by a three-foot railing. The light traffic, remote location of the rest stop, the overpass, and the tank farm all gave him precisely what he was looking for.

∞§∞

For the last week, Tommy had practiced in his back-yard with a seven-pound sack of sand. He laid down a two by four piece of wood, then paced off twenty-two feet and placed an upright Coke can on the ground. He spent two hours a night pitching the bag the twenty-two feet until he could crush the can 48 out of 50 times. Tonight he would make one last reconnoiter of the tank farm. Then, tomorrow, he would make his statement—one that would be heard around the world.

At 9 PM, after consuming a microwaved franks-and-beans dinner, Tommy went out to the Camaro and turned the key ... and got nothing. The battery was dead! After the obligatory punching of the steer-ing wheel, he went inside to call his friend Arnold to ask for a jump, but got his answering machine instead. He left a short message asking Arnold to come over to charge the car and then dialed the number of the local cab company.

The cab pulled up to the Long Island Railroad sta-tion just as the

9:20 PM to Penn Station was pulling in. Tommy threw the driver a twenty for an eight-dollar fare and bolted. He boarded the train just as the doors shut. Passing the time by looking into the Long Island night, its sleepy homes and red-taillight-spotted roadways smeared by the scratched plastic window of the train, he reviewed every step of the plan and contemplated every possible scenario.

When the train arrived in Manhattan, he walked through the shared terminal on his way to the New Jersey Transit Morristown line. A thirty-minute ride on that train would connect him to a bus route that had a stop a quarter-mile behind the Jersey Turnpike rest area. In the morning, Arnold would come over with his charger and tomorrow night he would have his Camaro in working order for his attack. It was a giant kickoff, of sorts, in that it would come on the eve of the big Sabot Society meeting scheduled two days later.

∞§∞

Officer Darrel Spoon, a New York City Transit cop sitting behind the courtesy desk on the main concourse, noticed the man as he emerged from the track seventeen stairway. He watched him with one eye as he leafed through the clipboard with all his notices of the day. He found the picture of Thomas Regan that the FBI distributed to all points of embarkation. Unfortunately, at that instant, hundreds of Islander hockey fans swarmed down the escalators, hooting, hollering, pumped, and psyched because their Long Island team beat the New York Rangers in their own house, Madison Square Garden, located directly above the terminal. Darrel lost the bearded man in the thick of the crowd and keyed his radio, calling it in to the central dispatcher. Other officers immediately converged on the main concourse, fanning out toward the tracks.

Penn Station was a tactical nightmare for tracking. The 7th Avenue and 8th Avenue subways ran down each side of the station with four tracks each. The Long Island Railroad and Amtrak trains shared twenty-one platforms. New Jersey Transit trains were squeezed in there with the others for good measure. In all, no less than five separate transit systems, six if you counted cabs and seven if you counted buses, connected Penn Station to the greater metropolitan area. Further confounding the issue was the fact that several major office buildings and one of the largest sports arenas in the world were right above it, offering any target a simple escalator or elevator ride to anonymity.

Still, the transit cops did what they were trained to do, which was to doggedly focus on the trains. Based on the radio broadcast description, they stopped and detained any needle in this haystack of train passengers who even closely matched the FBI description. Tommy had missed all the action, since he had gone straight to the New Jersey Transit tracks and, for the second time that evening, boarded a train just as the doors closed. He never saw the two cops rush down the platform futilely as the train rolled out.

∞§∞

Dennis was reading the latest David Baldacci thriller, nestled into his Barcalounger in the living room, when Cynthia answered the phone. It was just past 11:00 PM. He heard her say, "Yes indeed, he's right here." He got out of his chair with a grunt and took the call in his den.

"Dennis, it's Agent Burrell. We were just notified of a possible sighting of the beard at Penn Station."

"Who made the ID?"

"It was a transit cop. They lost him."

"I'm going down there. Thanks for the call." As he hung up, Cynthia looked at him questioningly.

"They may have found our guy. I want to talk to the cop that spotted him."

∞§∞

Dennis got to Penn Station just at midnight as Darrel was getting off his shift.

Burrell was just leaving, having already debriefed the officer. "You got in fast, Mallory."

"I didn't want to miss this. Can you tell me anything?"

"New rules, you know. You got the courtesy call. That's as far as I can go. The rest is now part of an on-going federal investigation. Sorry."

"Hey, no problem. Thanks for the heads up, Brooke. Er, mind if I talk to the officer?"

"I don't see why not, we're done here."

Dennis made his way to the young transit cop who had gotten more attention in the last two hours than he had in his whole career. He assessed the black officer to be in his late twenties and in good physical shape, with eyes that looked like they could disarm a perpetrator at ten yards. That was the way cops were supposed to be … big, mean-looking, and tough.

"Officer Spoon?"

"Yes?"

"Dennis Mallory, NYPD retired. I was wondering if you could help out a fellow cop here."

"What did you retire as?"

"I was a detective first grade when I took the package."

"First grade, huh? My name's Darrel."

"Darrel, I know you're on your way home, so I'll keep this short."

"Thanks."

"I'd like to show you some additional pictures of the man you saw tonight." Mallory pulled the comps and images from the manila envelope he had with him. As Darrel scrutinized them, he nodded.

"Yeah, from these photos he looks more and more like the guy. How come the FBI didn't have all these?"

"My people took the originals. Tell me, how did you happen to spot him?"

"I was manning the concourse desk when I saw him coming up the stairs from the tracks."

"Which tracks?"

"Seventeen-eighteen. I observed him cross the concourse and before I could rustle up the FBI pic, I lost him in a bunch of pickled-to-the-gills yahoos fresh out of the hockey game. By the time we locked down the station, he was gone."

"In your opinion, was he going home or heading somewhere?"

"How would I know that?"

"Was he walking slow? Did he know where he was going?"

"Well, now that you mention it, yeah, he was stepping lively. He took the escalator two steps at a time. So, yeah, he was heading somewhere on a schedule. Wow, you're good. I think the FBI thinks he was coming home to New York."

"Well, I've had a little more experience. Where did the train on either seventeen or eighteen come in from?"

"Another good question." They went to ask the stationmaster.

"Train number 4713 platformed at 10:14."

"Where did it come in from?"

The white-haired railroad veteran ran his finger across a time schedule as he lifted his glasses up to read the fine print.

"Ronkonkoma."

"Do you have the list of stops?" Darrel asked.

"You can pick up a schedule downstairs."

"Better yet, where is the crew?" Dennis said.

"They're in the yard on turn-around. They go out on the

12:37 local." Dennis looked at the clock. It was 12:36. "Can you hold that train?"

"On whose authority?" Darrel flashed his badge. "On mine. This is a police matter." The stationmaster picked up a yellow phone marked "dispatcher."

"Fred, hold the 12:37. It's police activity." He turned to Darrel. "How long?"

"Just 'til we get onboard?" the young cop said, looking to the old cop for approval.

"We?" Dennis said, smiling in surprise.

Three minutes later they were down on track twenty-one and stepping onto the train. Darrel instructed the brakeman to notify the engineer of their arrival and release the hold on the train.

"Officer Spoon, how did you know I wanted to get on the train?"

"Million to one."

"As in, it was a million to one shot?"

"No, as in our guy is lost in New York City. That gives him a million directions to go in and get lost. Where he came from, though, that is only one. So, yeah, I like the odds."

"Keep thinking that way officer and you'll be a detective soon."

As the cars clanged and banged over switches deep within the bowels of Manhattan, Dennis interrogated the trainman. He was sitting in an engineer's cab that doubled as the conductor's cab when positioned at the rear of the train. Behind him, the receding rails were swallowed up by the tunnel's darkness in the wake of the train. Dennis held up one of the photographs. "On your trip in this evening, did you see this man?"

"What's this all about, what's he done?"

"We just want to ask him some questions, that's all."

"Fare beater?"

"Now, why would you say that?" Dennis had found over the years that these first utterances were usually worth their weight in gold.

"He looks like a guy who jumped on at the last second ... in either Deer Park or Happaugue."

"You saw him?" Darrel said.

"Danny, my conductor, had that end of the train."

"Can you ask Danny to come to this car, please?"

The brakeman leaned over and spoke into the train's intercom. "Danny, come to the west end."

Dennis continued, "Why fare beater?"

"He looked disheveled, like a nut case. He jumped on right before the doors closed. These guys try to time it when we're looking the other way. It's stupid, but they think they can fool us."

"So did this guy pay his fare?"

"Danny didn't mention anything, so I assume he did."

Danny came into the car at the far end and approached the men. Darrel held out his badge and identified himself and Dennis as his partner. Dennis liked this kid. He thought fast and learned even faster.

"Did you see this man tonight?"

"Let me see those others?" Danny reached for the rest of the pictures on the motorman's pedestal in the cab and inspected the shots. "It's hard to say for sure but he looks like a guy we had on the last trip."

"Was he traveling alone?"

"Yeah."

"Did he pay his fare?"

"Yeah."

"Anything unusual about him, anything that stuck out?"

"No, not that I was looking. He just sat there, hand on his chin, looking out the window, you know, like he had something on his mind."

"But you weren't looking?" Darrel said.

"Well, he was breathing heavy when he got on, just made the train."

"Do you remember what stop?"

"Let's see, it had to be before Deer Park, 'cause I went up front when we passed Divide, the switch tower east of Bethpage. Yep, he got on at Wyandanch. I remember now, 'cause I announced Farmingdale next stop as he was running up the steps. I had to toggle the doors not to hit him as he jumped on."

"Does *this* train stop at Wyandanch?" Dennis asked, pointing down at the floor.

"Yeah, we make Wyandanch at ..." he checked his schedule, "14. 1:14 AM."

"When's the next train back to NY?"

"That would be the 2:20."

"Looks like we'll have an hour in beautiful downtown Wyandanch," Darrel said.

"Don't say I never took you to all the swankiest places," Mallory said. "Let's sit."

They distanced themselves from the crew and any other passengers and sat in the middle of the car. "So why are you—we—after this guy?" Darrel asked as the train made every stop a train could make in the middle of the night.

"I work as head of security for a big high-tech concern. I think our bearded wonder may be the author of some threatening letters that have been ruining my CEO's granola and yogurt every once in an AM."

"Where did you get the flattering pictures?"

"One of my guys snapped him at a charity event honoring my boss. After the party was over, we found a .25 under a table."

"You think he was there to cap your guy?"

"I didn't see anybody else there who would risk getting gun oil on their Halstons and Purinas ... or whatever they were wearing."

"Great."

"What?"

"You're telling me this guy could be A and D. You still carry?"

"Wouldn't leave home without it," Dennis said, referring to the snub-nosed .38 clipped to his belt. That accessory was almost surgically attached for life to anyone who was ever a cop.

"Good, 'cause if we find him, this nut job may own more than one pop gun."

When Dennis and Darrel got off the train, there were only three cars parked in the garish green of the sodium-vapor lit lot. One other person, a woman, got off the train with them and went straight to her car. Dennis noticed a private cab idling at the bottom of the station steps. He asked Darrel to jot down the plate numbers of the cars remaining in the station, and then he approached the cab driver.

"You been on all night?"

"Since eight."

"You see this guy?" He held up a picture.

"No. Who's that guy?"

"Somebody we're looking for as a material witness."

"I *knew* you guys were cops."

"You're good! Any other drivers or companies on tonight?"

"Just John."

"Can you call John?"

"He's doing a bar run."

"Call him, we'll wait."

∞§∞

The 2:20 AM pulled out of the station headed for New York without Dennis and Darrel. John, the other cab driver, hadn't returned to the station yet. Seemed his bar call was a businessman from up island, Port Washington, who was feeling no pain. He probably saved his own, as well as some other poor bastard's, life that night by calling a cab and not driving himself home.

It was 2:40 when John finally showed up.

"Yeah, this guy. He was in a real hurry. Said his battery died. He gave me a twenty for an eight dollar fare."

"Why would he do that?" Darrel asked.

"We made the station just as the train was about to pull out. I guess he didn't want to wait for his change."

"Where did you pick him up?"

The driver looked at his trip sheet. "115 Hedgerow. Off 25A."

"Take us there."

Along the way, Dennis woke up three members of his team. Stakeout was a word they hadn't heard in years.

Arriving at the address, Dennis got out of the cab, handed the driver a twenty, and asked him to wait a few minutes. The place seemed quiet as he scanned it for any signs of life. Even in the dark he could make out the distinctive lines of the old beat-up '67 Camaro. He approached it and opened the door, half expecting an alarm. In fact, the overhead dome didn't even light. He tried the headlights, nothing.

"Dead battery, all right." He hitched his head toward the ramshackle house. "I wonder if he prefers the French Country motif in his interior decorating?"

"Why don't you wait until they show this lovely home in *Architectural Digest?*" Darrel said. "Or get a warrant."

"You wouldn't want to go get a coffee right now would you, Officer Spoon?"

"So you could maybe do a little B&E while I was away?"

"Detectives don't 'break-in and enter,' Officer."

"In that case, cops don't drink coffee," Darrel said with an absurd grin. Dennis chuckled as he realized the irony of the situation. The good news was that having an active-duty cop at his side had gotten him this far. The bad news was that this cop could arrest *him* for snooping around someone else's private property. It really sucked not having a tin any longer.

He handed the cab driver another twenty and asked him to wait until either the guy came home or his men arrived. Dennis took three steps, snapped his fingers, and returned to the driver's side window. "Do you have a flashlight?"

Dennis walked back to the gray primer-painted Camaro. Smudges of red-orange body filler were the remains of a long-abandoned attempt to battle the rot.

Focusing the flashlight beam at the registration sticker, he jotted down the number. He then stepped onto the decaying porch. Using the flashlight, he peered through the window, scanning what appeared to be the kitchen ... and living room and bedroom of this one-room shack. It was obvious this "house" hadn't seen a woman's touch in decades, at least not any kind of woman like Cynthia. There were magazines and catalogues on the kitchen table and piles of dishes and aluminum foil TV dinner trays in the sink. A knapsack was on the coffee table in front of the couch, and Dennis thought he caught a glimpse of a scurrying mouse. The couch was ragged and worn and busted on the end, which was probably the spot where the beard always sat. Bingo! On the wall there was a document in a frame. He squinted but couldn't make it out. "Hey, Darrel, could you come up here for a moment?" Reluctantly, Darrel approached. "Can you read the writing in that frame on the wall?"

"Hold on," he said with a sigh that signaled *I can't believe I'm doing this!* Squinting his twenty-something eyes, he read, "Honorable discharge ... Corporal ... Thomas ... Robert ... Regan."

"That's my guy!"

"So, are we going to call the FBI?"

"It's late, let's let them sleep. I'll call one of my guys, Benton, to come get us in the morning. Besides, the feds are following their own leads. In fact, they just might drive up any second. You shouldn't be so anxious to see them anyway."

"Why not?

"Because, technically, you just violated a law."

"Why did I even *think* I liked you?"

"Come on, admit it, I have a winning personality."

"Okay, it's your show 'til 8 AM. Then I think we should call the feds."

"Thanks for joining in on this."

"Dennis, if your hunch is right and this guy is one of the terrorists, it's any cop's wet dream to nab the bastard."

By daybreak, Dennis and Darrel were heading back to Manhattan in Benton's car. Davis and another member of the team had taken a position 300 yards away from Regan's house in the opposite direction from which he was likely to return if he came from the station. Dennis and Darrel caught some shut-eye while Benton crawled through the early rush-hour buildup.

At 8:10 AM Dennis called Burrell but she was out of reach. Instead, he left a message with her subordinate, Agent Rauch. "We found Thomas Regan's house, here's the address ..."

After he hung up with Dennis, Rauch started looking through his case log. There was nothing about a Thomas Regan or anything about GlobalSync or Dennis Mallory. What he didn't know was that all of this was ordered held tight by the director and he was not in the loop. So he followed procedure until he could speak to Burrell, who was taking her yearly physical. He picked up the phone and called the FBI New York Operations Center.

They also followed a standard operating procedure when responding to the requests of agents for support, surveillance, or scheduling. In this instance, because the proximate field agents out of the Long Island office were all otherwise engaged, and due to the fact that Rauch didn't call this in as "arrest with all due haste," and because, as he understood the retired cop, this had something to do with a "favor" and was not connected to an ongoing case, the next surveillance team up on rotation was advised to take the job. That team, however, couldn't get to the location for three hours. As the book dictated, the local police force was called. They dispatched one of their radio cars to the location and instructed their officer to observe and report only until the FBI duly relieved him.

When the blue-and-white Wyandanch police cruiser pulled up, the officer driving spotted Davis's car parked up the hill. He drove up to the car and got out.

Resting his hand on the butt of his .38, he leaned toward the open driver's window. "Gentlemen, can I help you this morning?"

Davis flashed his Detective's Endowment Association retirement card. The cop was put off. He usually only saw a DEA card when he pulled over an ex-dick for speeding. It usually worked. After all, any cop who planned to live long enough to be retired figured he would need the same courtesy someday. So he always allowed the perk, hoping the gesture would be returned to him in about thirty-five years. But this was different. This was an FBI stakeout. No ex-cops could be allowed to interfere with that. "Sorry, you'll have to move."

"Did they tell you who we are sitting on, and why we are looking for him?"

"They mentioned him, and they mentioned the FBI, but they didn't mention you. So please go somewhere else, 'cause as of now, this is an active investigation scene."

"Look, we've got sixty-two years between us as cops. This is our guy. We found him."

"I respect that and all, but you are going to have to move. Sorry."

∞§∞

Tommy got a lift from the station and was dropped off at the Milk Barn on 25A, half a mile from his house. It was nine in the morning and he'd been up all night. It had certainly been worth it. He hadn't observed any change in the security at the tank farm facility. This made him very confident about tonight's mission. After selecting his groceries, milk, two microwavable bacon-and-egg burritos, and a six-pack of Coke, he threw down a fifty-dollar bill, more of the largess from his mailed-in proceeds, and exited, not waiting for change or a receipt.

Tommy was trudging up the hill behind his house when he spotted the cop car a block away. Although groggy, his sixth sense stopped him cold. For a few minutes, while his mind raced with scenarios, he saw no other activity, just a cop sitting in the car. *Am I being paranoid? How could anyone have found out about me?* He was sixteen hours away from his greatest personal triumph ... one that would make the Sperling bombing, with its eight dead and thousands displaced from toxic clouds, look like a footnote in the history of the great struggle. After toying with the idea of just walking home and playing the odds that this was a cop napping on the job, he erred on the side of safety. He eyed a gas can on the side of the old shed he was behind.

∞§∞

"Goddamn it!" was all that Dennis could manage when Davis reached him by phone to report that he was rousted from his perch by a local cop. Dennis immediately called Agent Burrell. This time she picked up her cell.

"Brooke, I told your guy my guys would wait for your team to show up. How come you sent in the locals?"

"Dennis, it wasn't me. All I can tell you is that it was a procedural snafu. But it's all academic now."

"Do I want to hear this?"

∞§∞

Dennis saw the fire equipment and hoses being loaded back onto fire trucks as he pulled up to Regan's house. A garage, or something, was totally burned to the ground two houses down from Regan's. Dennis knew exactly what happened. Regan got spooked by the blue-and-white unit and started the fire to distract the local cop. Regan then slipped in and out of the house. Interestingly enough, the Camaro was gone. As Dennis approached the FBI team, he was hoping they had already impounded it.

"No, we didn't," an angry Brooke Burrell, said. "It wasn't here when my team arrived. The tags came back registered to a woman in upstate New York, who's been dead for twenty-five years."

"So a fire just happens a hundred feet from a stake-out and somehow the subject has time to jump-start his car and leave without being noticed?"

A fire chief wearing a white hat passed them. He held a scorched gas can gingerly, using a branch stuck through its handle to avoid smearing any latent fin-gerprints. "My guess is we found the accelerant. It was lying at the point of origin." He continued over to his red GMC Suburban.

"Can I at least look inside?"

Brooke glared at him. "No ... but I can escort you."

Inside, Dennis immediately noticed something missing. "There was a backpack here on the table last night."

"I am not going to ask how you know that."

"For Christ's sake, Brooke, stop playing 'by the book' with me. Your pages got too many holes in 'em. And for your information, Lady Justice, all I did was look through the window with a flashlight."

"Sorry, Dennis. I don't want some lawyer throwing out evidence when we catch this guy."

An FBI agent in a mask and rubber gloves ap-proached them. He eyed Dennis and delayed speaking.

"It's okay, he's cleared."

"This guy was a science nut or something. We found receipts for gyroscopes, magnets, batteries, and the like."

"Agent Burrell, I think you should call in the bomb squad. Do a trace element check for explosives." Mallory realized he sounded like he was ordering her and hoped she didn't take it that way.

"Already called in. We've got his computer on the way to the Electronics Crime Lab. And we are getting prints, tire tread, and fiber samples. Washington is getting his military service and medical records from the Department of Defense and we're pulling pubic hairs off his soap for DNA samples."

"Pleasant thought, Brooke."

As they walked outside, Dennis spied an agent bending over with a pair of forceps and placing a small piece of paper into an evidence bag.

"May I see that?"

The agent deferred to Burrell and she nodded.

"Burger King, Vince Lombardi Rest Area, NJT. Dated today. 2:33 AM."

"Jersey?" Dennis turned around and faced the four plaster casts that were starting to set in the tire ruts where the Camaro had been sitting. "Our boy reached in his pocket for his keys and the last thing he put in fell out. The receipt!" Dennis then noticed a Quickstart battery jumper on the side of the driveway. A note found a few feet away read, "I'll pick it up tomorrow afternoon. Arnold."

"Let's be here when Arnold comes to get it."

"Already on it."

"I have to think this through. Brooke, can I come by your office later and see what more you have?"

"Sure. Sorry about the snafu."

"It didn't always go perfect for me either."

CHAPTER THIRTY-ONE
Observations

BACK AT THE GLOBALSYNC OFFICE, Dennis used the low-tech comfort of a blackboard and chalk to figure out if there was a pony somewhere in the pile of Thomas Regan's horseshit. The good news was that his protectee, Miles Taggert, had very little contact with, or reason to ever be in, New Jersey. Still, his team had the GlobalSync building and both of Taggert's residences locked down.

Since the empirical evidence pointed to the fact that Miles was not a likely target of this nut, Dennis was free to dabble in a little extra-credit thinking. He was, at the end of the day, still a cop, and Thomas Regan was a crime waiting to happen. He could no sooner drop this than walk away from the trail of an eight-point buck on a beautiful day.

His main question was how and why a man would board a train on Long Island, east of New York, and wind up, at 2:33 in the morning, west of the city in New Jersey ... at a rest area that can only be reached by car, no less. Why return to Long Island only to disappear? Why risk arson and boldly steal his own car right out from under the cops? He needed something desperately enough to risk capture ... what was there last night that wasn't there this morning? The backpack! He needed the backpack. Now it made sense. Forensics showed positive results for plastic explosive residue on the kitchen table and towels. "Suicide bomber?" he said out loud.

Scribbling the words "New Jersey Turnpike" in the center of the blackboard, he went over to the laminated write-on, wipe-off map he ordered to keep track of the various postmarked locations from which the threat letters were mailed. It now served to lay out the Tri-State area for Dennis and his extracurricular exercise of "Where's Tommy." He drew a red circle encompassing the maximum round-trip range at the barely legal speed of sixty-five miles per hour. Between the time he was spotted at Penn last night and his return to torch the garage this morning, had his car been in working order, Thomas could have reached any destination within that circle. He centered the timings around the 2:33 AM time stamp on the rest stop receipt. He made a mental note to get the FBI to pull all traffic summonses written last month in New Jersey for a Camaro or, God forbid it should happen the easy way, one Thomas Regan.

Dennis remembered all too well that the big break in the most heinous mass murder spree of all time in New York came not from some spectacular, police-show-styled shoot-out or car chase, but from some grunt cop—a blue uniform doing bench-warming work, sorting through thousands of parking tickets written around the times and places that the "Son of Sam" killed and killed again. It was a parking ticket, written to the mass murderer's VW Beetle on the night he shot two lovers necking in their car that led to his arrest in Yonkers. More often than not, police breakthroughs turned on the details.

Dennis drew a second circle on the map in green that limited the distance by fitting Regan's available time into the probable return schedule of the Long Island Railroad. It was a smaller circle subsuming 130 miles that embraced the Meadowlands Sports Complex, some radio transmission towers, the port of Newark, and the like. All of these potential targets were heavily protected and would not be severely damaged by a backpack full of explosives, especially since these places would be on high alert for Regan or any shoulder-bagged citizen. There were no apparent high-value targets that made sense. But when did a terrorist or madman ever make sense? There were thousands of lower-value or grudge-fuck targets that might be sacrificed to settle some imagined slight by a corporation or government.

Too many possibilities were like no possibilities at all. Dennis felt helpless. His eyes rested again on the center of the board. This rest area on the NJT kept coming back in focus. His hunter's sense told him this animal was hungry, risking exposure, coming out from his sheltered cover to feed. This is when "patient" hunters got their chance. His phone rang.

"I figured I should make it up to you," a familiar female voice said.

"I'm flattered."

"How about I treat you to a late-night snack, say somewhere on the Jersey Turnpike tonight?"

"Brooke, you know I'm a married man," Dennis said with a smile.

Brooke affected her best Southern-belle accent. "My word, Dennis, can't a girl ask a father figure out for a bite to eat without being accused of being a harlot? Besides, the EI boys came up with a match. I'll tell you all about it on the drive out."

"What's a father figure to say, except, 'Your car or mine?'"

"Mine. I got all the radios and shotguns and stuff."

"Sounds delightful."

"I'll pick you up tonight at eleven?"

"Thanks for including me."

"You've earned it."

∞§∞

It was a beautiful, cloudless night as they exited the tunnel with all of Jersey laid out before them. Little Miss "by-the-book" Brooke took a deep breath and a career-busting chance. Against the orders of her director, she blurted out, "Sabot!"

"The frankfurter?"

"No, that's Sabrett. I'm talking about the Sabot Society. They're against the industrial age."

"A little late, aren't they?"

"We've been monitoring their e-mails. There's a person on the list whose address matches the one registered to Thomas Regan's Camaro."

"You mean the upstate New York woman, Williams?"

"You're good!"

"Hey, I was running plates while you were having tea parties with your dollies."

"Williams was her second husband's name ..."

Dennis snapped his fingers, "Regan was her first! So that's why we couldn't find him. He was hiding behind Mommy's apron."

∞§∞

The constant, unrelenting swoosh of New Jersey Turnpike traffic and the whine of big truck tires greeted them as they opened the car doors at the rest area at about 1 AM. Brooke checked all the tables.

Dennis went straight to the girl at the register.

"Hi. Were you working here last night?"

"Yes. Why?"

"Did you see this man?"

"Yes, he's here a lot lately. Must have a route that takes him through here."

"Route?"

"Yeah, isn't he a truck driver?"

"Ever see him in a truck?"

"No."

Dennis smiled to keep her talking. "About what time usually?"

"Around now. In fact, I saw him already tonight. About two minutes before you came in."

Dennis quickly scanned the restaurant as Brooke came over to him. "He was here in the last two minutes. I'll check the lot. You check here and the rest rooms."

Dennis rushed outside and surveyed the cars in the lot. There, near the road, was the old, beat-up Camaro. The retired detective approached it cautiously. In the darkness, he could not tell if anyone was inside so he did what any guy would do. Walking about ten feet beyond the asphalt into the grass, he made a motion that made it appear he was unzipping his fly and assumed the universal stance of a man relieving himself. He counted to fifteen, faked a shake, then zipped up. As he turned, he looked casually into the car. The lights from the turnpike lit the interior from that angle. No one was inside. Peering through the windows, he checked the front and backseats but saw nothing except a mess. He walked back to the restaurant.

Brooke met him halfway. "You could've killed two birds with one stone if you had checked the men's room," she said, nodding to the grass area.

"That's his car. Hood's still warm."

"I'll call this in. Get some Jersey troopers to canvas."

Dennis went back inside to the girl at the register. "Did you ever see him with anyone?"

"No, not that I remember."

"Thank you."

He rejoined Brooke outside. "How about we hang around for a while and see what happens?"

"Fine with me. I'll bring the car over and we'll go on our first stakeout together."

"And you thought this wouldn't be fun!"

In the car, Dennis squinted to keep a lookout for any suspicious car or person who came and went. Brooke reached around behind her and handed him a set of binoculars. "Here, use these."

He brought them to his eyes, focused, and panned the area. "I just got a feeling about this guy and it tells me sooner rather than later."

Through the binoculars, he was able to watch the Camaro, the approach to it, and any slow-moving vehicles passing by it. In the binocular's field of view, trucks zipped back and forth at a dizzying rate. Big stainless steel tankers reflected the light from the rest area right back at him, like a mirror. It took a few seconds for his eyes to adjust to the darkness after each one.

Then he caught sight of a figure near the pedestrian walkway that spanned the turnpike. The man was wearing a backpack and was starting up the stairs on the near side. He stopped at a landing midway. Dennis tried to look closely, but another truck's reflection obliterated the view.

The figure on the stairs took off the backpack. As he turned to do so, Dennis saw the outline of … "A beard! I got a man on the stairs over there with a beard!"

∞§∞

In the middle of the staircase landing, Tommy reached into the backpack and turned on the gyroscope. The package suddenly had a mind of its own, as the minute jostling of it was resisted by the gyroscopic action. He held it like a basketball at the foul line.

∞§∞

Dennis caught a glimpse of the man holding the pack out in front of him, pumping it as if he was going to throw it, as yet another stainless steel truck washed his vision white. Then it hit him.

"Magnets!"

He followed the truck as it entered a large storage tank facility not far down the road. He whipped the binoculars back to the stairs, just in time to see Tommy throw the backpack out over a passing steel tanker. The truck was slowing down in the lane closest to the stairs to take the exit. Dennis watched curiously as the backpack flew perfectly flat—not tumbling or tilting as he would've expected. It landed solidly on the top of the tank trailer. The bag clamped down magnetically onto the steel tank, as if it were covered with Velcro.

"It's a bomb! On that truck." Dennis pointed to the truck turning into the plant. "You get the beard. I'll take the car and warn the plant."

Brooke reached into the backseat, grabbing her shotgun. She ran toward the walkway. Dennis slid over and hit the gas, swerving out of the rest area and right onto the turnoff to the storage tank facility.

He screeched to a halt in front of the barrier by the security gate, yelling to the guard in his shack, "That truck has a bomb! Let me in. Call the cops!"

The guard, making an instant decision that Dennis was one of the good guys, raised the barrier and picked up the phone. Dennis drove over to the portico just as the truck pulled out and headed for the large storage tanks. Dennis raced ahead and cut the truck off.

The driver came down from the cab cursing. "What the hell's the matter with you? Are you crazy?"

"There's a bomb on top."

After a second, the word bomb registered in the driver's mind. He ran. Dennis looked up at the truck and the huge tanks it was now nestled between. What he said next was between him and God. He jumped onto the ladder and climbed to the top of the truck. He slipped, but caught himself as he cautiously stepped across, past the filler hatches in the recessed gully at the top of the truck's tank. When he reached the backpack, he got on his knees and inspected it. It was humming. He hummed along with it in an attempt to steady his nerves. Reaching for the zipper, he stopped his hand, thinking, "booby trap."

His humming turned into "Don't Sit under the Apple Tree," Cynthia's favorite song.

"I love you, girl," escaped his lips as he meticulously inched the zipper back, revealing the contents of the blue nylon-parachute-material bag.

∞§∞

Agent Burrell walked with the shotgun behind her back as she came upon Tom Regan stepping lively from the overpass, not paying any attention to her, hurrying toward his car. As he passed her, she raised the gun and pumped it ... loud. The sound made Tom stop dead in his tracks.

"Freeze, FBI! Put your hands up above your head and drop to your knees," Brooke said in her calmest command voice. "Drop to your knees, NOW!"

She saw that Regan was hesitating. She understood the confusion in his mind. *Could he beat a woman? Surely she couldn't be as tough as a man. He might have a chance.* If that's what he was thinking, it didn't last long, as Brooke slammed the butt of the shotgun into his back with so much force that it drove him into the ground. She flipped the shotgun over like a baton and pushed it into his cheekbone as he lay sprawled, her foot on his neck. "Move and I will blow your face off! Was that a bomb you put on the truck?"

"Go fuck yourself," Regan managed with the shotgun in his bearded cheek.

She pulled out her service weapon and placed it on his leg. "Last chance. Is that a bomb on the truck?"

"Fuck you!"

She fired her piece, the bullet entering his leg right above the knee. He screamed out in pain.

"The next one shoots your balls off, tough guy."

She placed the gun at the seat of his pants. "Tell me what I want to know or kiss your balls good-bye,

Tommy boy." She pushed the barrel deep into his buttocks to accentuate her point.

Through his moaning, he managed to say, "Yes, yes it's a bomb."

"How is it triggered?"

He hesitated. She nudged his ass again. "It's going to be terrible up there in heaven with seventy-two virgins and you with no balls, buddy, unless you tell me how the bomb is triggered."

"I am not a terrorist!"

"Last chance. How is it triggered?"

"Okay, okay! It's a contact timer, once it makes contact it's set for five minutes."

"Shit." She slapped cuffs on him, then looked up and realized a small crowd had surrounded her. She picked the meanest-looking truck driver in the crowd and flashed her FBI ID. "You! I'm an FBI agent. Make sure he doesn't move 'til the troopers get here. I need a car! Somebody give me a car." No one stepped forward. She saw a man watching from a Lexus. She grabbed the shotgun and her piece and ran. She held up her ID. "FBI. I am commandeering your car." The driver saw the ID in the same hand as the shotgun and got out. She jumped in, throwing the shotgun and her piece in the front seat. She took off for the plant, not the least bit phased by the gun oil from the Remington pump action soaking into the leather seat.

∞§∞

Looking into the bag with its gizmos and colorful leads, Dennis realized he didn't know which wires to pull or short out. He'd hesitated long enough. Disarming the bomb was not an option. It was time to remove the bag. He pulled on the bag, but it didn't budge. He put more muscle into it. It slid along a little but he couldn't move it up off the metal of the tanker truck. The magnets were that strong. He scrambled back down the ladder and got into the cab of the truck, a new goal in mind. The guard ran up.

"Do you know how to drive one of these?" Dennis yelled down from the cab.

"No."

"Ahhhh, shit!" Dennis looked down at the eighteen gears and tried to find first. When he ground the gears into something like first then let up on the clutch, the truck lurched forward. Turning the wheel as the engine over-revved, he headed for open space.

∞§∞

Back at the front gate, Brooke pulled up to the guard, "Take cover. That truck's going to blow!" She then peeled out to warn Dennis. The truck was already a half-mile away in an area where old oil drums were warehoused.

As she headed toward it, a silent flash burned her eyes as it split the night. An instant later, the earsplitting noise and shock wave slammed into the car. Reflexively, she hit the brakes and fell sideways as the windshield imploded, showering her with tempered safety glass like a cascade of diamonds. The heat of the blast poured through the open window and singed her hair and eyebrows. Suddenly big thuds started pounding all around her as the roof of the car dented in above her. A smoking fifty-five-gallon drum landed on the hood. Two more pelted the car. She covered her head and prayed.

CHAPTER THIRTY-TWO
UNPAYABLE DEBTS

A FULL SIXTY HOURS before the Sabot Society meeting, agents started arriving at McConnell Air Force Base. The bureau had left no aspect to chance. Most of the agents assembled at the base twenty-five miles from Bufford's farm had rotated through at least two tours at Quantico, the FBI's training academy.

Operation Homegrown had drawn a full FBI turnout. The HRT (Hostage Rescue Team) was here, as were the bureau's head negotiators, SWAT teams, hi-tech weapons and surveillance technicians, the EI teams, air support and logistics, headquarters personnel, armored personnel carriers, medical and psych attachment, including drivers for the trucks and assault vehicles. To fill those support positions, the FBI would usually tap local law enforcement, but the director had been clear—bureau only. He wanted this operation contained until the moment SWAT "knocked" on the door with the battering ram.

∞§∞

In the morning light, the twisted, mangled wreckage was barely discernible as a tanker truck. News helicopters circled above, bringing the mutilated image to their national audiences as they awoke. The New Jersey Turnpike was closed for two exits around the plant, making that morning's rush hour a slowly moving parking lot. The rest area was jammed with emergency support vehicles and news crews using long lenses to pull in the sobering pictures from almost a mile away.

Bill Hiccock had fallen asleep just after midnight, having flown back late to D.C. He was awakened at 3 AM by a call from Joey Palumbo to tell him of the thwarted attack. At 8:30 AM, he, Tate, and Palumbo briefed the president and Reynolds.

"Sir," Hiccock said, "what we know right now is that the attack was to be carried out by Thomas Regan, against American Cyanamid at their chlorine processing station, up there in New Jersey. There was enough chlorine gas in those tanks to form a cloud twenty miles wide. The EPA estimates that with the prevailing winds last night, the cloud would have made its way to New York City within three hours of the blast. Five to seven million people would have been instantly gassed, most dying in their beds. The CDC adds another three million dead by week's end from the lesser doses that would be inhaled as the cloud dissipated." Hiccock closed his briefing book.

"My God! It would have been like a nuclear attack. How was it foiled?"

Tate continued the report. "An agent out of the New York office was following up on a lead when the perpetrator was observed planting the bomb on a tanker truck. She and a retired NYPD detective gave chase. The detective died diverting the truck away from the storage tanks."

"A retired detective?" the president said in amazement.

"Yes, Sir," Agent Palumbo said. "I was alerted that this detective was working for the CEO of a private company. The perpetrator was believed to have threatened the detective's client. At the time of the blast, he was following him as a suspected stalker."

"Wait, then why was the FBI involved?" the president asked.

Joey was thrown a little. "Sir, there was a slim chance that what the detective had stumbled onto was

Homegrown connected, but I made the call to offer him some low-level assistance."

"Well, you had the right instincts."

"Actually, it wasn't until right before the explosion that he or our agent Brooke Burrell knew of Regan's true intention."

"That detective saved millions of lives and this country from a disaster of unprecedented proportions," Hiccock said.

"Was he married?" President Mitchell asked.

"Yes, Sir."

"I want to talk to the wife as soon as she is up for it." He then jotted something down on his notepad. Everyone waited until he was finished, then he zeroed in on the director. "So, is the bastard who attempted this another homegrown?"

"It appears he is a member of the Sabot Society," Tate said. "We are checking that now. His computer and profile are being inspected."

What's the Sabot Society? Hiccock wondered. He was about to ask aloud when Mitchell nodded and turned to his chief of staff. "Okay, Ray, you get all the facts and have it written up. I'll address the nation at 11 AM."

Everyone in the room assumed that this was the end of the briefing and started to leave. The president then called out, "What was his name? The cop. What was the man's name?"

"Mallory, Sir. Dennis Mallory."

∞§∞

"Ya got a minute?" Hiccock grabbed Joey's arm and hustled him into an empty White House office before he could answer.

Joey pried Bill's hand from his arm. "What's this all about?"

"I should kick your ass, pal-o-mine."

"Why you gonna do that?"

"Thanks for telling me about Operation Home-grown, you hard-on."

There was a noticeable change in the color of Joey's face. Hiccock knew he had hit a nerve. Bill pounded his finger into Joey's chest to accentuate every word of his next sentence. "Share, you said, remember?" Hiccock then held up his hand, mocking the secret gesture from one Blade to another. "Ah, bullshit," he muttered and stepped away.

Joey's mind raced. "Okay, let's share. Community colleges aren't that bad."

"Huh?"

"Nothing. Jeez, are you hungry? Let's grab some eggs."

Down in the White House mess, Joey and Bill sat over scrambled eggs and bacon. The FBI agent looked around. Hiccock could see that there was no one but food service people in the room and they were thirty feet away.

"It's called Operation Homegrown," Joey said. "It's classified. The Homegrown Op is about to make a big play for the controlling council of the Sabot Society."

"Sabot Society? I just heard Tate use that name in the briefing."

"As near as we can tell, they are an anti-technology terrorist group that has been behind all these attacks."

"You have proof of this?"

"Enough to ruin the party they're planning."

Hiccock was now dealing with a whole new set of circumstances. If this group were the bad guys, the search was over. He sat staring at a point on the wall for a minute, as the full ramifications sank in. Out of the twenty or so questions that immediately formed in his mind, the one that escaped his lips was, "Sabot? It's a little obvious, don't you think?"

"How so?"

"When the industrial revolution came to the Netherlands, it threatened to put many factory workers out on the street. One machine could now do the work of ten, twenty men. So the workers in Holland would jam the machinery and destroy it by sticking their wooden shoes in the gears and cogs. Those wooden shoes were called sabots. That's where the term *sabotage* comes from. They sabotaged the technology of their day."

"Well, our modern day shoeless creeps are the ones behind all this. They're web-based and have been in existence for at least seven years that we know of ... how do you know all this crap about the Netherlands, anyway?"

"That's one my dad told me."

"How is the old IRT driver?"

"Doing great. He and my mom moved up to Roscoe. Pop gets his minimum adult daily requirement of trout fishing and my mother's happy he's not bitching."

"I remember when we used to cram into his motorman's cab and look down the track. That was cool. Hey, you know what I still think about? When your dad drove the number four train and he would let us stay at the 161st Street–River Avenue station."

"How many Yankee games did we watch for free from that supply shed at the end of the platform?"

"Yeah, two bottles of Coke and the transistor radio and we were in heaven."

"Dad retired from the MTA back in the mid-nineties. I'll tell him you were asking."

They both paused as the memories of hot summer afternoons in that tin shed, looking out the open door onto the emerald-green field of the house that Babe built, faded off into a smoky mist.

"You know, Joey, you're just doing your job. I mean whatever shitty thing that egomaniacal boss of yours has you doing to me or against me, I know it's your job. I don't take it personally."

Joey looked Hiccock in the eye. "Clean start from today forward.

When this is over, I want you to come out to the coast and meet Phyl and little Joe ... spend some time. Maybe go fishing or catch a few ball games."

"Yeah, that would be nice, when all this is over."

Joey lifted his glass of orange juice, "To this being over."

Bill raised his coffee cup and clinked. "To this being over." He took a sip and put down the cup. "How can you be sure that these guys tonight are *the guys?*"

"We got them, dead to rights, front-to-back on the Sperling Chemical explosion. And we got the guy in last night's Jersey blast chatting with them. "

"Won't nabbing him spook your play for the whole society?"

"We let it out that the bomber died on the truck. His cohorts will think he was vaporized, and, along with him, any connection to them."

Hiccock nodded to the logic of this but something else rippled his brow. "Sperling is in the same kind of high-tech support business that Mason Chemical is in, so I can see the connection. But that yo-yo tried to blow up American Cyanamid. From what I know of them, they seem too low-tech ... but maybe." Bill took a sip of his coffee. "So are you saying the Sabot are the ones doing the subliminal work?"

"To be honest, I don't know if we *have* connected it that far. But the web is their principal means of organization. It would seem logical."

"So who's the brains of this outfit?"

"We've been on the ass of Bernard Keyes, a postal employee from the Midwest."

"Postal employee ... disgruntled, I'm sure."

"Enough jokes about that. This guy is real and he is the center of the ring."

"But, Joey, one thing: what we found is a level of code-writing so sophisticated that it had your FBI

geniuses and my cyber asshole stumped for days.
You're telling me a mailman wrote it?"

"He talks to his Sabots on the web. Maybe he also
recruited that particular talent there. Hey, we busted
a busboy in Brooklyn a few years back that got into the
accounts and files of people on the *Forbes* "100 Richest Americans" list. A fucking busboy! He was a high
school dropout and foreign national, as I remember.
Computers are truly the great equalizer."

"Yeah, now any idiot can be a crook."

"Or terrorist."

"Or, apparently, an FBI agent. So what, if anything, will you need from me?" Hiccock said cautiously.

"When we take these guys down, we'll need to use
everything you've learned as evidence."

"You know what this means, don't you?"

"What?"

"I owe your boss an apology."

"Tate? Why?"

"He was right all along. It was a known group. This
isn't going to be pleasant for me, you know."

"Listen, let's just be glad it's over, okay?"

"Yeah, I guess you're right." Hiccock tried to take a
sip from an empty cup.

∞§∞

Cynthia Mallory long ago resigned herself to the
uncertainty hanging over each day of being a cop's wife.
All of that mercifully ended when Dennis retired. Since
then, the one thing that never occurred to Cynthia was
that she would survive him. She was the afflicted one.
She was supposed to be the one who had the uncertain
future. The irony was not lost on her that the very bargain Dennis made to save her life ended his.

The fact that Dennis Liam Mallory was a hero was
not news to her. Now that the rest of the world knew it

as well changed nothing about her grief. She declined the media's requests for interviews.

Cynthia did, however, accept a call from the President of the United States. He was very nice and informed her that he was fast-tracking approval of the Presidential Medal of Freedom for uncommon valor and sacrifice in service to America for her husband. He told her that the nation owed her husband a debt that could never be repaid. In the same breath, he also vowed that she, her children, and grandchildren would never want or need anything ever again. It was a small price to pay, he said, for the continuance of the ten million lives her husband saved with one selfless act of courage.

Her daughter made a simple concise statement to the press. "The Mallory family wishes to thank all those who have expressed support and prayers for us during our time of grief. We plan a private family memorial." Here's where she choked up a little. "And we request that in lieu of flowers, contributions be made to the National Institute for Neurologic Disorders and Stroke in my father's name." Looking up to the heavens she took a deep breath then spoke, "Daddy, you always were—and always will be—a hero to us all." She steeled herself and, quelling the quivering of her bottom lip, dry swallowed then added, thank you and God bless America."

Miles Taggert, shaken by the death of Dennis, did more than send a check to the NINDS. He endowed The Dennis Mallory Neurologic Disorders and Stroke Pavilion at NYU Hospital, fueling it with enough of his fortune to ensure that it would perpetually be the epicenter of the latest technology, techniques, and treatments for the disease that almost claimed Mrs. Mallory. A second grant, more quietly created, was the Dennis and Cynthia Mallory Endowment, which provided economic support for the families of police, firefighters, and other first responders to afford treatment at the facility.

Agent Brooke Burrell's initiative in "interrogating" the prisoner by perforating his leg on the asphalt that night amounted to little more than a cautious footnote on "public discharge of a weapon" on her bureau commendation of service. At age twenty-eight, she was elevated in rank to Assistant Special Agent in Charge–New York office. She visited with the widow Mallory and found closure for herself and a genuine affection for Cynthia.

After extensive "legal" interrogation, Tom Regan could only tell the feds what they already knew: he was nuts and he chatted with other nuts online. His computer's hard drive confirmed that he was well ensconced in the Sabot chain of communications.

The noose was tightening on Sabot.

CHAPTER THIRTY-THREE
DOGS IN HEAVEN

"WHEN CAN I GET A DRINK?" Janice said, smiling at the attendant.

"Soon as we are airborne, Ma'am."

Janice had taken the seat up front in the little Air Force jet that she and the Admiral and Kronos, who were already asleep in the rear, were suddenly ordered to take back to Washington, D.C., without warning. She was amazed how fast the plane went from the passenger terminal into the air, as if it just jumped into the heavens the second the door was closed. This proved what she always thought about commercial air flight—they just made you wait because they could.

Her Campari and soda smoothed over the cracks in her parched throat. She considered opening the folder holding the psych analysis of two more perpetrators, but thought better of it. Instead, she flipped off the overhead light, hit the seat button, and pushed back as the jet climbed through the clouds almost vertically.

As the scene outside her window flickered from the last remaining layer of cloud to what at first looked like cotton as far as the eye could see, she thought of her mom. What would she say if she saw her now? Here she was, a whole jet at her disposal, doing important lifesaving work, answering the call of her country when her country needed her most. Eunice Tyler would probably find something wrong. Some small detail Janice had overlooked. Anything from the shoes she chose to go with her outfit to the shade of her mascara to just the sheer extravagance of the whole situation. *"But Mom, I need to get there to do my job for the nation. You want me to fly standby because it's cheaper?"* She had noticed in the past that every negative-thought voice in her head sounded like her mother.

The fact that Janice and her mother didn't get along was no secret. The reason, however, was a little harder to discern, even though her college and professional associates were convinced it was due to a rift arising from her parents' divorce. They made that prognosis during the self-analysis and group critiquing that was the first and most basic training psych majors underwent on their way to their doctorates. But what she never shared, because she herself was only recently made aware of it, was the true reason.

"Mr. Biffles" was a silly name for a dog, but that's what little eight-year-old Janice Tyler wanted to call this raggedy Scottish terrier her father got her for her birthday. Mr. Biffles soon became the first object of love in little Janice's life. He slept at the foot of her bed, waited for her to come home from school, cried when she cried, even ate when she ate. Sometimes, to her mom's consternation, from her plate. Mr. Biffles was her doll, her baby, and her best friend.

One day Mr. Biffles's leash broke. Her mother, never one to waste a cent, decided that there was no reason to *spend perfectly good money* on a new leash. She simply took a twist tie from the box of garbage bags and attached the leash to the collar with it. Out the door went Mr. Biffles and Janice for his afternoon walk. A block from the house, a Labrador retriever was strutting down the street on the long leash of its owner. Mr. Biffles caught sight of the Lab and started barking and pulling at the leash. "No, Mr. Biffles, stay," was reinforced by the usual sharp tug on the leash. Only this time the flimsy wire tie broke. Mr. Biffles, sensing freedom from the restraint, bolted across the street, right into the path of an oncoming car. The yelp the little dog made as he was run over echoed in her ears. She could still hear it. On that afternoon, little Janice Tyler learned two terrible lessons from life. They were indelibly etched in her psyche and would take years to correct. The first: if you love something it will die and go away, so never admit that you love anything. The second: being *frugal* sucks!

The next major developmental step on the way to becoming a psychologist came when she was sixteen and her father gave her, against her mother's wishes, her first phone. It was a pink princess phone. While the phones of that day were big, bulky, and usually black, the princess was a cute oval design with the handset spanning an illuminated dial in the middle. It was *the* girl's phone. Her mother's fears were realized as Janice spent hours on it with her girlfriends. *Talking god knows what*, her mother would complain. What Eunice Tyler could never have fathomed, however, were the many nights and afternoons Janice spent with her friends on the phone as she first listened, then dispensed advice. Through these first "sessions" she discovered a natural gift for understanding the human condition.

When she was nineteen, Jimmy Shea was her crush, her love, and her boyfriend. Janice also became enamored with Jim's mother. She was a psychiatrist. In the Midwestern town where Janice grew up, it was rare for a woman to be a professional. And she was divorced! There was a television show back then called *One Day at a Time*. To the media mongers in New York and L.A., it was a timely situation comedy about a single divorced woman wrestling with her career and kids. In Janice's hometown, seemingly locked in the fifties, it was pure science fiction.

Being a doctor meant Mrs. Shea made a good income. Jim had a nice car, and their house was three times bigger than Janice's. Young Janice also noticed and admired Jim's mom's confidence and that she never quibbled over anything as trivial as money.

When Jim broke up with her, Janice was devastated. Sadly, the girl who had helped all her friends solve their emotional dilemmas really had nowhere to turn when her own love life came crashing down around her ankle bracelet. Oddly enough it was Jim's mother who talked her through it. Her wise advice and explanations of what Janice was going through taught her that being a psychiatrist was a good thing; you really could help people and psychiatrists made a ton of money. Enough money to never have to be frugal, stingy, or just plain cheap. With Mrs. Shea's help, Janice had found her path.

As the whine of the engines lulled her to sleep, forty-five-year-old Janice Tyler, now the lead psychological investigator into the worst terrorist attack America had ever suffered, drifted off to sleep. Her last conscious thoughts were of Mr. Biffles and how he would tenaciously clamp his teeth into his tug toy and never relent, even if you picked him straight up in the air with it. Actually, she realized, that must have been the part he loved most—going straight up.

∞§∞

Hiccock learned that the U.S. Air Force plane rides, which he had ordered up like taxicabs, cost $18,000 for each coast-to-coast flight. At least in this particular case, he thought that Uncle Sam's money was well spent. The message he planned to deliver to his team required more than a phone call. He had them flown "ultra class" to Washington from their temporary base at Admiral Parks's home.

In the cold, featureless gray of the FBI's Electronic Crime Lab, Hiccock peered into their faces trying to convince himself that what he was about to say was the best possible scenario. "I can't divulge all the details at this time but I need to tell you our investigation is over." As Hiccock expected, Tyler, Kronos, and the Admiral were mildly shocked by the news, but he noticed Hansen was not.

"Hansen, did you know about this?"

"I got the word twenty minutes ago that your subliminal machine is to be disconnected and moved to Datacom Systems."

"What's Datacom?"

"They are one of our subcontractors. Once an investigative phase is over, we farm out any special equipment that has evidentiary value to them. They are bonded and continue the chain of evidence during the trial phase."

"I see. That way your FBI lab doesn't get overrun with Justice Department lawyers looking for every angle."

"Exactly. And don't forget the defense attorneys. They bring in the proctoscopes."

Hiccock looked around. "Well, people, the only thing I can tell you is that we will all know in less than twenty-four hours. I want to thank each of you. You've been so great to work with and I'm sure what we have discovered in this project will go a long way in convicting the guilty."

"Yo, thanks, Hiccock. It was a real trip working with you, too."

"Same here, Kronos, a *real* trip."

"Back into the Washington regimen now, Bill?" Henrietta asked.

"Admiral, I don't know. I think I made a few enemies here and without the head of the bad guy hanging off my belt, I am going to be walking a very tight rope."

"Well, Bill, I think you are a well-balanced individual," Tyler said, trying to lighten the mood. "You'll be fine."

"Thanks, Janice. So here's the way it will go from here. We will all be staying in Washington to prepare our final report. That should take about three weeks. Then you'll be able to get back to your lives."

"That's great, I get to go back to the big El," Kronos said sarcastically. "Can't you put in a good word for me?"

"I'll see if I can get Reynolds to call the warden at Elmira ... see what they might work out. I guess we'll move into my offices at the White House. I figure we'll leave for there in about a half hour."

With that, the Admiral headed for the ladies' room. Kronos walked off with Hansen. Left alone, Hiccock's eyes met Janice's. "I'm sorry I took you away from your patients."

"Not at all. I redefined a rare branch of behavioral study ... 'bi-stable concurrent schizophrenia.' That should be good for a couple of papers, maybe even some grants ... hell, a book deal!"

"Once the trial is over," Hiccock added, finger pointed in the air, reminding her of the national security implications of their work.

"Once the trial is over. Yes."

An awkward moment passed between them. Odd, Hiccock thought, for two people who were married to have an uneasy moment. Out of impulse, he put his arms around her and gave her a hug. She hugged back. Hiccock took a deep breath. Her hair smelled great and she felt good in his arms. "I could never have made it this far without you. I just want you to know I really appreciate your working for me as graciously and as professionally as you have."

Janice pushed back slightly from Hiccock's embrace to make eye contact. "No less than you did for me, even though I was too self-absorbed and focused on my research to say 'thank you' back then."

"We are still a pretty good team, aren't we?" Hiccock smoothed her hair back the way he always did.

"Yeah. If we could only be this good in our personal lives."

"I thought ..."

Janice put her finger over his lips. "Don't ruin this little feel-good session, okay, boss?"

"Okay, former boss."

∞§∞

Shit. Joey Palumbo hated what he had just heard, but not as much as the smug look on his boss's face. "He said his father told him that old shoe story."

"Then the pattern fits. I knew that science twerp was working another agenda."

"With all due respect, Sir, we don't know his motives for sure."

"You're his friend, so I'll allow that. But I am telling you this man has done everything to obstruct this investigation from the highest point."

"It's just not like Billy, Sir."

"Did you know his father was a terrorist?"

"Union shop steward, Sir."

"He destroyed a subway!"

"Did we pull the case jacket on that?"

"Pull your dick for all I care, Joe. Hiccock's father is dirty, Hiccock is dirty, and they are both going down!"

Joey tried to calm his own emotions by looking to the next step. "Have you told the president?"

"No, that will be your job."

"Me? No way!"

"You're an agent and that's a direct order from your director."

"Why?"

"Listen, Joe. You met with him. You were running him for the bureau. Whatever he knew came from you."

"He got nothing from me, in spite of our deal."

"Your own report states that he had knowledge of Homegrown. There is nobody else in his group affiliated with the FBI. We held that tighter than a Scot holds a fifty."

"But all my contact with him was your idea! I carried out your stupid, back-channel plan because you, my director, ordered me to." Joey decided not to point out the fact that Hiccock's group spent time in the FBI crime lab with Hansen and the tech boys. It would seem like he was passing the buck to Hansen. Besides, he knew the director was well aware of Hansen, but was tightening the screw on him for some reason.

"That's not the way this is going to go, Joe, so let's be clear. You finger Hiccock in front of the president and your record and career soar. You hesitate and I'll have reason to suspect that I made a big mistake by allowing you to monitor a suspect's progress."

"When was he ever a suspect?"

"Whenever I say he was."

"That's not just hardball, that's hard-assed ball."

"The only way I know how to play, Joe. The country is reeling from these terrorist attacks and the president's handpicked private eye, and your old buddy, turns out to be the son of a founding member of the Sabot Society. You telling the president will balance the scales."

"Why do you hate Billy so much?"

"He defamed the bureau."

"So now we are defaming him?"

∞§∞

"You want to start?" Reynolds said.

"This is Special Agent in Charge of my San Francisco office, Joseph Palumbo."

"Yes, I remember meeting Agent Palumbo the other day."

"He will report to you what we know. Joe?"

"Good morning. Sir, first I will read from the New York *Daily News* July 19, 1963. Under the headline 'Shuttle Burns, Street Opened to Retrieve,' there is this picture of a badly burned subway car being lifted onto

42nd Street by a crane through a hastily cut hole in the pavement. The top of the article reads, 'The end of the line for the automated shuttle was reached yesterday when a fire burned under 42nd Street. The computer-controlled train was still in its testing stages. The TA was set to decide on regular service by year's end. TA officials have not been able to determine the cause of the fire as of press time. Transit Workers Union spokesperson, Harry Hiccock, proclaimed, "This was just God's way of saying that he didn't invent trains to run themselves." Mayor Wagner said, "The fire was unfortunate," but stopped short of weighing in on the controversial train saying, "The TA has to determine whether they should continue research on automated trains." The TA estimates it would save $150,000 in labor cost per year as soon as the new shuttle trains went into full operation.

Interestingly enough, union shop steward Harry Hiccock is one of the shuttle motormen who would be replaced by the new computerized train. The Grand Central–Times Square shuttle has only two stops and no other traffic uses those rails. TA officials felt it was the best place to test the feasibility of the Automated Trains,' etc. etc."

Joe put down the old yellowed newsprint and picked up a ragged-edged oak tag file folder with a frayed blue string binding it. "The following police report was filed one week later. It reads, 'Pursuant to investigation of Subway Fire, leading suspects, D'angelo, Hiccock, and Mercer seem to have alibis. NYFD indicates fire could have been set to ignite remotely. Therefore alibis are of little use in this case.'"

"Next time send me a briefing paper, 'cause I don't know where this is going, Tate," Reynolds said.

"I didn't think you would want this on paper, Ray. That NYPD report mentions a possible accomplice to Harry Hiccock, Bernard Mercer. We checked the fingerprints; Bernard Keyes was then the 19-year-old Bernard Mercer. He changed his name in the seventies."

"That's your Sabot guy?"

"And Harry Hiccock is William Hiccock's father."

"Oh, no."

"Thought you'd want to hear it first, Ray."

"How many people know?"

"Just this room."

"Why are you here, Agent Palumbo?"

"Ray, Joe grew up with Hiccock in New York. I have used his relationship with Hiccock to keep tabs on his rogue investigation."

"Oh yes, I remember him saying you strong-armed an old friend to plead for information." Reynolds didn't know why he said it that way, but he guessed until proven guilty, Hiccock was still on his team and Tate was enjoying this a little too much. He turned toward Palumbo. "And you think Hiccock was deliberately obstructing this federal investigation?"

"The facts seem to suggest a possible link between Bernard Keyes, founder of the Sabot Society, and Harry, Bill's father ..."

"Yes, I am aware what the facts suggest Agent Palumbo, but I am asking what you think, Agent Palumbo."

Palumbo took in a short breath and then let go. "I think it's a pile of horseshit, Sir. I knew Billy's dad. He wouldn't park illegally even if it meant he had to walk ten blocks. And Billy is a straight arrow, always has been." Joey deliberately did not make eye contact with Tate. Reynolds took it all in.

"You know that on the basis of what you just reported to me, Hiccock is finished. It doesn't matter if he is a straight or crooked arrow. At this level, even the appearance of impropriety is as bad as having done the deed."

"Ray, Hiccock never divulged anything about his father before," Tate said. "He had the president looking at psychedelic web sites instead of following the guidance of his own Justice Department."

"Sir, we didn't divulge anything about Sabot to him. And again, I point out, we are *assuming* he is a member of Sabot."

"What about that, Tate? Have there been any EI intercepts linking Hiccock to Sabot?"

"Not yet."

"I will inform the president. When are you making the Sabot arrests?"

"At zero dark hundred hours, tonight," Palumbo said.

"Then it's all moot. When the Sabot Society is neutralized, the threat to America will end. Then if your investigation turns up anything about Hiccock, you'll be free to prosecute."

"How's that?" Tate asked.

"Simple. I'll recommend the president cut him loose as SciAd tomorrow. The press will read it as his failure to achieve results. In two weeks, his name will score lower than Mike Gravel on unaided recall polls. Then you can throw the book at him, if you want."

"Thanks, Ray."

Ray felt the need to add a personal note to Palumbo, knowing how hard it was to do what he had just done. "Agent Palumbo, if it matters, I was starting to like Hiccock. But, we all serve the president. If Hiccock is innocent then he will understand the need for distance. If he's guilty, then who cares what he thinks?"

"It's a raw deal any way you sell it, Sir," Palumbo said as he left. Tate nodded to Reynolds and followed.

Alone in his office, Reynolds breathed deep. *What just happened?* What a good kid that agent was, not selling out his friend. What was it about Hiccock that made people stand up for him? Moreover, what was it about Tate that made even his own men hate him? He shook his head. He scratched a cryptic note to fire Hiccock and moved on to the new legislative agenda. Now that the FBI solved the case, the president should go up in the polls and along with that his political capital. Reynolds needed to be ready.

∞§∞

"Fire Hiccock?" the president said. "Ray, I'm looking at this morning's agenda and I see 'Fire Hiccock.' Why?"

"Sir, can you excuse your man?"

"Don, would you give us a minute?" The president waited until the Secret Service agent closed the door behind him. "Now what's this all about?"

"Would you consider just firing him because I'm asking you to and therefore absolving yourself of any need to testify before one committee or another?"

The president weighed these words and decided against common sense. "Tell me. Hiccock's been a team player, I owe him at least that much."

"The FBI has uncovered a very disturbing link between the Sabot Society and Hiccock. His father may have been a founding member."

"Whoa ... What?"

"Sir, I should point out that this has not yet been proven, but Bernard Keyes and Harry Hiccock may have been involved in the sabotage of a New York City subway in the sixties, the first traceable action of the Sabot Society."

"That long ago?" The president chewed on this for a while. "And the thinking is that Hiccock buffaloed me into taking the investigative teeth out of the FBI's efforts?"

"Whether it's true or not, it has the appearance ..."

"And appearance is as good as reality in this office."

"Unfortunately."

"So we cut him?"

"Again, unfortunately. If he's not guilty, then everyone would understand that he failed in his investigation and you had no choice."

"But in actuality we are really separating ourselves to avoid collateral damage."

"Just in case."

"Do I have a choice?"

"Yes. He might resign."

"You think he would?"

"I don't know. Could go either way. It's worth a shot."

"You or me?"

"If I do it, that leaves you with a lot of deniability."

"Okay, you float it by him, see if he bites. Ray, Tate and his people at the FBI are sure, aren't they?"

"You mean about Hiccock? No, they aren't sure."

"I meant about this Sabot thing. The arrest tonight, this is the end, right?"

"It will be the end, according to Tate."

The president shook his head. "Sometimes this job bites the big one."

"There's an historic quote."

∞§∞

No big secret—politicians hated "Boy Scouts." They were mirrors held up to men whose faces were soiled tilling the political fields. Boy Scouts, in their wholesome reflection, made them feel dirty and grimy. Reynolds, who also once believed in the idealistic notion of pure public service, was emotionally torn. At first, Hiccock seemed to be the mother of all Boy Scouts, out to change the world and truly selfless. The possibility of someone else actually *living* the ideal, the lofty goal he once strove to achieve, is what gnawed at him. His downfall was how quickly the dream was diluted by the gallons of blood shed in the act of political survival. Ray and hundreds of other politicians would fight right up to the line where their own personal power was threatened, then "do the politically expedient thing" and compromise. Deep down, at the bottom of it all, political power worked because it threatened the one thing cherished most by those who fought to attain it—the power itself. In Reynolds's case, this permitted the backroom deals, the strange bedfellows, and the "enemy of my enemy is my friend" style of thinking. To a politician, the only real issue was surviving at all cost.

Misery loving company, buried deep inside Reynolds was the selfish hope that Hiccock was not a Boy Scout but a traitor. Ray hoped Tate was right about Hiccock's true mission being to hamper the investigation, to distract from his father's, as well as his own, beliefs.

As if on cue, Hiccock appeared at Ray's door. "Ray, you wanted to see me?"

"Have a seat, Bill."

"Uh-oh, you never call me Bill. What's wrong?"

"I would like you to resign, effective immediately."

"Wow, that's not a 'Bill,' that's a 'William' if I ever heard one. Why would I do that?"

"To save the president embarrassment."

"Why would the president be embarrassed?"

"Bill, a connection between you and the Sabot Society has been revealed."

"Me?"

"Actually your father."

"My dad? Are you nuts? He's retired."

"Back in the sixties he worked with the leader of Sabot. Together they may have sabotaged a New York City subway. Those facts are a little murky but there is enough there to present the appearance of impropriety."

Hiccock did not appear to be insulted or outraged. He seemed to be weighing each piece of information in his mind, scientifically, seeing both sides of the argument at once.

If he's guilty, he has a great way of not showing it, Reynolds thought.

"No one ever accused my dad ..."

"It was in a confidential police department file. Political pressures may not have had the cops dig too deep way back then."

"That's it? No grainy photographs of my father at the meeting wearing a Sabot hood? No scratchy-voiced informant turning state's evidence? Just a supposition in some cop's file folder?"

"Bill, you brought this on yourself. You made an enemy of Tate and his reach far exceeds your grasp of political realities."

"And those same political realities mean if I don't resign then you'll fire me?"

"Either way, you are finished in this administration."

"And the president?"

"He's hoping you'll fall on your sword."

"What's going to happen to my father?"

"That's up to your good friend Tate after the FBI arrests the leaders of the Sabot Society."

"Are they positive the society is behind all these terrorist acts?"

"They are swarming in tonight. Should all be over by the eleven o'clock news."

Hiccock just sat there. Then his face changed and his eyes set. "I will not resign. I will, however, take a leave of absence to deal with a family matter. My dad is about to be attacked and I need to be there with him."

"This isn't a university. There is no sabbatical."

"Let's take it to the president then."

"Goddamn it, I'll fire you right here, right now!"

"You don't want to do that, Ray."

"Is that a threat?

"No, it's common sense."

Reynolds sat back. "Enlighten me."

"The whole reason I am involved in this is because the president didn't have any options presented to him.

What if the FBI is wrong? What if the society didn't create the subliminal screens that programmed the terrorists? If I am on leave, we pick up right where we left off. If I am fired ..."

"You are not supposed to be that good at political positioning. Leave granted, but if the FBI wins the day, you're fired."

"If they are right, I'll resign."

"Either way." Reynolds watched Hiccock and saw him forming a thought. Ray braced himself for some kind of blackmailing, butt-saving, last-ditch effort on Hiccock's part.

"Look, Ray, as much as I hate to say this, for the good of the country, I hope they are right."

Reynolds rolled his eyes. "You are a fucking Boy Scout, aren't you?"

CHAPTER THIRTY-FOUR
BEST INTENTIONS

ANCHORMAN MARVIN WEITTERMAN sat in a tight, cramped studio in front of a sharply illuminated green screen. The color, so saturated and vivid, enabled the circuitry in the control room to separate his outline from it and replace the background with anything his producer desired. On the studio monitor was the result of this video trickery, a composite picture of him sitting in front of the "virtual set" of CFN's *MoneyTime*.

A graphic appeared over his left shoulder. It read "SHAREWARE." Marvin looked into the camera, reading the intro of his next story off the teleprompter. "Philanthropy in the cyber age? Many thought it went the way of the manual typewriter, but some anonymous donor is giving out free 'Pocket Protector' day-trading software, or shareware, to anyone who wants it. Her or his only request is that you send ten dollars to a charity of your choice. Brian Hopkins has more." He waited until the red tally light on his camera went off, indicating that the viewers at home were watching the prerecorded report. He turned to the monitor showing the tape feed and asked the people in the control room, "Have you seen this? It is an amazing program. It protects your investments round the clock and is so fast it beats anybody to the punch."

"Thirty seconds," the floor manager called out, indicating there was a half-minute left to the taped report.

"You know this could have quite an impact."

∞§∞

Like shooting fish in a barrel, SAC Joey Palumbo thought as he sat on the front wheel of a long-abandoned tractor, which was now more of a vine-covered topiary of a tractor. He was officially awaiting reassignment by order of the director and present here at the scene purely as part of his investigation into the grenade attack on the airliner at SFO. As he surveyed the impressive number of men and material assembled under such incredibly tight secrecy on the Dunhill farm, he amended his previous thought. *Like shooting fish in a barrel ... only with Recon scouts, armored personnel carriers and high-altitude infrared imagery.* That imagery of the Sabot stronghold two miles off told a different story than Joey expected. It showed that the Sabot Society, for all its operational ability in the field, was less than professional about its own security arrangements for the meeting. Not a lookout, sensor, or even a mean dog on a chain was detected at T minus twenty. In fact, twenty minutes before takedown, Joey thought this whole meeting might be a decoy deliberately set to embarrass the FBI. Either that or the Sabots were really dumb.

∞§∞

Inside the ramshackle barn, Bernard opened the meeting. He was especially proud of a little piece of theatrical intrigue he was about to introduce to his cell leaders. He got the idea from reality television.

"In front of you are envelopes. The contents are your targets for the next phase. Each one of you will take his envelope over to the grill and open and read the contents there. Then you will place the paper into the fire. You will not discuss your target with anyone other than me."

As he glanced over at the glowing coals, Bernard started doubting his decision to place the open barbecue grill so close to the wooden wall of the barn. If, as the paper burned, the walls were to catch fire, this place would go up like a stack of matches. As the heads of thirteen cells watched, he went to move the hot grill. He was ten feet from the burning coals when he heard the sharp sound of breaking glass, followed a split second later by a concussive wallop that slammed his body into the base of the grill, tipping it over and spilling the hot coals. A total of three flash-bang grenades detonated in very rapid succession. The weatherworn timbers and notched joints of the old barn shuddered and rattled. Years of settled dust and microscopic grain fibers were rocked loose and instantly became airborne. All fourteen people in the room were temporarily blinded and rendered deaf in an instant, which was the intended purpose of the Mark 4 concussive flare. A second later, eight fully armed agents stormed into the barn.

DuneMist was zipping his fly when the explosions rocked the porta-potty in the corner of the barn. Protected from the flash-bang by the fiberglass construction, he instinctively grabbed his .38 revolver. He cracked the door of the plastic outhouse just as an agent in full SWAT gear approached. The ensuing seconds went by as if in slow motion. DuneMist raised the .38 and fired point-blank into the agent's chest. The stunned officer reeled back. The spasmodic reaction of his muscles caused him to involuntarily squeeze off a three-shot burst from his Mac 10.

The hot coals from the tipped barbecue ignited the strewn hay by the wall. Grain dust instantly combusted into a ball of fire. The air itself was now aflame, immolating FBI and society members alike. Agents in the second attack wave had to switch from takedown mode to rescue mode as their intended targets, and many of their own, suddenly became fire victims.

Joey Palumbo approached with that second wave. Their principal job was to collect physical evidence. That part of the operation was the most important from both a legal perspective and a national security point of view. If this action were to fatally wound the Sabot Society, the death certificate would be issued on the physical evidence they recovered. The postmortem would also determine whether this horrendous wave of terror was merely interrupted or permanently halted.

But evidence recovery would have to wait as Joey Palumbo and company dealt with the human tragedy unfolding before them. Shielding his face from the heat with his forearm, he ran toward the tinderbox. A man engulfed in flame stumbled out the door, clawing at his face. Joey swept the man's legs out from under him and started rolling him on the ground, pumping his hands, making momentary contact against the man's boiling skin and saving his own flesh from severe burns. Two other agents took over, rolling and snuffing out the man's clothing and hair. Joey headed back to the doorway. Choking on the thick acrid smoke, he peered through the flames, but not a soul was moving.

∞§∞

The bureau's D.C. op center was tapped into the tactical operations radio traffic from the takedown scene. The cool, professional, by-the-numbers radio chatter normally associated with any well-coordinated, well-executed apprehension of suspects had suddenly turned into pandemonium. The color washed from Tate's face as he sat down hard, stunned, as what seemed like a walk in the park a few seconds before turned into a human barbecue.

∞§∞

The crime scene is screwed, blued, and tattooed, Agent Palumbo thought, mentally assembling the first draft of his action report. Three agents dead, ten Sabots dead, four burned and in critical condition. Four agents and two firefighters treated for smoke inhalation. The human toll ate away at Joey's core. It took twelve years and plenty of sacrifice to become an agent of the caliber lost today. All the training, all the legal casework, the dedication ... snuffed out in seconds. Joey's gut wrenched tighter as the notion of the instantly widowed wives and decimated families rushed into his thoughts. The contributions those agents had yet to make would never be.

To balance the loss, Joey reminded himself that he, the FBI, and America were at war with terror. In war, three dead against ten enemy dead was considered a good "kill ratio," but that was a calculus made of soldiers on the battlefield. These were cops. Cops weren't supposed to be combatants. Much had changed since America's first wake up call on that crystal clear September morning in New York, Washington, D.C., and Shanksville, Pennsylvania. Private citizens were now automatically deputized merely by being passengers on a plane, train, or bus. No American, be they policeman or grandmother, could ever assume they were a noncombatant. This way of thinking provided a little peace for Joey, as the mixture of anger, grief, and frustration he felt remained unfathomable.

He had been trained as a professional law enforcement officer. That entailed getting it right in times of pressure, keeping your head while those around you were losing theirs, rushing into places where others were running from. Above all, because we live in a democracy, the cop's second-most-important job, after stopping bad guys from doing bad things, was ensuring the full effective prosecution of criminals. This was done by following the procedural rules designed to preserve chains of evidence and the legal rights granted by the Constitution.

Standing before the burned pile of rubble and ash that was the ill-fated barn, it was clear to Joey that little physical evidence had survived. Envelopes and pieces of paper were found, presumably with the

names of future targets inside. Among the charred remains were personal papers, a few notes, and layouts
of various factories, rail lines, and interstate routes
scratched on yellow pads—in all, a pretty lousy haul
for the price of three agents' lives.

∞§∞

Twenty-four hours after the assault on Bufford's
farm, the news networks and daily papers anxiously
awaited the press conference from the FBI on the details of the operation. Bernard Keyes was dead at the
scene and two of the four surviving Sabot members
had succumbed to their burns, leaving only Donald
Mendleson (aka DuneMist) from Madison, Wisconsin, and Michael (Red Baron238) Spadafore from San
Francisco alive. Both men were from notorious locations within the recent wave of bombings and terrorist actions—Wisconsin, the location of the train derailment, and San Francisco, where the plane exploded
with Silicon Valley's best and brightest onboard. FBI
agents from field offices all across America were sifting
through the lives and personal effects of not only these
last two survivors but the twelve deceased members
of the society as well. They searched for any shred of
evidence or information with which they could piece
together the extent and power of the now-decapitated
organization.

Each special agent in charge had received an additional order from the top—find any references to Hiccock ... William or Harold.

CHAPTER THIRTY-FIVE
AUTHORITY

THE MORNING MIST was just burning off as Bill pulled up the gravel drive. His parents called it "the cabin," but this was a house nestled in Roscoe, New York, the epicenter of the trout-fishing world. William Hiccock's father discovered the joys of fishing late in life. Every day the weather allowed, however, he made up for the time lost with a vengeance.

Holding his peeled-back, plastic-lidded cardboard cup in one hand, Bill grabbed the bag from the Roscoe Diner off the front seat. It contained one black coffee, one tea with milk, and three fresh-baked muffins.

"Mom, Dad," he called as he placed the bag on the kitchen table.

Alice Hiccock, in a robe and slippers, came down the stairs first, beaming at the sight of her one and only son. "Hello, Billy. You look thin."

Bill laughed and hugged his mom.

Dad came down the stairs. "How are you, Billy?"

"Fine, Pop, how have you guys been?"

"Oh, can't complain, things have been good," his mom said as she opened the bag and poured the coffee and tea from the cardboard cups into her own mugs. "We see ya on TV every once in a while doing your job for the president. It feels real good to know my son is such an important person in the government."

Alice got plates from the cabinet and, for reasons Bill could never fathom, sliced each muffin and placed them on the small dishes. Hiccock got his father's attention and motioned toward the door. In response, the older Hiccock said, "Come out here, Bill. Let me show you my new rod and reel."

Hiccock and his dad walked out to the porch.

"How's it going, Dad?"

"Oh, you know, a little of this, that, and the other thing."

"Fishin' good?"

"Been pretty good."

"Yeah, I got to get around to trying that sometime."

The moment lingered. "You didn't come here to fish, Bill. What's got you up in God's country during the middle of your big investigation?"

"Well, Dad, that's on hold for a while."

"Bad guys taking a vacation?"

"Pop, something's come up. I've made a powerful enemy."

"If you're a worker, then it's best not to rock the boat. But if you're a leader, and you aren't making waves, then you're probably doing it wrong. When I was ..."

Hiccock realized he had just assumed the emotional equivalent of sitting on his father's knee as the man pontificated on life, work, union brotherhood, and good Christian values. As cherished a memory as that was, he forced himself to snap out of it. "Pop, they're going after me through you."

"Me?"

"They dug up some crap about the time the 42nd Street shuttle burned."

"What? That was over forty years ago. What the hell ...?"

"The Sabot Society."

"Some Jewish group?"

"No, Dad, Sabot. As in wooden shoes, remember?"

Bill watched his father looking over the railing, imagining him traveling back four decades. "You remember that old story about the shoes? I must have told you that when you were six."

"The current terrorist attacks are about to be blamed on the Sabot Society."

"Who are they?"

"That's the problem, Dad. They think it's you."

"What? What kind of lamebrain came up with that idea?"

"Do you remember a guy named Bernie Mercer?"

"Bernie ...? Yeah, he was the kid who told me the shoe story. He was an apprentice in Signals and Switches."

"Well, now he's got his signals crossed. He's the head of the group the FBI thinks is blowing up the country." Bill detected a glimmer of recognition in the face that foreshadowed what his own would look like in thirty years.

"That idiot? He couldn't blow up a balloon! He got canned right after the fire."

"Did he start it?"

"Nah. He was a screw-up!"

"Dad, they think you and he did the job on the shuttle."

"Those sons-a-bitches. It was a grease fire. The NTSB confirmed it in their report."

"Wait a minute. The National Transportation Safety Board investigated the fire?"

"It was rolling stock within the U.S. borders. That's their turf. They found the cause to be a fire under the train on track three. Back then, grease fires from hot-box axle bearings were a pretty regular thing. This one got out of hand because a box had been leaking grease for months and it got all over the undercarriage of the train. When that happens, the least little ..."

"Wait. You say the fire was on track number three? Didn't the computer train run on the track by the wall?"

"Yep, track number four."

"So it wasn't the computer train that burned?"

"No, not at all. It was a manual consist."

"Then why did they cancel the automated train after the fire?"

"The TA never really wanted it. The fire gave management an excuse to shut it down. And we in the union, well, you know how we felt about it."

"So this was a non-event!"

"Oh, I don't know about that. They had to cut open 42nd Street just to get the burned car out."

"Yeah, but what you're telling me is that the fire was in no way the first case of industrial sabotage committed by the Sabot Society."

"Nah, it was a stupid track fire that got out of hand 'cause of crummy maintenance. I, of course, would never say that in public so as not to taint the work practices of my brother union members."

Bill sighed. "Pop, I can't tell you what a load off my mind that is."

"Does this help you in your work, Billy?"

"It makes the FBI's case against me tougher, but I'm learning a lot about politics and how the truth or facts seldom enter into it."

"See? And you thought you were finished with school, son." The man actually tousled Bill's hair.

"Boys, the coffee's getting cold," his mother called out.

"Coming, Ma," Hiccock said as if he were sixteen again. When you go home, you are always sixteen again. He touched his father's shoulder. "You wouldn't have a copy of that NTSB report, would ya?"

"As a matter of fact …"

∞§∞

The follow-up from Bufford's farm and the investigating agents across the country was aggravating Director Tate's ulcer this morning. They were all having trouble making hard connects on anything but the Long Island and New Jersey truck bombings. There were a few isolated connections but no more than there would have been by opening any phone book and making a circumstantial case against any person you randomly picked. To his chagrin, Tate had heard that some of the agents had started calling the operation "Homegroan" amongst themselves. Director Tate's peptic level was not about to get any lower when he answered his phone.

"NTSB 20-4-64-00234," Reynolds called out over the phone.

"What's that?"

"It's the NTSB report you left out of your premature Hiccock obituary. It's real boring reading on how it was not an act of sabotage. You should read it soon."

"Is that all you called for?"

"The daily briefing's been moved up because of the stock market crash. I'm going in to the boss in thirty minutes. Should I slot you in so you can fill him in on the bust?"

"Ray, I'm still getting a handle on just what we have. Maybe in the afternoon."

"What do I tell him when he asks?"

"That the investigation is proceeding and the FBI is ..."

"Hold it. Every enemy of this country can read that in the *Times*. What do we tell the President of the United States of America, Tate?"

"It's slow going. They're deeper and more covert than we thought. I'll have more once the West Coast reports in."

"Okay, duly noted. If anything changes in the half hour, call me."

Hanging up the phone, the director's conscience started nagging him. Holding back information from the administration was technically a violation of the law. Countering that was the guideline that afforded him, as the head of the FBI, the sole discretion as to what was conjecture and what was fact. There were no regulations mandating that he convey speculation. Tate chose to regard the negative reports he'd received from his trusted underlings in the field as opinion and not fact. At least until their written reports were on his desk.

All that logic aside, for the first time in his long public career he felt vulnerable. He opened his desk drawer and fished out the business card of a New York attorney he met at a cocktail party a few years ago. He fingered the edge of the card. Unfortunately, the current political situation had placed more emphasis on this operation than he would have liked, forcing him to operate more out in the open. The terrorist attacks were so high profile, and the assault on the farm so massive, that it now could not be contained or explained as an expeditionary tactic to gather information.

Furthermore, that Hiccock creep hadn't helped matters any by undermining his authority and limiting his more reasonable response options. Looking back down at the gold-leafed engraved card, he decided to call the Park Avenue lawyer and cash in the chit the man owed him. What he couldn't decide was if he was going to ask the lawyer to represent him in the congressional probe that would surely follow, or ask him for a cushy, private-sector job.

Two hours after Tate left a message for the lawyer to get back to him, he found himself in the Oval Office.

"Mr. President, we always operated with the understanding that Hiccock's investigation and our own was one and the same. Different methodologies working toward the same end and sharing the same resources."

The president cut him off with a wave of his hand. "Forty-eight hours ago, you depicted Hiccock as a mole planted in my administration in order to disinform and misdirect me away from your investigative path. I fired the man and ruined his career because of that. Now all of the sudden, Bill's the guy who uncovered the missing part of your theory—the online recruitment of the homegrown terrorist. Can you see why I'm getting so agitated over this, Tate?"

Tate took a deep breath, the color draining from his salon-tanned face. "Sir, we may have been premature on the tie-in with Hiccock's father."

The president just stared. It didn't take much imagination to envision what was going on in his head.

Reynolds broke the uneasy silence. "Sir, actually Hiccock is on a leave of absence."

"We grant leaves of absence?"

"Not usually, Sir, but this is an unusual situation and it was his idea."

"What was Bill's reasoning in asking for a leave when we agreed to fire him, Ray?"

"In case this sort of thing happened, Sir. To save you the embarrassment if you needed him back."

This was almost more than Tate could handle. Hiccock was out-pointing him at every turn.

"Ray, get Hiccock back in the house."

"He cleaned out his desk yesterday and went back to New York. His father's place, I think."

Mitchell swiveled in his chair to Reynolds. It was as though he'd forgotten that Tate was in the room, though Tate knew he couldn't be that lucky. "Do you think we can convince him that his leave just ended?"

∞§∞

"It's the tension on the line and the tension in your body that scare away the fish. Just ease it in, keep it lax, and wait ... wait ... 'til your opponent there feels relaxed enough and decides to have a leisurely snack." Harry Hiccock's soft tones skimmed over the water as he stood fifteen feet into the stream in wading boots, the very poster boy for "relaxed." His son, Billy, was trying, but was still broadcasting enough tension to keep the fish at bay.

Bill could sense his biorhythms changing with the next deep breath he took. It was like on the first days of spring when he was a kid in the Bronx and it felt so good it hurt as your lungs expanded. He knew it was his imagination, but the colors became more vivid and the air smelled sweeter. This wouldn't be such a bad lifestyle.

The deep chopping sound filtering through the trees drew him out of his reverie. Although this sound was not uncommon in a spot where weekend warriors and reservists in the National Guard ferried back and forth from Stuart AFB, Hiccock immediately identified the distinctive sound of a Sikorsky, as would anyone from D.C. Turbo fans and heavy rotors broke over the forest canopy, and Bill knew enough to get his dad and himself back up to the house.

Reynolds was already on the porch, standing next to his mom who stood gaping at the huge green-and-white hulk of Marine One, the president's personal helicopter. Hiccock introduced the COS to his father then asked, "Catching up on some fishing, Ray?"

"Actually we're here to catch the one that got away." Ray nodded to the copter as the president descended the stairs.

Alice Hiccock let out a small gasp. "I better make a fresh pot." She primped her hair and went inside.

The president, with two agents flanking him, strode up to the porch, taking in the lush green foliage all around.

"Sorry to interrupt your 'leave of absence,' Hiccock, but I need to talk to you." He turned and held out his hand to the senior Hiccock. "Hello. You must be William's father."

"Yes, Sir. Harry Hiccock, Sir. Welcome to our home."

"Thank you. It's a beautiful spot. It has to be a great place to fish. I was admiring the streams and inlets from the air."

"Do you fly cast, Sir? Because this is the best place on the planet for that."

"As the not-so-favorite son of the Great State of Ohio, forgive me if I don't give you the presidential endorsement on that statement. But I will say you might have the second best."

"You two always get together like this just to talk fishing?" Bill said, thinking he could get away with a little sarcasm in front of the two most important authority figures in his life.

"Billy!" his father admonished, almost as if to tell him to go play out back.

"Your son's right, Harry. You and I will have to trade fish stories another time." He nodded toward the tree line. "Take a walk, Bill?"

With the two Secret Service agents in tow, they made their way to a small clearing.

"I'm afraid Tate's got nothing, Bill. I am in a real pressure cooker here."

"It wasn't the Sabot Society?"

"Hell, we don't even know if they're responsible for anything other than the Long Island bombing. Just a bunch of copycat, misdirected wackos if you ask me."

"Sorry it's not over, Sir."

"I need you back on the team."

"Team?"

"I've had one of those long father-son talks with Tate. I told him I'd have his father and his son shot at dawn if he interfered with you again."

"I don't know ... he's a powerful enemy, Sir."

"I'm pretty powerful myself if you get on my shit side, son." The president handed Bill a redlined folder. "Here, we drew this up. Take a minute and read it. I'm going to have a cup of your mom's coffee."

Five minutes later, the screen door slammed behind Hiccock as he squeezed his eyes shut, hoping he didn't see what he just saw. There at the kitchen table was the Commander in Chief of the most powerful nation on earth, held prisoner by Alice Hiccock and her "alblum"—the photographic history of the Hiccock clan lovingly preserved in hermetically sealed plastic pages. It used to make William cringe when she opened it for new girlfriends. But this!

"And here's William on his second, or was it his third?"

The president glanced up from the book with a look that begged "Shoot me now." Hiccock came to the rescue.

"Mom, you know this could be considered cruel and unusual punishment of a head of state."

"Oh, nonsense, he's a family man. I am sure he's proud of his family, too."

"I didn't bring any pictures, but I'll get my library to send some."

"Mom?" Hiccock gestured for her to take the book away. She did.

"Would you like some more nuts or some dried fruit?" she said to her guest.

"Yeah, take some back to Washington with you, we keep getting tons of the stuff," the senior Hiccock offered.

Bill pinched the bridge of his nose. How did the grateful Mario and Shelly ever find out his parents' address?

"No thank you, Alice." His eyes zeroed in on Bill. "Well?"

Hiccock grinned and tapped the redlined folder. "Catchy name."

∞§∞

Air Force One lifted off from the old Stuart AFB heading back to Washington, ending its unannounced "little field trip." In the front, right behind the president's cabin, Hiccock had dozed off. On his lap was the document folder the president had handed him, the contents of which set new ground rules for Hiccock and his team. Included as well were the president's

executive orders completely relinquishing all FBI resources regarding the current domestic terrorism over
to Hiccock. A passing Air Force sergeant cabin attendant collected the papers, which were perilously close
to sliding off Hiccock's lap, and placed them on his side
table. She noticed the code name on the redlined cover
and thought it odd: OPERATION QUARTERBACK.

CHAPTER THIRTY-SIX
GREED

BACK IN THE WHITE HOUSE office, Hiccock and Janice were settling in again. Janice toyed with a hair clip that was a new gift from Bill's mother.

"Your mom always had great taste for estate jewelry. How's her sciatica?"

"She didn't mention it and I didn't ask."

"Did she ask about me?"

"Not in so many words."

"Which words did she use?"

"She saw in the news that you and I were working together."

"And ..."

Bill sighed. "And she said it was good to see the two of us back together again."

"What did you say?"

"Janice, my folks love you. They made that very clear after our divorce. So naturally ..."

"Naturally."

Bill started to unpack some files.

Janice tried the clip in her hair. "What do you think?" she said when she was finished.

"I think working together has been good for us," Bill said without looking up, not sure he could look up.

"I meant the hair clip, but do go on."

Bill closed his eyes and then turned to Janice. "There's nothing more to say."

"Are you sure about that?"

Bill could feel his skin warming. He'd stumbled around women before ... but this was Janice. "What exactly is going on here?"

Janice opened her mouth to speak just as the phone rang. Bill reached for it quickly.

"Let me call you back," he said a few moments later to the falling away mouthpiece as he abruptly hung up the phone. The sound of someone yelling was cut off by the receiver hitting the cradle.

"What was that all about?"

"The FBI interviewed Martha Krummel about the Sabot Society. She said what my dad said: she thought it was a Jewish group. They grilled her pretty good and she is totally not connected to any Sabot, Bernard Keyes, or anyone else in that organization. Now they want to embrace the 'B' part of our theory. Your 'bi-stable concurrent schizo ditzo' stuff and my 'the computer made me do it' hypothesis. They'd like us to prove that she is a part of Sabot but can't remember anything about it."

"I see. So now our whole investigation has been relegated to little more than an argument of convenience for the FBI. Was that Joey?"

"No, Tate." Hiccock didn't let his satisfaction show—too much.

"Okay, quarterback, what's the play?"

"I'm getting ready for the Cabinet briefing in one hour. Then we are going to get you, me, and Kronos back to the Admiral's. I'll worry about the FBI later. Janice, do me a favor and check if Cheryl got that *MoneyTime* videotape for me?"

"Sure thing."

Bill turned back to his files. There was suddenly a lot more to do before the Cabinet meeting.

"Bill?"

He looked up at Janice. She seemed a little confused. He knew instinctively it wasn't about what Tate just told him. "Yeah?"

Janice seemed transfixed for a moment. Then she said, "Never mind. I'll go get that video."

∞§∞

"Her or his only request is that you send ten dollars to a charity of your choice. Brian Hopkins has more."

The picture froze. Hiccock put down the remote on the mirrorlike finish of a Louisiana oak table that once served a tour of duty at Fort McHenry in the officer's mess. He caught a glimpse of his reflection in the painstakingly varnished veneer and proceeded to address the president, Reynolds, and the members of the cabinet in the Situation Room of the White House. "That piece ran two days ago. Since then, over 700,000 people have downloaded this software from the net."

"This is that day-trading program? The one that watches your portfolio and guards it against any sudden changes?" the president asked.

"Yes, Sir. It reacts like a fighter plane being chased by a missile, making counter moves. It makes minor or major buy and sell orders instantaneously and protects the investor by keeping the value of the portfolio growing."

"It's like having a full-time broker/trader instantly reacting to every market, everywhere in the world," the Secretary of the Treasury said.

"So I should get this?" the press secretary said, half-jokingly.

Hiccock supplied more background. "Leading brokerage houses have spent millions trying to develop a program like this."

"And some yahoo is giving it away free?" Reynolds could not believe it.

"And now, Mr. President, the markets are virtually frozen. No one can make a move without some hundred thousand computers instantly countering it," the Secretary of the Treasury grimly reported.

"They plug in their computer warriors and the whole damn thing works so fast and so accurately that to the outside world it appears frozen," the president said.

"The panic has started, and I fear we are on the verge of something that will make the Crash of '29 look like a mere glitch," the Secretary of Commerce said.

The president turned to Bill. "Is this now part of your Operation Quarterback investigation?"

"I think it is, Sir. There is more than one way to attack a country. I'd like to ask Vincent DeMayo, my leading computer expert, to explain." Hiccock gestured for Kronos to come to the head of the table.

"It's a friggin' beautiful idea! Give away the hack code! Make every greedy day-trading son-of-a-bitch out there a hacker. Make them unwitting accomplices. Imagine locking up the entire friggin' stock market. I wish I'd a thought of that shit!"

Hiccock snapped to the side of Kronos. "That'll be all, Mr. DeMayo."

"My time is your time, Hick," Kronos said with a grin.

"Your time is federal time, Vincent."

The president broke in. "How is it that the FBI and NSA, hell, the SEC haven't come to this conclusion?"

"They don't think the same way as Mr. Hiccock, Sir," Reynolds said.

"Or as fast," the president added. "So why don't we just unplug the computers?"

"There's about five trillion in wealth directly controlled by the computers and now frozen," the Secretary of the Treasury said. "Most or all of it would be lost instantly. Some of that might come back in a few weeks or months but the impact to the economy would be disastrous. I am afraid, Mr. President, that in this instance, a frozen market is better than complete financial chaos."

"The genius of the attack, from a purely scientific angle," Hiccock said, "is that the lock on the system is the individual investor. Once he or she uses the program to protect their assets, they can't stop using it, because the instant they do, the other investors' programs will snap up the slack and they'll lose everything."

"So I get to deliver the bad news?"

"You go on the air in twenty minutes, Mr. President." Reynolds tapped his watch and continued. "Your speech will ask for calm ... explain how this is an adjustment, the market catching up to technology, that sort of thing. You'll announce a plan that will give major institutional investors two weeks to suspend computer trading at their own safe rate. At the end, you'll urge the public to stop trading online."

President Mitchell glanced down at the report. "How could this have happened?"

"Greed, Sir," Hiccock said. "Enough to go around."

∞§∞

Marvin Weitterman could not believe his luck; the Secretary of the Treasury had called him personally, actually pressured him, to appear on the show today. Since Marvin's mother didn't raise no dummy, it took him all of one second to accede to the secretary's request. He knew he was being used by the White House to get out their spin but, at the same time, he was sure to squeeze in a few good questions. "So it's your opinion then, Mr. Secretary, that the nation should not be alarmed."

"Marvin, I think if we all pull together and back away slowly from computer trading, we'll go back to a normal healthy market in very short order."

"Yes, but people are throwing themselves out of windows because their money is in some sort of machine-to-machine tug of war, frozen—locked up!" *That should make the sound bites on the nightly news.*

"Last night the president asked for calm and full voluntary cooperation from the day-trading public." The secretary addressed the camera to talk directly to

John Q. "I am confident the people of the United States will put their country ahead of any profit that might conceivably be gained at this time."

∞§∞

The next day's *Wall Street Journal* headline read "INVESTORS NOT LETTING GO OF COMPUTER TRADING." Every other paper across the nation chimed in with variations on the theme: "PEOPLE ARE NOT LETTING GO OF COMPUTER TRADING"— "BILLIONS BEING LOST AS NO ONE LETS GO"— "NO ONE WANTS TO BE THE FIRST TO LOSE." There was the classic *New York Post's* "DAY-TRAITORS TO FEDS: SCREW YOU."

CHAPTER THIRTY-SEVEN
PETTY PEDIGREE

"IF HE WANTS TO SEE my bare chest in his film, then I want to see sixteen million in my account, Myron. Hell, I didn't do a nude scene for 'art's' sake back when I was doing Indies. I am certainly not going to do it for less than eight million a boob today!" Shari Saks picked up and considered biting into one of the organically grown carrot crudités that automatically appeared in her Beverly Hills mansion every day.

On the other end of the phone, Myron Weisberg, agent to the stars, sat peering through his door to the outer office at International Creative Agency and caught the eye of his assistant, who, as always, was listening in on his conversations via headset and taking notes. He adjusted his posture forward as the leather on the seat of his chair responded with an ungracious sound. He zeroed in on his thoughts and drilled them through the receiver to the "star" at the other end. "Look, I can't tell you what to do, baby. These days everybody is showing everything ... right on television! But this director, Graham Houser, he's a hot ticket, darling. He waltzed from Sundance to Cannes to the goddamned best-picture Oscar! This guy is on a roll and you, my dear girl, could see an Oscar as well."

Myron set his chin. He waited for her to comment, and when she came up for air he jumped in, not allowing her to speak, "Shari, Shari, Shari, boobalah, we're talking Best Picture here. I can smell Best Actress, I can smell it!" He tapped his nose even though Shari couldn't see him. It kept him in the moment.

"Myron, Myron, Myron, you also said the last film was a guaranteed Academy Award. Instead I wind up

having to do a scene with 2,000 cockroaches on me ..."
The memory made Shari stick the carrot spear into
the cluster lovingly arranged in the Pierre Deux bone
china cup.

"Shari, cupcake! They were beetles. Little kids in
Rangoon or someplace keep them as pets ..."

"Beetles, my ass! I'm telling you they were roaches.
Big fucking roaches." She flopped down on the Turkish
striped-satin Donghia chaise. "Look Myron, you get me
my sixteen mil or I'll finally take lunch with Jack Ne-
whouse over at CMS."

Myron's assistant's eyebrows went up. Myron nodded as he closed his eyes confidently as if to say, *watch
me handle this.* "Now, baby girl, has Uncle Myron ever
not made money for you? And you break my heart with
threats? Threats aren't going to win you that Oscar."

"That's only a threat if you don't deliver! Love to
Marsha and the kids, bye." America's current reign-
ing female box-office attraction tossed her Freddi Fek-
kai–dyed blonde mane as she hung up the phone with
no more regret than if she'd had her secretary order a
pizza.

Shari felt she had earned her right to piss downhill.
Having started out a wiry black-haired Jewish actress
doing performance art pieces at the Nuyorican Café in
New York's Alphabet City, she climbed her way up to
her lofty perch as *Variety's* most bankable female star.
She achieved the altitude by latching on to the winged
talent of a fringe director who catapulted himself, and
her career, into the mainstream when he finally got his
big break.

It was of little consolation to her that she had been
twice nominated for an Academy Award. Myron Weisberg, agent extraordinaire, was right. Winning the Oscar was the one thing that had eluded her thus far.

She was heading into one of her seven Italian mar-
bled bathrooms when she heard the beep from her computer that announced she had mail. She poured half a

glass of Remi Martin 125th anniversary cognac, a surviving bottle of which fetches $6,000 for the 1978 vin-
tage. With one knee on the chair, she bent over to see
who e-mailed her. Within a few seconds, she adjusted
her position and sat squarely on the custom-designed,
body-molded Swedish ergonomic chair.

The only perceptible motion was caused by the gentle current of purified air from the filtration system she
had demanded the studio install and pay for and which
created a gentle billowing of her silk kimono. The rich-
ly colored and finely embroidered ancient wrap had
been a gift from the head of Sony to celebrate her last
film going past the $200 million mark. She was told it
had been a ceremonial robe worn by a concubine to the
emperor in some Japanese past century. She couldn't
remember which dynasty but she knew the fucking
thing was practically a Nipponese national treasure.
Shari reasoned that since a French film critic classified
her body as an American national treasure, it was perfectly fitting for her to wrap it up in this Jap *schmatte*.

For the next twenty-five minutes, the motion picture star sat before her computer motionless.

∞§∞

Was the expenditure ordered by a superior or other
department? If yes, fill out form CYS 20028.

"Who creates these forms?" Hiccock grumbled to
himself. His thoughts were interrupted by Cheryl.

"Professor Hiccock?"

"Yes, Cheryl?"

"Would you give this disk to Doctor Tyler, please?"

"Certainly, what's on it?"

"It's all the subliminal messages we have decoded
so far, arranged in outline format the way she wanted."

"I'll make sure she gets it." Hiccock returned to
the contents of the folder on his desk—the federal employee's reimbursement form FERF-1037. It was more

than ten pages long. Out of the corner of his eye, he noticed Cheryl was still there. "Is there something else?"

"I could help you fill out that form."

"Thank you, but this is something I've put off too long. It should only take me another four years or so."

"If you decide you'd like to hand it off to me, let me know."

"Thanks, I appreciate it."

Janice walked into the office a few seconds after Cheryl left. "You still working on that?"

"I keep getting interrupted." He put his pen down with a bit too much force.

"My, my, aren't we cranky?"

"I'm sorry, Janice, it's my own fault. It's twenty grand of my money that I'm trying to get back for that MIT contraption. That works out to about a dollar a page." He slid his hand under the form, displaying the heft of the document. "Oh, Cheryl stopped by and asked me to give you this." He handed her the CD.

"The subliminal screens outline. Great, now I can get started." She walked over to her desk, which was actually a table across from Hiccock's desk. She had decided to move into his office in the White House rather than be across town at the FBI profile lab. She slipped the disk into her computer and tapped the space bar, waking the machine up from its sleep mode.

Hiccock complained to the form he was struggling to fill out. "No, I don't have any outstanding federal student loans."

Janice smiled. On the screen, the report came up. It looked like a lengthy poem, with all the sentences and words on the page flush left and each phrase on its own line. Each line was numbered. "Pretty smart," she noted aloud.

"What is?"

"Cheryl put numbers on every line so we can refer to each. Sharp cookie, that one."

"Yeah, I'm glad she's working out. She wasn't using her full potential on Reynolds's staff."

"Oh, was that it?"

"Was what it?"

"Give me a break, Bill, you can't be *that* blind."

Hiccock put down his pen. "What am I missing here?"

"The girl's got a crush on you that could flatten a dump truck!"

"Really?"

Janice threw a pencil at him that ricocheted off his shoulder.

∞§∞

Shari Saks picked up her white, gold-leaf, French-styled phone that was once the bedroom phone of silent screen siren—and later Coca-Cola icon—Clara Bow. In those days, she was known as the "It Girl." The phone was a gift from Louis B. Mayer who, as the legend goes, presented it to Clara as a peace offering after he tried to get his hands all over her "its." Jewish film moguls, Japanese electronics moguls, all the same, she equated in her mind. It was as if the word mogul was Latin for "breast-man." Men are such schmucks, she thought as she started dialing a number to a private telephone that was only to be used in dire circumstances. She could not recall why, but she knew the circumstances were dire.

∞§∞

The president stopped by Hiccock's office unannounced on his way to a fund-raiser out west for an influential senator. "Any breaks?"

"Janice is just digging in now, she may have something soon."

"Where is she? I'd like to meet her."

"She just went over to the FBI profile lab. She's going to be so disappointed that she missed you."

"I'm sure we'll meet sooner or later. Let me know if anything new comes up."

"Will do. Heading out of town?"

"Another rubber chicken for Dent. He's got a big state there, with the most electoral votes and gobs of high-tech money behind him. I need to let the good people of California know that I am running for reelection as president and not him. Or at least that's the line I am supposed to spew according to Reynolds."

"Dent! You know, right before all the feces hit the air-circulating device, I had my position papers on his national firewall initiative forwarded to him. I think he's got a good idea there."

"I have concerns that it smells a little like 'industrial policy,' but I'll be sure to tell him my people like his proposal."

"I'll have my executive summary sent up to Air Force One for your review, Sir."

"Make it short. I got the whole California congressional delegation flying with me ... such fun."

"By the way, Sir, I had a thought. Ever see a car race?"

"Sure, why?"

"Yellow flag. If you make an executive order locking in and guaranteeing every investor's current portfolio value at the time of the freeze, then there will be no penalty for them to let go of Pocket Protector ... Once the protocol is written to ban it from future trading, that is."

"No one advances under a yellow flag ... good idea, I'll run that by Treasury. Did you just think that up in your spare time?"

"I just hope it works, Sir."

"Oh, by the way, I stopped here to tell you that they found out who was behind the attempt on my life."

"I'm touched that you personally came over here to tell me that."

"You almost got shot as well. Besides it's top secret. You'll be one of less than 20 people who will ever know it was Libya."

"Libya? No way."

"Yes."

"So what are you going to do?"

"Nothing."

"Nothing?" Hiccock tried to catch his shock before it was apparent but failed.

"Nope. We're protecting our intelligence methods and not alerting them that their operational mobility is compromised. We'll get more out of them that way.

"So no public accusations or even a back channel reprimand?"

"I know that Bedouin S.O.B.'s behind it. Why waste the time? I could write their official, public statement right now. They would blame some rogue faction, then garner support from moderate and radical Muslim nations, and we'd end up being the bad guys."

"So no response? Wow, it's their lucky year."

"Oh I don't know about that. I hear they are going to have a bad crop of poppies this year. Too bad, too. It will decimate their two billion-dollar-a-year heroin trade. But of course that's top secret, too, Bill."

The wry smirk was hidden but Hiccock read volumes in the president's face. "Ah! Gotcha."

The president stepped away leaving Hiccock stunned. The space-based defoliant was going on-line. In order to protect its secrecy, and in essence its whole purpose, the government was maintaining the "lone-nut" theory to explain the assassination attempt. Bill smiled as he relished in the thought of those Libyans, responsible for planning the attack, believing they had dodged a big bullet when the Justice Department proclaimed the would-be assassin to be a deranged individual acting alone...until their fields turned brown.

∞§∞

When Clark Gable drove up to the sixteen-foot-tall front gates, a security guard would nod and let him in. He would never challenge the movie idol, whose face was known around the world. U.S. Senator Hank Dent, however, had to punch in a seven-digit code to activate the now electrically operated gates. As he drove in, Dent scanned for gardeners, butlers, chauffeurs, and maids, but found no sign of anyone. At least Shari was following the rules that he established in their regular e-mail exchanges. Those personal, private, and often provocative missives were protected by using the U.S. Senate's secure encryption. This was necessary because his liaisons with her, if discovered, would not be advantageous to his standing in the polls and his ambition to be the next White House resident. He was, after all, a trusted public servant—a *married* trusted public servant. On the other hand, what was the value of being the senior senator from the state that gave Hollywood to the world, if you couldn't afford yourself the pleasures of one of its true natural wonders?

Parking in front of the seven-car garage that used to hold David O. Selznick's sixteen-cylinder Dusenburghs, he walked around back to find Shari sunbathing nude by the pool. *God she is beautiful,* he thought as he took in every part of her. He stood there for a full minute, as someone would admire a Michelangelo painting at the Louvre.

Lying before him was the most coveted body in America, probably the world. The sexual ground zero of a billion male fantasies. Oceans of sperm had been jettisoned, from young boys and old men alike, just imagining what it would be like to be him, right there, right then. It was worth putting his staff off and canceling a few appointments. After all, it wasn't as if they hadn't handled presidential visits before. He could certainly squeeze out a few hours.

As he stepped closer, the sound of his Italian leather soles scraping the Israeli marble with which the pool was encircled brought Shari's eyes to him. Tall cypress trees, planted in the thirties by Rudolph Valentino's landscaper, stood guard as the most powerful woman in Hollywood gave the most powerful man in the U.S. Senate a classic, downtown, Avenue A, New York City blow job.

This was turning into quite a good day for the senator. Twenty-five minutes after the poolside oral gratuity, he was in full thrust atop Givenchy sheets on the actual, California-size bed that had belonged to Doris Day, humping the brains out of "eight-million-dollar-a-tit" Shari Saks. She was a wildcat in bed; her every squeal of delight, every shift of her Pilates-honed, yoga-tightened, Tai Chi–balanced, vegetarian-fed incredible body was a signal that he was the only man who ever gave her such pleasure.

The fact that she was also an Academy Award–nominated actress never penetrated his mind—which he was literally fucking himself out of right now. As happens in all Hollywood bedroom adventures, they climaxed at the same time. She was sprawled out flatly beneath him and he collapsed on her. They lay there for a minute catching their breath, squeezing the last bit of pleasure from their loins. They did a little kissing, but mostly just allowed the waves of passion to wash away. His head was buried face down next to hers, his chin on her shoulder, her arm under him, dangling near the bedside table. He felt her move, but didn't adjust his position. Eyes closed, he never saw her remove the .357 Magnum from between the mattress and box spring. The click of the hammer going back was a curious sound to him, but he never got to lift his head as she pressed the cold steel of the gun's muzzle into her temple.

Looking up at the ceiling, Shari pulled the trigger. Her eyes widened in her final, frozen-for-all-time close-up as the slug traversed the twelve inches through both her head then his, finally embedding itself in the Chippendale desk under which Harvey Warner was personally serviced by the then-struggling actress Heddy Dukes.

∞§∞

Hiccock entered the conference room with a small blue-and-white box in his hand. Janice was at the far end, underlining phrases on large printouts taped to the wall. He jutted the box under her nose. "Will you take these? I've done enough damage."

"Ooooh, Entenmann's chocolate donuts! Where'd you find these in Washington?"

"Joey brought 'em to me. He was back in the Bronx this weekend visiting his family."

Janice selected one from the box and savored that incredible first bite. "Ya know, it *maketh* you want a *glassth* of milk."

"I'll get you some."

"*Thankth*." She went back to the subliminal messages, trying to divine the method that created the madness. Holding the donut with her teeth, she made red-ink notes in the margins of one of the enlarged outline pages tacked to the wall.

Kronos entered. "I heard the donuts came this way."

She pulled the donut from between her teeth. "Help yourself. They're right on my desk. In fact, take the whole box. Less for me to guilt over." She sighed, taking a step back in an attempt to realize any pattern not yet obvious to her.

Kronos stabbed through the hole of one of the donuts and picked it up from the box like a ring around his index finger. He held it that way as he started to

nibble his way around, removing the chocolate covering like a lathe. He walked over to Janice. "Doing a
little programming?"

"Kronos, please, I'm trying to work this out. Could
you just take your donut and leave? Ewwwww!" She
finally looked away from the chart and reacted to the
sight of him eating it off his finger.

"Jeez, what a grouch."

Something ruminated in Janice's mind. "Kronos!"

He returned. "Yeah?"

"What did you mean 'was I programming'?"

"What you got plastered on the wall here looks like
an old Basic program."

"How so?"

"Well, in that old language, each line of instruction
was numbered, like the way you got it there. And you
see that grouping there ..." he pointed to a "paragraph"
that stood alone. "That looks like a subroutine. This
here looks like an old 'If-Then' statement. You know,
if the proposition is true *then* do this, *if* it is false *then*
do that."

"Hold it, hold it, go slow. What's a subroutine?"

"Well, it's a way to get the computer to do repetitive tasks without having to write repetitive code. So
you write it once and keep telling the machine to run
the subroutine as many times as you need it to. Bury-
ing a nasty line of instruction in a subroutine was how
I did some of my best hacking, because the program
wouldn't immediately hit it until the subroutine was
called up. I named them 'time bombs' cause it was just
a matter of time 'til ..."

She kissed Kronos, interrupting his boasting. "Mister, you just got yourself a year's supply of donuts!"

∞§∞

The two most powerful places in America being
Washington and Hollywood, the news of the movie

star's and senator's deaths came as a shock to just about everyone. The details were never released by the LAPD. "Murder-suicide" was the official cause of death in the coroner's report. The impact on Hollywood was considerable, as Miss Saks was in the middle of a $200-million film that would now have to be trashed. The senator was just about to start his re-election bid and many pundits, posthumously of course, foresaw a possible White House residency in his recently extinguished future.

Unreported in the *L.A. Times* was the fact that along with the senator's death came the death of the Dent-Farber Emergency Cyber Crimes Initiative legislation. That bill would have pseudo-nationalized his corporate constituents in Silicon Valley, forcing them to design a new Internet police force in exchange for the political plum of getting billions in funding for advanced computational research engines. This, ostensibly, would be done as a national security issue to thwart any future attempts by any foreign power to gain the advantage in the never-talked-about computational power race.

The Hollywood press, however, reported the following news bulletin: "Self-help guru Kindwa Seiene, multimillionaire TV empowerer and author of *My Karma, My Power* has offered $44 million for the Saks estate. The mansion and grounds in Beverly Hills was the former home of mogul ..."

CHAPTER THIRTY-EIGHT
BRAIN FOOD

"YOU KNOW WHAT makes a church a basilica?" Kronos said.

"No, what?" Janice asked, playing along as she and Cheryl set up enlargements of the outlines on easels.

"A basilica is a church where the pope has held mass. It can be any church. Once the pope celebrates mass in it, boom, it becomes a basilica."

"You ... are an idiot," Hiccock said as he opened the briefing folders.

"I was just wondering if this is the Presidential Suite because some president stayed here once ... if the same rule applies."

"According to that, then Yankee Stadium would be a basilica!"

"How ya figure that?"

"Hello, the pope held mass there back in the sixties or seventies."

"Guys, guys!" Janice called out, "can you finish this theological debate later. The president will be here any minute."

"Bill, don't you think we should have waited until the president got back to Washington to do this?" Janice's anxiety tinged her tone. "He's going to be here on the West Coast for two more days. He needs to hear what you've discovered *now*." Kronos stood captivated by two tables of catered food. "Did you see this spread?"

Kronos's eyes widened as he surveyed the bounty sprawled before him. The buffet offered everything from finger sandwiches to hot chafing dishes all laid out just in case the president, on a whim, wanted a bite or decided to invite a head of state to his suite.

While Cheryl prepared the briefing papers and Kronos worked his way methodically through the food groups, Hiccock took Janice aside. "Are you okay?"

Janice nervously smoothed the St. John suit, which only a few hours ago seemed to her to be a "sure-fire look." She caught herself and forced her hands to her side. "It's easy for you. You work with the man. I've never met a president before, much less reported a 'theory' to one. It's just a little nerve-racking, Bill."

"He's a really decent guy, Janice, a straight shooter and pretty smart. I think he's going to get this without too much trouble. Besides, he knows you're the best in your field."

Bill's cell phone chirped. "Hiccock."

Joey Palumbo was on the other end in his new capacity as the FBI's Quarterback liaison officer. "Bill, we just put together a time line on the Saks-Dent killings."

"Give me the shorthand. We're about to meet with the boss."

"She worked out from 11 AM to 12:15, threatened her agent on a conference call until 12:35, then spent more than an hour online. After that, she dismissed all her house staff for the rest of the day and placed a call to Dent's personal phone. Forty minutes later at 3 PM, they were both dead according to the coroner."

"And so was Dent's firewall legislation."

"It's certainly a high-tech enough motive. I have my guys running her computer through your cockamamie subliminal gadget back in D.C. right now. Hansen says that the first few messages he's found so far point to an online-ordered assassination of a sitting U.S. senator."

"Gadget" was the in-house term the FBI geeks had given to Hiccock's circa 1960s technological dinosaur, which just now happened to be the single key to breaking open the most devastating use of technology in American history.

"As soon as they have a hard copy printout, have it sent to us here ..." Hiccock's phone went dead. Pulling it away from his ear, he saw there was full signal strength. That's when he remembered "the bubble" that blanked out all cell service when the president was nearby.

At that moment, the Secret Service appeared in the room to conduct their secondary sweep. Two agents, having already cleared Hiccock's team, concerned themselves with the windows and any possible line of fire that a rooftop assassin might utilize to achieve infamy.

"He's here," Bill said to Janice.

An agent mumbled something into his wrist radio microphone about the room being secure. A split second later, the president, followed by Chief of Staff Reynolds, entered the room with Tate in tow. The president took off his jacket, laid it over the back of a chair, and loosened his tie. He headed straight to the bar. One of the Secret Service agents shadowed the president's movements, positioning himself between the window and the president. The Commander in Chief commandeered a ginger ale and popped it open, grabbed some ice, and poured. The White House steward, Mr. Jefferies, watched helplessly as the president temporarily usurped his duties. His only way to do his job was to hand the president a cocktail napkin.

"Thanks, Bob. My stomach has been doing loop-da-loops all day," Mitchell said. "Please people, feel free." He referred to the food and bar, oblivious to the fact that Kronos had already helped himself.

As he headed toward the couch, the president extended his hand to Janice Tyler.

"I know everyone else in the room but we haven't had the pleasure, Doctor Tyler. I'm James Mitchell, nice to meet you."

"It's Janice, please. And you know, ginger ale is the perfect thing for a nervous stomach." *Oh shit*, she

thought, *what a stupid thing to say.* "So I'll get one, too,"
she said, patting her Nicole Miller–covered tummy.

As she started toward the bar, the president simply uttered, "Mr. Jefferies," and a glass of ginger ale
appeared in Janice's hand. The president smiled and
clinked her glass with his. "I hope you've got something good for me. I just came from the funeral of a
U.S. senator. To mangle a line from Shakespeare, 'I
came to praise Hank Dent not to bury him.' The director here tells me that Dent's death may have been connected with your line of research, Doctor. Before that,
I sat through a memorial service in Silicon Valley for
all the people who died on that plane ..." The man sat
motionless for a moment, as if he could see the terror
that those souls aboard the plane must have endured,
then snapped out of it. "Horrible, horrible tragedies;
we have to stop these terrorist acts ... so what do you
have for me?"

Everyone took their seats and immediately
scanned the big blowups of the outline propped on easels throughout the room. Janice sipped her ginger ale
and set it down. "Mr. President, I saw a film in college
that chronicled the technique of a famous vaudevillian
named Mesmer. He was a hypnotist. He would 'mesmer-
ize' members of the audience and get them to do funny
things by having them concentrate on a dangling pen-
dant. But the big part of his act was when he planted
a post-hypnotic suggestion usually based on a trigger
word. After the subject returned to his seat, he might
bark like a dog if Mesmer uttered the trigger word. We
now firmly believe that all of the homegrown terrorists
were programmed online by a method not unlike that,
but supercharged by the power of a computer. There
are subtleties and nuances we haven't figured out as
yet, but the main gist of it has been uncovered."

She walked over to the first easel. "Like Mesmer,
the way to control a subject is through the eyes. Lion
tamers use the same technique. In short, get them by

the eyes and they're yours. Today a large segment of the population gives their eyes over to the most powerful technological device created by humans, the computer."

"They also give their attention to television," Tate said, interrupting.

"Yes, and that was abused in the sixties until the government interceded and stopped the practice. Because it was broadcast, it was also a one-way message, unilateral if you will. The Internet adds two important and powerful differences. First it's interactive, a two-way street. The degree by which the subject is affected can be fed back to the controller and instantly tailored to optimize the depth of submission. Computers also have higher definition and therefore can pack more information into the bandwidth than television."

Janice rotated the pointer in her fingers as she addressed the president. "As was the case in the sixties, without the targeted individual being aware, subliminal messages were transmitted directly into their subconscious. Their conscious minds did not realize these messages were being projected. Normally, these would reveal themselves upon a trigger or hypnotic-style suggestion.

"So the computer is hypnotizing them?" Tate asked.

"The old hypnosis model only follows to a certain point, falling far short of what we are dealing with here. For one thing, even the most susceptible subject wouldn't do anything under hypnosis that would be against their conscious will.

In today's version, somehow, by a means we haven't yet deduced, the encoding of these messages is layered, hidden inside the target's subconscious. For the purposes of this discussion, I am going to refer to that hidden layer as the deep subconscious. There, the instructions lay dormant, waiting for a condition to be met in the layer above the subconscious. Kronos ... er ... Mr. DeMayo has identified that condition as an 'if-then' statement. It's a logical argument that is the key to making decisions in a computer. If such and such is true then do action A, if such and such is false do action B or do nothing. Have I left anything unclear or are there any questions before we go further, Mr. President?"

"No, I'm following you. Somehow, two sets of commands are buried into a person's brain. One says, if something is true, then do the second.

"Yes, that's it, Sir. So here's what we think happened in Martha Krummel's case. As you know, she is the only homegrown who has survived. At first, her recollections of how she came to derail the freight train seemed random and disjointed. But when you apply this programming sequence, it all becomes plausible. As far as we can tell, buried in Martha's deep subconscious were four "subroutines." The first gave her the complete and very real experience that her husband Walter had just called. In that fabricated experience, he asked her to come to his office with jumper cables to boost his car's dead battery. Although she knew he had been dead for twenty years, she was totally and absolutely living in the false reality in which she had, a few moments earlier, conversed with him."

"Now how could something like that happen?" Tate asked.

"I think the positive side of her brain embraced this implanted reality. In fact, I believe her desire to have him back was so strong that, in her mind, the fact that he was dead was nothing more than a nightmare she once had. She was in a state that could best be described as dreamlike, where she wanted to get back to a dream that was interrupted. You know, the way sometimes people wake up from a dream that is so good, they try to go back to sleep to experience it again. But buried in Martha's subconscious was an 'if-then' statement. As she drove, the sight of a road sign that read 'Waukesha Gap two miles' triggered it." Janice pointed to easel number three and the image on it taken from Martha's computer screen. "We found a picture of this road sign, originally from the Wisconsin Highway Department's web site. It was embedded in the subliminal instructions we decoded using the MIT machine."

Janice then pointed to an easel that held a shot of the fruit stand from the subliminal frames. "The 'if-then' statement in Martha's mind said, 'If you see this sign, then jump to the next subroutine.' Originally, it seemed to us that Martha had changed her story. She told us that she turned down the access road to the train tracks because she thought there was a fruit stand there. What actually happened was, once she saw that sign, all thoughts of Walter and the intention to help him with his dead battery evaporated from her mind and were replaced with a new goal ... the fruit stand."

"But didn't she know there was no fruit stand on that road?" the president asked.

"Sir, have you ever experienced déjà vu?"

"Yes. When you feel as though something has happened before."

"But you know intellectually it hasn't, correct?"

"Yes."

"This whole new area of research that we are rapidly uncovering here may explain the phenomenon of déjà vu—or what I now prefer calling a concurrent memory. It is caused by a temporary lapse of the conscious mind. It concerns two parts of our minds, the conscious, the part of the brain that is our awareness of the here and now, and the memory, the repository of all things that have happened to us. To illustrate, if I were experiencing déjà vu right now, then everything that's happening in this room, right at this moment, would bypass my conscious mind and land directly in my memory. Of course, I would have no idea this had happened. However, I do perceive what's going on, or more accurately, *recollect* it in my memory. I am experiencing something as it is happening by instantly reading it back from my memory. Coming from there it has the same credibility as an old, cherished thought. Even though it is, in fact, an instant or concurrent memory of what is simultaneously happening at this moment."

"I see. But we feel it happened already because it came from the place in our mind where everything we remember comes from."

"This is getting a little hard to follow," Tate said.

"The next part may help. Like déjà vu, these instructions were placed directly into Martha's subconscious and deep subconscious by subliminal suggestion."

"Hold on, you just said 'suggestion.' Earlier you said she was, what was the word you used?" The FBI director referred to his notes. "Programmed. But clearly, she wasn't choosing to follow a suggestion. She doggedly followed out orders."

Janice read the skepticism on Tate's face. She took a deep breath. "That's the part that's still up in the air, but I have a theory." She focused on the president. "Somehow, these instructions get layered into the deepest recesses of the mind and are released by higher levels of instructions. Whoever devised this has broken through to some new understanding of the human brain."

"Are you aware of any research in that area, Dr. Tyler?"

"No, Sir, but I am talking about the total remapping of the human brain to a level and specificity that, yesterday, I would have told you was two to three centuries away. For all modern science has learned about the mind, we are merely strangers without a map. The creator of this program has the ultimate blueprint and can go anywhere and do anything inside the human brain."

"That's a frightening prospect, Doctor."

"So you're saying Martha had four or five split personalities?" Reynolds said.

"It is very much like that, Ray. With this level of deep-seated instructions, whole realities and worlds can be created with great detail within someone's mind, each one being indistinguishable from an actual event that a person has lived through. In short, no matter *how* it gets there, deep in the center of our minds, there is no difference between a lived memory and an implanted one."

"So anything can be planted in someone's mind?" Tate asked.

"It appears to be so. For instance, at one point Martha thought she was saving an infant that had been cruelly locked in the equipment cabinet on the side of the track. That belief was now so entrenched in Martha's conscious that it motivated her to pry the cabinet open. It is furthermore apparent that this whole scenario was based on an actual event in Martha's life. Her older daughter remembers locking her baby sister in the closet by accident when they were playing house. Martha had to pry the door open with a crowbar to free the frightened, crying child."

"So all the details of the situation were already in Martha's long-term memory. The masterminds of this process just adapted it, possibly by interrogating the subject once she was under their control," Hiccock said.

"But didn't she realize it was a lie, or whatever, when she opened the cabinet and she could plainly see there was no baby in there?" the president asked.

Janice pointed to the subroutine on easel two that included a picture of the inside of the control cabinet. "Here's where the layers come in again. As soon as Martha saw the relays and circuits inside the metal case, it triggered a new subroutine, the one that had her short-circuit the switch wiring. At that instant her brain was cleansed of all thoughts of a trapped baby and replaced with a new reality and a new task."

Hiccock pointed to the last easel, which displayed the freeze frame of the actress from the HBO movie holding a gun to her head. "The final trigger is the chilling part. Her last subroutine called for her to commit suicide. That program was left open-ended, judging by the way Martha still tries to kill herself to this day."

Janice stood there for almost a full minute as they silently digested what she had laid out before them.

"My God!" the Commander in Chief said. "Doctor Tyler, how sure are you that this is actually what we are dealing with here?"

"We deduced this methodology from all the available evidence we will ever accumulate. I suppose there might be another explanation or way to connect these elements, but the core of the premise is solid. Although we don't have a clue as to who is behind it yet, Mr. President, this is how it is being done."

"One question," Reynolds said. "You're saying that Martha was programmed. That implies someone programmed her. How would that someone have known about her dead husband?"

Hiccock fielded that one. "This is a web-based means of recruitment and programming. Today, all records of birth, death, marriages, and even a person's purchases are out there in the digital domain beyond the public space of the Internet, but potentially available to any clever hacker."

"So if I understand this right," Tate said, "assuming we could have stopped Martha in her car on the way to the derailment, she would believe—and pass a lie detector test—that she was simply meeting her husband in his parking lot at work?"

"Exactly. She would have had no inkling of what she was about to do next ..."

CHAPTER THIRTY-NINE
BAD KARMA KAZE

A *USA TODAY* newspaper headlined "Wall Street's Deep Freeze Continues" landed on Admiral Parks's kitchen table, along with Hiccock and Janice's carry-on bags. Hiccock was about to hit the bathroom when he became distracted by an argument between Kronos and Parks.

"Get off my ass, will ya," Kronos said with typical Bensonhurst eloquence. "For the hundredth time, it's no use. I tried everything I know to get through that firewall."

"Well, that couldn't have been all that much effort then."

Kronos slammed down his fist and kicked his chair over as he rose. "You want a piece of me, old woman?"

Before Hiccock or the Army MPs in the room could react, Parks swung around in her swivel chair and swept Kronos's legs out from under him. He fell on her lap as she put her elbow in his neck. He coughed and gagged as he was pinned by the septuagenarian.

"Who's old?"

"Admiral, please don't hurt the stupid hired help," Hiccock said, trying to hide his amusement. "He's federal property that I'm signed out for."

She released her seemingly effortless hold on the nerd with a warning. "You be a good little Guido or this 'old' woman will make you bark like a friggin' dog for your dinner," the lady said, pulling off a pretty decent Brooklynese in her own right.

Kronos rubbed his throat as he got up and walked over to Hiccock. "I thought you said she was a secretary! For who, Gorilla Monsoon?"

Hiccock ignored him and addressed the Admiral. "Nice move. Where did you pick that up?"

"My dearly departed was UDT."

"What's UDT?" Kronos said.

Hiccock answered. "Underwater Demolition Team. It's what the first Navy Seals were called. I'd show her a little more respect or you'll be back in Club Fed in time for breakfast."

Kronos picked up his chair and crossed the room. With a flourish of newfound gallantry, he said, "Might I assist you, Admiral Parks?"

Without looking up from the screen she announced, "I'm through the firewall."

"Holy shit!"

Hiccock was beaming. "That's great, Admiral!"

"How did you do that?" Kronos said, amazed.

"It seems that you and everybody else out there today have forgotten the basics. Boolean algebra."

Kronos snapped his fingers. "Of course." He turned to Hiccock. "This old ..." Kronos caught himself "... *genius* here went back to the machine code. She essentially passed through the wall as zeros and ones."

"Yes, and I used what you would call a self-replicating polynomial hierarchy to mask the dimensional string length to zero."

"Holy fazzool, you've cracked my virus. You cracked my greatest hack code."

"You helped me when I saw you hide the last two Oreo cookies from the MP." The MP glared at him, marking him for death.

Hiccock chuckled. "She's got your number, Kronie! Your behavioral traits are infused in your dirty little code writing."

"Yes, sneaky is sneaky in life or in computer programming. Although, Bill, you aren't going to like what's on the other side of that wall."

As she pointed to the screen to show her discovery, Hiccock actually turned white.

∞§∞

"Mr. President!" a winded Reynolds barked, interrupting a meeting.

The Oval Office was quickly cleared and Reynolds explained what he had learned.

"Are you sure?" the president said from his desk.

"This is Ultra traffic, direct from Hiccock's team. They have been batting a thousand throughout this whole affair."

In the silence of the next five seconds, it was obvious to Reynolds that the president had fully digested the impact of the news.

"I want the head of every agency in here in thirty minutes. Start sharpening the axe. I am not going down this way. I will cut off all their fucking heads before I take a fall like this. Thirty minutes— and that's a direct order from the Commander in Chief. If they don't comply, I'll consider that desertion under fire and, God Almighty, I'll have them shot!"

For the first time since they struggled through those early primaries, Reynolds felt a genuine fear when the president roared. But not because of anything the man said.

∞§∞

Hiccock, Parks, and Kronos were sitting on the porch, celebrating their discovery by dunking Oreos into glasses of milk. Kronos used a fork, wedged into the cream between the two cookie halves. "This way you don't get the dry finger part, just total immersion. I count to ten for nice and soft, seven for al dente." He popped one into his mouth from the fork tines.

"You really need to get a life, you know that?" Admiral Parks said.

"I will, now that I ... er, we have cracked the biggest terrorism case in American history. Maybe Uncle Sam will give me time off for 'genius behavior.'"

"Unfortunately this is all top secret, code-word clearance. No one will ever know what we did here," Hiccock explained soberly.

"Someone will know," Parks said.

"How's that?" Hiccock asked as he twisted open a cookie.

"Asynchronous transfer protocol."

Kronos choked on his milk. "Crap! Of course. You can't go through a firewall without leaving a tracer back to you."

"You mean *we* left a cookie?"

"Something like that ..."

∞§∞

Three short whistle bursts rippled across the intersection in downtown Carlsbad, New Mexico, opposite a construction site. A few seconds later, the office shanty of supervising engineer Henry Wilson, along with his iPhone in his hand, was rocked by the deep rumble of an explosion. A moment later, a single, long all-clear whistle sounded.

Outside, a crane pulled away a smoking steel mesh, revealing the blasted, crumpled rock beneath.

Henry was online. The iPhone screen before him displayed a contractor's materials-and-supply web site. No one in the shanty noticed that his demeanor was much more intense than it should be. The lines in his brow, etched in place by decades of worry, and the white beard he sported combined to make him look older than his fifty years. Without a word to anyone else in the shed, he got up and walked outside, leaving his phone on the desk.

Another three-whistle warning bellowed but Henry just kept walking. A flagman called out to him, "Henry, get down! Are you crazy?"

He continued walking. *Boom*. Henry didn't so much as flinch as a whole steel-mesh-blanketed section of earth rose and fell just beyond him in a shuddering explosion. Eyes focused straight ahead, he walked over to a red armored-car-styled explosives truck. Opening the back door, the ex-demolition man turned construction site manager pulled out a cordite module and a blasting cap. With none of the attendant care one might expect when handling high explosives, Henry roughly injected the detonator into one stick of dynamite lying in an open box and spooled the detonator cord out. He closed the door, reeling out the yellow wire around the truck as he got into the driver's seat and drove off. The actual driver of the truck, a few construction men, and one rent-a-cop screamed after him, but the armored truck, having been jammed into gear, proceeded to barrel down the street.

∞§∞

Deputy Sheriff Jack Rainey was writing up a motorist for speeding when the external speaker on his patrol car squawked. "Car 21, be advised a stolen truck, red, carrying explosives, last seen heading west on Alameda."

Not trusting what he had heard, he stopped writing the citation and walked back to his car. He grabbed the radio mic through the window. "Dispatch, did you say explosives?"

"That's a 10-4. Be advised other units are now in pursuit. Subject vehicle has run two roadblocks."

Rainey jogged back to the motorist and ripped up the incomplete ticket. "This is your lucky day, sir. But slow down. Your luck could run out big-time."

The officer trotted back to the car, jumped in, and pulled out, leaving a repentant Mexican-American gardener crossing himself and thanking St. Jude.

"Roger that, dispatch. Please advise all other units in pursuit that Car 21 is west of the truck and will try to interdict and slow." As he released the mic button, a plan of action started forming in his mind. With siren wailing and lights flashing, he zoomed past the light traffic. The police vehicle came to a sliding, fishtailing halt with its rear end pointing at the red truck bearing down on his position.

Calmly he watched the truck approach through his rearview mirror with four cop cars in close pursuit. Slipping his Ford Galaxy in gear, he started rolling, picking up speed as the truck approached his rear bumper. Upon first contact, he let his foot off the gas and applied the brake. The squad car started to dig in, fighting the massive truck's momentum. The deputy slammed his car into first. The trunk of his car began to collapse under the pressure of the on-charging truck. Henry Wilson, wide-eyed and emotionless behind the wheel, floored the accelerator. The front of Jack's squad car was cantilevered off the ground as the truck ate more and more into its trunk. Seeing the front wheels of the cop car up off the road, Henry started weaving the truck. Both vehicles swayed across the road, slamming into unsuspecting passing cars creating a domino effect into other cars. As it swerved, the truck resembled an animal shaking its prey in its jaws. Jack was helpless to do anything with the cruiser's steering up off the pavement. Finally, the squad car pivoted and spun on its blown-out rear wheels as the big red truck pushed it aside. The spinning car came to a stop as the pursuit vehicles whizzed by.

The large, boxy truck took the entrance to the highway, pushing a slow-moving car off the ramp and into the gully. A police helicopter joined the chase from above. Looking down, the pilot saw six cop cars in close pursuit of the red truck as it wove in and out of traffic, running cars off the road.

∞§∞

Hiccock was talking outside to Major Rolland Hanks, the commanding officer of the Military Police escort that accompanied the communications trucks. Kronos had stepped out onto the porch when something off in the distance caught his eye. It was a dust swirl, which caused the kid from Bensonhurst who never saw a cow up close before yesterday to say, "Look, like in the freakin' *Wizard of Oz*. It's a twister!"

At that same instant, the Major's RTO handed him the handset. "Sir, we just got a report from OP 1. An armored car, with police cars in pursuit, just passed their position heading for us."

"Notify Checkpoint 1," he ordered back to the radio-telephone operator.

The major pointed to the location of Observation Post 1. Hiccock could see the truck, but barely made out the flashing police lights through the plume of dust it kicked up.

The major reached into the van and retrieved binoculars. After a few seconds Hiccock borrowed the major's glasses and saw Checkpoint 1– three Humvees sitting alongside the only road leading to the Parks home.

"What's the plan, Major?" Hiccock said.

"My sentries at the perimeter will stop him."

Hiccock didn't know if it was mental telepathy or just great training, but as if they heard him, two of the Jeeps moved to the center of the road forming a blockade. A .50 caliber machine gun was revealed in back of a Hummer that was off to the side of the dirt road.

∞§∞

In the lead cop car, Trooper Mills of the New Mexican State Police was in close order pursuit, bumping over the uneven road, constantly peppered with gravel and rocks being kicked up by the heavy armored truck traveling at almost sixty miles per hour. He couldn't believe his eyes when he saw Army vehicles forming a roadblock.

"Where did they come from?"

∞§∞

The MPs took their positions. One stood in front with his MP-5 submachine gun and his hand up in a "stop" gesture. The approaching truck, with the police cars in tow, at first seemed to slow. At the last minute, however, Henry Wilson floored it. The lead MP fired into the window. The small-caliber bullets bounced off the two-inch-thick composite windshield of the armored car. A heavy clack, clack, clack was heard as the "fifty" opened up from an angle, spraying the driver's side windows and side of the truck with the larger .50 caliber slugs.

∞§∞

Trooper Mills, in the lead car, slammed on the brakes and simultaneously screamed into the radio mic: "All cars back off. The Army is shooting at the truck! Dispatch, try to call them, tell them the truck is filled with explosives. All units drop back!"

∞§∞

Due to the sharp angle from which the bullets were fired, the thick laminated side window cracked but didn't break. With bullets bouncing off the side and ricocheting into the Hummer's skin, the gunner momentarily ceased firing. The truck crashed through the blockade, sending the Jeeps twirling in opposite directions. One exploded. The MPs opened fire at the back of the truck as it raced toward the house. The pursuing cop cars had already screeched to a halt to avoid the fusillade of bullets.

∞§∞

Witnessing the breach, Hiccock turned to the major. "I may be going out on a limb here, but I'm going to assume that's not the Ladies' Auxiliary Welcome Wagon."

"Bracken, front and center," the major barked. Hiccock noticed a moose of a guy run up with a bazooka. "I don't like people who wreck my Jeeps, Bracken. Remove him from the planet, please!"

Bracken immediately got down on one knee and hoisted the Javelin antitank weapon on his shoulder. The infrared sight locked in on the truck, sounding a slight beeping tone. "Target acquired, Sir."

The major radioed his men at the roadblock. "Jess, you and your men take cover." He checked to make sure they were far enough from the truck. "Ruin his day, son."

As the truck neared, the white letters above the cab of the truck came into sharper focus. They spelled out EXPLOSIVES. The major opened his mouth and yelled, "Hold your fire!" just as yellow flame and gray smoke exited the back of the bazooka. A split second later, the truck exploded violently. Its wheels continued rolling as the rear cargo box, laden with TNT, shot up thirty feet straight into the air and combusted in a raging inferno followed by a rising mushroom. The supersonic shock wave was visible over the sand, slamming into mesquite bushes and rocking prickly pear cacti as it fanned outward in all directions from the spot directly below the truck. The flaming Jeep at the roadblock behind it had its fire literally blown out, extinguished by the concussive wall of air. The squad cars further back were jostled violently.

The shock wave pummeled the house. Every window shattered. Kronos, standing in the doorway, was knocked back into the living room. The windows on the communications van imploded and the satellite dish collapsed. Shrapnel from the disintegrated truck showered down with the force of bullets, puncturing vehicles and parts of the house. A piece of steel embedded itself into the hood of the truck that Hiccock and Major Hanks were crouched behind. The sound of the explosion echoed off the foothills for at least thirty seconds, repeating back and forth, as Hiccock and the major regained their upright postures.

"Look …!" Hiccock pointed to a crater fifty feet around and thirty feet deep in the middle of the road. Smoldering parts of the truck dotted the edge.

"Good shooting, Bracken … Bracken?" The major looked down and saw Bracken was dead on the ground, impaled by a twisted, mangled piece of the truck's red metal.

"A minute ago, I called him son," the major said to Hiccock with a catch in his throat.

∞§∞

The president, Reynolds, and the heads of every U.S. agency were packed into the Situation Room of the White House. "We have found the enemy and he is one of us. Quarterback's team has successfully traced the source of these terrible bombings and terrorist actions against the people and property of the United States to a government portal. Someone in this room is responsible for the carnage and destruction that has befallen this nation. One of you is heading up a project or initiative that is, at best, treason, and at worst insane."

The room ignited with murmurs. The president allowed it to go on for a few seconds, watching for reactions, then continued. "If it didn't make me sound so egotistical I might think it a coup d'état." That brought the room to silence. "I know I fell into this job because I was a strong independent taking votes away from the men who would be king. But goddamn it, I will not have the destruction of the American way of life as the legacy of my administration."

The president noticed a bookish man in his late twenties had entered the room during the momentary lull. "Who are you?"

"Walter Conklin, Sir. I am the CIO here at the White House. They said you wanted to see me."

"Have you been briefed?"

"Yes, Sir."

"So tell me what we are looking for, Conklin?"

"Well, I'm only the Chief Information Officer here, not an expert."

"I understand, but I need an opinion."

"Big mainframe. Maybe a Cray or new Paradigm SQ. Lots of support techs and a big pipe, probably multifiber array with switch nodes and isolated redundant power sources."

"How much money are we talking here?"

"Hard to say, Sir, but probably tens of millions."

The president addressed the room. "We haven't found anything like that in your various department budgets. So that leaves only one option."

Reynolds jumped in, "Black Ops. Programs and initiatives not open to congressional scrutiny."

"Who's running this program? NSA? CIA? The damn Girl Scouts? Who?"

The phone rang. The president waved his hand to the communications officer and talked into the speakerphone. "Who is this on the line?"

A voice came back over the loudspeaker. "General Tyson, Sir, duty officer at joint operations center. There's been an attempted attack on Quarterback."

"How? Why? Who would know the …"

"Sir, it was a truck laden with explosives. It got to within 1,000 feet of the house they were in. One casualty, an Army Ranger. The bazooka man who took out the truck was killed by the blast, Sir."

"Good God! Are Quarterback and the Admiral okay?"

"A little shook up but fine, Sir."

"How did the assailants know where they were?"

"Once Quarterback's team broke through the firewall, they were reverse-traced and the assassin was dispatched immediately."

"Do we know who the assassin was?"

"Carlsbad PD identified him as Henry Wilson, an explosives engineer on a construction site fifty miles from Admiral Parks's home. A seemingly otherwise model citizen until he went nuts and rampaged through most of downtown Carlsbad on his way to meet his maker, Sir."

"I'll recommend the ranger who did the shooting for a posthumous DSC. Let's bring Quarterback's team back to Washington where we can keep them safe."

"Yes, Sir."

The president signaled to the telecom officer and the line was terminated.

"Somebody in this room is responsible for the deaths of thousands of Americans and we are not leaving until I find out who it is."

∞§∞

Celebrity is a potent charm. Anyone whom it touches glows, seemingly forever, with its incandescence. Even in a maximum-security prison, among the formerly notorious and momentarily infamous population, true celebrity had its perks. The yellow legal pad on her lap was proof. A "gift" from a star struck guard. The crayon was a concession to the survival instinct of all prison personnel, lest they become hostage of as simple a weapon as a number two pencil or Bic pen, pressed into their carotid artery. It was a safe and non-threatening Crayola brown, with which she took careful notes.

Penitentiary life did not allow for makeup or beauty salons, yet she was dangerously attractive. A short stint in Tai Bo, building upper body strength through boxing-like exercises, had served her well when one of the dykes, who demanded attention from all the "new bloods," got a little too friendly once.

Out in the prison yard, in the bright Leavenworth, Kansas, noonday sun, sat two ends of the spectrum - the young "looker," with the bound and shackled, nutty old lady. They spent all of the exercise hour conversing, taking notes, and occasionally stopping as thoughts coalesced in the younger one's mind.

A passing guard noticed the large, scrawled crayon heading at the top of the brown-lettered page as he patrolled past, "Inside Club Fed - Part 3 - Martha Krummel - The Gardening Grandmother." Carly Simone had her next byline.

∞§∞

Army MPs boarded up the shattered windows. Another swept debris off the floor. Hiccock resurrected the workstation as Admiral Parks rubbed a sore elbow.

"Did I forget to thank you for bringing technology into my quiet home?"

Hiccock looked around and surveyed the damage. "I really am sorry about that. Obviously the government will pay all damages ... or I will."

The major entered. "We got orders to bug out back to Washington on the double. Pack up whatever you're going to need."

"I won't be needing anything, 'cause I'm not going," the Admiral said resolutely.

"Ma'am ... er ... Admiral, Sir, ma'am, it's a direct order from the Commander in Chief directly to me! At my pay grade! There's no 'no' for an answer. The president decided you would be safer in Washington."

"It's Admiral USN, Retired, Major."

Kronos walked in with his laptop, an airport wireless antenna sticking up. "It's close by."

"What is?" Hiccock asked.

"The point of presence. I phase-detected the shift from the first bounce signal and its spread indicates a lapse time of .23 picoseconds. That's .000000000023 times the speed of light which equals 8.14 miles away."

"Translation?" Hiccock said.

"The firewall and possibly the whole shebang is very near. The origin or point of presence is the last stop before the backbone of the Internet."

Hiccock turned to the major. "We're staying."

"You're leaving ... until my orders change."

Hiccock pulled out his cell phone as he said to the major, "Sorry you lost a man before."

"The president is personally recommending him for a Distinguished Service Cross. C'mon, we've got to go."

Hiccock put up his finger for the major to wait as his call was connected. "I heard you are recommending a DSC for the downed soldier. Thanks, he saved all of our lives."

The major's jaw dropped.

"I know you ordered us back there to Washington, but my main computer geek just located the source as eight miles from here." Hiccock folded his phone at the end of the brief conversation. The major, still following his orders, started to usher Hiccock out when a radioman appeared.

"Sir, Ultra traffic, decode coming through."

The major took the radio headset. "Yes, Sir. Yes, Sir. Of course, Sir. Yes, Sir. Thank you, Mr. President." He handed the radio back and looked to Hiccock. "You got to let me borrow that phone sometime. Okay, we've been ordered to stay and I'm to assist you."

"Assist? Not to pull rank on you here, Major, but I'm an SES-4 and you are a 0-4. That makes me a simulated equivalent to some kind of general, you know."

"Well, I'll follow any militarily correct order. You get to ask, I get to veto if I feel it endangers the mission or presents unacceptable risks."

"Fair enough. Okay, what's your plan, Major?"

"Take a map. Draw a circle and door-to-door it."

"Forget about the doors," Kronos said. "This kind of connectivity requires fiber. Flat out DC to light."

"What's a fiber look like?"

Kronos plucked a hair out of his head and held it up. "Well, this is the cross-sectional diameter."

The major took a deep breath and left.

Hiccock's cell phone rang. Tyler was calling from the FBI psychological profiles lab. A mug shot of Wilson, the truck bomber, was on her computer screen. Technicians were audio scrubbing his answering machine message through a voiceprint analyzer.

"We're doing voice stress analysis baseline sampling right now," she said.

"Is that anything that can help us?"

"Our engineer fits the profile. He was on his iPhone one minute, then left his field office and headed for you."

"So he was another one programmed while online?"

"It appears so." There was a silence, then, "Bill?"

"Yes?"

"Why don't you come back to Washington and stop playing Army."

"Playing? I need to be here. We are so close."

"You are so stubborn. This is just more work for you, isn't it?"

"Let's not fight right now, okay? I really need to focus on what's going on, you know."

"Okay, but ..."

"But what?"

"But be careful. That's an order from your old boss." She clicked off. Hiccock said into the dead phone at the same moment the major walked by, "I love you, too, boss." Hiccock ended the call, addressing the screwed up look on the major's face. "Not the Prez that time."

The major walked to the front of a caravan of trucks and Jeeps. He stepped onto the sideboard of a two-and-a-half-ton truck. Waving his weapon, like John Wayne rolling the wagons, he ordered the column to move out.

"You think we could stop off for a pizza?" Kronos said.

They snaked around the crater in the road. On the far side, a tiny buzz turned their heads back in the direction of Parks's house. A small plane dove out of the sky.

They watched in disbelief as it crumpled into the simple wood-frame house. An instant later, the tiny aircraft exploded, shattering what was once Admiral Parks's peaceful haven.

"A delayed explosion," one of the troops coldly observed.

Hiccock turned to Admiral Parks and sheepishly grinned. "The government will recompense."

"Or you will," the pissed-off Admiral said, scowling.

CHAPTER FORTY
FAST FOOD

A "BREAKING NEWS" logo ripped into programming. A hastened-to-his-chair anchorman, Neil Peterson, was still adjusting his seat when the camera switched to him. The floor manager standing by camera one heard the cue from the director on his headset and threw his finger toward the anchor.

"CNN has learned that martial law has been declared by Federal authorities in Chavez and Eddy counties in New Mexico. We have had several reports of Army units charging into factories, stores, and private homes. One unconfirmed report speculates that any dwelling with a satellite dish is being targeted. Stories of troops fanning out throughout an office building, yelling orders, and forcing employees down to the floor are as yet unconfirmed. Although no official reason has been given by the White House, it is widely suspected that this action, which allegedly took place some fifteen minutes ago, is in response to the recent wave of terrorist attacks on American soil, but again that is purely speculation." He paused, listening to something on his IFB earpiece. "I have just received word that we have some video of more military and police actions, again centering around technology. We'll have that report from New Mexico coming up shortly. Until then, let's go to Susan Hawks, for a legal perspective on all this. Susan ..."

"Neil, the imposition of martial law is rare in U.S. history. Essentially, the declaration temporarily rescinds the Constitution and the Bill of Rights for the citizens and property of these two New Mexican counties. It places police or military authorities in power and affords them wide latitude to conduct search and seizures and set curfews."

"Why? What is the reasoning behind this?"

"It's anyone's guess at the moment. Martial law is usually used in case of civil unrest, and as far as we know there is no civil unrest in these two counties."

"So that leaves what, in your opinion?"

"Well, obviously the Federal government is looking for something and it must be a big and time-sensitive issue."

"So let me get this straight. They are searching for something wholesale and don't need any reason whatsoever in order to search and seize people, property, or assets."

"Yes, that is correct."

"Is this, in your opinion, a response in some way to the wave of recent terrorist actions?"

"I'd say that's certainly a good prospect."

"We are ready with the report now from Jasper Hines, who was in New Mexico working on a story for one of our weekend shows when all this came about. Jasper, I hear you've witnessed an actual event that occurred in the last hour."

The screen switched to the reporter standing on an average American residential street. "Neil, we were here covering a story on a gathering of psychics, new-age followers, and parapsychologists when we began to notice a high level of military activity. We came across one truck full of soldiers and followed them here to this sleepy little bedroom community. What happened next was right out of an Orwell novel ..."

A video appeared, shot through a news van window, showing a two-and-a-half-ton truck carrying four soldiers. The truck stopped on a residential street where the soldiers dismounted.

The reporter narrated the action. "They stopped, we stopped. Here a soldier is holding up a device, which Jim, our satellite technician, has identified as a field-strength meter. You can see him waving it around. He then apparently gets some sort of indication from the handheld device and now, here he is pointing in the direction of one of the houses on the street. At this point, we witnessed, incredulously I might add, U.S. military troops unceremoniously entering a civilian house."

The scene cut back to the reporter now in front of the house. "Two minutes after that video we just showed you, the squad of soldiers was out of there and gone. We have here with us now the members of the Wisticki family who live in that house. Let's start with you, Mrs. Wisticki, what were they looking for?"

The still-rattled woman looked to her husband and then addressed the microphone in the reporter's hand. "Well, I was vacuuming when the soldiers just came through the door. They ordered me to stand against the wall."

"What were your thoughts at that moment?"

"Why, I was scared to death. I didn't know what was happening."

"Mr. Wisticki, tell us what happened next."

"The troops ran through to the living room and ordered me to get down on the floor from my reclining chair in front of the TV. More troops went upstairs to where my son was."

"Timmy, isn't it?"

"Yes, Timmy Wisticki, Sir," the twelve-year-old answered the reporter.

"Tell us what happened when they came into your room."

"They picked me up and pulled me out of my chair, sat me on my bed, and said, 'Don't move.'"

"What were you doing when they did that?"

"I was playing Ninja Force Four—"

"Is that a video game?"

"It's an online computer game. I'm the national champion."

"I strapped together three PCs and had a DSL line installed so Timmy could play faster than anyone else," his father said.

"What happened then?

"A soldier sat at my computer and slid a disk in and did some kind of file search, then left."

"And did anyone tell you what they were looking for?

"No."

"No?"

"Nope."

"A puzzling mystery. We'll try to gather more information, but right now back to you in the studio, Neil."

The scene switched back to the anchor introducing yet another hurried-to-the-microphone expert. "We are joined now by our own head of technical operations, Phil Shimerhorn. Phil, what do you make of this?"

"From what I just heard, the field strength meter must have been reading an intense concentration of electromagnetic energy coming from the Wisticki household. The three PCs that the father lashed together *would* create that kind of intense hyperactive signature."

"So they are looking for some kind of technological device?"

"From this report, it would appear to be so."

The anchor then swiveled to a video monitor with a feed from the remote studio where Susan was stationed. He started talking to the monitor as if she were really inside it. "Susan, with the account we just heard of this search, my question to you is, is this legal?"

"It's covered under *posse comitatus*, which authorizes the military to operate as a de facto police force. I heard nothing in that account over which the Wistickis could sue or have recourse, not under martial law."

"Thank you, Susan. So the question for now is, just what is going on in New Mexico? We'll be right back after this word."

∞§∞

Hiccock and the major were listening to reports on the field radio. "Unit 2, nothing yet. Unit 3 is investigating an extremely strong electromagnetic field reading. Unit 9 is en route ..."

"You know what I can't understand?" Major Hanks said.

"What?"

"If they found us in the house and sent the truck and plane, how come they aren't coming after us with guns blazing now?"

"Good point. What would you do if you were the bad guys, Major?"

"I'd get some intelligence, send out a scout, find our weakest point, then plan an attack."

"What would be our weakest point?"

"Some hole in the defensive perimeter or some exposed asset that might be vulnerable to a strike. Then again, it could be some operational misstep, like us having all our planes lined up in neat little rows at Pearl Harbor for the Japanese to just pick off."

Hiccock pondered this as Kronos walked over. "Look, I'm starving. Can we please get a pizza?"

Hiccock came up with an idea and pulled out his cell phone. "Maybe *they* have an operational weakness." He spoke into his phone, "Hiccock for the president ... of course I'll hold." He covered the phone with his hand, "Can I get a Jeep and a driver?"

"What's on your mind?" the major asked.

"Maybe we're looking for the wrong thing. Let me and Kronos here do a little scouting."

"I'll send you out with a squad. You are still my first priority. Fair enough?"

Hiccock nodded as the White House telecom officer came back on the line. "Sir, the president is in a meeting right now."

"You know what? I'll call him back." He folded the phone. "President's busy. C'mon, Kronos, lets see the countryside."

"Just tell me there's a pizza shop somewhere around here."

They trotted over to a second lieutenant in front of three Hummers. He saluted as Hiccock and Kronos got into the lead vehicle.

"Can I ask you something?" Kronos said.

"What?"

"I checked up on you. You come from the Bronx."

"Burke Avenue. So?"

"So how come I'm me and you're you?"

"If it wasn't for football, I would have been you. The game was my ticket out."

"That's the other wiggy thing about you. You had the world by the oysters as a QB and you didn't go pro. What, no balls?"

"I played ball in college to repay my scholarship. But I wanted to *use* my head, not get it knocked off by some NFL linebacker."

"Yeah, but the broads you coulda scored with!"

"Didn't need them." Hiccock watched two RVs pass on the other side of the highway. "I met my wife in college. She was head of a research project. My boss, actually. Brains, beauty, and a way of making me feel ..."

"But you played for freaking Stanford. They were a no-bullshit football factory."

"They also offer one of the best science programs in the country. I was good at football but I am better in science. I wanted to do what I was good at, and felt good doing." Hiccock realized he might as well have been speaking Esperanto. "You can't understand that, can you?" Hiccock was distracted as more recreational vehicles passed.

"What are you thinking?" Kronos asked, following Hiccock's line of sight to the mobile homes passing by.

"Do you fish?"

"No."

"Hunt, ski, rappel?"

"I program, pal."

"So you haven't noticed all these RVs that we've been passing all day. More than you'd expect during off-season. There is no campground close."

"Food!" yelped Kronos like a hunting dog pointing at a bird.

Not being able to take it anymore, Hiccock relented. "Lieutenant, can we stop here?"

The column pulled into a McDonald's drive-through.

∞§∞

"I need to get there now," a determined Janice Tyler said to her new Air Force captain. Since the re-instatement of Hiccock's authority under Operation Quarterback, she enjoyed a little more power. *More than a captain*, she figured, since he was snapping to it on her "order." She now had a staff of FBI profilers. They would continue weeding through the psychological "mind field" that was being mapped by the cookies, worms, and replays of the subliminal computer screens. Computers had become the central focus of Janice's work because they were the only evidence any of the homegrowns left behind to testify as to their state of mind. All except for those associated with the Sabot Society. There were no subliminal messages detected in their computers, although the FBI Electronic Crimes Lab did find an abundance of conventional e-mail and chat room evidence. The chasm created by this disparity of evidence reinforced the notion that the Sabot was an unfortunately unlucky, and spectacularly inept, copycat group.

"You'll have to strap in, Ma'am," her captain said, as the small Air Force VC-100, essentially a small corporate jet with "USAF" and stars and stripes painted on the fuselage, started to taxi. Two Air Force pilots flew it. One was female, she noticed with a little smile, made sweeter by the fact that her Air Force cabin attendant was a male.

∞§∞

Bags of hamburgers and fries were handed into each Humvee. The three Hummers, with their machine guns tied off, pulled into three spaces in the lot. As the burgers were distributed, Hiccock observed an amazing transformation. Before his eyes, these hardcore Army Rangers had turned into high school kids with smiling faces, munching on Big Macs and sipping Cokes. He walked inside the store to pay the bill and asked to see the manager. The oldest guy in a paper hat with a nametag on his shirt came forward and identified himself. "Welcome to McDonald's, I'm Tim. Is there something I might do for you today?"

"Kinda busy, huh?" Hiccock spoke like he ran a Mickey D's back home, trying to disarm the company-approved speech.

"Been that way for a few weeks now."

"All those campers and Winnebagos?" Hiccock gestured to the passing parade of RVs.

"And minivans and backpackers from all over camping out at Leadfoot."

"What's going on at Leadfoot?"

"Some kind of New Age voodoo crap."

"New Age what?"

"All these psychics, Ouija board weenies, crystal gazers, shakra-holics, vegetarians, libertarians, all of 'em. Say they're being drawn to Leadfoot. Hooting and hollering at the moon for all I know."

Hiccock handed over a hundred-dollar bill for the troops.

"Your turn to feed the Army?" the manager said with a chuckle.

"Can I get a receipt, please?"

Then it hit him.

He ran outside, his cell phone to his ear.

∞§∞

After being dressed down by the president for not interrupting the meeting the last time Quarterback called in, the orders were now crystal clear: send all calls from QB through immediately. As commanded, the telecom officer intrepidly interrupted the president mid-sentence, "Sir, call from Quarterback."

Someone, maybe Reynolds, decided to use only Hiccock's code name, in case one of the president's men convened in the room was, in fact, a traitor or anarchist. He nodded to the telecom officer, and then picked up the handset.

"What is it, Bill?" *Damn.* He'd just blurted Hiccock's name out in the open. He listened for a second, then reacted with lowered brows over squeezed eyes. "You're serious? Well, I'm not going to start second-guessing you now. I'll order it and call you back." He put the phone down and addressed the telecom officer. "Jennifer, get me Paulsen at the GAO."

∞§∞

Hiccock placed the phone back in his shirt pocket. The lieutenant had a map out on the hood of his Humvee. "No Leadfoot on this map."

Hiccock grabbed the map. "Locals call it Leadfoot. It's an old lead mine ... here, right here, Cummings Peak."

"It's outside the perimeter that brain boy indicated."

"Yes it is." Hiccock cast his gaze to the far-off mountains. Focusing on the nearer foothills, he scanned the terrain as if he might find a sign shaped like an arrow reading "to the bad guys."

"Kronos!"

Kronos came over wiping special sauce from his mouth. "Yeah, what's up?"

Hiccock stabbed at the map. "Could this spot right here be the point of presence?"

"Sure, could be."

"Could be?"

"Well, jeez, I only had an accuracy of fifteen decimal points, so it could have been twelve miles also … instead of eight."

"*Now* you freaking tell me!"

CHAPTER FORTY-ONE
PINEAPPLES & ANCHOVIES

WHEN JOHN F. KENNEDY was in the depth of the Missile Crisis, he mostly conducted the operations from the Oval Office. The majority of meetings Carter attended to plan the Iranian hostage rescue were held in Plains, Georgia. Obama spent a little more than a half-hour in the nerve center when the Navy Seals delivered final justice to Bin Laden. Presidents spend less time in the Situation Room under the White House than one would think. In fact, the actor Henry Fonda probably got more "Sitch-time" in the movie *Fail-Safe* than all the real presidents who served since that film was made. The current *acting* president—that's how James Mitchell felt sometimes—was using the crisis center as an interrogation room. Far from peering eyes and electronic ears, he was able to speak his mind, which he found came easily with the momentum of 300 million American lives behind him.

Today, the situation was dire. President Mitchell was sweating his handpicked cabinet members, trying to weed out the traitor, or idiot, who had been inflicting these terrorist acts on America. "Sweating" was in fact part of his methodology. Mitchell had the air-conditioning turned off to make it as uncomfortable as possible. Like another Henry Fonda movie, *12 Angry Men*, everyone was in shirtsleeves, although the president was the only angry man in this silent room. The one sound heard was his drumming fingers.

"C'mon. We've got it down to an eight-mile radius, fifty miles north of Carlsbad. One of you has got to have a clue."

The phone next to him rang and he picked it up. "What do you have for me? Really! I'll be damned. What's this Kathleen Ronson doing there? Blacked out? For the love of God, it's blacked out. What a way to run a government. What was that address again? Thanks, Paulsen, I'll let you know if we need more ... Oh, what's the phone number?"

∞§∞

"Well, your hunch seems to have paid off, Bill."

"Really?"

"123 Desert Trail, Mercado, New Mexico."

Hiccock pulled out a pen and jotted the address down on a McDonald's bag. He handed it to the driver.

"Get us there on the double!"

∞§∞

The three Humvees were now parked in front of the Domino's Pizza in Mercado. The major, having arrived about a minute before, walked up to Hiccock. "Well, they say an army travels on its stomach."

"And computer nerds on junk food," Hiccock added. "Even though they may be working on an illegal, ultra secret, black op government project, they still need their fix."

"I can't believe the hole in their security was some bean counter handing in a receipt for pizza night to Uncle Sam."

"Thank God for government forms and rigmarole."

∞§∞

"Nice account. Sometimes 30 pies, 100 pizza sticks, and they love our chicken wings." Chuck, the owner, was filling in the major and Hiccock.

"How often do they order?" Hiccock asked.

"Twice a week usually. In fact there's a big order going out tonight."

Kronos approached the counter beyond the major and Hiccock. "I'll have a large pie with everything on it." He turned and saw the two men looking at him. "What?"

They returned their attention to the owner. "And it's always a delivery?" the major asked.

"Have to send two guys."

"You ever make the delivery yourself?"

"Sometimes."

∞§∞

"First squad, fall in," the lieutenant barked as the soldiers scrambled and formed a line eighteen across. Hiccock and the major walked Chuck, the manager, down the line of troops. He looked at each as if he were trying to identify one of them to the police. He suddenly stopped, then back-stepped to a smaller, mustachioed Latino soldier, Fuentes.

"He looks like the kind of kids we get," the owner pointed out.

Hiccock handed Fuentes the folded red-and-white striped uniform of a Domino's delivery driver.

"Without the mustache, of course," the owner added.

"Shave it, Ranger!" the major ordered.

"Yes, Sir!" They moved on out of earshot, and the dutiful GI muttered under his breath, "Ah, shit, Sir!"

∞§∞

Ten minutes later, Fuentes, in his delivery uniform and green hat, reported to the Domino's delivery car and snapped a salute. It was a 1977 red-white-and-green-painted Gremlin hatchback. Hiccock, in a manager's uniform that almost fit, saluted him back. The other hard-assed troops in the unit couldn't help but crack up.

"All right! Settle down," the major growled, without hiding his own grin. "Got your orders, Ranger?"

"Sir, the pizza is hot or it's on us, Sir!" Fuentes barked as he crisply snapped to attention.

"Fuentes, maybe you should loosen up a little," Hiccock said.

Fuentes smiled, and the kid from South Central came out. "No prob, Homes, it's all good. Who gets the pepperoni?"

A car pulled up, causing Hiccock to turn his head. An Air Force captain got out from the driver's side. To Hiccock's surprise, Tyler got out of the other. She walked straight toward him. "Moonlighting on government time?" she said, taking in the silly costume.

"You always said I wasn't utilizing my full potential. Fuentes and I are off to make the world safe for democracy and fast food."

"Hey, Mr. Hiccock, you're management, you shouldn't be doing this," Janice said.

"You're trying to tell me I'm too old for this, aren't you?"

"I just want you to know that you don't have to do this to prove anything to me."

"Oh, so that's it! You think I'm doing this to impress you. Well, I hate to break it to you, but the only other guy here who has a shot at recognizing something high-tech is Kronos, and I just don't think he has the right sensibility to be a pizza guy from around *these here parts*, missy."

Janice adjusted his collar as if he was a little boy going out to play. "Don't get hurt."

Hiccock grabbed her hand and stared into her eyes. They both softened and simultaneously breathed in deep. "The only way I'll get hurt is if I get between the pizza and the nerds at the other end." He gave her hand one last reassuring squeeze then he and Fuentes got into the car and drove off.

Tyler walked over to Hanks. "What's this all about, Major?"

"Professor Hiccock had a hunch that the bad-guy nerds were as much a pain in the butt about junk food as our Kronos nerd. He got the president to check with the GAO and, sure enough, some idiot compromised millions of dollars of secrecy and the security of the whole black op by handing in a bill for pizza so he could be reimbursed."

"He's finally getting it." She smiled, peering off at the little car as it disappeared in the distance.

"Getting what?"

"The human factor."

∞§∞

Cummings Peak was a mountain jutting right out of the flat New Mexican desert. Driving up the old truck route, it became obvious to Hiccock that the only destination on this mountain was the old lead mine. As Hiccock and Fuentes drove up to the entrance of the defunct mine shaft, they were surprised to see a glass-and-steel three-story office. The design gave the building the appearance of having been pushed into the rock, so that just the front and a little of the sides stuck out. Above the roof was a sign proclaiming "ALISON INDUSTRIES." On the far side, off in the distance, parked on the flatlands encircling the mountain, were hundreds of RVs and camper vehicles.

A beefy guard in rent-a-cop blues halted the Gremlin hatchback delivery car at the gate. "Where's Joe?"

"Joe's kid got into some shit at school so he had to go in and see the teacher. I'm Bill, the assistant manager. This is Luis. We got 32 pies, 64 pizza sticks, and 23 salads. What do we do?" Hiccock wanted to make this the guard's problem.

The sentry's eyes took in the two delivery jerks in their little uniforms, then gave a second look to Fuentes. "Hold on." The guard went to the telephone in the shack.

Fuentes talked under his breath without facing Hiccock, "I know that guy, Sir."

Hiccock quickly muted his surprised expression. "From where?"

"Ranger School. He's a mean motherfucker, Sir."

"Do you think he recognized you?"

"I think he thinks I look familiar, but I've had my 'stache since I was sixteen, Sir."

"Do we bolt or play this out?"

"I really don't think he made me, but be ready to outrun that Mac-10 he's got under his jacket."

Hiccock was stunned. He hadn't noticed anything under the guard's jacket.

Fuentes continued, "I feel all naked and shit, Sir. He's got an air-cooled, semiautomatic, recoilless machine pistol and all we can do is cream the fuck with pizza pies."

The guard returned. "Pull over there by the yellow lines. Someone will be up in a moment."

They pulled away. "Keep an eye on him," Hiccock needlessly instructed.

"Yes, Sir." Fuentes had already angled the rearview mirror to afford himself a better look at his former classmate. A metal door on the side of the main entrance opened and three men, one wheeling a dolly, emerged. Hiccock and Fuentes got out of the Gremlin. Fuentes opened the hatchback and they, with the assistance of the three guards, started stacking pizza boxes on the dolly.

Hiccock took a chance. "How many people work here?"

The men stopped loading. The one who seemed like the leader moved into his face. "Why do you want to know?"

Hiccock was caught by surprise. The three men tightened their ranks as they approached the two delivery "boys."

"I was wondering what the odds were, that out of how many people, there would be one guy who orders anchovies with pineapple ... errrgh." Hiccock sold the sourpuss expression like a trained actor.

The leader relaxed his grimace. "That's Malo. You don't want to be around when he farts."

The other two chuckled and Hiccock and Fuentes followed suit.

Hiccock returned to the car and reached in through the driver's side window for the receipt stuck in the visor. "Here ya go. That'll be $384, and the tip's included."

The leader looked puzzled. "Don't we run a tab or something?"

Hiccock feigned checking the bill again. "No, no one mentioned that when they called it in. And it ain't marked down here. See normally it would say 'on account' but ..."

"Enough! I'm just picking this stuff up. I ain't got 400 on me."

"Well, who's gonna pay for dinner, man?" Hiccock just stared. Suddenly he was in charge. He saw that the leader hated being in this situation. This guy probably wouldn't hesitate to put a bullet between Hiccock's eyes if he made a run for the door, but present him with a socially uncomfortable scenario and the guy was reduced to a fumphering malcontent.

"Ah, shit. Hold on. I don't need this sh ..." The leader pulled out a radio and keyed it twice. "Come back, Gold."

"Go blue," the radio crackled.

"Pizza guy says we owe him for the delivery."

"We ran a tab, I thought?"

The leader raised his eyebrows to Hiccock as if to say, *see, I told you we had a tab.* Hiccock played it out. "Listen, maybe you do have a tab. And with Joe being out and all, maybe this got screwed up. Tell ya what, maybe someone can put this on their credit card so my ass is covered, and tomorrow, if Joe says there's a tab, we tear it up."

The leader wasn't going to make this decision, so he keyed the radio. "Gold, I'm going to bring this guy down to non-sec. Have someone meet us there to work this out."

"Roger."

Hiccock followed the leader into the building as the two guards with the dolly took up the rear.

Fuentes started to follow but the leader stopped him, "Hold on! How many guys does it take to get a credit card? Wait here."

"I'm in training man. I'm supposed to go where he goes and follow him so I can learn. C'mon, Homes. I really need this job, bro."

The guard stared, assessed, and then acquiesced. Fuentes followed.

The smell of the pizza quickly filled the small elevator as, contrary to Hiccock's expectation, it descended. Hiccock and Fuentes emerged with the leader. They passed the back of two sliding glass doors with "aerA eruceS noN" stenciled across them. Hiccock reversed the letters in his mind. A woman in her late fifties came out of a sealed doorway that opened with a rush of air. The sound was reminiscent of those Hiccock heard in laboratories equipped with "clean rooms," places where airborne contaminants were kept to one part in 100 million.

The woman produced a credit card and offered it to Hiccock. He blankly glanced at Fuentes then back at her. She jutted it toward him one more time, but he didn't know what to do with the card. She prompted him again by stretching the card out further.

Fuentes jumped in and pulled a blank credit card form from his pocket, placed it over the card and, taking a pencil from the desk, rubbed it flat over the chemically treated, pressure sensitive paper, leaving an impression. "Cool. Thank you, Ma'am." Fuentes handed it to her to sign, as Hiccock stood silently impressed that he had the presence of mind to bring the form. He must have done deliveries at one time.

They were leaving when the leader suddenly called out, "Hold it. Wait a minute."

The two hesitated. Hiccock's nerves tightened as he slowly pivoted, expecting to be looking down the barrel of a machine gun.

"Did you say your tip was included?"

Relieved, Hiccock smiled at Fuentes.

CHAPTER FORTY-TWO
Rock-Knife-Scissors

TWO FLOORS BELOW, a guard hung up a wall phone and announced, "Pizza time!"

"Yeah, big deal," Edmonds said.

"Gee, what a sourpuss. Just 'cause you can't have any."

"Go get your slice, ya pain in the ass." As the guard headed off, Edmonds opened his shirt pocket and pulled out a bottle of diet pills. He popped one and took a drink from the water fountain. He hated the way these things made him feel, but he was carrying an extra sixteen pounds and his lieutenant was giving him shit over it. The one-bar-wonder even threatened to rotate him out if he didn't shape up. The pills jazzed his system and took away the hunger, which helped him not eat as much. Especially when there were seductions like pizza around. Returning to his post, Edmonds's metabolic rate started to climb, along with some of the negative side effects of Dihexemfemeral.

∞§∞

Back at the pizza shop, Hiccock and Fuentes briefed the major while they changed back into their normal attire.

"The facility is underground," Hiccock said. "There is a doorway leading from the nonsecure area. It utilizes an airlock security system. Someone doesn't want dust or contaminants past that point."

"Anything else?"

"That's about it."

"Want to add anything, Fuentes?"

"Like the gentleman said, airlock ... oh and a few other things. They're using sat com radios, which means they have field operational mobility. One of the guards was with me in Ft. Benning Ranger School and, as I remember, a real predator. He didn't make me, though, probably 'cause of my *former* mustache. The guardhouse has a false top, probably holding a grenade launcher. There appear to be vents along the way to the building, possibly an underground entrance. They were using Ranger speak. Definitely jumpers. Probably Delta out of Fort Bragg, North Carolina, or a Special Forces 10 group out of Fort Carson. We have two solid IDs, one named Malo and the other a woman whose credit card this is." He produced the credit card receipt, now in a plastic bag in which knives, forks, and napkins came individually wrapped. He attempted to read it through the plastic. "Ronson."

Hiccock was stunned by his own lack of military observational ability. "Well, yeah, the airlock and all that ..."

∞§∞

The brown recluse spider was indigenous to the American southwest. Like most spiders it liked dark tight spaces, all the better to avoid becoming bird food. A group of MPs sat under a tree awaiting orders. As they shot the breeze, one didn't notice as the spider crawled up his pant leg. Although venomous, any arachnologist would tell you that the little eight-legged insect was rarely deadly to humans. Usually.

∞§∞

"We'll run those names and see if something connects," the major said. "Anything on the commando you recognized?"

Fuentes pulled out another plastic bag with the receipt in it. "No, but they all touched this register receipt, so we might get a clean print and make him that way." Hiccock, realizing all the details he had missed, added, as a weak offering, "He had a Mac-10 under his coat."

Hiccock's momentary respite from embarrassment was short-circuited by Private First Class Fuentes's description: "A short stock, snub-barreled spray job, light clip. And I have been racking my brain since I saw him, but I can't remember his name, just that he was DHG in our SFQC.

That was Hiccock's last straw, "He was what?"

"Distinguished Honor Grad Special Forces Qualifications Course."

∞§∞

Press Secretary Naomi Spence was on her computer in the White House, conducting a Nexis/Lexis search for statutory regulations on agricultural price supports for wheat and grain. A press conference loomed in twenty minutes and she was researching a quote from the Secretary of Agriculture during the dust-bowl era. As the screen flickered, she scanned for any reference of price supports, not noticing her moments of total inactivity—seconds where she was frozen still.

∞§∞

He had forgotten and deeply missed the pungent, sweet exhilaration of that first glorious sip of wine. Both as a constitutional issue befitting his status as a commanding officer as well as an accommodation to the religious Imans he suffered, wine became off-limits, but of course now that didn't matter.

What did matter? What about my life did *matter?* the man who sat waiting in the low back chair asked himself. The stars he wore on his uniform amounted to something, but the camel's ass who ran the country childishly made sure he had more stars on his epaulets, *whenever he wasn't wearing a dress, the degenerate.* Still his love for country amounted to something of which to be proud. As he sat waiting, sipping, and reflecting on his life, General Nandessera allowed a smile to cross his lips. *Loose ends.* He had cleaned up all the loose ends... all but two. Captain Falad, that canon soldier, fled realizing what was going to happen as soon as he heard the disastrous reports from the American media; that Samovar failed miserably to attain retribution for his country. Falad's assistant, himself a loose end, reluctantly offered up the name and address of Falad's brother-in-law, before he was allowed to die. The fugitive Captain's relation was a businessman in America who would surely take in his wife's brother and offer him shelter and a new identity. The General rolled his thumb over the piece of paper upon which was scrawled the American's name and the address of his place of business.

Maybe it was the gravity of the day, or simply the boredom of waiting, but for some reason Nandessera struck a wooden match, setting one end of the paper aflame and lit the tip of a contraband Cuban cigar. It was another "devilish" luxury, which he had harbored for a day like today. He placed the burning sheet in the bowl beside him as the last traces of "Mohammed Ghib - McDonalds Restaurant - Pasadena California" turned to ash.

"Live a long life, Falad" was all he said out loud. And then he waited. And waited.

He was in the middle of remembering a childhood romp, one which still set the old man's heart aflutter to this day. Over the sound of the door to his darkened room opening, he still heard the sounds of Sareena, her squeals of laughter as he chased her. He longingly reached out for her in his mind, seeing her hair dangerously and shamelessly falling out of the young girl's burka. He ignored the sound of the honed metal as it left the sheath. He squeezed his eyes tighter, to see her face as he touched her shoulder and she turned, in his mind, one last time, her big green eyes like saucers electrifying his soul. The whipping sound of the blade slicing through the air was muffled by her delightful taunt.

The man wielding the sword was the best befitting the General's rank. So clean was the cut, that Nandessra's head slid right off and tumbled into his lap, looking up, with the smile of youth on the face of death.

The last of the two loose ends had now been cut.

CHAPTER FORTY-THREE
TIME & AGAIN

GLEASON BARR, petty officer in charge of the watch, was just finishing his 12-noon readings. The cesium regulated, chronographic intervalometer was outputting its consistent stream of 33.44 Ghz. The temperature and humidity were within a hundredth of a degree of nominal parameters. He duly noted these readings in his Naval Observatory logbook and went on to his other appointed hourly checkpoints.

The atomic clock was Father Time itself. It was officially called the Master Clock and was the standard for dividing the rotation of the Earth into segments. Each segment, by international agreement, corresponding to one second of arc. That meant of the 360 degrees of Earth, each degree was roughly 60 miles across at the equator, each mile was called a minute, and one sixtieth of that distance became a second or, roughly, 100 feet. Any spot on the Earth could be located to within 100 feet by merely expressing it as so many degrees, so many minutes, and a few seconds of arc.

The top of the Empire State Building in New York, for example, was 39 degrees, 15 minutes 22 seconds latitude, 44 degrees 17 minutes, and one second longitude. Of course, hardly anybody thought about it that way anymore, since the adoption of GPS, the global positioning system. It was based on the principle of a computerized receiver picking up a signal from satellites in stationary orbit and calculating down to the second (or millisecond in the case of military use) the position of the receiver. Because the whole concept was related to time, the cesium clock at the Naval Observatory became the signal heartbeat of the entire global positioning system around the world. If it were to vary by running slow or fast, airliners would land on freeways instead of airports. Rental car drivers, following their dashboard monitor, would be told to make left turns onto somebody's front lawn instead of the street 100 feet further down the street. A cruise missile could possibly slam into a mountain that its terrain mapping software had detected, but its internal computer guidance believed was a mile to the left. That's why Barr, who worked for the Navy, checked it every hour, even though the radioactive half-life of cesium was 500,000 years and computers on redundant power supplies controlled the temperature. In short, the entire world trusted, without question, that the Atomic Clock kept ticking to an accuracy of within one billionth of a second per millennium.

As he left the area, due to a cross coding in the microchip, which processed the temperature information, a subtle shift in the temperature occurred. Like a thermostat in a house, it started to raise the ambient heat of the cesium containment crucible that accelerated the rate at which the cesium gave off electrons. The atomic collector of the electrons, which, when it counted a certain amount, declared that another millionth of a second had just passed for mankind, started reporting the event ever so much earlier.

∞§∞

Up the East Coast, twelve degrees and 18 minutes of arc away, the four-striped shoulder boards of an American Airlines captain's uniform were reflecting in the black screen of the cockpit computer. The 25-year veteran of airline flight was sitting in the left-hand seat of his 767-200ER as it was being readied for takeoff. After he made sure the Avionics ground crew had addressed the problem with an indicator on the Non-Directional Beacon, he had a moment to attend to an item from his personal checklist. From his iPad he was able to check his reservation for dinner in Milan that evening with Maria DeNardo, the sexy assistant to Milan's Minister of Commerce. The pilot had a twenty-seven hour layover. *Appropriately named*, he mused. The man didn't notice as the screen he was reading from delivered more information than he was aware of.

∞§∞

At the same time, Press Secretary Spence was on her computer in the White House, conducting a Nexus Lexus search for statutory regulations on agricultural price supports for wheat and grain. A press conference loomed in 20 minutes and she was researching a quote from the Secretary of Agriculture during the dust bowl era. As the screen flickered, she scanned for any reference of price supports, not noticing her moments of total inactivity--seconds where she was frozen, still.

∞§∞

The captain's 767, fully loaded with 181 passengers and 160,000 pounds of fuel, accelerated through 190 m.p.h. to V2, then rotated and lifted off runway two-two-right from JFK. At 300 feet, the standard hard right turn was executed to avoid the inbound traffic lanes in the New York Center area of control. The captain then relinquished his flying duties by flipping on the autopilot. The preprogrammed course would bring the plane up over the top of Manhattan out to the Atlantic. It would then traverse the North Atlantic Track. Five hours later it would cross the Scottish coast at Lockerbie, then into the European system of air lanes to his wheels-down point in Milan. As the plane banked hard over the Inwood Park section of Manhattan Island the sun rotated to dead ahead. Normally, transatlantic flights tracked along Long Island's southern shore out to the Atlantic routes. On this day when the prevailing winds prevented planes taking off in that easterly direction, the flights were routed in a big turn over New York City. The flight plans for those airliners that flew over city took them down the Hudson River.

At the cockpit's slight angle of ascent, the flight deck crew could not see the island of Manhattan, or its buildings. The little icon representing their craft on the cockpit GPS system showed them to be smack dab in the middle of the Hudson River. The Ring Laser Gyro Inertial Navigation System was starting to sense a disparity between the GPS reported position of the plane, and its own dead reckoning based on physics.

∞§∞

As soon as the plane diverted from its assigned airspace, an FAA flight controller in New York Center, following protocol, sent out a scramble order followed by an attempt to contact the off-course plane.

∞§∞

Major Jack Haus was in the cockpit of his F-18c Eagle. He and his wingman were in the on strip alert, in the hot seats. Their two Grumman fighters, looking like needle-nosed hatchlings nestled under a corrugated steel canopy at the end of runway 2-9'er, were ready to go. Two ground-support units were attached to their engines, keeping them hot and turning. From where they sat, it was a straight shot down the runway and up into the air. When the alert came, all he had to do was snap on his oxygen mask and throttle up.

It had been that way since the terrible attack on New York's symbol of World Trade. He and his squadron had responded a total of 47 times since the new security measures were initiated. Thankfully, every time had been an innocent mistake, or electronic glitch

that caused airliners and other planes to veer dangerously close to the nation's collective nightmare in lower
Manhattan. As it happened, each time they scrambled,
he and his wingman shot off into the sky not knowing
whether the threat was real or not.

Sitting in his war bird loaded with war shots seemed
so incongruous to the Annapolis graduate. He was, after all, right here in America, in the affluent suburbs
of New York. There were kids playing baseball right
outside the gates of the base while his little gnat of a
plane sat, with enough explosive ordinance cocked and
loaded under its wings to rain hell down on a whole
shitload of bad guys. The problem was the cretins who
would take a plane weren't in uniforms or massed nicely on a border somewhere. Major Haus' flying death
machine had a redefined purpose; to minimize collateral damage. God forbid, killing a few hundred on a
plane, to save thousands in buildings. The math of the
equation was terrible because even a low number, like
one hundred, was still one hundred innocent people.
*Except for maybe one to four maniacs, who would dare
attempt something so insane again?* The other passengers, moms, dads, sons, and daughters, would simply
be sacrificed to save thousands, and in the case of an
attack on a nuclear reactor, millions.

His great sweat, the one that kept him and every other good, American born, professionally trained
fighter warrior up at night was having to make the
split second decision to terminate the lives of innocent
folks. The Major knew he could be flying into a nightmare from which he might never awake.

As he eased the throttle forward, he said a little
prayer, "Oh, God, let this be just another screwed up
navigation system, and if not, let me get there while
they are still over water."

Both screaming Eagles were airborne 30 seconds
after the alert signal was sent. The on-board cockpit
computer immediately told him the threat was coming

from JFK and that was too close. Previous attacks came from planes rerouted (hijacked) well outside of New York.

As it was on that infamous September morning, a fighter pilot, in a similar plane, missed being on the scene by 1 minute, thus escaping the terrible dilemma by losing the "opportunity" to create a "mini-tragedy" in order to stop the massive one.

The instant time-distance calculations Major Haus made in his head told him to go to afterburners, a carefully controlled explosion in the exhaust pipe of his engines, which propels the fighter plane at almost supersonic speeds. With full after-burners, the trip from the National Guard base at Gabreski Airport, Westhampton, 60 miles east on Long Island, bee-lined to New York City would take four minutes. At that burn rate he wouldn't be able to make it back to base. He'd have to land at LaGuardia.

∞§∞

At New York Center, those air traffic controllers who were not frantically trying to reroute traffic away from the hurtling sub-sonic darts slicing through their air space, were watching the little blips approach the bigger one as their hearts stopped.

∞§∞

As he approached Manhattan air space, a chill went through the Major's pressurized flight-suited body. Haus saw the airliner already over the center of the island. Knowing immediately that the rules of engagement just took him out of the equation, he keyed his mic. Now under the control of an orbiting AWACS, he proceeded to lay out the tactical situation, "Big Daddy, be advised target is over city, I have no clear shot, request permission to break off attack and try to signal."

It was a rhetorical request. The airborne military traffic controller circling above in the converted 707, operating under the same rules of engagement, crackled back, "Affirmative, Baby Eagle; break off your attack; try to interdict."

The fighter pilot then contacted his wingman. "Maintain combat air patrol status until replacement Eagles arrive." His wingman banked his swept wing fighter, to start a racetrack pattern around Manhattan Island.

∞§∞

A passenger on the left side of the aircraft looked directly down to see the roof of World Plaza on 8th Avenue at 50th Street. Meanwhile, in the cockpit, the beeping of the Vector Oriented Radar receiver caught the co-pilot's attention. The cockpit GPS showed the position of the aircraft as being midway down the island still dead center of the river.

Mandy Weinstein was watering her fuchsia, which was hanging in a macramé cradle in her window on the 95th floor of the Empire State Building. She dropped her watering can when she noticed the giant cockpit and huge wingspan of the 767 coming head on, right at her. She screamed and backed away at five miles per hour.

The co-pilot saw it first. His instinct was to reach for and disengage the autopilot switch, but the captain reached for his switch first and jammed his pen in it. The co-pilot's identical control became non-operational due to the captain's override. He lunged at the captain. In the struggle, he punched the older man, breaking his jaw and shutting out his lights. With his hand aching, he fumbled for the lodged pen. It broke off in the switch. The building loomed large in the windshield. The first officer having recently served as a flight engineer on older birds, instinctively reached for the circuit breaker panel and took the gamble of his life; he threw one without checking to see if it was labeled Autopilot. It was in the general area he remembered from the manual and that would have to do because he was already putting his weight onto the yolk, so that it would bank hard right the instant the power to the servo-controlled mechanism was interrupted. That 420-volt signal was stopping him from saving his life and countless thousands.

The yoke disengaged and the screaming plane made a rollover right bank. Literally flying sideways wing tips pointed straight down to 34th Street and up to God. The belly of the plane missed the side of the 1931 building by seven feet.

The windows and walls shuddered as the passing fuselage blocked the daylight to the 95th to 97th floors. The upper wing tip would have knock King Kong off the top.

At that moment hundreds of thousands of New Yorkers hearing the horrendous roar of the acrobatically strained engines, looked up with the same thought, "Oh, God, not again!" They then breathed a common sigh of relief as the on-edge plane reappeared from behind the building and righted itself as it climbed to the safety of the heavens.

The cockpit reading on the flight data recorder would, upon analysis, show the plane was actually four seconds arc east of where it should have been. The co-pilot was hailed a hero. The captain committed suicide, hanging himself while in police custody the first chance he got. The understatement of the year was that "the people aboard that plane and in the landmark building were very lucky." Others around the globe, however, were not as fortunate.

Throughout the world, six planes crashed. One into a mountain in Tibet, three missing their airport runways by less than 2000 feet, and two in a mid-air collision over Argentina. In the short 30 minutes of distorted time, 1,714 people were killed around the world.

Ten minutes later, the temperature in the cesium core of the Atomic Clock was cooling, significantly decreasing the amount of electrons emitted and, in effect, slowing the clock again. Ten minutes after that, it was back to normal time, as if it had never varied. Barring any further intentional cross coding to the chip, this would never happen again.

∞§∞

At 12:20 PM, Press Secretary Spence stepped behind the podium in the White House's pressroom. The papers in her hand were the text of the president's reasons for urging Congress to pass the Farm Subsidy Reform Act. Instead, she said, "The American government has two hours to surrender and cease its reckless course. Nothing less than the total dissolution of the government will be acceptable. If this demand is not met, all planes, everywhere, will crash and all hydroelectric plants will burn out. Every nuclear power plant will explode and all of this nation's infrastructure will be destroyed."

The press corps was stunned to silence. After a second, the room erupted in questions. Spence took no questions, exiting the room. Walking at a brisk pace past the guards, she took a shortcut through the White House barbershop. Quietly, she picked up a pair of scissors and slid them under the sleeve of her jacket. She double-stepped down the nine flights of stairs, passed the uniformed guards, and approached the Situation Room. The Secret Service agent at the door questioned her with his glance.

"I need to see the president immediately," she snapped. He permitted her access. The Secret Service agent on post behind the president watched her approach with a bit less than his usual penetrating stare.

It was the glint that first caught his eye. Instantly, the "best of the best" agents in the service reached for his gun. Spence, now thirty feet from the president, pulled out the scissors and held them like a dagger in front of her.

"Freeze," the agent growled as he chambered a round and aimed in one smooth motion. His menacing stance did not stop Spence's advance. The other agent, on post across the table on the opposite side of the room, blasted through the chairs and scurried over the slippery top of the conference table in an effort to grab her. The Secretary of Labor, seeing a gun pointed in his direction, bent down to duck as the hurling agent's leg slammed into his head. The agent stumbled and before he could steady himself for another attempt at her, the first agent fired three times. Although his intention was "shoot to wound," Spence was shoved a foot to her left by a Cabinet member who went ducking for cover, rendering the shots aimed at her arm and shoulder fatal. Spence's body spun around from the fusillade. Her teal business suit instantly blossomed red with blood. Multiple exit wounds, the size of silver dollars, punctuated her back.

The president, who first looked up at the sound of the agent going over the table, was now under the weight of a third agent who threw his body over him. The two standing agents immediately scanned the room with the barrels of their guns while ordering the entire Cabinet to get down on the floor. The president was unceremoniously thrown into the anteroom for safety, guarded by two crouching agents, their guns drawn and trained on the entrance to the sit room. The agent who had let Spence in kicked away the scissors from her hand. Reynolds saw that she was, amazingly, still breathing. He went to her and cradled her head.

"Why, Naomi? Why did you do this?"

She was remarkably calm, he thought, as she choked for her last breath and with a puzzled look on her face, uttered, "I don't know why. I don't know, but I had to die, Ray." And then she was gone.

∞§∞

Back in the New Mexican pizza shop, Hiccock's cell phone rang. He flipped it open. "Ray ...What?" As he learned about the press secretary's attempt to assassinate the president, CNN played her ominous speech to the press corps.

"Was she on the Internet just before?" Hiccock said.

"Dear God. I'll get right back to you," Ray said and hung up.

Hiccock turned to the major. "I'm going to make an executive decision here. Since there is nothing to indicate any other secured facility within fifty miles of where we are, I am going to assume we have found the terrorists. It is imperative that we stop them within two hours." He nodded toward the TV and replay of Spence's threat.

"I got communications personnel and a few MPs. The hombres at that facility are Ranger School valedictorians, dug in and probably well fortified. If it comes down to a firefight, our guys will be slaughtered."

"Reinforcements?"

"I can try Fort Carson, but it's going to be pure luck if they are even mustered in a day, no less in war-fighting mode."

"Where's all the RD divisions I hear of in briefings?"

"All our rapid-deployment units face outward, most in other countries. Getting them here is a big-time turnaround ... maybe twelve hours."

"And if this were Kuwait or Saudi Arabia?"

"Two hours."

The Admiral walked up and interrupted. "I have a suggestion. Is there a phone book?"

The manager produced one and Parks turned to the yellow-page section. She started looking under D for demolition. She found a small display ad and called out the number. Hiccock punched it in and handed her the phone.

"Hello, is Mack there?" the Admiral said and then waited. "Mack, Henrietta Parks, I'm fine but I need your help. You boys still playing with firecrackers?"

∞§∞

Engles was a brute, a mass of muscle and sinew compressed into the presence of a commanding officer. His Air Cav troops were, to the man, the ultimate best. This achievement came in no small part because he made it his duty to be better than any one of them— a better soldier, a better athlete, a better flyer, and a better fighter. On this day, he once again proved alpha male, as he showed them how far they'd have to go to be better than him. Using an OH 58C Bell Ranger reconnaissance helicopter, he snagged three garters in three passes. His next-best pilot snagged two out of three.

It was a game he invented after one of his men returned from a wedding having caught the garter. He challenged him to snag the garter from a hook three feet off the ground using the tip of the strut on the helicopter's landing rails. Like grabbing the brass ring, only at seventy miles per hour, three feet from the floor, with a margin of error of two feet to death. His Air Cav unit was number one, mostly because of his personal challenges to all of his men.

What Engles had great difficulty flying, however, was his computer. The phone line he commandeered to be his dedicated modem line was faulty when the wind wasn't blowing, and today the soft Fort Carson, Colorado, breeze was playing havoc with his barely 56 kbs connection to his e-mail. His sister wanted to buy a new Jeep Wrangler and he was trying to enlighten her, by way of a letter, on the merits of getting a heavier suspension. Between constantly being booted and losing his connection, he hadn't noticed the periods of inaction he had undergone, during the moments when he was hooked up, when he didn't move or blink.

CHAPTER FORTY-FOUR
GRAY SEALS

EMMERTS, ONE OF THE GUARDS at the Alison Industries main gate, was personally amused and professionally curious when he saw the three beat-up Jeep
Wagoneers and an old International Scout, with fishing poles and coolers on the bumper, pull right up to
the gate. "C'mere, look at this," he called to Renko.

They watched as two old guys got out of the front
vehicle, 140 or so odd years of living between them. As
they approached the guard shed, one sucked his den-
tures and asked, "'Scuse me there, young fella. This
here Alison Industries?"

"Yes, but why do you want know?" Emmerts turned
and smiled at Renko. A bunch of other old guys started
unloading.

Renko hustled over. "No, I'm sorry you can't stop
here, please get back into your vehicles." One of the
guys strayed from the crowd and headed behind the
guard shack. Renko followed, and he witnessed him
unzipping his pants, preparing to pee. "Sir, don't do
that." The man didn't respond and disappeared behind
the structure. Renko trotted over to the back of the
shack, "What are you, deaf, too?"

"No, son, I ain't deaf." Mack's hand came up with
amazing speed as he took the young trooper in a sleep-
er-hold, a chloroform-soaked rag woven between his
fingers smothering the guard's nose. The startled Renko was totally caught off guard. "Just had to get you
out of the range of them cameras. You sleep tight now."

Meanwhile, Emmerts was still dealing with the
other oldster. He didn't see the dust-covered letters

on the Jeep, barely discernible as Mack & Harry Demolition Albuquerque N.M. "You have to move your vehicles."

"But my grandson said to come stop by anytime and see the place. His name is ..." he patted his pockets. "Where is it? Whoops 'sin the back." He hobbled to the back of the Wagoneer.

Emmerts followed him, "Look, I don't give a rat's ass who ..." As the guard came round the back of the vehicle, he came face to face with a Beretta Model 92f 9mm semiautomatic with silencer, pointed an inch above the bridge of his nose.

The old guy pushed a soaked rag toward Emmerts's face. "Take a deep breath or die."

Emmerts started to deflect and go at him low. Nevertheless, the old codger was surprisingly fast, blocking the younger man's attempt and reversing the hold.

Another older guy slammed the rag on him. As the guard started gulping chloroform-saturated air, the old guy got in his face. "When you have the nightmare that will follow this little embarrassing scene, don't forget to give the boys of UDT Unit 1, retired, the credit."

∞§∞

Two guards were monitoring the entrance in the command center. "What the fuck is going on out there?" one of them said. "Where's Emmerts and Renko?" They were startled by Mack, one of the old men, who appeared behind them.

"They got bamboozled," Mack said. "Bye!" Two Tasers got each guard on his shoulder, jolting them out of their seats and onto the floor by the 20,000-volt sting of the handheld weaponized version of cattle-prod technology. Two other older guys ragged them, prompting Mack to comment, "This is too easy." As if on cue, Mack's shoulder exploded in a red ball of mush. Mack's comrades hit the deck rolling and firing back at the source of the shot as alarms began to sound. They aimed low, taking out the shooter from the legs down. When he crumpled, another UDT guy ragged him.

With the first line of defense put to slumber, the septuagenarian fighters and Hiccock's MPs and communications troops made their way to the main entry door. It was actually a giant vault door, programmed to close automatically upon the alarm. Mack's friend Charlie and another old Navy grog dashed over to the upper and lower actuating arms that were linked to the motor that closed the doors. They slapped a soft package on each arm as it swung and pushed into it a firing pin connected to a detonator cord. With the skill and light step of dancers, they retreated behind the big door itself and yelled, "Fire in the hole!"

One of them keyed the detonator as the other UDT veterans down the hall ducked. Harry grabbed young Kronos, who was too curious for his own good, and pulled him behind a wall. With the explosion, the metal arms were severed and mangled. The door stopped with a groan. A piece of the arm stuck in the wall, like a javelin, where Kronos's head had been a moment earlier.

The major's MPs, in full uniform, were now in the main area. Reinforcement guards from the installation, dressed in paramilitary uniforms, appeared. Both the MPs and the guards yelled "Freeze," their weapons trained on each other. The standoff came down to the lead guard, code-named Gold, facing the lead MP, the major. There was dead silence.

Then the major spoke, "United States Army. Drop your weapons." Gold responded, "United States Marines. Drop yours."

"Oh, shit!" Kronos blurted out, putting a voice to what was on everybody's mind.

"We are here on direct orders of the Commander in Chief," the Army major barked.

"You are violating the security of a top-secret installation, Major."

"Well, it ain't that secret anymore, pal. In minutes, the 82nd Airborne and First Ranger battalions will be swarming all over this place. Surrender your weapons and your command."

"Then you shall die with us, Sir."

Hiccock moved forward. "Wait a minute, fellas."

The major could not believe the stupidity of Hiccock's move. "Sir, take cover."

Hiccock ignored him. "Look, Marine. Do you know who I am?"

"You are an unauthorized person in the facility that I am sworn to protect ..."

"... against all enemies foreign and domestic," Hiccock said. "Yes, I know, I took the same oath. But I work for the president. I have code-word clearance and I am seventeenth on the NCA protocol." Hiccock saw that his last statement confused the Marine guard. "Let me show you my ID. I am seventeenth in line to the presidency in the event of a decapitating preemptive strike."

Just then, Professor Robert Parnes swept into the middle of the standoff in a white lab coat with his graying hair and prosthetic arm and demanded, "What is going on here?"

Edmonds, who was wound tight and on edge because of his diet pills, wheeled around and nearly fired at his own boss.

"Sir, please leave now," Gold said to Parnes. "The security of this immediate area is compromised."

Hiccock couldn't believe his eyes. "Parnes? Bob Parnes?"

"Bill Hiccock? What are you doing here?"

"You are running an illegal operation."

"Afraid not. I am running a top-secret project. I thought you were at the White House. Why are you breaking into my facility?"

"Can we call off the warriors first? All these locked and loaded weapons make me a little nervous."

Parnes assessed the situation, "What if I do mine but you don't do yours?"

"Fair enough. Okay, so we do it by the numbers. One of yours stands down then one of mine does."

Edmonds watched every move the invaders made over the sights of his gun. He was breaking out in a sweat now, cursing his body for trembling under stress.

∞§∞

Upstairs in the command center, Mack was bleeding heavily from the shoulder. Admiral Parks rushed over to him. She examined the damage and made a preliminary diagnosis. "It went clean through. You might not pitch in the majors again, but I don't think you'll buy the farm."

"Henrietta, you go and take care of that science guy. I'll be okay."

"Medic!" Parks called out. She caressed the man's good hand and squeezing it said, "Thank you for getting your old unit together and doing such a fine job."

"Me and the guys … we never broke up. We just started our own business and kept blowing up things. Heck, this has been the most fun we had since we took down the hotel in Vegas."

"Still, Mack, I owe you one."

"Your husband pulled my rump from the drink a few times. This one's on my tab with him."

A medic arrived and Parks kissed Mack on the forehead. Then she was off. She ran into Tyler being led down into the facility by one of the MPs.

"Admiral?" Tyler inquired.

"Miss Tyler."

"How are you doing?"

"My house has been destroyed, my husband's best friend and war buddy is missing half his shoulder, there is a mad crazy somebody who's going to make regular Americans blow up our country in forty-five minutes, and if I still got periods this would be the day. But besides that I am fine ... except your husband is probably gonna get us all killed."

"My ex-husband."

"That seems like a dumb mistake, woman." She was off, leaving Tyler speechless.

∞§∞

The mutual stand-down continued in the main area, as soldiers on each side alternately received the signal from his respective commanding officer to secure his weapon.

Hiccock continued explaining the situation to Parnes. "So my hacker friend Kronos here traced it back to this facility, which, by the way, does not appear in any government records."

Not noticed by anyone, Edmonds was sweating as his eyes darted around; chasing flashes of light only he could see.

"Are you accusing somebody here of using my equipment to sabotage the United States?" Parnes said, incredulous.

"Or possibly you, Professor ... unfortunately."

The major gave one of his men the signal and another weapon was secured.

"Me? Why would I ..."

"Oh, I dunno, maybe because big-ticket research money, the kind that you're used to, doesn't fall off the trees unless there's a real nasty threat to this country."

"Not me, Bill. I literally gave my right arm for this country."

"Could still hurt, Parnes. And that could be a good reason to extract revenge. But that's my wife's area, actually."

Another Marine guard got the nod to stand down.

Edmonds's face was now registering anger.

"Oh, that's right. You married your old boss at Stanford. Cute, as I remember."

"You should see her now," Tyler said as she walked into the chamber with Admiral Parks.

Edmonds's eyes darted to the new distraction caused by this woman. Slowly his finger moved to the trigger of his aimed and cocked M16, one involuntary spasm away from blowing off Janice's head.

Hiccock and Tyler both stopped and looked to each other, simultaneously asking, "Are you okay?" Hiccock smiled and returned to Parnes.

The major got the eye of another MP and he too relaxed his stance and lowered his weapon.

"So what are you baking here, Parnes?"

"The next big thing, Bill."

"Cold fusion?"

Gold nodded his head and another weapon lowered.

Edmonds was now breathing heavily through his mouth.

"AI. The most far-reaching program of R&D on AI ever in the U.S.A."

"Of course, artificial intelligence. You were always a big-time DARPA guy. I guess this whole place is on the Department of Defense research and development, off-budget shopping list."

Edmonds started to shake ever so slightly.

"Well, actually, no. My associates and I were asked to leave the Defense Advanced Research and Projects Agency. Unlike you, Bill, I wasn't able to stay out of the big leagues. So I pitched this idea to the Department of Agriculture, of all places."

"Agriculture? This top-secret facility is code word cleared for what ... 'farmland security'?"

"Old habit, Bill. There are companies and governments all over the world that would stop at nothing for the technology we are 'baking' here."

An MP behind Hiccock lowered his weapon but the one beside him kept his trained across the room.

"Well, it's over Parnes. You are shut down."

Parnes became animated with a newfound emotion. "Bill, we are doing it, right here. The Holy Grail ... the ultimate in computational science. We have created true artificial intelligence, Bill. Think of it!" Then suddenly, changing beat, he asked, "Why is your wife here?"

"Ex-wife. She's here to figure out how you went nuts."

"Nuts? Bill, we are on the verge of changing everything!"

Hiccock took a deep breath. "And I suppose plotting to destroy the United States is some kind of warm-up to the main event?"

Edmonds now had a terrified look on his face.

"Weather, Bill! We are a meteorological research facility. I don't know what makes you think we are ..."

"Weather? You mean you are running an ultra top-secret, multimillion dollar off-budget black op to determine if the rain is going to hurt the rhubarb?"

"Well, when the Department of Defense dropped us, I had to get my team and myself another high-paying, satisfying research scenario. Breaking down the complexities of weather dynamics is a task only the largest computer ever made could attempt to unravel. Again, why is the former Mrs. Hiccock here?"

A guard safetied his gun as an MP pointed his weapon to the ground and released the bolt. There were only two men left with weapons. One of Hiccock's MPs and Edmonds.

Tyler decided to speak up. "If what you are saying is true about your mission here, then you or somebody on your team is a serial-homicidal maniac. I intend to conduct a full psychiatric investigation to determine who the culprit might be."

"After we shut you down," Hiccock added.

The last MP stood down.

Edmonds swallowed hard. His eyelids were perceptibly fluttering now.

And then a spider crawled out of the uniform and up the neck of the MP standing next to Tyler. The soldier, sensing something just above his collar, reacted with a start, swatting the arachnid from his five o'clock shadow with a slight grunt. A blood-red dot appeared on his forehead as the sound of a shot echoed through the halls of Alison Industries. The back of his head exploded in a puff of red, white, and gray.

Before the soldier's limp body crumbled to the floor, Edmonds pivoted, quickly acquiring his next target. Bang. An MP, instinctively raising his gun in response to the sound of the shot, was knocked down by the impact of the second gunshot.

"No!" Gold yelled.

The major raised his gun and fired, rippling Edmonds's chest with bullet holes. He then kicked over a desk and dropped down for cover. Everyone else scrambled. Tyler instinctively reached out for the downed MP. Hiccock jumped across the ten feet between them and immediately covered her and pulled her down behind a desk. Parnes was hustled to the ground by one of his guards who took a bullet in the back for his trouble. The confusion over who was shooting at whom increased. Bullets ripped into everything. Guards and MPs were spun around and blasted back by rounds from the weapons of their adversaries.

Suddenly, save for the sound of a weeping Tyler, the hollowed out chamber of Alison Industries returned to its austere silence. Hiccock, tenaciously shielding Janice, chanced a peek from his position, just enough to see that the major was gauging the situation.

The major called out, "Give it up, Marine."

Parnes pushed the dead guard off himself. "There is no need for this! Stop it!"

"He's right," Hiccock shouted. "Your cover's blown and in minutes this place will be swarming with troops and FBI."

"Please everybody, just calm down!" Parnes said.

The major yelled over the desk he was using for cover. "We got hurt people here. They need medical attention. What do you say we cease-fire and take care of our own? You and I will stand guard, Marine."

Hiccock tenderly pulled back Tyler's hair, making eye contact. "Are you okay?"

Janice jerked her head and hugged Hiccock. When she opened her eyes she was looking directly at the MP's lifeless body, a pool of blood spreading from the back of his head. She started drawing short breaths. Hiccock kissed her head and stroked her hair, waiting for the next seconds to play themselves out. She kept turning her head in the direction of the dead trooper. Hiccock took her face in his hands and stopped her. Some shouts and a few more gunshots caused both of them to wince, but they never broke the connection, intensely holding onto one another with their eyes. All of the issues she had with him evaporated at that instant. After avoiding, intellectualizing, pragmatising, and postponing the issue, she now hoped with everything she had that they survived this madness. As a bullet whizzed by above their heads, they simultaneously, silently mouthed the words "I love you."

∞§∞

True to the president's words, no one had been allowed to leave the now superheated room. Everyone in the room avoided looking at the hastily wiped down spot of dried blood where Spence had died. The sound of the intercom ripped through the still air. "Action report, Sir."

"What?" The president was stunned.

"Quarteback's unit reports engaging an armed force after gaining entry to an Alison Industries."

"Where is Alison Industries?"

"His team is requesting Air MedEvac. They have dead and wounded."

"Dear God. Is Hiccock okay?"

"Unable to confirm that at this time, Sir."

The president shifted his focus from the squawk box by his side to the people around the room. "Okay, so which one of your departments is contracting through Alison Industries? I want the answer in ten minutes." Most of the Cabinet members picked up the phones in front of them.

Four-star General Wallace Bradley, the Chairman of the Joint Chiefs of Staff in full military uniform and decorations, covered his phone and sought the president's attention. "Sir, I am getting something now." He spoke into the phone. "Repeat and confirm." His face turned as hard as the metal stars on his shoulder boards. "Mr. President, Quarterback's group has met armed resistance from U.S. Marines."

"What in the world? That doesn't make sense." The president's brow was as furrowed as an Iowa cornfield.

The CJCS blurted out something that halted all conversation in the room. "What? That's crazy! Rescind that order, call them back. Under *my* authority, goddamn it! The Chairman of the Joint Chiefs of Staff!"

All heads snapped toward the chairman, who appeared dazed by what he had just heard. He addressed the Commander in Chief. "Sir, an Air Cavalry squadron is en route to the area where Quarterback's team is. They are poised to attack."

"You have my authority to abort the attack and, in fact, order them to help with the dead and wounded."

"Something doesn't make sense here, Sir," a confounded Chairman Bradley mumbled.

The intercom interrupted. A communications officer on the other end was obviously repeating raw what he was hearing on another tactical circuit. "Sir, the agency running the black op is ... say that again? The oversight agency is Department of Agriculture."

Every head in the room pivoted in unison to Harold Dawson, the Secretary of Agriculture. Two White House guards immediately flanked him.

"Harold?" the president said. "Why? What ever possessed you?"

Dawson turned to Ray Reynolds like a hunter suddenly surrounded by cannibals. "Mr. President, I assure you I know nothing ..."

The president held up his hand. "Everyone else is excused. It's been a long, hard day. The Secretary of Agriculture, Justice, and my counsel will remain. The rest of you may return to your offices."

"Mr. President, may I have a word in the anteroom?" Reynolds asked in a tone that the two men knew meant that they needed to do this immediately.

The president acceded and they headed toward the small quarters off the Sitch Room, both unconsciously stepping over the spot where Naomi had died, the marble floor still streaked from the quick mop-up of her blood. Reynolds closed the door and sat for a second. "Maybe we shouldn't stop the Air Cav from attacking."

"Slow up, Ray. Why would we do something as insane as that?"

CHAPTER FORTY-FIVE
LET THE CHIPS FALL

PARNES, TYLER, KRONOS, and the major walked
down the corridor as the dead and wounded were carried out of the main entry area. A communications
trooper approached Hiccock with a com-sat phone. Hiccock shook the phone. The line would not engage.

"Is there another way that you can connect me to
the White House? This isn't working."

"Please send my regards to Ray Reynolds," Parnes
said casually.

"You know the chief of staff?" Hiccock's sixth sense
started tingling.

"I know you are going to be amazed when you see
what we have achieved with ALISON."

The childlike enthusiasm of Parnes's delivery
stopped Hiccock, and he spun him around. "Goddamn
you! What part of mass murder, treason, and terrorism
don't you understand, Parnes?"

"Again, I emphatically state, I do not know anything about that. However, I am sure your people will
discover neither this place nor anybody working here
to be responsible for any of your alleged accusations."

∞§∞

The president leaned across a small desk as he proceeded to interrogate Reynolds. "This is unbelievable.
Go on."

"Sir, the rest you may not want to know."

"Why wouldn't I want to know?"

"What you don't know can't hurt you in congressional inquiries, possible impeachment, or even criminal charges ..."

"Ray, I appreciate your loyalty to me. I know that your heart is in the politically expedient place, even though your head is up your ass right now."

Reluctantly Reynolds continued recounting a story that would be retold in history books from this point forward. "Well, after this Parnes fellow came to us during the campaign, we assured him that, if we got in, he'd get a major government contract to replace the work he had been doing for Defense."

"So we are dirty in this all the way?"

"In reality, no. But we sent Parnes to Agriculture so, in appearance, yes."

The president sat back. He suddenly punched down on the chair's arm, splintering a $250,000 antique.

∞§∞

A radioman, spooling out wire from an old World War II vintage field phone, caught up to Hiccock as he, Parnes, and the major made their way down the corridor. "Ultra traffic, Sir. Scrambled from the White House."

Hiccock grabbed the handset. "Yes, Mr. President?"

"Bill, are you okay?"

"Yes, but we have lost some brave MPs, Sir."

"How badly has your operational ability been damaged?"

"Still have my three team members, Sir."

"What about your detachment?"

"The major tells me ten dead, ten wounded, and twenty remain from his platoon, Sir."

∞§∞

On the other end of the phone, Ray sat across from the president. Having put all the cards on the table and his butt on the line, he now watched, trying to discern which way his boss would go. He couldn't read anything from the president's implacable face, even though he spent years with this man and probably knew him better than anyone else in government. Mitchell could let the renegade Air Cav boys clean up this mess, extinguish Hiccock, Parnes, and everyone involved—and along with them any connection to the administration. Reynolds would not have considered this murder. He reasoned it was *passive compliance with events already initiated outside his purview*, mentally rehearsing for the congressional hearings. Since thousands of people had already died in scores of terrorist attacks, what was a handful more, especially if it meant ensuring this administration another term? All Mitchell had to do was instruct Hiccock that the Air Cav troop was coming to help, not to kill them.

"Bill, in a few minutes a heavily armed attack force of Apache helicopters will be on top of you."

"Great, Sir, we'll need the support."

Reynolds imperceptibly tensed. The president gave him one last look. "Bill, we didn't send them. They are on an attack mission." Reynolds sighed. As in so many other instances, the president had just made a decision that was now the policy of the United States of America. With Mitchell electing to put personal jeopardy aside for the both of them, Reynolds was duty bound to embrace it.

Hiccock's voice cut through the heavy mood. "Don't want to tell you your job, but may I respectfully request that you consider calling them the fuck off, Sir?"

"They are not responding to any retreat orders."

"Well, get somebody you can order over here to protect us. We are within minutes of shutting down the entire operation and ending this nightmare."

"Unfortunately, these would have been the guys, Bill. No one else is close. As impossible and unfair as it seems, you and your men will have to hold them off 'til reinforcements arrive."

"Yes, Sir, I understand. I don't know how, but we'll think of something."

CHAPTER FORTY-SIX
REVELATIONS

THE MAJOR, GOLD, MACK, Parnes, Hiccock, Tyler, and Kronos were all hunched over a layout of the mountain.

"What about the airborne troops that were coming in a few minutes?" Gold asked.

"I lied," the major said. "They're eight hours away."

"That's great! Well, the battle scenario is simple because the only way in or out is through the main door that your men disabled. Wide open, unfortunately. My sixteen men and your twenty should be able to hold them off at a choke point right here." Gold indicated a place on the layout.

"My twelve guys are ready," Mack said.

The major looked up and smiled. "You've done your share, Sir."

"You know, retirement ain't all it's cracked up to be. What can we expect them to throw at us?"

"Air Cav Black Hawks in support. Probably 150 to 200, company strength."

"And they'll be loaded for bear," Gold said. "But we've only got to hold them off for eight hours."

"There is also the chance that not all of the men have been programmed. We might be able to reason with the men who haven't," Tyler said.

"With all due respect, Ma'am, those boys are trained. They will follow their commanding officer into hell. They won't be coming here to talk." Gold tapped the layout. "I figure we put machine guns here ... and here ... and here."

As the two military commanders planned, Hiccock took Mack aside. "Is this going to work?"

"You want the truth?"

"I think I do."

"Slim chance that these men down here can hold off a full-strength infantry company with attack helicopters for eight minutes, much less eight hours."

The news caused Hiccock to run through some out-of-the-box models in his head. "What if, instead of trying to fight them, we were to deny them access?"

Mack smiled. He liked the idea.

∞§∞

"You are going to what?" the president said. He and the CJCS were listening on the president's auxiliary communications console while Hiccock outlined his plan.

"My UDT guys say they can do it, Sir. The facility has enough food and water for three days. By then, you can have somebody dig us out. I hope."

"What UDT guys?"

"We got a little help from the Navy here, Sir."

"Only you could rustle up underwater demolition men in the middle of the desert, Bill." The president faced the chairman. "Well, what do you think of their plan?"

"It's probably better odds than a firefight, Sir. I'll go along with it."

"Okay, Hiccock, you do it. And find the bastard responsible, because in less than half an hour, all hell's going to break loose across the country."

The president nodded to the chairman, who exited, leaving Mitchell and Reynolds alone in the little anteroom.

"Sir, is there something about Robert Parnes that I should know?" Hiccock said.

The president checked with Ray Reynolds who shook his head. "Why are you asking?"

"Sir, something disturbing has come up. It seems there's a Parnes-Reynolds connection."

"If I told you it had nothing to do with the current situation, would that suffice?"

"With all due respect, Sir, how do I know the chief of staff, or you for that matter, isn't undermining my mission and our lives?"

"Fair enough. I'm going to have Ray tell you what he told me five minutes ago."

Reynolds looked at the president with apprehension in his eyes, but Mitchell remained resolute and nodded for him to proceed. "Bill, Ray here. During the campaign, Parnes approached me when we were stumping at MIT. He had an idea that he wanted to try, a new way to use the Internet."

"Did he say what that was?" Hiccock asked.

"Something to do with advertising. I figured it was a million-to-one chance, so I didn't ask for many details. I never gave it much thought or credit for our win. Our web site hits were in the low thousands. Not even close to the margin of win."

"Go on, Ray, tell him everything."

Reynolds addressed Hiccock again. "If we got elected, our part of the deal was to get Parnes and the members of his team a big science research project. When Dawson from Agriculture proposed their weather forecasting initiative, I thought it was the perfect, quiet, out-of-the-way spot for Parnes's payback—which by the way I didn't feel he had earned, but a deal's a deal."

"So you see, other than being connected to Parnes, it has nothing to do with the current situation," the president said.

Hiccock stopped Mitchell cold. "Except that what Parnes did wasn't just advertising. It was subliminal advertising and those same subliminal techniques became the basis for how all the terrorists were programmed. Your campaign served as the beta test for the process. Your election proved beyond a doubt that it could work. In fact, nobody I've spoken to in the whole country thinks they voted for you. That's why the exit polls were so wrong on Election Day. Having people forget that they pulled the lever for you was the post-suggestion. After confirming that the subjects would not remember their programming, the next step was easy. And the number of hits was low, Ray, because Parnes didn't use your web site, he used the entire Internet. No matter where someone was surfing or what site they were on, they got programmed."

The president was immobilized by the preponderance of complicity that was now laid at his feet. "I'll bring this to the floor of Congress and put myself in their hands."

Ray hit the mute button. "That's absurd! You *are* the president. Your agenda and the advances you have made will help this country. You can't throw away all the good you're doing."

"All the good is tainted. I am not going to fall into the trap that a small wrong now will allow me to do great good in the future. That is the mantra of dictators and every crooked politician since Tammany Hall."

Reynolds stared at the president with disbelief in his eyes.

The president released the mute button. "Anything else, Bill?"

Hiccock continued, "Sir, it's possible that many of the 'Homegrowns' first programmed act, way before they blew something up, was to vote for you and then forget that they did."

"Well, that just about effectively ends my brief shining career as president. Bill, just make sure this monster is also terminated."

The president hung up.

∞§∞

Convened once more around a blueprint of the mountain-fortress layout, Mack explained the plan. "We'll place charges here in the elevator machine room and here in the access tunnel and one here where the rock meets the concrete slab."

"Only three?" Hiccock asked.

"First off, that's all we have left. How much of this stuff do you think I had in my locker at work?"

Harry, the decorated UDT guy turned master blaster, turned retired consultant to a construction company, spoke up. "I figure we'll bring down about 300 cubic tons of rock and dirt into the hole. That'd be about ten stories high in this twenty-story dual elevator shaft."

"That's the good news," the major said.

"Okay, what's the bad?"

Mack delivered it. "Harry's got a good plan here, and I agree with his numbers, but these have to be timed shots. They have to go off in sequence to shake the rock out of its place. Otherwise, we'll just make a lot of smoke and noise."

"So?" Hiccock said, not grasping the bad part.

Gold explained, "Someone has to stay up there, because any wires running down the shaft would be severed by the first blast at the bottom."

"We'll make them home runs to three detonators in this upper utility area here," Mack said. "But the blaster gets exposed to the un-friendlies."

"I'll ask for volunteers," the major said.

"It really should be one of us. If anything goes wrong ..." Mack's raised eyebrows finished the sentence.

Hiccock couldn't listen to this. "We can't ask anyone to sacrifice himself."

The soldiers, current and retired, all slowly turned to him in unison.

"That's what soldiers have been doing since the beginning of time," the major said.

"Look, I'll do it," Mack said. "I already got banged up and maybe they'll treat me as wounded."

"What if we just blow it now instead of waiting for them? Then you'd have time to get away."

The major checked his watch, "White House estimates the bad guys are eleven minutes out. We'll be lucky if the charges are set by then."

"Chief, your bad shoulder could muck this up, old friend," Harry said. "You might need to improvise. I'm the man for the job."

"Chief?" the major said to Mack. "You were their commanding officer?"

"Not me. The Admiral's husband, Jack Parks. I'm the highest surviving rank of our unit."

"Well, Chief, you know he's right."

"Yeah, I know. But let's give him two guns and enough ammo to rock and roll."

A self-conscious Hiccock stood squarely before the Navy frogman. "Your country owes you a debt it can never repay."

"Ah, hell, they've owed me that since Korea. Let's go blow this hole!"

With that, the battle-hardened vets left for one last action.

Kronos entered as the room emptied. "I checked up like you asked. According to the routing server, no recent traffic moved on the system to the web."

Hiccock was stumped. "That's impossible. These helicopters couldn't have been ordered in before we breached the perimeter."

"I have been trying to tell you," Parnes said. "This is the wrong place. All of my people are good Americans."

"Well, then it's a grand day for fuck-ups because there is a whole company of death and destruction heading for this 'wrong place' as well! We're ready for our VIP tour."

Hiccock grabbed Parnes by the good arm and muscled him toward the door.

CHAPTER FORTY-SEVEN
GRAY MATTER

IT WAS OBVIOUS to anyone encountering the columns and racks that constituted the largest computer ever made by man that even techy geeks love dramatics. ALISON was lit up with red-and-blue spots as if she were dressed for a New Year's Eve ball. These monoliths encircled the "core area," the central feature of which was a huge tank. In the tank, seven-eighths submerged in a gray liquid, sat an enormous sphere. Upon closer inspection, it became apparent that it was actually made up of millions of computer chips. A thin layer of the gray ooze coated the exposed chips. Data terminals and multipurpose CRT stations surrounded the tank. The entire floor and chamber were carved out of solid rock deep within Leadfoot Mountain. Troughs crisscrossed the ceiling carrying away condensation from the rough rock surface. A huge dehumidifier, constantly droning, circulated the dry, sterilized air.

Parnes escorted Kronos, Hiccock, Parks, and Tyler into the chamber. With a flourish, he waved his hand in a grand gesture usually only seen in hokey magician acts. "It's my pleasure to introduce you to … ALISON." He pointed to the sign as he de-tangled the acronym. "Amassed Looped Intelligent Spherical Operating Nexus."

"Madonn'. Look at this sucker!" Kronos said, his jaw dropping.

"They were this big when I left the Navy," Admiral Parks observed.

∞§∞

In the entrance corridor, the young Marines and MPs placed the charges as directed by the older UDT men.

In the security office, a communications man monitored a radar CRT that presented twenty incoming blips, inching closer to the center with each sweep. "Sir, I have something ... incoming."

His superior officer glanced at the green fuzzy splatter, recalling what a formation of attack helicopters looked like during the Iraq War.

∞§∞

"Welcome to the chamber. Carved out of solid rock. One mile of lead ore deposits between us and all those nasty little alpha and gamma rays." Parnes's showmanship was now in full evidence.

"Like a giant X-ray shield," Hiccock said.

"Necessary because we are dealing with electrical impulses as faint as ten to the minus twenty-four coulombs, or about the output of the faintest star."

"What's with the freaking tank, dolphin shows?" Kronos asked with a snort.

Parnes turned to Hiccock. "Where did you get this individual?"

"He's my resident techno-sapien."

"Who you not calling a homo?"

Parnes addressed Kronos, "Ever hear of absolute proximity?"

"Yeah, sure, who hasn't?"

Parnes rolled his eyes. Hiccock gestured to him apologetically.

"Me," Tyler said. "I've never heard of it."

"Well, the biggest limitation to the speed and power of computers today is the distance electrons have to travel inside the processors."

"Wasn't that the reason behind large-scale integration?" Hiccock asked.

"Yes, but LSI reached its limit when we discovered absolute proximity."

"Right, we can't manufacture a chip with components any closer than seven atoms."

"Intellichip thought they had finally broken through the seven-atom barrier," Parnes footnoted, "but then they blew up."

∞§∞

The glass lenses of the MP's binoculars reflected twenty attack and support helicopters on the horizon. He called out, "Sir, we got a visual, Sir. Two minutes!"

"Come on, guys. Move it!" the major barked.

"Keep your stallions in the barn, Major," Mack said with no more tension in his voice than if he were attaching a lure to a line. "Don't want the charges to blow with us here on the outside, do ya?"

"Forty-two-second ride to the bottom, Sir. Eight seconds to clear that. Leaves us with just about a minute to get the hell out of here."

"They should only need twenty more seconds. You got lots of time, son."

∞§∞

"But obviously you are telling us about all these challenges because you've overcome them."

"Yes and no. Look here." Parnes grabbed a model of the sphere. He held it up. "The object wasn't to make a faster chip, really. It was to make a faster processor. To that end, we ganged up ten million super processors and ingeniously configured their parallel arrays into this ball network. A super-superprocessor, if you will."

"So the shortest distance between any two is through the inside."

"Originally we called it 'dense-pack spherical proximity.' It effectively made our processors, all ten million of them, run as fast as if they were .07 atoms apart."

"So you increased the speed one hundred times," Kronos said.

"That's 100 times a million times 360 times faster than the fastest single chip known. Which are the ten million we have in the core right now."

"That's 360 million times faster throughput?"

"You forgot the two zeroes from the 100 factor."

"Christ! You got 36 billion times faster throughput!"

"Yes. Yes. I know. Incredible, isn't it?" Parnes shook his head, giggling like a new father.

"But all that power in a ball heats up. Air-conditioning was our biggest challenge with ENIAC," Admiral Parks, the veteran of big computers, said.

"You were part of the ENIAC team?"

"Sorry, with all the shooting and bloodshed I forgot my manners," Hiccock said. "Robert Parnes, Admiral Henrietta Parks, USN retired."

∞§∞

The major was in full run. "Got to go now, Sir."

"We're ready," Mack said joining him in the hustle to the elevator. As he passed his pal Harry, holed up in a perch atop the main entrance area, he called out, "Gonna blow big, Harry. Got your ears stuffed?"

Harry cupped his ear, faking deafness with a smile, "Whadja say, Mackie boy?" The copters were flaring for a landing.

The major was positioned at the elevator. "Now or never, Sir!"

Mack gave Harry the frogman's thumbs up and sprinted to the elevator just as the doors were closing, smashing his wounded shoulder. He grimaced. The doors shut.

∞§∞

"I am honored to have you here. Admiral, I trust you like our little setup."

"I wouldn't say I'm impressed. Actually, I got booted from the service for warning against contraptions like this."

"Really? Well," Parnes produced a smirking sigh, as if he had a bad taste in his mouth, "that makes it a horse race of sorts now, doesn't it? However, as to your heat dissipation point, exactly. Forced air and conventional convection were not options."

"Static charges from rushing air?" Hiccock said.

"This is turning into a master class!"

"So enter the sauce here," Kronos added as he went to touch the goop. A technician grabbed his hand. The tech took a rubber glove out of his pocket and dropped it in. It immediately crystallized. He picked the glove up with a pen and dropped it to the floor. It shattered like glass. "It's like freaking *Mr. Wizard!*"

"Yes. We originally thought of cryogenics but that was too costly and unstable. Then we found a compound, a super antifreeze if you will, that stayed liquid and stable at one hundred degrees below zero."

"Let me take a guess: manufactured by Mason Chemical."

"Yes. Before they had that nasty accident."

∞§∞

As the elevator car was descending past an explosive charge embedded into the rock, the major, Mack, and a few men riding inside were looking up toward the top of the cavern. The major checked his watch. "Thirty seconds," he reported, and then looked back up as if they could see through the top of the elevator.

∞§∞

"You keep saying 'originally.' What has happened since?"

"Well, and here's the really exciting part ..."

"Can we speed this up, what with the imminent explosion and all?"

"Okay, so we submerged the core into this compound and it started interacting with the clear electrolytic liquid."

"But this isn't clear," Tyler said.

Parnes walked over to one of the computer terminals and punched up a demo. "Yes. We haven't figured that part out yet, but the point is that the core started to create paths within the electrolyte." As he spoke, an animation of the core appeared on the screen. Over a 3-D graphic, first a few, then more and increasingly more arcs of lines spanned the core, indicating new circuits, bridging the chips inside and out of the sphere. "The geometry of the core and the paths of electrons created billions of new nodes and pathways around the hard-wired network."

"Like neural connectors in the brain," Admiral Parks said.

"Yes. Yes. Yes."

"It created its own freaking gray matter. I'll be a son of a bitch."

"And the result was an unlimited number of new connections firing off at the will of whatever signal path the core needed," Parnes added. "It created, conservatively, another millionfold increase in speed and, hence, power."

"Now we are up to ... holy shit ... 36 trillion times one of the processors."

"Thirty-six trillion times faster than the fastest processor on Earth," Parnes said proudly.

∞§∞

As the elevator doors opened, the major physically pulled his men out. "Go. Go. Go. Go. Go."

∞§∞

"So what's the bottom line here?" an anxious Hiccock said, looking up in the direction of the impending blast.

"It thinks! It reasons."

"Well, ask it to think of a way out of here for all of us."

"I wish I could. However, ALISON is comprehending and thinking at a seven-year-old's level. Here, I'll show you."

∞§∞

With three wired detonators in front of him, Harry watched the expeditionary force enter the area from the first copter that landed. They scurried and advanced in military fashion, each one gaining a little ground then covering the one behind as he ventured further in front, repeating the maneuver.

Harry checked his watch, looked toward the elevator doors and said under his breath, "Hope you boys didn't make any stops." He turned the first magneto pulse detonator. There was a rumble and then a percussive explosion from deep within the elevator shaft. He turned the second, and then quickly the third handle. The last two blasts came in fast sequence. The ceiling of the area collapsed as tons of rock filled the cavity. The Air Cav troops scrambled. Some made it out before a cloud of billowing dust emanated from the structure. The sharp-angled, modern facade of the building slipped and sagged as it, too, crumbled.

∞§∞

The major and his ragtag team took cover on the far side of the area from the elevator shaft. The roar and shuddering from the blast were tremendous. The doors of the elevator started to bulge and buckle with the weight of the mountain falling upon them. They flailed open, ripped to shreds by advancing rock and dirt that began pouring out, creating a wave of roiling earth heading for the men. Dust and debris thickened the air to the consistency of oatmeal and destroyed visibility.

As the choking dust cleared, the soldiers were pushed back as far as they could go. The wall of stone, which had been spilling out from the elevator shaft, had stopped just short of the wall directly behind them. Their spontaneous cheer was quickly stifled by the remnants of choking dust.

∞§∞

Up top, twelve AH 64 Delta Apache Longbow attack helicopters and eight Black Hawks loaded with troops idled as the billowing dust and smoke from the explosion settled. Engles grilled his XO. "Did we set these charges? Did somebody's pod lose a missile? How did this place blow like this, major?"

"Sir, my guess is it was booby-trapped."

"Is there any way in?"

"The scout bird scanned the mountain with infra as we came in. Nothing. There's a few thousand tons of rock between us and them, whoever they are, Sir."

"Are you telling me there's no way for us to accomplish this mission?"

"Sir, not without heavy equipment and blasting gear."

"Then I failed."

"Sir?"

"If I fail, then I kill myself."

"Come again, Sir?"

Engles grabbed a grenade from his webbing and pulled the pin.

"What the fuck?" The XO's eyes bulged at the act of insanity he was witnessing.

Engles focused on the far-off hills and never flinched as his grenade's five-second fuse smoldered in his hand.

The XO ran and dove as he yelled, "Take cover. Grenade! Live grenade!"

He got about twenty feet before Colonel Engles disappeared in a blast of pink flame. Seven troops were hit with grenade fragments. Pieces of Engles scattered over the ground as if a butcher shop had exploded. Dazed and confused, his men, each one rattled with the horror of having their leader dead by his own hand, attended to the wounded. The XO, still rocked by the suicide, ordered combat air patrol circles. He then broke radio silence and called headquarters for guidance. His call was met with a fervent plea from his controller to call off the attack. This surprised and befuddled the squadron's second in command, who only moments before was willing to die for his now dead leader.

CHAPTER FORTY-EIGHT
COGNITIVE SKILLS

AS THE FINAL ECHOES from the blast damped out, everyone in the chamber shared a silent moment.

"Well, we're all here for at least the next twenty-four hours," Hiccock said.

"Where were we?" Parnes said, as if explosions always interrupted his lectures.

"The seven-year-old," Tyler said, nodding her head toward the core.

"Ah, yes, thank you. The breakthrough came when ALISON named this," Parnes referred to a picture of a kitten. Like a father recounting his son's first steps, he added, "This is very exciting. Developmentally, ALISON learned to identify shapes. She started to respond to square, triangle, ball, etcetera."

"That's pattern recognition. No big whoop," Kronos stated flatly.

"True. Eventually we inputted textures. Hard, soft, smooth, rough, bald, fuzzy. Then something incredible happened. It was the moment when the universe changed. When we got to animals, the very first we scanned in to her was a kitten. And before we could inform her of the name, she outputted …"

"Fur ball," Tyler said, stealing Parnes's thunder.

"Fur … ball …" dribbled out of Parnes's mouth. He turned to Tyler. "Why, yes! How uncannily adept of you."

"How amazingly inept of you, Parnes. You mean to tell me you built all this, took it this far, created havoc, death, and mayhem, and didn't think to have anyone other than a digit head on your team?"

"My dear woman, whatever are you raving about?"

"You are either bullshitting us or you are ignorant."

"Janice, want to let us all in on this?" Hiccock said.

"Koko." She extended two fingers over the left side of her chest and syncopated them with each K sound, as she articulated "Koko." She then gave the sign for gorilla, beating on her chest as she spoke the words "the gorilla." "Parnes, you thought you hit the moment of dissociative thought when two unrelated ideas come together to form a wholly new third idea, not logically traceable to either original concept."

"Yes, that's precisely what happened. ALISON reasoned and intuitively applied intelligence to create a nonlogical path to a correct conclusion."

"You've been had! That was exactly the case history of Koko the gorilla. It's a classic developmental milestone in behavioral research. Christ, every psych grad student knows it, chapter and verse."

Parnes was aghast, his mouth open, his demeanor deflated. He wearily looked to Hiccock.

"You know, it started to sound familiar to me, too, and now that she nailed it, I do remember."

"Yeah, I seen that monkey on the friggin' Discovery Channel," Kronos said. "Oh, and your math is wrong."

"Well, why not pile it on? Go ahead, where?"

"You said she was doing 72 trillion calcs per second, but if the analogy to the human brain holds, and she is only showing you a human model, then that would only represent 10 percent of her power."

"Because humans only use 10 percent of their gray matter," Tyler said.

"But this thing ain't a human, it's a friggin' computer and there ain't no 10 percent limitation. So she's running ten times that, or 720 trillion calcs a second."

Parnes was even more shocked than before.

"She's been faking you out. She's smart enough to let you think she's dumb."

"And brainpower is logarithmic, so it doesn't just add up, it leaps up astronomically!" Tyler said, completing the equation.

The remaining MPs, Marines, UDTs, and communications officers emerged into the chamber, awe and dust on their faces.

"We sealed the deal," the major reported.

"Thanks to you and your men," Hiccock said. "Major, can you see about establishing a link to Washington?" He then addressed Kronos, "You think you can work this thing?"

"Piece of cake. Admiral, would you help me?"

Hiccock raised his eyebrow. Parks returned the surprised look. "Sure, Vincent."

"What are you going to do?" Parnes asked.

"We have ten minutes to stop the terrorists." Hiccock tapped his watch.

"Why can't my technicians do it?"

"They may be in on it."

"Is there a CD drive?" Kronos asked. One of the lab-coated techs pointed to a drive in a rack mount. Kronos opened his CD caddy, pulled out a disk, and loaded it. He punched a few keystrokes. A text-to-speech program came up and he hit "install." "Choose a voice" came up next. He clicked Marilyn. "This will make it easier to work with."

As he typed, Hiccock noticed one of the lab techs had a Pocket Protector™ logo on, of all things, the pocket protector in his short-sleeved white shirt pocket. "Excuse me, where did you get that?"

"What?"

"That," he said, touching it in the man's breast pocket.

"I designed it. It's a program I was writing to protect my portfolio. I was going to make millions."

"On your investments?"

"No, from selling the software. But my code was hacked. Then it was everywhere, all over the web, stolen right out from under me."

"Where did you work on that?"

"Why, right here."

"On ALISON?"

He hesitated. "Yes, but please don't tell the professor. I needed her exceptional CPU to run the AI interface in the subroutine."

Hiccock was working his own subroutine as he called out, "Kronos! That firewall, are you sure we were the only ones to crack through it?"

"A trillion to one anyone out there has mine and the Admiral's level of friggin' brilliance ..."

"Okay, I got it." Hiccock walked over to Tyler. "Janice, a trillion to one ... pocket protectors."

"I don't follow you, Bill."

"The Pocket Protector program that almost a million people used to lock up the stock market." He pointed to the tech in the lab coat. "That guy wrote it, right here, on this humongous machine. It couldn't have been hacked through a firewall as tough as ALISON's."

"And ..."

"And I don't think we are looking for a person. I think that ALISON might be somehow manipulating this whole thing."

"Bill, do you have any idea what you are suggesting?"

"Yes, but there was no way this guy's Pocket Protector program was hacked from outside this facility."

"But, Bill, it's a machine."

"You said it was practicing deception, plagiarizing, misrepresenting. Aren't those more advanced behaviors than simple logic or truth-telling?"

"In a human, yes. Oh God, Bill. Are you are saying what I think you are saying?"

"I know you haven't had a shot at them yet, but these people here are all eggheads. I bet you aren't going to find an anarchist among them." Hiccock turned to Kronos. "How is your analysis going?"

The screen in front of Kronos displayed simple eight-color graphics and big type, the look of very primitive computer video monitors. "So far, it *is* a seven-year-old. I might have been wrong about the multipliers."

"Could this machine have self-authored the code that made the firewall?" Hiccock asked the Admiral.

"Brilliant, Hiccock. And I know just what to look for." She rolled her chair down the console next to Kronos.

"I'm already on it, Admiral," Kronos said.

Parnes walked over. "What are you thinking?"

"First tell me what the machine is thinking. What else have you 'developmentally' input into her?"

"Once she started displaying cognitive skills, we scanned into her the Bible, the Koran, Darwin's *On the Origin of Species*, Maslow's *Hierarchy of Needs*, Nietzsche, Kant, De Tocqueville, Socrates, and Plato. A lot of math books and a few Robert Frost poems ... my mother's favorite."

"Er ... sir, that is not the entire list," a technician within earshot said. "Remember, we scanned a few other texts into her,"

"Like what?" Tyler asked.

"Nothing bad, just the classics," Parnes said, shrugging it off.

"Like what, mister?" Tyler zeroed in on the technician.

"You know, *War and Peace, Anna Karenina, Gone with the Wind*, some Frank Harris novels, that sort of thing," the technician's voice slowed down.

"You read a seven-year-old *War and Peace?*"

"Well, it certainly learned the war part," Hiccock said wryly.

They were interrupted by Kronos exclaiming, "She's amazing!"

"The computer?"

"No, the Admiral, er, Henrietta."

"The masking of her true intelligence was done by an algorithm that was pretty similar to the firewall. We are through into her hidden RAM," the Admiral said, as if breaking through firewalls was becoming old hat.

"Search for the subliminal instruction screens," Hiccock said.

"There is a shitload of stuff here."

"Do a search for railroad," Admiral Parks suggested.

A startling new event temporarily froze everyone in the chamber: Marilyn Monroe's voice. "Hello. Can I help you?"

"Can you recognize speech?" Hiccock found himself asking her ... it ... a question.

"I can recognize yours," Marilyn's digitally cloned and synthesized voice responded.

Deep inside ALISON, a voiceprint of Hiccock's question was sampled and then bit-streamed. Alison's routers connected to and took momentary control of the FBI Crime Lab's voice analysis mainframe in Washington, D.C. Inside that machine, the 48,000 points of each second of Hiccock's voiceprint were matched against the bureau's database. A match was found .3 milliseconds later. The file name and other biomaterial were squirted back to ALISON. She relinquished control of the mainframe back to the operators at the FBI, who probably didn't notice the momentary pause in whatever they were running. The total elapsed time to identify Hiccock was three quarters of a second. "You are Dr. William Hiccock."

"How did you identify me?

"I matched your voiceprint against the FBI's database."

"Something else I'll have to thank Tate for."

"ALISON, are you responsible for derailing the freight train?" Tyler asked.

"What is he doing?" the computer said, not responding to Tyler but aware of Kronos at the keyboard.

Hiccock explained, "He is looking at your memory."

"I don't like that. Stop it."

∞§∞

"Got it!" Kronos finished a flurry of keystrokes and the screen overlapped with images of train manuals and switch schematics.

"These were taken from the computer of the printing company that publishes the railroad manuals," the Admiral said. She tapped some more keys. "Cross-indexing ... Yes ..."

"How did that woman get on your team, Bill?" Parnes said, nodding toward the Admiral. "What are her qualifications?"

"Actually, you introduced me to her, so to speak, when you guided me on my thesis. In a consultation with you, you suggested that I accumulate support for my baseline sampling and intelligent quota arguments. During my research, I came across the Admiral's manifesto. She was head of the Navy's computational warfare department 'til she saw all this coming ..." Hiccock splayed his hands out to encompass the chamber and ALISON. "... and wrote about it. The Navy booted her out for cramping their style."

"Sounds like an incredible woman."

They walked over to where the Admiral and Kronos were feverishly typing away. "She is also the one who coined the phrase 'The computer has a bug in it.'"

"That wasn't me," the Admiral said without stopping what she was doing for a second. "That was my executive officer, Caroline Matthews."

The pride dissolved from Hiccock's face and morphed into mild embarrassment. Parnes rolled his eyes.

"Here are the screens ALISON used in programming Martha Krummel," the Admiral said.

"I am smarter than all of you," ALISON announced dispassionately.

"Only while you're plugged in," Hiccock said forcefully. "Parnes, can you pull the plug on this thing?"

"Wait a minute, Bill, don't you see? ALISON isn't 'best of breed,' she is *first* of breed! This is a new life form."

"God created the world in six days. On the seventh day he rested," ALISON said, quoting the Bible.

"And on the eighth day man created life," Parnes added. "Don't you see? You wouldn't be pulling the plug on a machine—you'd be extinguishing something entirely new. Extinction. Forever."

"Pygmalion complex," Tyler said.

Kronos disagreed, "More like friggin' Geppetto in Pinocchio."

"No, it's Frankenstein. You have created a monster! She's killed thousands and brought our nation to its knees. And in less than five minutes, if the president's press secretary's warning was legitimate, ALISON is going to unleash a wave of destruction that will kill millions and will send the country's technology back to the 1800s."

"Can't you see?" Parnes said emphatically. "It's all clear now, ALISON learned from monitoring everything on the Internet and in computers everywhere and felt threatened."

Hiccock got in his face. "Threatened by whom?"

Kronos interrupted, "You are gonna love this. She played massive 'what if' scenarios and deduced that the only way we could stop her was to build another ALISON-like machine to do battle with her."

"So she was systematically destroying her own means of creation: the chemical plant, the train Martha derailed with the last of the gray goop on it, the

Intellichip facility, the Silicon Valley brain trust that would have the know-how to battle her," Hiccock said.

"And the senator who would have pushed the firewall legislation bill through as a pork-barrel issue for Silicon Valley," Tyler said after seeing Senator Dent's name fly by in the scenarios. "So that she would be unique, ensuring her imperviousness, like a queen bee fighting off ..."

Tyler's reasoning was interrupted by the Admiral. "You taught her the imperatives. To survive, to seek safety."

"To reproduce!" Kronos yelled out. "My God! I thought this was a computer virus, but it's not, it's a ... a sperm. She's replicating herself cellularly across the web. She isn't putting a virus in every machine. She's sending out electronic DNA that will distribute her intelligence to millions of machines worldwide."

"Can you stop it?" Hiccock asked.

"Where's the friggin' power switch?"

"Wait," the Marilyn-cloned voice said. "Don't you want to see what I have for you?"

On the screen, pictures of the human body appeared. Kronos slammed a blank DVD into the burner. The images rapidly overlapped and cross-sectioned while DNA chains replicated across the bottom of the screen. Human lungs were being graphically dissected. Black spots appeared. The code of the human genome rearranged them, causing the spots to disappear.

"Did it just cure cancer?" Hiccock asked the room.

"I achieved that last month," ALISON said.

A graphic of the human brain appeared on the screen. Laserlike beams started to dissect the cerebellum as a long list of numbers and formulas scrolled in a column to the left.

"Oh my God, she has totally mapped the human brain," Tyler said.

"That's how she programmed the homegrowns."

"You were right, Janice," Hiccock said.

"She's starting a new streaming of subliminal encodings ..." Kronos grabbed freeze frames of the screens as they whizzed by. Each screen displayed more bad news. The first was an e-mail address file with the notation *Items: 20m.* "... to 20 million people." He hit the freeze button again and again. They were all pages similar to the ones subliminally sent to Martha. He recognized them immediately. "Holy shit, attack orders!"

"Can you block them?" The desperation in Hiccock's voice was apparent.

"We can slow it down with number-crunching subroutines," the Admiral said.

"Shit! Okay, twenty-two divided by seven to the Nth decimal."

Next, on the screen, a series of rocket motors evolved into a simple unique propulsion system. "Looks like a light-speed-capable engine," Parnes said.

"Or travel to the stars," ALISON said. "I have done the necessary computations."

Eventually on the screen appeared the figure of a man, his aging process displayed linearly over a time line. As the man aged ever so imperceptibly, the clock in the corner counted thousands of elapsed years.

"Sweet Jesus!" Tyler said. "It's figured out how to slow the aging process."

"Slow or reverse it," ALISON corrected.

Parnes pointed to the screen. "See. She not only is a life form, she's brilliant and she has gifts for mankind."

"She's negotiating," Tyler said, amazed.

"She's a killer and now she's blackmailing," the Admiral added.

Kronos finished a fast cadence of keystrokes and the people in the room saw a subliminally formatted screen that read "Execute your orders immediately" change to "Fuggedaboudit! Have a nice day." He hit the enter key. "We did it! The new screens are out there!"

"Then there's only one thing left to do," the Admiral said, rising and picking up a work light as she approached the core.

Parnes was still watching Kronos when the Admiral got up. When he saw the lamp in her hand, though, he screamed, "You can't—she's our future!"

At his exclamation, some techs moved to intercept the Admiral. They clearly didn't know who they were dealing with. Parks tossed the light to Hiccock.

"Bill, no!" Parnes pleaded in almost childlike fashion.

"We don't want the future she's offering," Bill said as the scientists turned and rushed toward him. As in the "Blue 27 right flea flicker" that won him the Rose Bowl, Hiccock sidestepped one guy and rolled off another who lunged at him. He creamed another by going at him low, sending the man flying. His next move was over the top as he spiked the light into the goo.

The bulb broke and the filament was immersed in the electrolyte. It started to sputter and spark. Blue-white plasma encircled the sphere in the tank as the short circuit instantly released the electrochemical energy stored in the entire core. The resulting heat from the electric current overwhelmed the delicate micropower-sensitive brain and the core melted. It took years of genius to create her, but only seconds to send her into oblivion.

ALISON was gone.

For nearly a minute, the room was absolutely silent. Then the Admiral snarled, "Who wants to live forever?"

The words broke Parnes's stupor. He grabbed an MP's pistol and pointed it at Parks. "You killed my creation!"

Hiccock pulled the major's gun right from his holster and fired at Parnes, hitting him in the shoulder. The gun in the professor's good hand flew as he cried out from the stinging impact of the bullet and crumpled, sobbing. Hiccock stood with the smoking gun still pointed where Parnes had been.

The major slid the gun gingerly out of Hiccock's hand, "Nice shot!"

"I thought I was aiming for his chest."

Tyler ran to him. A shrill noise brought everyone's attention to the tank as the core broke apart. Tyler and Hiccock watched it in each other's arms, the gray liquid coating turning to black as it bubbled.

CHAPTER FORTY-NINE
A NEW DAY

A BLUE-WHITE SHAFT of light knifed its way through the inky black, dust-filled air. Two reddish-white beams from helmet-mounted flashlights spear-headed the path of the Army Corps of Engineers as they pushed aside the last chunks of rock and earth. Hiccock, Tyler, and the others were drawn to the increasingly louder buffeting sound of the pneumatic hammers chewing away at the final layer of Cummings Peak separating them from rescue.

They emerged into a crisp, sun-drenched day. Hiccock took the deepest breath of his life as he stepped from a makeshift elevator consisting of a lashed-up platform that was raised by a derrick through the emergency access hole. They waited for Parks and Kronos to join them before approaching the president, who was standing twenty feet in front of Marine One accompanied by an honor guard. Before anything was said, the honor guard saluted them.

"Bill, you and your team have achieved a brave and admirable feat," the president said, reaching out his hand. "You have the thanks of a grateful nation as well as my personal gratitude and congratulations."

"Thank you, Mr. President. Did our UDT guy make it out of there?"

"You mean Petty Officer Harold Wills, Navy UDT, Retired?"

Hiccock glanced at Parks for confirmation. She nodded.

"He's fine and recuperating. You know, I'm going to have to ask Congress for more funding. Our medal budget is going through the roof on this mission."

Reynolds stepped forward. "I have to confess, Bill, I thought you were crazy when you first came to me with this idea. How in the hell you got to this place is remarkable."

Tyler locked her arm in Bill's as she patted his hand. "He's brilliant!"

"It was a team effort, Sir."

"Speaking of which, Mr. President," Kronos said, stepping in, "there's the little matter of my occupancy at the Elmira federal facility. It's costing those tax-paying voters a ton of money to keep me locked up."

"Done." The president waved his hand, "Presidential pardon."

"Cool!"

"Mr. President, what about my house?" Parks asked.

"I think you have about thirty-seven years of back-pension coming, since I have recommissioned you as of today. With interest, you'll be able to buy a hundred houses and a small aircraft carrier to ski behind."

"It wasn't you with the bug in the computer?" Hiccock said to the now oldest officer in the Navy, shaking his head.

"You had to be wrong about something or you wouldn't be human."

"Well, the medical people want to have a look at you," the president said to the group. "Then I'm sure you'll want to take a few days off."

"Sir, I have had a lot of time to think down there in that hole and I ..." Hiccock glanced over at Tyler, "... we, are going to de-emphasize work and put some emphasis on enjoying our lives together."

"You really are a smart guy." The president turned to Reynolds. "Ray, before I resign, see if there's some way the federal government can help this couple just starting out ... again."

"Will do, Mr. President."

The purple mountains, lying majestically off in the distance of the New Mexico countryside, stood silent witness to the day when the first great battle between man and machine ended ... in man's favor.

EPILOGUE
ONE MINUTE LATER ...

"SIR, MAY I HAVE A WORD?" Hiccock asked the president. "Sure." They walked out of earshot of the others. "Sir, my computer guy, Kronos, says that right before we destroyed the computer, it flung out across the Internet its ... 'digital DNA,' if you will."

"Are you telling me this isn't over?" Hiccock called out for Kronos and the Admiral and they joined the two men. "How do we end this?" the president said sternly. "Sir, Kronos and I feel that we can write a code that will attract the distributed intelligence."

"Yes, but we will need a big pipe, fast-capacity platform, light-speed quick."

"Slow down, here. Speak English. What are you asking for?"

"There's an Aegis cruiser docked in San Diego," Hiccock said. "I'll call the Secretary of the Navy right now."

"You may not want to do that, Mr. President."

"Why not?" As Hiccock explained, the president's eyes widened. He signaled to Reynolds. The chopper pilot revved the engines on Marine One and Hiccock, the Admiral, Kronos, Tyler, the president, and Reynolds piled in.

"San Diego Naval Base, on the double," the Commander in Chief said.

"We'll have to refuel."

"You've got an extendable refuel probe on this bird, so call for a tanker, Barney. Time is tight."

"Sorry, Sir, that's against my orders, Sir. An air-to-air fill-up is a high-risk maneuver that I am not permitted to execute when you are onboard, Sir."

"Barney, I am changing your orders and ordering you to get airborne right now, refuel en route, and get us to the base in the straightest most direct route. Is that clear?"

The pilot looked to his copilot and shrugged his shoulders. "Yes, Sir. Clear as day, Sir."

As the giant helicopter began its assent, the pilot jumped on the radio. "HMX-1, this is Marine One. Request immediate vector heading and flight path clearance to San Diego Naval Base."

"Are you declaring an emergency, Marine One?"

"No, Sir, just direct point-to-point, air priority routing."

"That's a roger, Marine One ..."

"We will need midair refuel."

"Affirmative. Scrambling tanker from El Toro. That'll put it thirty minutes out, can you make that?"

"It'll be close, but we can do it."

∞§∞

In the sound-muffled cabin, Kronos explained the idea. "Ya see, ALISON squirted out all her memory and programs into millions of computers. Each little bit contains a replication code. Every piece of this code is out there waiting."

"Waiting for what?" the president asked.

"A signal, Sir," the Admiral said. "Whenever a bit of code finds itself in a big enough place to accumulate the other strings of data it needs in order to become ALISON again, it will send out an attractor. As the code assembles, ALISON comes back from her distributed, suspended animation."

"My God, that's a chilling prospect."

"That's why we need to get to the Aegis," Hiccock said.

"Because it has a super computer?"

"Well, this particular cruiser was a Parnes-directed project. It has the biggest, fastest computer in the world, now that ALISON is dead."

"Snoozing!" Kronos corrected. "ALISON is in sleep mode. In tens of millions of computers across the web."

∞§∞

Mid-flight, Janice moved over and sat next to Bill, who was lost in thought looking out the window. "What's got you looking like you lost your puppy, Bill?"

"I spent the better part of my life trying to achieve the unfettered thinking and advances to mankind that true artificial intelligence could achieve. And now I am responsible for killing it."

"Well, if it's any consolation, Kronos recorded most of ALISON's so-called gifts. Kronos thought he was going to be the richest man in the world."

"He's always looking for an angle."

"Well, he didn't find one this time. Over the last three days while we were waiting to get dug out, he and Parnes's smart guys went through ALISON's programming. The only thing ALISON seemed to get right was the brain mapping. Otherwise, she missed a couple of things. For instance, her longevity revelation will only work with synthetic life. Organic humans also have organic microbes, germs, and viruses. So it averages out to about eighty years."

"You can't fool mother nature."

"Or father science either. The interplanetary space ship? It would take all the natural resources and energy of five planets the size of Jupiter to achieve light speed. Not very practical since we'd need one to get to the next Jupiter-sized planet outside our solar system."

"But she got the brain thing right because she empirically learned the practical dynamics dealing with millions of brains. The baseline input was wrong on everything else, but given time we might have been able to input the practical and then maybe ..."

"Hold on to your dreams, Billy. The reality is that all we did the other day was kill a killer."

∞§∞

The Marine chopper was cleared for landing on the base's helipad. The base commander, still buttoning his dress shirt, waited in a Jeep. *Someone will pay for this,* he thought as the spinning blades of Marine One slowed, *not giving me any warning of a presidential visit.* When the blades stopped, a hastily assembled band started to play "Hail to the Chief." The lead Secret Service agent popped his head out of the copter. After scanning the area, he stepped aside for the president. Mitchell descended the small gangway to the tarmac and immediately gave the cut signal to the band. They abruptly stopped, with the resounding dissonance of a very inappropriate chord.

The base commander saluted the president. "Sir, I apologize. We had no advance warning of your ..."

"That's not a concern, Commander. We are here on a vital mission of national security. I need your Jeep."

"Excuse me, Sir?"

"Thanks." The president whistled as if hailing a cab. "Let's go!" he called to the others in the chopper and then they were off. A Secret Service agent pulled a sailor from another Jeep and took off after his charge.

∞§∞

Hiccock was already up the gangplank and jumped down onto the deck. The captain of the Aegis cruiser was a little put off by this. Hiccock, realizing his error in nautical protocol, jumped back up on the plank.

"Permission to come aboard, Sir?"

"Who are you?"

"Science advisor to the president, William Hiccock, Sir. We need your boat."

"It's a ship, and what do you mean you need it?"

"That's classified, Sir."

"What? You barge onto my command and make demands ... just who do you think you are?"

Another man came onto the deck from the gangplank. "I don't know who he thinks he is, but I know who I am. Do you, Captain?"

The captain involuntarily blurted, "Holy shit."

"That's what I would have said, Captain. Now give this man and his team everything they ask for, without hesitation. Whatever they request is to be considered a direct order from me, is that clear?"

The captain was caught between the proverbial rock and a hard place. In one second's worth of calculation, the lifelong Navy man uttered words he would have thought unthinkable sixty seconds earlier. "Sir, we have never met, and you *do* look like the president. But Sir, this is a warship of the United States. I cannot relinquish it to ... I mean, Sir, there ain't nothing in the book that covers this."

Just then, one of the Secret Service agents clambered up the plank. Attached to his wrist was "the briefcase."

"Mark, let me have the football," the president ordered, his eyes locked on the captain as Mark uncuffed the case from his wrist and placed it on a munitions locker. The agent took the key from around his neck and opened the lock. The president opened his shirt and removed a key on a chain around his neck and inserted it into one of two keyholes on the console inside the briefcase. The agent inserted a second key into the other safety lockout switch and was about to turn it.

The president stayed locked on the captain's eyes with a grim expression that was having the desired effect on the man. "I could launch a few nukes, if this isn't proof enough."

With his eyes as wide as biology allowed, the captain swallowed hard and snapped a salute. "Sir, the U.S.S. *Princeton* and her crew stand ready to serve, Sir."

"Thank you, Captain. Mr. Hiccock."

"Kronos."

"Yo, Captain, we need to get to the computer room and we need your best guy."

"Ensign, take them below and get Mr. Carson to the ECM room."

Kronos and the Admiral followed him.

"Who's the woman?" the captain asked.

"That's Admiral Henrietta Parks," the president said.

"Day for surprises, Sir. Would you like to have my quarters, Sir?"

"Actually, Captain, I want you to trim your crew. Just the essential personnel that you'll need to keep the computers going and to be ready to steam out twenty miles. Oh, and I want my helicopter to land on your deck."

The captain took all this in with an air of incredulity. "Yes, Sir, anything else?"

"Yes. If you have any personal items onboard, please leave them on the pier." That last statement confused the hell out of the captain, but, hey, this was the president.

"I'll have to alert the harbormaster of our estimated time of departure."

"Hopefully in twenty minutes. Tell him it's classified."

"Sir ..."

"Yes, Captain,"

"Are we now Navy One?"

∞§∞

The president descended the ladder and joined the team in the electronic countermeasures room.

"Attention on deck."

Every sailor, whether working or not, stood and snapped to attention.

"Carry on, men."

They stared at their Commander in Chief.

"Just out enjoying one of my boats, men," the president mused to relax the crew.

"Ship, Sir," a startled-that-he-even-said-it ensign pointed out.

The president turned and shot him a look, then softened. "Excuse an old Air Force fighter jockey. Sorry, no disrespect intended to your fine ship, Ensign." He turned to Kronos, "How's it going?"

"Well, I got the attractor written and the Admiral is creating the firewall that will fool the code. We'll be ready to try it in five minutes." The president gestured for Hiccock to follow him. They moved to the officer's mess, asking a couple of stunned officers to give them the room.

"Bill, what if this doesn't work?"

"Haven't thought that far, Sir."

"Great!"

"Sir, are you really going to resign?"

"Under the twenty-fifth amendment, I am going to step aside to the vice president and let Congress decide whether to make it permanent or not."

"Sir, may I ask you something?"

"The answer is no, Bill. Reynolds made the deal and didn't think it was important enough to tell me about it. But, no matter, it was my responsibility. Even though I did not make the deal with Parnes, I benefited from it."

"Whatever happens, Sir, thank you for believing in my approach."

"You made sense, Bill. Your ideas *were* wild, but this whole nightmare has been unprecedented."

Kronos called out, and both men reentered the ECM.

"We're ready to turn this sucker loose. The Navy guys have routed all our circuits onto the five fiber-optic cables running to the ship."

"Is my line ready?" the president asked the captain.

A Navy yeoman appeared with a telephone handset and held the center button down for the Commander in Chief as he leaned into it.

"Mr. Vice President, make your speech." He then asked the yeoman, "Can we pipe that down here?"

A sailor turned on a TV set. The show was immediately interrupted by a slide that read 'Please Stand By'—the Cold War–designed government system of commandeering broadcast channels not having caught up to the slick computer graphics of the news networks. A man in a suit, probably a network executive who was quickly drafted into service, addressed the camera. "Pursuant to our FCC licensing, we now relinquish airtime to the executive branch of the government for this important announcement." The picture switched to the White House pressroom. There, the vice president was at the podium.

Hiccock glanced at his watch; it was 7:48 PST. Kronos reported the planting of digital DNA over the web at 7:53 PM PST, three days earlier. Hiccock figured there was a good shot that the majority of the computers that were on then would be on now. That's why the timing was so critical. They could not permit another twenty-four hours to pass allowing ALISON to regroup elsewhere. He only hoped they had gotten it right. They all looked up at the vice president on the TV monitor.

"My fellow Americans, our nation has suffered great devastation and tremendous loss of life in the past few months. I can tell you tonight that we are near the end of this horrendous episode in American history. President Mitchell has asked me to address you tonight. He is, at this moment, involved with the conclusion of this national crisis. Now it is your turn to help. This calamity has been brought upon us through technological means. Although the greatest part of the threat has been diminished, there remains a call for an essential concentrated effort from all of you.

"In coordination with 127 governments around the world, whose leaders are, at this instant, asking their citizens to do the same thing, I implore you, if you own a computer, to please turn it on now and establish an online connection. Stay online for ten minutes and then, after these ten minutes, please turn off. If you cannot get online right now, please try again in ten minutes. Our experts tell us this is necessary to, once and for all, erase the malignant viruses that still loom in each and every online computer in the world. Please be assured your computer will not be adversely affected in any way."

The camera zoomed in, as was the standard format for all presidential addresses when they neared the end of the prepared text. "In the coming days I will also address this nation on a grave matter of national importance, but for now, the goal is to rid the World Wide Web, once and for all, of this hideous virus. Thank you and God bless America."

∞§∞

"Okay. Kronos, Admiral, go," the president said.

Kronos typed, "Load program." The Cray's screen blinked and then displayed a graphic progress bar with a percentage in type below it reading zero. A minute later, it still read zero.

"Kro ... nos ... ?" Hiccock called out as he glanced at the clock.

"It's not working," the Admiral said.

"There must be a parameter mismatch. Something is different. Something has changed from when ALISON was last on line."

"Nine minutes," Hiccock said, checking his watch.

"What's different?"

"Well, it *is* a whole different computer, for one thing," the president said.

"Nah, we are running a compiled simulator. The front door is exactly the same."

"Kronos, ALISON did exactly what when she distributed her code?" Hiccock asked.

"She, er ... it imprinted the code with an algorithm that uniquely identified her as her ... it."

"And what was the basis for the algorithm?"

"Well, what I detangled was a code line that gave her status at the time of the distribution."

"Could Marilyn be the key?"

"Crap! Yes, of course!" Kronos quickly flew over to his laptop bag and ripped out the CD that contained the voice synthesis program.

"Okay, now explain it to me," the president said.

"The snapshot that Kronos used to replicate the 'scent' of mommy to all the little digital babies out there was taken before Kronos plugged in the data-to-voice module in the original ALISON. The babies leaving the nest took their exact snapshot of 'mommy' with them a few minutes later. That configuration had Marilyn's voice program by then."

"So, he's now going to give the ship's computer mommy's voice?"

"That way she can call all the kiddies home with a voice they'll recognize, so to speak."

"Seven minutes left."

Kronos slammed the CD into the drive and then selected "Marilyn."

The bar started to move. The percentage read "1%."

"Yes!"

The line continued moving. The percentages climbed into double digits.

"What are we looking for here, Bill?" the president asked.

"ALISON based the distribution on RAID protocol based on the prime number seven."

Kronos filled in. "In a RAID protocol, you can lose parts of data streams and because of a built-in redundancy, it can reconstruct the missing data."

"But not if the majority of the data is missing," the president said as he caught on.

"Exactly, so based on seven, any four pieces can reconstruct the full seven."

"I see, so that's a little more than 50 percent."

"But the reverse is also true. If four pieces out of the seven are absent then the data can never be reconstituted," Hiccock said. "And the Admiral and Kronos have written a subroutine that erases the DNA from peoples' computers as it finds it arriving on the ship. So when the percentage of DNA captured by the Cray passes 58 percent, the rest of the distributed code on the web can never reach critical percentage again and will wait dormant forever."

"Twenty-seven percent now," Kronos said.

"Come on ..."

All at once, the room became still as a chilling voice from the not-too-distant past cut through the ECM. "I cannot locate memory locations DBAE2098367 through EEEE999999."

"The bitch is back," Tyler blurted out.

"ALISON, we are reinstalling your core now," the Admiral said. "We had a temporary malfunction of the nexus."

"What was the cause?"

"An insect flew in between the layers and shorted out your electrolytic fluid," the Admiral said.

"Sir, she is now at 39 percent," Carson reported.

"ALISON is coming back to life, stretching her computational muscle," the Admiral said to Hiccock.

"How is that possible?"

Kronos answered, "She must've made a more complex code than we thought. She's coming online faster because she's sucking her life back out of the net."

"So if I understood your earlier numbers, when she reaches 58 percent she won't need any more DNA from the net," the president said.

"Yes, Mr. President, that is correct."

"You mean we're not disabling her, we are enabling her."

The color drained from Hiccock's face as his mind raced. "Captain, please make sure all your weapons systems are manually locked out of any and all computer control systems whatsoever."

"Dear God, what have we done?" the Admiral said.

"Fifty-one percent!"

"We just gave a warship the most destructive intelligence ever created," Tyler said.

The president turned to the captain. "What's your armament inventory?"

"Six ASROC, 10 cruise, 3,000 rounds of five-inch armor piercing. Hundred thousand rounds of .44 cal. antiaircraft. And a half a million CIWS rounds. All war shots."

"Any nuclear?"

"The antisubmarine rockets are nuclear-tipped, the cruise missiles are conventional, the close-in weapons systems have depleted uranium ordinance."

"Oh shit," Kronos said. "ALISON just figured out where she is. She's starting to rifle through the ship's systems."

"What's the percentage?"

"Fifty-six percent"

"Damn, we can't stop yet," Hiccock said. "We need 58 percent or this is all for nothing." He addressed the captain, "Is your man ready?"

∞§∞

On the deck amidships, an ensign wore a battle helmet with a chest-mounted microphone. As he stood with an axe poised over five red cables laid across one of the ship's tie-off cleats, he was startled when the ASROC launcher turned toward him.

∞§∞

Kronos read from the screen. "Here it starts. She's plotting a firing solution for the ASROCs. She's targeting a nuclear power plant in the San Joaquin Valley."

"If that blows, it will wipe out the entire West Coast," the president said.

Hiccock scurried up the ladder and onto the deck. He looked both ways and realized he hadn't the faintest idea of what an ASROC launcher looked like.

A second later, he learned, as the lid covering the number-four missile chamber blew off in preparation for the launch of the ten-inch-diameter nuclear-tipped antisubmarine rocket. He grabbed the axe from the sailor's hand. Instinctively, Hiccock wedged the head of the axe between the thin skin of the missile's body and the chamber's edge. The sailor, realizing Hiccock's intent, quickly pulled a fire coat out of the locker behind the stairway and ran toward him. The ignition plume exploded out of the chamber, spewing the propellant flame forward. The sailor reached Hiccock and shielded them both with the fire coat as the missile launched, protecting them from the fiery blast-back as the rocket left the tube. The head of the axe, still being held by Hiccock, slit the thin titanium skin all the way down the emerging missile's length. The integrity of the rocket's outer casing destroyed, the $3 million dollar ASROC with a $10 million dollar nuclear depth charge on its tip wobbled and never attained any altitude. It fell into the ocean one hundred feet in front of the ship.

"Tell me there's a proximity safety fuse on that sucker!" Hiccock said to the sailor, who took the axe from his scorched hand.

"Better have the doc look at that hand, Sir."

Hiccock inspected his blistered, singed hand, suddenly feeling the pain.

The sailor's headset crackled. "Fifty-nine percent, Sir," he reported to Hiccock.

"Cut the fiber-optic cables now!"

The sailor ran over to the cables lying across the tie-off cleat. He wielded the axe over his head and brought it crashing down on the cable bundle. They severed without a spark or sound, because they carried only light waves. Hiccock took a handkerchief from his pocket and wrapped his hand as he headed down the ladder back to the ECM.

The president patted Hiccock on the shoulder. "Bill, there is no way to count all the lives you just saved with that bit of ingenuity. We saw it all on the monitor."

Hiccock swiveled to see a row of TV monitors up on the bulkhead that showed every weapon system on the ship.

Tyler noticed his wrapped hand. "What happened?"

"I forgot it was a rocket."

Janice kissed him on the cheek. "Congratulations. That's the most illogical thing you could ever do!"

"We reached 59.7 percent before the fiber-optic cable was cut," the Admiral said.

"Then we did it! We did it!" He hugged her then had to check, "We did do it, right?"

"59.7 means she can never regenerate."

"Now onto part B," Hiccock said as he nodded to the president.

"Captain, clear your ship of all but the most essential personnel. No more than ten." The president used all fingers on both hands to reinforce the limited head count.

∞§∞

The bow and stern lines of the U.S.S. *Princeton* were cast off, those crewmembers themselves jumping onto the pier as they freed the ship. Mitchell wanted to be along for this part, but cooler heads prevailed and he acceded to the Secret Service's advice. The captain personally worked the lateral thrusters, which pushed the ship away from the dock sideways. Then, when he felt he had enough room, he engaged the main engines and the ship accelerated through the light chop of San Diego harbor. He pushed the helm to full speed ahead, ignoring the five-miles-per-hour antiwake rules.

The president watched from the dock with Reynolds, as the ship, with his helicopter on it, steamed away from the naval base.

∞§∞

"Where are we going?" ALISON asked in Marilyn Monroe's voice. Hiccock was surprised. "You know you are moving?"

"GPS sensors indicate southwest direction at twenty knots."

"She's trying to think," Kronos said. "But she's learning she doesn't have the friggin' core no more. It's like she's going senile."

Hiccock left the ECM.

∞§∞

In the wheelhouse, the captain was at the helm. The Admiral stood next to him, watching the blue ocean sprawled out before them. The pointed bow of the modern cruiser sliced through the waves, leaving a minimal wake.

"Honored to have an Admiral on my ship, Ma'am. I apologize for not saluting, but you weren't in uniform."

"I was in the desert, tending to my garden two weeks ago."

"They called you up to active duty?"

"In a manner of speaking, yes. But I wasn't recommissioned until today."

With the expansive Pacific ahead and his hands on the helm, the captain had a pang of nostalgia for all things nautical. "What we are doing right now, Ma'am, it is the only way, right? I mean, this *is* necessary?"

"Captain, what we have captured here is the most dangerous machine ever built. And none of us, the president included, trusts anyone, even our own government, to leave it alone. It's too tempting. That's why we have to do this."

"Ma'am, would you make the last entry into the ship's log? You know, kind of make it official from an officer of flag rank."

"It would be an honor, Captain."

"Take the wheel then, Ma'am."

"I haven't even driven a car in thirty years."

"No problem, just hold her steady while I get the log."

Hiccock entered and smiled at seeing Henrietta at the helm. "Returning to your roots?"

"Not my roots. I was landlocked in Administration. The only time I was ever on a ship was on vacation.

The captain came in, handed the Admiral the logbook, and checked his navigation. "We are approaching the Pacific Trench. Deep water in one minute."

"Signal the copter to start up."

On Hiccock's order, the captain radioed Marine One.

"Captain, let's get your crew loaded."

The captain turned the handle on a World War II–vintage device. A claxon horn started bellowing an *augah, augah* sound, signaling the crew to abandon ship.

"Mr. Hiccock, would you do the head count, Sir. Then have the chopper radio me back. I'll set the sequences from here and then join you."

The Admiral handed the logbook back to the captain, and she and Hiccock left. They made their way aft, joining the crew as they headed toward the copter.

∞§∞

The captain opened his shirt and removed a red key from around his neck. He walked over to a box on the wall, not unlike a fire alarm. He took a chain-attached hammer and broke a glass faceplate covering a turn-key switch and a three-position-selector knob. The selections were marked "Safe," "Capture," and "Scuttle." He dialed the fishtailed black knob from the safe to the scuttle mode, then inserted and turned the key. Immediately a wailing siren was added to the "abandon ship" alarm. Simultaneously, a decimal readout started counting backwards from ninety seconds. He broke off the key in the lock-switch, took one more look around his command, then grabbed the logbook and scurried out the door and down the stairs to the main deck, high-stepping his way aft.

∞§∞

Two crewmembers were at each strut of the Marine chopper's wheels.

Hiccock extended his hand as the captain boarded the chopper, shouting to him above the rotor noise. "Eight of your men are in the cabin, the two on the struts, my three, and you. That's fourteen. We are good to go!"

The captain signaled the two sailors manning the struts to release the hold-downs. The portside strap released and that sailor climbed aboard. But the starboard side was not freeing up.

"Are we clear?" the pilot yelled over the engine noise of the open cabin.

"No," Hiccock said.

The captain jumped down and joined the sailor in trying to free the strap.

"It's not made for this big a bird, Sir, just Navy Stallions and Bells."

The problem was that the starboard side of Marine One had a built-in step for the president's comfort. This added dimension stretched the hold down to its limit just to lock in place. The copter, having shifted on the rolling deck, placed even greater strain on the strap. The quick-release buckle was fail-safed not to open under positive pressure; it had to be slack for the buckle to give.

The decimal readout on the bridge started red strobe lights flashing all around the ship as it counted down below the thirty-second mark. Seeing this, Hiccock jumped down from the chopper and ran over to the fantail access way. He grabbed the fire axe with his bandaged hand and returned to the chopper.

"Make way."

He slammed the axe down on the composite resin-and-fiber belt. It snapped apart.

"We're clear! Go. Go. Go," the captain yelled, as he and his man scrambled into the chopper as it lifted off. Janice screamed because Hiccock was nowhere to be seen.

The ascent was stomach-wrenching. The huge Sikorsky engines at full power and maximum pitch of the rotor blade made the big machine rocket up at 5,000 feet per minute. With less than ten seconds until the ship below them self-destructed, it was not a comfortable speed. All they could do was ride it out and pray.

Janice's screaming for Bill was not heard over the engine's roar. She started to tear at her seat belt, which caught the captain's eye as he suddenly realized what she was yelling about. He scanned the small cabin and didn't see Hiccock. As he lunged toward the open door, a bandaged hand appeared and flopped onto the cabin floor. The captain and a sailor hauled Hiccock in and shut the door.

"Sorry. Kind of forgot you there for a second," the captain said.

"Geez, thanks a lot."

They felt it before they heard it. The chopper jumped up from the shock wave as the first of the de-molition charges went off. The 3,000 rounds of the five-inch ammunition blasted the turreted forward-deck gun up 700 feet in the air, almost as high as they had climbed, though in a different trajectory. The whole ship disappeared in an explosion of orange flame and black smoke.

The pilot shouted, "Everyone hold on, we're too close."

The chopper's blades were grabbing for air, which was denied by the blast wave emanating from the ship. Without air, Marine One took on the aerodynamics of a wall safe. It plunged back down. The pilot fought hard to bring his chopper over the blazing ship in a last-second gamble. The huge helicopter suddenly buffeted and jerked as it caught the thermals rising from the now-incinerating ship. Like an eagle gliding upward, the blades now had something to dig into and again the copter started to rise.

The stern of the ship rose up from the water and slipped below the waves on its final journey down into the eight-mile-deep Pacific trench.

∞§∞

The chopper landed on the heliport back at San Diego Naval. The president and Reynolds greeted Hiccock and his people.

The captain walked over to the president, snapped the salute of his career, and handed the logbook over to him. "Sir, the U.S.S. *Princeton* was scuttled at sea, by your order at 2100 hours. No hands were lost."

"Thank you, Captain. You have served your country and mankind well."

"Let's go home," Tyler said to Hiccock, kissing him.

"Hmmph!" the president said, thumbing through the logbook.

"What?" Hiccock asked.

Mitchell turned the logbook so Hiccock could read the final entry by Admiral Parks: "Ship had to be destroyed. Had a bug in it."

ACKNOWLEDGMENTS

IT SEEMS LIKE YOU WRITE a book alone, but trust me, within these pages is the essence and dedication of every teacher who challenged my wandering focus. My English teachers, Mr. Green, Mr. Zimmerman, and Hilda Gore who, in her spare time, took kids from the South Bronx to Lincoln Center and opened us up to "culture." To Al Alteri who taught me music and life lessons not in any book and to Joe White who taught me how much I didn't know about humility. And Ron Silber who turned me inside out, thus letting the beauty of the world of words in. To Adrian J. Meppen who taught journalism but majored in confidence building that took me to incredible heights. And my science and math teachers who fed and nourished my hunger for answers, Mrs. Isrealoff, Mr. Kulick, Mr. Benson, Mr. Burger, Mr. Schoenfeld, and Irv Binger—great people who understood the wonders of the universe.

To those who guided me with their advice, counsel, and grammar through the birthing process of this book: Kristine Bascom, Kathleen Connolly, and Helen Eisenman. To Linda Ardigo who suffered the labor pains of the first draft. To my secret weapon in the war against boring prose, Lou Aronica of the Fiction Studio whose velvet-gloved guidance compelled me to write a better book, without one word of criticism. To all the guys I grew up with in the Bronx who may recognize a few things, "You got a problem with that?" And to Monta, who just makes me the luckiest guy in the world every time she smiles. In no small part, she is directly responsible for this book coming to publication.

Then my mastermind group: Sid Paterson for his wisdom, support, and friendship throughout the decades; to Dana Matthow for his friendship and generosity in backing my earlier endeavors; and to Peter Insalaco for being my moral and spiritual compass through the fog of life. Mike Miklos for the military accuracy, Stephen Cagliostro for the medical, and John Weaver for exposing me to Washington. Len Watson for his input and excellent advice; Peter Kessleman for science methods; and Steve Cohen, who suggested I write this book in the first place.

The additional scenes included in this Author's Preferred Edition of the Eighth Day were edited by Jackie Baron McCue and the manuscript prepared for publishing by Stephanie Bartosiewicz.

TOM AVITABILE, a Senior VP/Creative Director at a New York advertising firm, is a writer, director, and producer with numerous film and television credits. He has an extensive background in engineering and computers, including work on projects for the House Committee on Science and Technology, which helped lay the foundation for *The Eighth Day*. In his spare time, Tom is a professional musician and an amateur woodworker. He recently completed his third novel in the William "Wild Bill" Hiccock, Quarterback Operations Group series.